# ENEMY

# ENEMY

## K. EASON

47N⬦RTH

Text copyright © 2016 Kathryn F. Eason

Published by 47North, Seattle

www.apub.com

Amazon, the Amazon logo, and 47North are trademarks of Amazon.com, Inc., or its affiliates.

ISBN-13: 9781503934498
ISBN-10: 1503934497

Cover design by M. S. Corley

Printed in the United States of America

*To Tan and Loren, who were there when it all began*

# PART ONE

PART ONE

# CHAPTER ONE

Smoke collected on the belly of the storm. It rose up in slim fingers above the tree line, coiled into a fist when it cleared the ridge. Hung there and spread against the underbelly of the clouds like oil across water.

If a man stood just so, facing into the wind, he might imagine that it was the forest burning. Except this was the wrong season for natural fires. Too cold, too wet, snow underfoot and more waiting overhead. It was the wrong smell, too, for burning trees. The wind brought a firepit stink, flesh and charcoal and dung. Village smells, which most days meant sure shelter, with a storm on the way.

Then that man would peer skyward and consider the clouds, and give thanks to his ancestors that the village was so near and that he had a sackful of tradables to buy his welcome. Snowhare skins, soft and white. A fine rack of antlers he'd taken off a bull elk that had broken through the snow-crust upslope a day ago, weak and furious and an easy mark for arrows.

Good fortune, Veiko had thought then. Meat and hide, horn and hooves. Worth the extra day spent above the trees while the storm gathered. Worth the weight on the hike down. A stranger did not walk into an Alvir village unchallenged, from the forest, looking like Veiko did. A stranger came by the road, with goods and hands on clear display, his axe on his hip and bow slung on his back.

Except on that road now, there was a column of soldiers jogging toward the crease in the hills, and the smoke, and the village. Their collective breath streamed out behind them like steam off a boiling pot. The standard-bearer's flag clung sullenly to its pole, wrapped tight against the gusts. Illhari legion, armed and armored and moving fast.

Now Veiko wondered if he'd caught the elk's unluck. Failed to appease its spirit. Because that was not village smoke collecting there above the trees. Nor was that the smell of village cookfires.

Charred meat. Charred wood. The smell of raiding.

Had Veiko not found that elk, he might have been in the village when the raiders came, and it might be his meat stinking on the wind. He shivered. Perhaps it was not unluck the elk had given him. Perhaps its spirit had repaid him in kind: saved him from a trap and slow death in return for relief from the same.

Beside him, Helgi heaved a deep-chested whine. Protest. Query. Distress, maybe, at the smoke-reek and the movement on the road. Veiko dropped a quick hand to the dog's head. Glanced sidelong and found Logi halfway out of his crouch, ears up and curious. Logi knew roads meant villages, people, new things, and warm sleeping.

But not that village, not now. Even if he might find walls still standing, or some shelter, the legion wouldn't welcome him. Tall, pale foreigner, with village houses burned and people dead, no, they would—what was the Dvergiri word for it?—*detain* him. And likely shoot his dogs. Maybe throw him in chains after and sell him in the city. He'd heard his elders' tales about Illhari justice. Best he get as far from the road as he could, as soon as he could. There were other villages. Let the raiders come for him, if they felt brave. Let them try to find him at all.

He took a handful of Logi's scruff. "No." He winced. Days since he'd used his voice. "Wait."

Logi sighed and dropped his chin onto his paws. Helgi chuffed and settled back to his belly. And the three of them waited, part of the snowscape, until the last trooper bobbed out of sight.

\* \* \*

Snowdenaelikk had just rolled the last of her jenja, lit it, and blown the first smoke that didn't stink like destruction, when Briel's sending came. A cascade of jumbled impressions crowded into her skull. A svartjagr's vantage, above the tree line and moving fast: dizzy twist of tree and ground, a flash of
*two legs*
color, the hollow-gut swerve and *there*, a
*clutch*
trio of troopers, marching ragged up the path above Davni. One trailed
*wounded/prey*
behind the others, who
*pecked*
kept heads together. Two male, one female. And because Briel remembered her training: an eyeblink's focus on the weapons. Plain legion blades, still sheathed. Short javelins in a sling on the larger man's back. Crossbow on the woman's. The night-and-blood diamond pattern on the tunics. They were from Cardik's garrison, that was no surprise. But to arrive at this toadshit village already, this fast—Laughing God, that *was*.

The sending ended, and the blindness came. Price of a svartjagr's sending, yeah, count it out in heartbeats. No need for panic. Listen to the sizzle where her jenja had landed, smell the sweet and spice. She thought about trying to find it, pat-pat in the snow. Salvage *something* of it. Swore instead and crouched, her hands flat to the wall of the ruined temple. Cold stone, slick moss, a dead Alvir god's face roughing her palms. She waited for the sunrise stages of vision, black to grey to, well, more grey, in the shadowless pre-blizzard twilight. This wasn't so different than the cave-dark of Below, without witchfire.

Overhead, a whisper of wings and tail. A thump as Briel found a perch in what remained of the temple's rafters. Soot sifted down from the impact, fresh stinging insult to offended eyes.

Snow blinked tears and blur as her vision crept back. "Fuck, Briel. Kill me someday, won't you, if you send when I need to see."

Briel hissed. One of her three primary utterances. Big talker, Briel.

Snow squinted up, scanned the rafters. Stone building, this one, the corpse of a temple gutted during the Purge. The walls still stood, moss-grown on the north sides, the tough mountain spine-vines on the rest. Most of the roof had spilled down between them. The thatch had gone first, collapsed and left a rib cage of crossbeams. Briel's hide matched the wood's greasy black. Invisible until she dipped her long neck and stared down at Snow. In the twilight, the svartjagr's eyes glowed like embers. Like the village had when the last of the fires sputtered to ash. She and Drasan had picked through the wreckage, expecting the odd bit of surviving silver and coin. Instead, they'd found all the wealth you'd expect in an Alvir village on a caravan route, wealth no raiders would have left behind.

So this had not been a raid, then. Something else. Big damn fire, yeah, fires and corpses and ashes. And now there was a motherless patrol coming upslope, and she didn't want to be here when they arrived. Grey skies, no shadows to weave and wear, no light to push and bend. The storm might conceal

*a retreat*

an escape, except it'd stalled out to flakes and cold spit, while soldiers clustered in the village and sent scouts to search buildings and—

"Briel."

"Chrrip?" Another of Briel's utterances, the one that covered everything *sssss* wouldn't. This version meant *now what?*

"Go," Snow told her. Waved a hand at the sky through the crossbeams. "Find us a safe place, yeah? Scout and come back. *No* sending! I need my own eyes."

"Chrrip." The svartjagr took a running scrabble along the beam. Launched a handspan from the end, arrowed into wind. Her wings caught currents and angled, and then she was up, gliding black against the brooding steel sky. She circled the temple once, then flapped and dipped and vanished behind trees.

Snowdenaelikk doubled back through the ruined temple. Squeezed through the gap in the wall beside the shattered archway and dashed into the courtyard. Old stone paths fought for territory with weeds, made for treacherous footing under the snow. She lightstepped a path across it, scuff and scrape. Drasan hadn't been so elegant, had gouged out a trail for any fool to follow. Careless, stupid, no surprise: Drasan was green, not even twenty. Needed seasoning. Tsabrak's special orders to her—

*Teach him something, Snow, will you?*

—when he'd sent them out. Because Drasan, the idiot, had cut the wrong purse in Cardik, and the wrong throat to go with it. Governor's consort, yeah, *real* smart. So it was a run into the Wild to meet Tsabrak's new courier in the hills above Davni village. *Take the long way,* Tsabrak said, *waste time.*

In winter. Funny man, Tsabrak, sending her out here with a sullen half-taught teenaged godsworn initiate and the unappealing promise of one of Davni's two taverns as reward.

Only Davni *wasn't* anymore, and the troops from Cardik had gotten here before coals were cool. Two unexpected events in as many days. Blame Taliri raiders for the first. Blame a dog-loyal Cardik commander for the second. A man from the Sixth with something to prove. A woman would've waited for the storm to pass, reckoning the raid long over and the village past any help. The detachment here now must've been running patrol, saw the smoke, diverted, and fucking *sprinted* to get here this fast.

Snow managed her own dash. More effort than she remembered, running. The seax banged bruises into her hip. Had to strap it down better. Adjust the motherless belt. It wasn't rigged for running. Neither was she. Her lungs seized on the cold air, coughed a cloud of protest.

Bad habit, jenja.

The tent sulked at the uphill edge of the temple grounds, between a cluster of young evergreens and a tumbled wall of fieldstones. Ragged stones ringed a center of burned wood and stripped bones. Last night's unlucky rabbit—thank you, Briel. A scene not unlike the village, down to the iron pan still resting in ashes. Drasan's turn to clean up, which she'd expected to do anyway, which no one would do now. She paused long enough to grab the pan's handle, used it to push the tent flap aside.

Drasan didn't even turn to look. He was busy sorting loot from the village, coins and chits divided into piles, and most of his own belongings scattered around him. "Did you enjoy your poison weed?"

She considered the back of his skull, imagined a cast-iron impact. "It's not poison, and no." She sucked another lungful of air. Blinked away spots. "We have to go. Now."

"The fuck?" Drasan looked at her now. Frowned. "The courier's not here yet. Tsabrak said wait."

As if she hadn't been in the room, getting the same orders.

*Wait for the courier in the old temple in Davni, yeah? She'll find you.*

No idea what the message would be, or if there was merchandise to go with it, or what the courier looked like. Probably nothing more than a package of uncut rasi, delivered by a scruffy Alvir bandit. Running rasi was dangerous work. The last courier had gotten herself caught by the Cardik garrison right before solstice, trying to sneak into the gates after dark. Tsabrak had been hunting a new courier since. He wouldn't be happy if she missed the meeting. Rasi was habit forming. Lots of people in Cardik who wanted a fix, yeah, and if Tsabrak couldn't deliver, some other cartel might. But she could come back once the legion was gone. No courier would come here with the legion camped out and swarming.

"Bigger problems. Briel saw troopers."

Attitude settled into Drasan's jaw. "Not likely. It's too soon for troopers. Your vermin is mistaken."

Vermin. Right. Briel wasn't the problem. Fucking stubborn *male* pride was, godsworn arrogance that didn't like direction from a woman, any woman, even a half-blood ally half again his age. Made her wonder sometimes if the foremothers hadn't been right after all, and the Reforms a soft-minded mistake.

She loosed a wrap of her patience. "I saw them, idiot. They're on the toadfucking *trail* to the temple, and you left a lot of marks. Now be quiet and move."

"Shit." Drasan forgot any pretense at authority. Listening to her now, moving fast. Random grabs at clothing, supplies, that would probably miss something vital. Busy scooping coins into pouches, too, clink and rattle.

She hissed a fair imitation of Briel—

"Leave that toadshit."

—and scooped her pack off its perch on the tent pole. Quick reconnaissance of the contents, a quicker scan of the surroundings. She jammed the iron pan in. More weight than she wanted, but more use than Drasan's priorities. It might stop an arrow loosed at her back. She settled the pack across her shoulder. Circled the tent, once and twice, on her way back for a third pass and a peek out the flap.

And knew. Premonition, certainty, too many years dodging armed and armored authority.

Clink. Rattle. Hiss.

Armor had its own resonance. The legionnaire's sword, its own whispers. And the troopers themselves, oh Laughing God, their own breed of arrogance that came with both armor and sword.

It was the woman's voice outside, command-solid and only a little breathless. "You. In the tent. *Out* now, and slowly."

As if Snow had any intention. She crossed stares with Drasan. Traded tiny slit smiles. The boy was a fool about some things, but he knew close-quarter fighting. And better than that, he knew when to run.

Like now.

* * *

Someone had been smoking jenja by the fallen wall. Kenjak smelled it before he saw the pale spiral rising out of a pile of dead leaves and twigs. He stopped beside it, under pretense of investigation, and caught his breath instead. Long, cold chestfuls of sweet smoke that didn't cut the memory of what he'd passed through. The village stench lingered in his throat. On his tongue. Cooked meat that had been *people*, in the streets and the houses and the shops.

*Fast death,* Ollu had muttered, and made a sign against ill luck that would've earned lashes if First Spear Rurik had seen it.

The villagers hadn't tried to run. Hadn't had *time*. And that wasn't like raiders.

Which made Kenjak shiver for reasons that had nothing to do with iced mud in his boot, or the blisters, or the jenja, which meant there *was* someone up here. Sudden death wasn't Taliri raiders, and sudden death might not answer to swords or spears. Might come back, and they'd never know it and die like the villagers had—

The Rurik that lived in his head looked down his long nose and sneered *coward.* And worse, *superstitious.*

The faces of abandoned gods peered out of the old temple's brickwork. Crude carvings, Alviri work. Kenjak felt a small surge of pride that the Dvergiri had never produced something so ugly. Since the Purge, the Illhari Republic relied on the wits of its people, not on superstition. He felt a twinge of something colder, too: there were snubbed candles pressed against the brickwork, and a smear of ash. Someone still prayed here, or had, until the raiders came.

But whoever had lit the jenja, whoever hid in a temple to dead Alviri gods—that person couldn't be responsible for what'd happened in Davni.

"Kenjak, you toadfucker." Ollu came around the wall, hand on his sword and scowling. "Why're you holding back? There's *tracks*. Fresh. Motherless toadshits are here."

"But—"

"Don't need to hear it. Salis went up, wouldn't wait, said I should get you." This while trading his sword hilt for a fistful of Kenjak's tunic through the gap in the armor, rough haul half around and half over the remains of the stone.

"Jenja—"

"Who cares what they smoke? They're here, rabbit brain. And we're going to get them."

Ollu let go and brought both hands down hard on Kenjak's shoulders, like he meant to drive him into the earth. "Listen. First time, scared's normal, yeah?"

The knot in Kenjak's belly didn't feel at all like fear. "Ollu, these can't be the ones who burned Davni. There's not enough of them."

"Maybe they're conjurors."

"And maybe we've got wings. No *way* there's a conjuror out here. It's too Wild."

Different light in Ollu's eyes now, different shape to the smile. Kenjak thought of the barracks cat, when it cornered something helpless. "We marched all the way out here and *up* here, yeah? Got to have something for it, or Rurik'll skin us. Come on."

Kenjak clipped off his protest. Nerves, that was all. Ollu was right.

At least Ollu didn't insist that they run the rest of the way. Kenjak followed the older man through the temple's ruined guts, dodged fallen timber and scuffed through the ash. There were indeed tracks stitched through the snow, by someone who didn't care who saw them. Kenjak was more and more certain the person who'd made those tracks hadn't a thing to do with the burning. Equally certain Ollu wouldn't listen. Kenjak's opinion didn't change when he saw the tent, either. Faded thing, ragged. Couldn't hold more than two people. Not a raiding party.

Salis had her crossbow cocked and leveled at the flap. Saw them coming and jerked her chin, as if there was any uncertainty of her destination or intent.

Ollu threw a hard look at him. Kenjak pushed his chin up and nodded and squeezed out his own scowl. Never mind the hammering in his chest, or the sudden premonition of bloodshed. He angled into his place on the tripoint formation. Drew his sword. Anyone trying to run would have to get past him or Ollu or Salis. He hoped they'd try it. Hoped they wouldn't.

His hand shook enough that the sword wobbled, and he steadied his blade with the other hand. Caught another look from Ollu, and a wink.

He could just make out voices from inside, male and female—

"You. In the tent. *Out* now, and slowly."

—that got quiet before Salis finished. No response.

*Maybe they don't speak Dvergiri.*

Except everyone did, even raiders. The Illhari Republic made that its price for doing business.

One beat. Two. Twenty, while breath steamed and snow turned from sprinkles to steady flakes.

Salis peeled a smile. Took a step forward, toward the tent flap. "I *said* come out. Savvy that? I'll shoot if you don't."

Kenjak pulled a deep breath. Closed his eyes for the exhale, willed his stomach to settle.

And in that moment's darkness, he heard the long, ragged sound of tearing canvas, and the thud-twang of a firing crossbow, and another ripping sound. A wet thud that sounded like steel in flesh, and a man's choked-off gargling scream.

*She got one.*

He opened his eyes in time to see Salis lurch sideways. See the hole in the tent, where her bolt had torn through. A second hole, wider, below it, where something had torn its way out.

Salis dropped to one knee. Her crossbow spilled out of her hands and into the firepit. So very few gaps in legionnaire armor, but a knife's hilt poked, triumphant, from just above her hip. Someone inside throwing metal at them, someone with good aim.

Kenjak broke formation. Instinct swung him sideways, out of range. Just the right angle to see the dull black flicker of Illhari steel come through the back of the tent and slice down. A long-legged shape stepped through. Dvergir-black skin, Alvir-fair hair, an eyeblink of nervous indigo turned on him.

*Half-blood.*

And then she was over the stones and into the trees. He took a step after her. Hesitated. Snow falling heavier by the heartbeat, they'd lose all trace if he didn't go now. But Salis was hurt, and you didn't leave your partners, and Ollu—

"Kenjak."

—was right on his shoulder. Flat-voiced fury: "The fuck is your problem? Got one dead inside, and Salis—"

"She's"—he stabbed at the forest—"running." He processed Ollu's report. "A second one. Running away."

"Shit." Ollu scowled. Glanced back at Salis, on her knees, fingers wrapped around the dagger hilt. Blood turned the snow red underneath her. "Can't leave her."

Salis swore. Spat: "I'll. Be. *Fine.*"

"Light a fire," said Kenjak. "Rurik will see it, he'll send someone up."

Ollu's turn to hesitate. He looked from forest to Salis and back. "I don't think we can leave—"

"*Listen* to the green, Ollu, *get that motherless toadfucker.*" All of Salis's breath at once. Ragged inhale on the back end, and a rough, "Order, savvy?"

"Savvy," said Ollu, and clapped Kenjak hard on the shoulder. And then they were running again, through trees this time, and Kenjak didn't notice the cold at all.

# CHAPTER TWO

It was the dogs who warned him. First Helgi, then Logi, went stiff and still and sniffed. Then Helgi growled, barely a mutter, and ghosted ahead, with Logi silent and tight on his flank. No barking, which meant Veiko did not drop his armful of dry wood and string his bow or unsling his axe. A man could freeze to death without a fire. That was certain. Whatever the dogs had upset—far less so. An animal, maybe a fox or a lynx. There was no reason to rush unless the dogs made noise.

Which they didn't. Veiko trailed their pawprints and their silence to the clearing, where he found Logi stalking, stiff-legged, around the spruce's wide skirt. Helgi, always braver, had thrust his head into the dark gash where the branches split. His tail poked up straight and furious.

Veiko considered. Something in there, yes, but there were no tracks besides his and the dogs' in the snow. Nor—he crouched and balanced the wood against his flat thigh—nor had whatever it was bothered his gear. He could see it, hanging where he'd left it, with none of the contents spilled out.

A less cautious man would have ducked under the branches and looked first. Whatever ran from dogs was not that dangerous. But there was a village smoking in the next valley, Illhari soldiers on the march, and only a fool rushed into things he did not understand. Men died from bad judgment.

He brushed a patch out of the snow. Stacked the wood carefully, one piece after another. There was no sound from inside the tree, no sound from Helgi, only Logi's breathless whining. A lynx, perhaps. A squirrel.

Veiko clicked his tongue, once and twice. Helgi returned without protest. Logi kept circling, until Veiko said his name. Then he whined and crept back, ears flat, darting glances over his shoulder. Veiko frowned. Grant that the younger dog wasn't Helgi's quality, but he wasn't a puppy, either. *Something* up that tree that was not squirrel or cat. He straightened. Stepped around the wood and strung his bow. Notched an arrow. The dogs were watching him now, hunter-tense.

"Go," he bade them, having neither hand free for signals.

Helgi mirrored Veiko's caution. Ears forward, ruff and tail stiff, careful stalking back to the tree. Logi abandoned all sense, bolted under the branches and hurled himself against the trunk, and, merciful ancestors, woofed up at the branches.

The branches hissed back at him.

Veiko had startled snakes before, sunning themselves on rocks. Had teased cats, as well. This hiss belonged to neither snake nor cat. A deeper sound, more resonant.

A bigger animal, then. And angry.

Helgi growled. Sat beside Logi and stared pointedly up. Veiko ducked under the branches. Gave his eyes a moment to adjust to green-blue shadow, and looked.

He might've been wrong about the snake. Maybe two man-heights up, where the branches were too slender for weight greater than squirrels, an arrowhead skull swiveled on a long black neck. Big eyes, ember bright in the storm-light, twin slit pupils. It hissed again, and Veiko saw fangs slivering white against black lips and gums. But no, not a snake. Wings, he saw, bat-fragile and folded, the claw joints dug into the bark. Tiny hind legs meant for tucking, for gripping, clinging to the branch. A tail as long as its neck, looped for balance around the trunk. The creature was almost as long as a rock leopard, he estimated, nose to tip, but not heavy. Not with the small branches stiff and unbowed.

No idea what it was, but that did not alarm him. The world below tundra and glacier held many new things. And yet. He had heard tales.

*And Hakkon the Brave did face the wurm with only his father's axe.*

Hakkon the Brave had been a fool, then. Small as this creature was, Veiko didn't want himself within range of jaws or tail. Nor did he wish to share his campsite with it. He raised the bow, pulled the arrow back to the corner of his mouth.

The creature squeaked. Recoiled and reversed and put the trunk of the tree between itself and his arrow. Peered around and hissed again, a much smaller sound. Protest. Indignation.

Unexpected.

Veiko angled the bow sideways. Kept it notched and drawn. Waited as his arms began slow, shivering protests, while the bat-snake ventured a little bit farther around the trunk. Veiko swung the arrow back, slow and deliberate. The creature ducked behind the trunk again and hissed like a sackful of vipers.

He relaxed his draw.

The head reappeared. Orange eyes looking at him now. Appraising.

"Chrrip?" Long utterance that ended on an up-note, that sounded for all the world like a question.

He had been alone too long if he was imagining conversation from an animal. And yet. Veiko released the arrow and replaced it in the quiver. Rested the bow against his leg and showed empty hands.

"I will not," he said softly, "shoot you."

"Chrrip." It came around the trunk. Paused on the branch and looked down, this time with its wings spread partway. For balance, maybe, or to make itself seem more impressive. It worked. Wings wide as his arms if they were fully stretched. Membrane and bone, like a bat's. Talons on the wing joints, on the hind limbs. Had he seen it flying, he would have dropped for cover and worried about shooting it later.

Which was, he suspected, one of its better defenses.

"You could fly away." His voice seemed too large for the evergreen quiet, like a drunken man's attempt at whispers.

The bat-snake came down the tree a bit farther, face-first. Slow blink, first one eye and then the other. Veiko swallowed sudden dryness. Animals did not talk. This creature did not, either, but it managed to make itself understood better than some people he'd known. And it seemed to understand him.

*Spirit-touched.*

And then he had a vision: of firelight dusting yellow off the branches, and snow sheeting solid on the other side of the branches. There, the dogs on the fire's far side. There, himself, stirring something in a black iron pan he did not own. And there, beside him, a woman with ice-colored hair and black Dvergiri skin stretched over a hostile nose and aggressive cheekbones. Not young, not old, and no one he had ever seen before. And yet his chest warmed and tightened, need and affection tangled together.

"Chrrip."

The vision faded. There was only the spruce-colored shadow now, and the luminous threat of the storm. No fire. No heat. No woman.

The bat-snake dropped suddenly. Plummeted like a stone for an arm's length before its wings snapped open. It streaked over Veiko's head, shot past into the snow. And came back in a tight circle to cling again to the tree trunk. That long neck twisted to find him. Eyelock and

"Chrrrrip?"

He had the sudden impression of trees flashing past him, of someone or something fleeing through the forest. His guts clenched around an urgency he had no business feeling. Not, he realized slowly, *his* fear at all.

"Chrrip." Softly now. Veiko thought its eyes might be glowing, faint and hot in the shadows.

Curiosity had much in common with bad judgment and could get a man just as dead. He didn't know what the bat-snake wanted. He *did* know that he needed supplies, and now the nearest village was a day south and west. He should camp. Wait out the storm. Find another village and resupply, because winter did not forgive *curiosity*.

Logi whined. Helgi pressed against Veiko's knee and sighed. As usual, the dogs already knew what action he'd choose.

"Go," he told the bat-snake. "I will follow."

* * *

Snow thought there might be two troopers after her. Hard to tell, between the pounding in her ears and chest and the rattling as she stepped on every dry twig in the forest. Tsabrak would laugh at her if he saw her now.

*Didn't I teach you better, Snow?* with his garnet eyes slitted and smiling.

Better, yes, and the lessons had stuck. There weren't many more-skilled than she was at quiet, at speed . . . inside walls, yeah, boots on stone, with or without a sky overhead. But this toadshit forest wasn't Cardik or Illharek, was it? There was fresh snow, and she had no shadows, and she'd left Drasan choking on a crossbow bolt back at the tent.

She ran along the top of a fallen log, paused at a bare place, and jumped. Left a mark that time, smudged on the border between snow and dirt. Doubled back and went the other way on the log and leapt again, from the other side. Uphill, this time, which they might not consider, not if they saw the first track. Might

*please, Laughing God*

assume she'd go down, headed for the road and the valley crease. Instead she pelted upslope, skidding and jumping from one needle-slick patch to another. Reached back one-handed and pulled up the hood on her cloak. Greys and browns and threaded black, meant to blend with stone and wood. With walls, of which she was painfully short at the moment. Only trees between her and them, trees and snow and the better part of a hillside. But the ridgeline above—that was rocks, scoured smooth in the wind, and her tracks wouldn't show. Had to get up there and over it before they caught her.

She fetched up against a tall pine. Crouched and dared a moment to breathe, with the cloak pulled across her mouth to hide the steam. And to watch as her pursuers flickered and dodged through the trees. And stopped, there, at the log. Heads leaned together, close enough she expected to hear helmets clink. Two men, yes, and armed, *yes*. But no evidence of crossbows on either of them. Swords and javelins, which they couldn't cast well in a forest. Small blessing, yeah, they'd have to run her down and spit her or catch her in the open.

She eased the seax around, took comfort in the solid curve of the hilt in her palm. Black steel from the mines under Illharek, and it held a wicked edge. Meant for Illhari street fights, turns and cuts in tight places. But it also had nearly the reach of a legionnaire's sword, and she knew where their armor was weak. She was tall, even for a Dvergir woman. Had reach on them both.

And *both* was the problem. Two of them, one of her, which meant an ugly fight that she might not win.

*So you don't fight, yeah?*

Yeah. She resettled the blade on her hip. Five steps between tree line and ridge rocks, another half dozen before she'd be over and out of sight. She needed only a few moments, a brief diversion, two backs turned just long enough.

". . . she went." The smaller one turned, dragged his voice with him and threw it upslope. Young face, young voice, and not at all out of breath. The half-light smeared his features a uniform Dvergiri black, his skin only a shade or two lighter than the queue rattailing from the helmet's lip. He had a highborn accent, too, fuck and damn. Some senator's whelp on a purchased commission.

"She's not far." The second voice, older and a little breathless. Another Dvergir face, shadow-dark in the helmet, but a Warren accent, which meant native Cardik, which might mean career soldier and someone less interested in risk and glory than a transplanted Illharek boy with his family honor to maintain.

The second one coughed, gut deep. He braced one hand on a tree, the other on his hip. Blew plumes of exhaustion into the snowfall and sent the flakes swirling. "Just hold. A minute. Yeah?"

"Yeah." Barely concealed impatience in the younger one. No— *anger*, slicing his movements short. He paced the length of the log. Stopped at the top and stared up at the ridge, and the bare rock. Didn't see her, no, she knew that because he didn't rush headlong. And this one would, damn sure, the moment he saw her. Entirely too young, just like Drasan had been, entirely too confident.

"Ollu! If she got up to those rocks, we wouldn't see tracks."

But smart. Fuck.

The older one

*Ollu*

had already started downslope, one hand still on his ribs. He twisted around. Shook his head and made his armor rattle.

"There's a print, boy. Down *here*. This end of the log."

"But—"

"This way." Ollu gestured sharply. "Rot your eyes, Kenjak, she left a *track*."

Kenjak hesitated. Snow watched his mouth open, watched his shoulders square up for argument. And watched his arm drop, fingers rolled into a fist. He turned around, started back toward Ollu, reluctant and stiff and obedient.

Something to be said, after all, for inbred male compliance.

*Thank you, Laughing God.*

Snow rocked onto the balls of her feet. Mapped and remapped her path to the rocks, through them, and over the ridge. Put her feet *there*, clear patches, keep low and hope the God's favor held.

*Please.*

Three, two, go. Short out-breath and then straight dashes from point to point, don't look back and don't think about javelins. Hard to hit a moving target. The boy wouldn't have the skill yet. Ollu might, but he'd be too far downslope and throwing against the wind.

*Please.*

She cleared the first of the rocks, the snow melting dark on the grey. It was slick, but she managed. City streets got wet, too, cobbles and bricks, same kind of treachery. She compensated for the pack's bulk, took shorter strides, kept her weight centered, hand on her blade's hilt to steady it.

*Please.*

Three steps from the summit now, lungs tight around air and fear, yeah, because the rocks here were slush-glazed. Couldn't slow down, couldn't afford injury, and oh Laughing God, so fucking *exposed*. That highborn brat might look back one more time, might see her. She was certain of that, suddenly, spreading-chill-in-her-guts convinced that he'd look up and—

*please*

"Ollu! There she is! *Ollu!*"

*motherless God*

—see her. Hell with caution, then. She overstretched, made two steps out of three. Fell and skidded over the summit, on ass and hip and one palm stinging through its glove. The other hand flailed and put itself between her face and an unexpected branch: knobby pine, twisted and lurking, growing out of a crack in the rocks. She bounced off it, wished her pursuer a faceful of branches and needles. Because that little toadshit was coming, damn certain. Wouldn't wait on Ollu, no, he'd be too afraid of losing her, confident he'd catch her up.

"Kenjak, wait!"

"I got her!"

No great gift to be right all the time, yeah.

Snow bared teeth, grin and grimace. Sucked air between them. Kept her momentum and slithered feetfirst down the slope. Smoother on this side, better and worse. Less chance she'd snap an ankle. None at all that she'd stop herself before the tree line. North-facing hill, storm-facing, slush hardened to ice. She pulled her knees up, tried for a controlled spin off the rocks and into the trees, tried to take the impacts on the pack and that motherless pan. Managed a half-turn that fetched her up hard against a taller, less knobby pine, with broken-off branches studded like spears about head height. She wished those on her pursuers, too. Grabbed one and pulled herself upright. Protests rippled through her hip, where the skin felt numb and the muscles too tender, where she wasn't entirely sure the leather breeches had held against stone and friction.

And then her vision tunneled. Black on the edges, a narrow pinspot of light at the end. But no blindness this time, no tumbled images through a svartjagr's eyes. Only a sense of direction, blurred by altitude and speed. North and east, Briel wanted. A sense of whiteness, of size. Maybe a cave, then.

Or incoming blindness, which she couldn't afford. She sent

*no, not now*

urgency at Briel. Got her own eyes back. Sharp snap to clarity, aches in both sockets, fuck but she hated that feeling. Briel wouldn't be happy on the other end, either. Would be scared now, and maybe angry, and that meant unpredictable. Briel might try another sending. Might come herself and attack the soldiers with teeth and tail-spike.

That wouldn't be unwelcome, no. Just real unlikely. Svartjagr were not brave by themselves. They were pack hunters, and Briel's pack consisted of one half-blood Dvergir in a lot of trouble.

She dared half a beat's rest to reorient. Briel wanted her going down this time, and so she would—down the hill and into the valley and angle up the other side. Bigger trees on the south face, more scrub, she might make it to cover before Kenjak saw where she'd gone. And maybe, here on the stones, in the rocks, she might dare a conjuring. Crazy-stupid, this far from a city, this deep in the Wild, but so was running blind in a forest in winter; and rocks were at least *like* the caves.

Any Dvergir could weave shadows, with a little guidance. But very few could do what *she* could, which was—

Crash and clatter of steel against stone. A yelp, in a young man's voice, and a pain-strangled:

"Stop! You there!"

—run, at the moment. Faster.

\* \* \*

The half-blood would've gotten away if Kenjak had listened to Ollu. *Fast* runner, long legs, and no armor. No hesitation, either, like she knew the forest. She must've had an egress already plotted, she and the dead man, which might make them Taliri agents, spies, part of the raiders who'd destroyed the village. Sure, he'd argued otherwise with Ollu, but maybe he'd been wrong. The half-blood's companion had tried to kill Salis, which no innocent citizen would. So this woman wasn't a citizen, or she wasn't innocent, and either way Kenjak meant to run her down and drag her back to the First Spear.

The how of that niggled at the back of his brain. He should've caught her on the downhill rush. Except his helmet found every low-lying branch, while she slid beneath them. His armor clung and slid and threw his balance; his scabbard tenderized his thigh. *She* wasn't having those troubles. Ducked and slid between trees like shadows while he dodged traitorous pines and leapt treacherous stones and, half the time, bounced into one or the other.

She knew the terrain, that was all. Had more experience. But he'd catch her on the next uphill, because she'd started up at an angle, was already slipping a little. Slowing down. He'd catch her up, and then he'd—

*Die, if you're stupid. Wait for Ollu. Don't run alone. A soldier never—*

Rurik's warnings, and Ollu's, the advice of every veteran he'd ever met. The half-blood could be leading him to ambush. Could be running him into a camp of raiders, maybe the same that burned Davni. They must be out here.

*And where are their tracks, then?*

They must be concealed. Which made it more prudent to wait for Ollu, and keep his eyes on where she went. Except Ollu would've gone the wrong way, Ollu had been doing exactly that until Kenjak had seen her running. And Ollu pounded behind him now, slow and fallible. Kenjak heard an occasional snatch of his name, other orphan syllables he could interpret as *stop* or *wait*.

Which he would not do. The snow was falling thicker now, sifting through the branches and dusting the forest floor. Her tracks trailed in front of him, smudged and shallow and far in between. Long legs, damn her. She'd clear the next hilltop again before he did.

He thought about Rurik's face if he reported an escape. The cold-eyed *what are you good for, little brother, except breeding?* stare.

He dipped his chin and dug his toes deep into the pine needles and mud and dirt. Dug deep in himself, too, and strained and found a little more speed in muscles that had been tired an hour ago. Gained ground, step by step, closed the distance. A dozen more steps and he'd have her.

*She tried to escape, First Spear, but I caught her—*

She must've heard him. Sensed him. Kenjak wondered if she had wings, or charmed boots, or if she'd been playing before. Mocking him by letting him get close.

*Setting you up, boy, that's what she's doing, it's a trap.*

He missed a step. Caught himself on one hand and lurched upright. That cost him an arm's length of ground on her. So she did get to the hill summit before he did. And instead of plunging over the top, she paused. Looked back and flicked a smile at him that made Kenjak think he should stop and wait for Ollu. Let her go. Then he saw the rings in her ears for the first time, and the tangled topknot, and realized, too late, what he'd cornered.

*Conjuror.*

The half-blood scooped a handful of earth into one gloved palm, clenched it, and uncurled her fingers. Kenjak had a sick-bellied split second to realize her hand was empty, that the earth had vanished, before the ground under his feet turned traitor and heaved.

He sprawled backward on the pine needles. Nearly brained himself on a stump. And saw, with his vision throwing pain-sparks, the forest ripple around him. Trees wriggled, bent. Straightened again, while the earth still shuddered under him. Kenjak expected a thunderclap. Smoke. Lightning that the stories said accompanied backlash.

He heard swearing instead, Dvergiri and inventive as any soldier. A crashing of a body through brush. When he looked up, the woman was gone.

And so was the crest of the hill.

* * *

Veiko followed the bat-snake south. It wasn't simple to track it, in storm-twilight and thick snowfall. It flew hunter-silent now, near invisible through tree limbs. But even when he couldn't see it, he could feel it. Knew where it wanted him to go, which was unsettling. And more unsettling: the bat-snake's intended destination was both south and west from his campsite, toward the burned village. That would put them closer to the legion than he wanted. Wrong direction altogether. He wanted away from that place, from the soldiers, nowhere they could find trace of him.

He thought about stopping, calling the dogs, turning back to his campsite. That was smart shelter, upwind so that any fire of his would be lost in the larger burn-stink. Turn his back and go, well, if not home, then at least to a place of his choosing. The bat-snake's need tugged at him, but he could ignore it.

Up ahead, Helgi slammed to a stiff-legged stop. Snarled at Logi as the younger dog crowded up on his flank. That was all the warning Veiko got before the ground bucked like a half-tamed takin. It twisted and rippled like water, dirt-slip and needle-slide, he and the dogs scratching for purchase. His skin tingled, itched and pebbled like the moment before a lightning strike. Wrong season for that, too, wrong weather altogether. And then that fast, the feeling was gone. Normal cold air, normal storm-swirl. Solid earth underfoot.

Helgi whined. Logi flattened himself to the snow. Veiko thought he might want to do the same.

The trees had moved. The hillside had. It felt just a little steeper now. A little more rugged. And maybe it was the snowfall blurring his vision

*no, it is not*

but the profile of the ridge ahead looked different, too, as if someone had gouged the earth away.

*And put it where?*

The bat-snake swooped and caught itself on the trunk of the nearest spruce, the same one that'd been seven paces left and downslope just moments earlier. It paused there, wings wide, and stared at him.

"Chrrip!"

Impatient, as if it couldn't grasp why the dogs were cowering, or why he'd joined them. As if it hadn't felt that flux at all, or didn't care. As if the earth rearranged itself regularly, nothing to fret over.

All right. Animals

*that thing is not, quite*

were a good judge of danger. If this one wasn't afraid

*and what about the dogs?*

then perhaps he needn't be. Maybe such happenings were common in the Illhari Republic.

*Tell yourself that.*

Veiko stood carefully. Nodded at the bat-snake, who *chrripped* approval. And then it was off again, a flicker of black in the snow. A new direction, too: down, into the grooves between the hills, in the direction the land-flux had come from. Going right to the source.

Of course. Veiko shook his head. He must be spirit-touched. Snow-mad.

*Curious.*

Which was just as dangerous. He resettled his pack and his axe and started after it.

"Helgi. Logi."

This time, the dogs let him lead.

\* \* \*

Ollu caught up while Kenjak was still scouring out his guts. Heave and gag. His ears wouldn't stop ringing, the world wouldn't stop moving.

Ollu hooked the back of his belt and hauled him roughly upright. Steadied him as his knees wobbled. As his stomach tried to climb up his throat again.

"Backlash," he said, and had to swallow hard. Wouldn't puke on Ollu's boots. Wouldn't.

"Yeah, I felt it." Ollu's face steamed, mouth and nose and skin. "She's desperate, to try conjuring out here."

Kenjak nodded. Of course. Desperate. He pointed a leaf-steady hand at the ridgeline. "She—"

"I see where she went, boy. Running slantwise up this hill. She'll keep that direction on the other side. Guessing she can still run, anyway. Backlash'll kill the conjuror, sometimes."

"What if the land's different on that side?"

Ollu snorted. "Conjuring doesn't remake the world, boy. It just rearranges what's there." He palmed the top of Kenjak's helmet. Twisted his head ungently. "See that crease? It's a gully now, but it's still following where the streambed was. Wraps around, yeah? We take that, cut her off. And if she broke something in the fall, or died . . . better luck."

"She's alive." Gulping now, to keep his guts steady. "I heard her swearing."

"So she's a tough conjuror, then." Ollu slapped an open palm on the back of his helmet. Said, clear through the new ringing in Kenjak's ears: "Twice stupid to chase her alone, boy. You're lucky so far. Now stay with me, yeah? See if you learn how to deal with her kind."

# CHAPTER THREE

Deep crevice she'd landed in, a winter-dry riverbed layered with snow and dead leaves. Might be rocks underneath, or frozen mud. Hell for footing. Which meant going slower, maybe, or risking what the fall hadn't managed. Snow thought about trying to climb the other side for exactly two rapid heartbeats. Thump-thump and no thank you. She could scale any wall that was solid. This—wasn't. Mud. Roots. Slip and slime and no fucking chance.

She squinted up through the cold-kiss flakes. Two voices up there, words smeared to useless with distance and altitude and the echoes and knives in her own head. Toadfucking backlash and the headache that went with it, worse than anything Briel ever gave her. At least she could still see.

The soldiers hadn't followed her over the top. The backlash hadn't left much of the hilltop, and only a fool would jump blind after her. But they'd be coming. Wouldn't abandon the trail. The Illhari legion didn't quit. Charmingly predictable, on so many fronts.

*So run, yeah?*

Yeah.

She gathered her balance and stood up. Took a test step and let her breath out slowly. Thank

*the Laughing God*

luck that she hadn't broken or twisted anything. Bruises, yeah, that iron pan in her pack had left marks, but nothing lethal. Now the backlash, that could've killed her *and* the soldiers and leveled a square league of forest. Lucky twice over all she'd gotten was a mudslide for her daring.

Her former instructors at the Academy would've beaten her for something that stupid. Broken her fingers so she couldn't repeat the stupidity and expelled her. Tsabrak, though, might approve.

*The Laughing God loves the bold, Snow.*

And the stupid. Apparently.

She picked the direction she thought was most easterly. Readjusted the pack on her shoulders. Should've left the pan in the ashes. Should've hit Drasan with it, first thing, and left him alive for the legion, gotten herself out. Might still be lost in the forest, but at least she wouldn't have soldiers on her trail.

*Where am I, then?*

Briel's sending answered that question, and then it blinded her.

\* \* \*

Veiko found himself chasing the curves of a dry riverbed that hadn't been there two days ago. He'd crossed this terrain already. It was— had been—familiar. A tiny creekbed scarcely wider than his foot, in a shallow dip between hills. Now it was much deeper, a gully carved through the hillside.

His chest tightened around a chill that had nothing to do with weather. He had heard tales of the southlanders' witch-wars, and how the spirits of the land had struck back at them. Hadn't believed those tales until now. A hunter, a crofter's son, had no business with spirits. Spirits were a noidghe's affair.

He licked his lips. He should turn around and return to the work of surviving a winter alone, without his village, his father and brothers, four solid walls. But he could feel the bat-snake's distress tugging at him. Knew, somehow

*spirit-touched*

that it wasn't that far away. That

*she/I/we*

it needed

*me*

help. Needed *him*.

*Fool.*

Battle sounds, sudden and close, from around a sharp bend in the channel. Steel-clang and shouts echoing off the embankments.

Heat and cold together spiked through his belly, spread to his fingertips, settled into the long muscles of his thighs. Battle tension, but not his, and another familiar surge of need. Of real terror, too, and a desire to

*dive*

rush forward, to

*strike*

protect and

*tear*

defend and

*fly*

escape all at once.

Helgi snarled suddenly, savagely. Logi barked and leapt forward, ears flat and furious. Veiko realized then that he had a fighting grip on the axe that he couldn't remember pulling out of its sling. Realized that he'd got two more steps toward the bend in the riverbed and that he'd cleared enough of the corner to see the woman from his vision, alone, unarmored, running from a pair of Illhari soldiers, one of them cocking his arm back, ready to cast a javelin at her back.

She skidded on what had been the stony bed of the river, awkward and unbalanced by the pack that slewed across her back and by the blade she held left-handed like a lantern in darkness. She looked up, shouted at the sky. Panic stripped her voice raw.

"Briel!"

A keening answered, like restless dead at midwinter, the forgotten and furious ancestors who would take a man's soul if they caught him. The bat-snake streaked down between the soldiers. Its tail whipped, and the javelin thrower clamped his hand to his face. Screamed as red spilled through his fingers.

The woman skidded on snow, bounced herself on palm and knee and back upright. Spun toward the source of the screaming, took a step and tripped on an obvious stone and staggered again.

And then Logi barked and the woman spun and slashed with the blade. Veiko's throat sealed around Logi's name, even as he lunged forward and swung the axe to block. Wouldn't get there in time; she was too close, moving too fast.

She missed. Cleanly.

The blade swiped over the dog's head. Caught Veiko's late-arriving axe on the backswing and stuck in the wood. The woman tugged at it.

"Fuck and damn," she said clearly. Her eyes swept across Veiko's face, stopped and hung on a point just above his shoulder. Wide eyes, blue as summer midnight and blank as fresh snow.

Blind.

\* \* \*

Kenjak lay on his belly in the snow, eyes squeezed tight. The svartjagr's wingtip had laid his cheek open, but its tail had taken Ollu across the face. Ollu had stopped screaming. Down to whimpers and moans now, which were worse. Kenjak wanted to go to him, wanted to peel Ollu's hands back and see what'd happened. Wanted to make that sound stop. But he couldn't move, couldn't make himself

*get up, K'Hess Kenjak, why are you lying there?*

go to Ollu, because he knew the svartjagr was still up there, still circling, and it could

*rip out your eye*

hurt him like that.

*Coward, aren't you boy?*

It'd missed his eyes on that first pass. Might not, with another chance. Better to stay flat, play dead, hope it left with the half-blood.

A dog barked, very big and very close. Kenjak's heart clawed its way into his throat. He risked movement, twisted his neck and looked, and yes, there it was. And not just the dog—the woman, too, and a tall Alvir man—no. Kenjak blinked. Blamed blood and tears for the one eye's blurring, but there was nothing wrong with the other. The man was no Alvir, for all the pallid resemblance. He wore rough-spun wool and fur and leather, pale hair sectioned into narrow braids, taller than anyone Kenjak had seen. Skraeling, must be, whose people lived on mountaintops and ate only snow and who spoke in the language of beasts.

The skraeling held an axe in both hands, leveled above the dog's head. The half-blood's seax was stuck in the shaft. The skraeling's face didn't say *friendly*.

"Fuck and damn," said the half-blood. She tugged at her blade. "I didn't just hit a *tree*."

The skraeling's eyes narrowed. "No."

"Right."

Kenjak pulled himself onto his elbows. Heard a deep-throated snarl and saw paws coming at him—

"Helgi."

—then watched the paws slew aside and circle back to the man, to the half-blood, to the second dog. He saw Ollu, too, gone silent now, uncurling limp, his face rolling toward Kenjak, and oh foremothers, he had no eyes, was nothing but ragged slash and blood, a whole river of it.

"You are blind," said the skraeling.

Kenjak gagged up bile and nothing, because he'd already heaved out everything. Coughed and spat and expected the dogs to rush at him, or the axe to cleave his skull, or—

The half-blood cleared her throat. "At the moment, yes. Briel, please? Ah, thank you."

"You talk to the bat-snake? Does it understand?"

She laughed. Improbable sound. Startling. The dogs' ears swiveled, and their heads. Heat started in Kenjak's belly, a tiny coal. Spread fast as flames in dry leaves. He lay with his cheek pressed into the snow, his blood leaking pink and the torn flesh stinging, and he listened. To her. *Laughing.*

"Yes to the first. When she pleases to the second."

The woman raised her right arm, and the svartjagr keened again, right overhead. It struck the woman's back and shoulders, claws first, and wrapped its tail around her waist.

And chirped. Like a bird. Like a pet. Like it hadn't just torn a man's face open.

"Kenjak." Ghost-whisper, barely louder than Kenjak's own heartbeat. He dared a side-eye at Ollu. Swallowed hard as the acid boiled up in his throat. Ollu's mouth looked raw and round as his eye sockets. Ollu's fingers stretched toward—him, maybe, or the javelin lying between them. Both out of reach.

"Boy," Ollu whispered. "You . . ."

Whatever else he said got lost under a pair of deep barks and a svartjagr's hiss, the skraeling's sharp "Logi!"

And in the echoes, the woman's voice.

"So, you talk to the dogs, do you? Do *they* understand?"

"Sometimes."

Ollu had slumped silent again. His fingers curled over his outstretched hand like a dead spider's legs. And maybe Ollu was dead, too,

*please*

and past pain. But he'd wanted something from Kenjak. Wanted—well, it didn't take much to guess it. Same thing Salis had wanted. The same thing Rurik expected.

*Do your duty, little brother.*

Kenjak wanted to tell Ollu he couldn't, because the half-blood wasn't alone now, that she had a svartjagr and a big skraeling with an axe and two dogs, while he had only a legionnaire's sword. She could conjure, too, and what chance did he have against that?

Ollu couldn't advise him. Kenjak stared, horrified, as the breath steaming out of the older man trailed to a tendril and stopped altogether. Soon the snow would begin to collect on his skin. Would bury him.

The javelin lay between them. Kenjak's sword, only a little farther. It would only take a little effort to reach one of them, only a little more to cross the snow and get her. Kenjak was that quick. He could do it. And maybe Rurik would find his corpse beside Ollu's, but Rurik would find the half-blood there with them. He'd know what happened.

*I did my duty.*

Kenjak surged to his feet.

\* \* \*

Her sight was creeping back, dragging a headache behind it, when the dogs growled. Sudden sound, savage, competing with Briel's violent wingbeats. Snow bit back a very undignified squeak. Nothing she could do if the dogs jumped her, except die. And then, next moment:

"Helgi. Logi."

Sharp syllables, accent like an axe chipping cold wood. Not-A-Tree wrenched her blade nearly out of her hands. She held on to the hilt, only just, as he brushed past her in a gust of leather and dogs and woodsmoke. The snarling boiled around her knees as she squinted into the snowfall, and yeah, there, maybe those were body shapes in the white-grey blur.

Red and black haze, that was an Illhari soldier. Winter-colored, that was Not-A-Tree. Something in his hand, slim and grey, with a darker steel blot on the end. Not a sword, no. Laughing God, was that an *axe*? She blinked. The world smeared into focus.

It was. An axe with a seax-sized cut in the shaft. The dogs, she realized—they were big animals, like wolves—had gone quiet. Briel, too.

The soldier had his weapon drawn and pointed. "Stand aside, skraeling, in the name of the Illhari Republic. That woman"—she could make out more details now, the boy's handsome highborn face and his terrible youth—"is a criminal, and by the authority of the governor of Cardik she is *mine*."

"No," Not-A-Tree said levelly. His Dvergiri sounded stiff and formal. "She cannot defend herself."

"She . . . you." For a heartbeat Snow thought the soldier would back down, walk away, declare defeat, and go home. He rocked back and started to lower his blade. Then he lunged at Not-A-Tree. Legion-standard maneuver that would have worked against an average bandit, a typical outlaw, someone who waited to meet steel with steel.

Not-A-Tree folded sideways, one neat step, as the sword stabbed past him, and swung the axe. Steel whistled, ending in the dull crack of breaking bone. The boy's blade flickered like a fish in the river and buried itself in the snow. The soldier himself crumpled where he stood. He curled around his arm and moaned.

Not-A-Tree stepped back. Lowered the axe. Breathed audibly for the first time. It sounded to Snow like a sigh.

Snow sheathed her blade. Managed not to slice off a finger. Blind and waving metal was one thing. Hands shaking like this, she was safer unarmed.

Not-A-Tree shifted stance and attention as she drew even with him. Staring down at her, yeah, and there weren't many men taller than she was. Well. Dvergiri men, which he wasn't, clearly. One of the northern tribes, whose names no one knew. Blue eyes, bright as witchfire, gone narrow and wary in a face not much past twenty.

The words spilled out of him like stones down a rock face. "You were blind. Now you are not."

Her throat felt too small. "It's temporary."

"That is fortunate." Suspicious. Foreign. Hell, no, *alien*, and holding an axe that could sever a limb as neatly as it broke bones.

If he meant to kill her, well, he could. Not a toadfucking thing she could do to stop it, yeah?

*The Laughing God loves the bold, Snow.*

Right.

She raised her chin and made herself step past him. Past his dogs, who lifted their muzzles and sniffed. One of them—the smaller one, fox colored—flattened his ears and whined. Friendly now, or curious.

She edged around and stopped closer to the soldier. He stared at a spot just in front of her boots, braced, dear Laughing God, like he expected torture, or brutality, or

*what he'd do to me, if he could*

a boot in the face. Anything but meet her eyes. Highborn habits broke hard. Insult her, sure, but he didn't want to lock eyes like an equal. Thank the old ways, and highborn conservatism, if it made her job easier this once.

She squatted and folded her arms on her knees. Made a show of looking at the bands of color on the top edge of his uniform. "Second Mila, is it? You seem young to be in the Sixth. What's your name?"

Silent. Defiant, this one, grant him that. Maybe grant him *brave*, too, although that looked a lot like stupid most times.

She peeled back a smile. "All right, Second Mila. *Kenjak*, yeah? That's what he called you. Your partner."

*Now* she had his attention. Horror in his eyes. "You. Killed. Him."

She glanced at the corpse. "No. That was Briel."

His mouth worked around something sour. "Half-blood."

"Yeah." Old anger in her guts, like shifting coils. "That's not a crime."

"Conjuror."

"Neither is that."

Tsabrak would've gutted the boy already, left him for the storm and the crows. Which she should do, too. Two soldiers meant more on the way, and Tsabrak's toadfucked courier was still out there. She came back without a new source of rasi, yeah, Tsabrak might leave *her* for the crows.

The snow squeaked a warning. The skraeling loomed suddenly at her shoulder, dull distressed leather breeches and oiled boots. Kenjak flinched.

"What," the skraeling asked, in his dusty, precise Dvergiri, "are you doing?"

She twisted her neck and peered up at him. Fuck and damn, tall man, and that axe too close to eye level for comfort. "Having a friendly chat."

He snorted. "He is no friend of yours."

"Noticed that, did you? Was it the sword gave it away? Or the threats?" She raised her hand, half surrender, half apology. "This one's highborn," she said. "From Illharek. Likely his mother's important."

Eloquent silence.

She sighed. Expect a skraeling to understand politics, yeah, expect the sky to rain cats. "Best we don't *leave* him like this, yeah?"

The skraeling squatted beside her. He studied Kenjak, narrow-eyed. "What do you intend to do with him?"

"Well. I don't think Briel will eat him. Do your dogs like fresh meat?"

"They will eat anything."

Laughing God, the skraeling had a sense of humor.

The boy's eyes darted toward his fallen sword, and she saw despair as clear as sunlight. Then he recovered his sneer, turned it fully on Not-A-Tree. "Skraeling," he spat, and this time found liquid to go with it. No range, fortunate for him. Briel hissed anyway, and the grey dog, the bigger one, growled. The skraeling said nothing at all, but those witchfire eyes burned holes into Kenjak's hide. Credit the boy, he tried to meet and match that stare. No shame that he failed.

Snow coughed a second time. "Second Mila, I don't mind your insults. My companion might. Or do you *want* us to kill you?"

Kenjak didn't move at all when she reached for him, when she pulled down the edge of his collar and exposed the House sigil inked into the skin under his collarbone. Fuck and damn. That wasn't just highborn; that was *political*. His mother was a senator. Killing him would have consequences. Sparing him, though—that might be worth something.

"K'Hess," she said. "That's an *honorable* House. Means you should've at least called warning. Asked surrender."

Sullen now and shivering, with cold or shock or both. "You attacked Salis."

"The soldier with the crossbow? That was Drasan, and she paid him for that."

She pried his fingers away from the wounded arm. Controlled her own wince. Visible bend between wrist and elbow, both bones snapped clean. She ran her palm over the sleeve. Felt the wound's heat like live coals through layers of leather and cloth. Blood spread dark on the fabric, which meant broken skin to go with the bones.

"You're lucky. That axe could've sliced just as easy. Broken arm, I can help. Severed, I can't."

The boy glared somewhere sideways of her. "I don't want your help."

"And I don't want to help you. But listen, Second Mila Highborn, I leave you like this, you won't fight again. If the wound rots, you'll die a lot slower than your friend. The poison on a svartjagr's tail-spike works fast. The poison your body makes, you'll die for days."

His pupils pooled black. She answered the question he hadn't asked, the one probably lodged in his throat.

"Hurts a lot, I think, dying like that." She twisted, looked up, caught the skraeling's witchfire stare. He hadn't moved. Watched her and waited. "Borrow your hands? He'll probably pass out, but I don't need a brawl if he doesn't."

The skraeling stared at her as if she'd just announced her intention to wear a cat on her head. "You will help him."

"I intend to set the bone, yeah."

"I do not understand."

No, he probably didn't. Tsabrak would've called her softhearted and sneered about charity. Asked if she liked the boy's face, was that it, and refused to help. But Tsabrak would not have cared what her reasoning was, either. So.

"Two reasons, yeah? His mother's a senator. Important woman. He survives this, House K'Hess might remember who saved him. Might repay the favor someday. Second reason: there's a First Spear in Cardik named K'Hess. So if this boy dies out here, like this, troops will scour this forest looking for revenge."

Blink. Nod. First time she'd seen his eyebrows settle back where they belonged. Not-A-Tree knelt beside her. Set the axe aside, deliberately and easily one-handed, and close enough to grab in a hurry. "What shall I do?"

# CHAPTER FOUR

Veiko pressed his body weight against the boy and tried not to listen to tearing cloth and wet flesh. Tried to ignore the screaming and kept his eyes fixed on the dead man, who had screamed, too, before he died. Long and loud, yes, but not so close to Veiko's ear.

Illhari soldiers, he decided, did not handle pain well.

*You think you'd do better, skraeling?*

A whisper, that, which Veiko should not have been able to hear. But he had, clear as if there were no sounds but snowfall and wind in the pines.

*How many battles have you seen, skraeling? How many wounds?*

The dead man's lips appeared to stretch in a smile that wasn't, Veiko knew, *real*. Shadows and storm, that was all. Just an accident of light.

*Tell yourself that.*

There were tales, stories—angry ghosts might haunt their death sites, it was said, refuse the peace of their graves. There were rites one could perform. Prayers and bindings. But Veiko wasn't a noidghe, and this was a Dvergir spirit. The ghost road's secrets belonged to the noidghe, and Veiko was a crofter's son, a hunter, an outlaw—

"Hey."

The woman's voice, her hand on his shoulder; her face dipped between him and the dead man. Abruptly he realized the screaming had stopped. He thought he had another corpse under him, until he marked the steady in-and-out of ribs against his own. The woman's hand patted reassurance, same as he might give his dogs.

"You can get off now. He's not going anywhere."

Veiko did, careful to avoid the dead man's stare. The wounded Dvergir's scent clung to his skin and clothing. Sweat. Pain. Fear. He clenched his fists and did not indulge the urge to brush at himself like a child who'd discovered an insect clinging to his shirt.

The woman seemed unaffected. Hadn't reacted to the screams or the thrashing. But she paused now to look at him. To frown.

"You all right?"

His stomach tightened. Settled as he pulled a deep breath.

The dead man laughed, a sound Veiko felt more than heard, like fishhooks in flesh.

*Feeling a little sick, are you? Some warrior.*

His skin prickled. He would not argue. It was unwise to encourage the angry dead. "I am fine."

"All right." She pointed her chin at the remains of the soldier's uniform. "Think you could cut that sleeve into strips? We're almost finished."

*And what after that?* Veiko did not ask. Did as she wanted him to, yet again. He'd already sacrificed one of his arrows for a splint. A small matter to hold the pieces against the boy's broken arm. Pay no attention to the grind and slip of what should be solid, no. Tie this. Pull that. Once she'd had him retrieve an herb—

"The mossy stuff, purple, little green bag—yeah, that one."

—from a pouch on her belt. He leaned in close and told himself that the Illhari had different customs, that was all. No Alvir he'd ever met, no trader or hunter or woman in the tavern, would have let a *skraeling* stranger so close. He tried not to notice the warmth and solidity of her, nor recall how long it had been since he'd touched something living that was not Helgi or Logi. He couldn't smell fear on her, only a faint sweet-sharp smokiness that he didn't recognize.

*She's a conjuror, skraeling. You know what that means?*

He would not look at the corpse. Found the moss and tried to give it to her, and found—

"Tuck it in there, yeah?"

—himself stuffing it into the wound instead. The boy's raw flesh steamed in the chill. Salt and metal stink that couldn't quite smother the stone-and-earth scent of her.

*Ask why she isn't afraid of you, skraeling.*

Because he hadn't wanted to harm her. Perhaps the bat-snake had communicated, somehow, his intentions.

*Maybe she reads your mind, skraeling. Her kind can.*

Her kind. *Half-blood,* the soldier had named her, and *conjuror. Not a crime,* she'd said to both.

The ghost laughed.

*Don't believe that. Might be your bones here with me next. Think she's safe, skraeling?*

No, he did not, but it was far less safe to speak to the dead. Veiko squeezed his eyes closed. Sudden chill, a lessening of snowfall, that meant the storm had finally dragged itself over the mountains. Close to sunset now, and that meant the spirit world would draw even closer. He wanted to be long gone before that, didn't want to see the ghost rising up and pulling its flesh after it, growing solid, growing real.

*I am not a noidghe, and I do not see spirits.*

Which would not save him if the dead man walked.

"Hey." The woman frowned at him. Asked, a second time, "You all right?"

He flushed. Lied, a second time. "I am fine."

One fine eyebrow arched. Almost white, stark against Dvergiri skin. "It's one thing to butcher an animal, yeah? Another thing to cut on something still living. I'm a chirurgeon. Most times I do this, there's drugs. Too hard to work on a thrashing body."

She paused. Waiting for a response, Veiko guessed. Some indication he'd understood that sudden flood of language. Which he had. Mostly. Except:

"Chirurgeon?"

"Trained in the Academy. You have no idea what that means, do you?"

It was like trying to run up a snowslide. "No."

A tiny smile curled the corner of her mouth. She plunged her hands into the snow and scrubbed it pink. "Means I know how to mend wounds, yeah? We're done here, soon as I build a fire. Can't have him freeze before help arrives. But he'll use that arm again. Hold a sword."

"He will not thank you."

"No. But he'll remember who saved him. Might be useful, someday, some highborn owes me a favor. And more important for you and me right now—whoever finds him won't waste time hunting for a murdering half-blood and a—"

"Skraeling?"

She flashed him a look as pointed as arrows. "Why didn't you kill him?"

"He was." Veiko paused. "Not a threat."

"To you."

"Yes."

"Until you got between us."

"Not then, either."

Veiko did not want this conversation. Did not want her gratitude, no, because that meant obligation. Meant connection, a twining of fates and lives. Better to settle debts now and be free of each other. Walk away *alone* and leave her to her fate. He looked at the dogs. At the bat-snake. He had spoken more in this short sliver of afternoon than he had in two long months.

His throat hurt. He cleared it. "My name is Veiko Nyrikki." His father might not permit him that name anymore. He might be only Veiko Clanless, now, Veiko Outlaw.

"Veiko Nyrikki," she repeated carefully. Nodded. "Snowdenaelikk."

Nothing about her was easy. "Snow. D'Naelikk." It sounded like a Jaihnu clan-name, maybe one of the settlements on the tundra's eastern edge. "Snow is your . . . House?"

He thought she would laugh. Saw the grin crack her features wide, heard the sharp hiss of breath going in. Only silence, coming out, and her teeth clicked together. "Just Snow, yeah? No House name. I'm not highborn. My mother chose the name. And by now I think my mother'd rather pretend I never happened, yeah?"

He nodded. She must be another outlaw, then, whose family disowned her. A man did not pry into another's business. Guess what she had done, yes, imagine it, but do not ask.

*Oh, ask her, skraeling. Blood on her hands, yeah, soaked to her wrists. That one is a murderer.*

*So am I,* Veiko thought. And said, over the ghost's laughter, "The storm is light now, but it will get worse. Be quick, whatever you do."

She tipped her face up. The snow collected on her cheeks, brief scattered white before turning to wetness. The wind caught the edge of her hood, pulled it down to her shoulders. Her pale hair was close-clipped around the lower half of her skull, with a long topknot gathered at the back. A trio of fine gold rings, and one heavier silver, flashed high in the curve of her ear. She was like no woman he'd ever seen, Dvergir or half-blood or otherwise. Like no *one* he'd seen in all his life.

"Yeah? How can you tell?" Looking at him now, head tilted, curious. "Veiko?"

He was, he realized, staring. Stopped and turned his face into the rising wind. "The air gets colder. There is a . . ." He couldn't find the Dvergiri word. Shrugged at her. "Feeling."

"Feeling. Right." Flash smile as she twitched her hood up again. She started collecting the dead man's javelins, which had scattered during his dying. Wedged them under her boot and leaned on them until the wood snapped.

Crack.

Like ice in spring thaw. He managed not to flinch at the surprising violence she brought to the task.

Crack.

She wore another smile now, small and grim. Didn't ask for his help, and Veiko didn't offer. Revenge was a private matter.

*That it is, skraeling. So why don't you run? That's my only warning.*

Maybe it was the spreading twilight that made Veiko think he saw a smile on the dead man's face. Maybe.

Crack.

Sweat beaded on his skin. Chilled there, through all the layers of wool and linen. Spirits could walk, after sunset. Wear their flesh and do terrible harm to the living. A hunter should have no business with them. A man should not see them or hear them, and he had done both.

Easy to step back, fade into the forest. Get far away from this Snowdenaelikk, this angry spirit, this wounded soldier who would live to remember them both.

And it wasn't imagining, wasn't twilight, the sudden stretch of a dead mouth, or the gleam of long teeth.

*Think I'll get up and chew your flesh, skraeling? Maybe I will. But her first, yeah? So run.*

Dust in his mouth. Ice in his chest. His heart was somewhere between them, fluttering in his throat. He forced words around it.

"You will perform the burial rites, will you not?"

Crack. Snow dropped two more pieces of javelin onto the small pile of broken wood. "For the corpse? Never mind. Of course for the corpse." She frowned at the body. "No. Let his own people handle that."

"You are Illhari. He is, as well. I have heard you burn your dead."

Her mouth quirked again, and this time it wasn't a smile. "You heard Mila Highborn, didn't you? I'm half-blood. And a conjuror. That's two different kinds of Illhari than he is. I think this motherless toadshit would just as soon I let him rot than touch him. I don't mind. And this makes no sense to you at all, does it, Veiko Nyrikki, who just happened to be walking through this particular forest and picked a fight on my behalf?"

Dizzying, baffling, the number of words that came out of her mouth. He seized on the ones he recognized.

"I am here because of the bat-snake—"

"Briel?" She laughed, for the second time in their short acquaintance. "Svartjagr, not bat-snake. I asked her to find me a safe *place*, not a person."

"She did. My campsite. You did not make it that far."

She stared at him, mouth open and, for once, empty of words.

Somewhere, hidden by soot-colored clouds, the sun dipped behind the mountains. Veiko grimaced. "Among my people, we cover a body in stones, to hold it to the earth. I do not think we have time for that."

He scooped up his axe in both hands and dodged around Snowdenaelikk, straddled the dead man, and hacked, once and cleanly. The blade slid through flesh, through bone. Only a little resistance at the end, before the head rolled clear. And it was not his imagination, no trick of light and shadow, that the dead man's face twisted hate for a heartbeat.

*Toadfucking skraeling.*

"Laughing *God*. Why did you do that?"

Veiko shook gore off his blade. Swiped it through snow and shook it again. Wiped it clean on the boy's remaining sleeve. Kept his shoulders turned so Snow would not see his trembling.

"It is sunset," he said slowly, so that his voice did not shake. "The angry dead can walk if they are not prevented."

"The angry dead. Worry about the angry living, yeah? No, not *me*. Fuck and *damn*. The legion, Veiko. The ones who were not supposed to come after us, because we didn't give them cause. Except now we have. Killing in battle is one thing. Desecration's something else."

"So we burn him in the manner of your people."

"You know that bodies don't burn like sticks, yeah? And that I don't know a fucking thing about building pyres?"

He did not, either thing, but: "You were intending a fire already."

"A little one so the boy won't freeze—oh here. *Fine*." She dropped to her knees, dumped her bundle of broken sticks on the corpse. "We'll need more wood than this."

Which would not be easy to acquire, down in a dead riverbed, when the nearest trees were a man's height up the banks and any fallen branches would be soaked and rotten. Veiko decided he did not need to tell her that. He retreated instead, dogs at his heels, to search for wood that he might not find.

*Run, skraeling.*

It might have been wind in dead branches. Might have been his own better sense talking. Easy to fade into the snow, to disappear. She would manage a fire. Would survive until searchers arrived.

*And then?*

It was not his concern what the legion did with her. He had intervened once already. They were not kin, he did not even know her clan-name, and—

"Chrrip."

He hadn't seen the bat-snake—svartjagr—move. Saw her now, closer than he liked, her head on a level with his. She clung to a tangle of roots in the steep bank. Solid black, darker than even a Dvergir, with a live-coal stare. Snowdenaelikk had sent Briel to find a safe place, and she had found him instead.

A wise man would have shot the bat-snake when he first saw it, but a wise man wouldn't have a mountain range and two seasons of exile between self and home. Fools involved themselves in others' business, and Veiko was, by that measure, already far down that path.

"Chrrip?"

His chest tightened with an anxiety he should not feel—and did anyway, because the svartjagr wanted it. Wanted him.

"I am not leaving."

"Chrrip." The tension eased abruptly, like a bowstring released. Well-being flooded after, warm satisfaction that was not his. That clashed with the knot in his belly and turned sour. Fools bargained with spirits. Fools, or noidghe.

He chose fool, for the moment. Under Briel's supervision, he collected a pathetic bundle of twigs, one still bristling with green needles. A recent casualty of wind, that one. Probably still green inside.

"This isn't enough," Snow said when he came back. "Not for a body."

"It will prevent him from walking."

She looked at him. Swallowed whatever she meant to say and didn't, if her expression meant anything, enjoy the taste.

She rummaged through her pack one-handed. Clinking. A rattle. A sound like dried leaves. And swearing, recognizable by its venom, even if he did not understand the words.

"You have a firestone?"

"Yes."

"Good. Drasan had ours." She pulled out a blown-glass bulb, very small, and shook it doubtfully. She squatted and drizzled the oil over the broken, meager kindling, dumped it more generously over the corpse's torso.

"Do not forget the head."

Narrow look, but she didn't argue. The oil collected in the crease between helmet and hair, like blood from a wound, glistened as it soaked into the dead man's black braid.

*Think I won't follow you, skraeling?*

Veiko knelt beside the corpse, turned the head facedown.

He struck flint to steel. Sparks mixed with snowflakes, brief alliance that ended in spitting flames and spots of damp on the wood. And—there. The oil caught. New flames flickered and spread and spat. Fought for territory with thick flakes that soaked in all the spaces the oil had left. Hiss. Spit.

He leaned over the fire. Tried, with little success, to shield it. Too much in the open here, too unsheltered. The fire would die, and the boy would freeze, and the dead man's spirit would not pass into the next world. Might follow them, haunt them, wait for a new chance at vengeance.

"Get back." Snow wedged her shoulder in front of him. Passed her hand in front of the fledgling pyre. Once. Twice. Shadows flowed away from the flames, liquid blackness, and the fire surged in their wake. Brightened and steadied and carved new shadows out of the twilight and drove them back in an ever-growing ring of heat and light. Oil pop, flesh sizzle, the stink of burning hair, the spirit's muffled shriek as flesh caught and burned.

Veiko edged away—from the flames and the corpse and her. Wished he hadn't, in the next moment, when she glanced at him sidelong. But it was one thing to hear about Dvergiri witchery, and another to see it, high flames where there had been flickering.

She offered him a smile worn thin on the edges. "Light to shadow, shadow to light. It's not even conjuring, yeah? Any Dvergir can do it. Even half-bloods. It's just most don't bother to learn."

He held the shiver under his skin this time. "There are stories about your people."

"Oh, I'm sure of that. We're stitched from the shadows, we're the living incarnation of malice, we're motherless, godless, heartless women who keep our men chained and gelded—ah. You hadn't heard *that* one, then? Don't worry. Been a long time since the Reforms. It's elective surgery, these days. Only ones who do it are highborn."

Unsettling notion. Veiko glanced at Kenjak. Frowned. "Did he . . . ?"

"Do I look like his family's personal chirurgeon?" Snow crouched behind Kenjak. Hooked her hands under his arms. Dragged him closer to the fire. "He's a soldier, so probably not. It's only the ones who aspire to politics or tradition who bother."

"It is a wonder any man aspires to either."

A snort. She settled Kenjak between the pyre and the riverbank. "A highborn man's aspirations matter only as much as his mother thinks they do. Most times, *politics* for a man means being a consort where his mother thinks he'll do the most good for her House. It's a little better for the lowborn, yeah? We just leave unwanted boys in the forest and have done."

"That is also tradition among my people. Only it is the girls who are killed."

"Yeah. Well. Taliri and Alviri do that, too." She seemed a little older then. A little tired. "You were serious about the angry dead. Ollu, there. He was dangerous."

"Yes."

She stared somewhere past the growing pyre. Through it. Into the spirit world itself, for all he knew. "So that's twice I owe you."

"You." *Do not owe me* shriveled in his throat. One thing to lie about small things. This was not small, and it did no honor to either of them to pretend otherwise. He offered an explanation instead, to excuse the obligation he'd laid on her.

"I did not—do not—think that you deserved to die."

She tilted her face toward him. Looked at him from eyes gone blacker now than her skin, as if the flames had burned the blue away. "And I thank you for that, Veiko Nyrikki, more than I can possibly express."

He had not wanted her gratitude, and now he had it. Had not wanted responsibility for her life and had accepted it twice. He would only add to her debt if he took her back to

*a safe place*

his campsite. She wouldn't freeze, not immediately, not with the pyre. But she had no firestone. No more oil. And she couldn't— wouldn't—stay here alone. The legion would come, and he could guess at their mercy, no matter what she'd done for the boy.

"We should go," Veiko said. "Now. My camp is not so far."

"We, is it?" She had not assumed, then. Hoped only, and wouldn't quite look at him. Veiko recognized *lost* when he saw it, and *fear*, and averted his gaze. Those things, too, were a private matter. He would not add any more to her debt.

"Briel believes so."

Flicker-smile. She nodded. Gathered her pack and waited, wordless, as he collected both dogs and his bearings. And she followed him, still silent, into the storm.

# CHAPTER FIVE

First Spear K'Hess Rurik was not an easy commander. Not loved, not liked. Feared, perhaps, by some of the troops, although First Scout Szanys Dekklis would not have admitted to that particular emotion. She'd have called her tangled guts *anticipation* if someone had asked her. The way a good soldier should feel when her commander summoned her out of her tent during a blizzard. Oh, not the commander personally, no: his optio poked her head into the tent flap, snapped, "Dekklis. First Spear wants you *now*," and jerked her head out of sight like a startled turtle. Snow swirled and settled in her wake, pindot wetness on the canvas floor.

The lamplight splashed across a dice game gone suddenly quiet. The tent reeked of wet wool and lamp oil and warm bodies. They'd been outside for hours, stacking the residents of Davni like cordwood, to finish on a proper pyre what the first burning had done only partway—had been inside, now, for not long at all. Boots still soaked. Cloaks still dripping.

A good soldier didn't say *toadshit* under her breath. A good soldier swallowed the sentiment and let it sour the dinner still warm in her belly.

"You have all the luck, Dek." That was Teslin, gathering up her dice, raising an eyebrow. "Bet he wants you to go out there, yeah? Look for that brother of his."

"This weather, that's suicide," Barkett said. He grinned, all teeth. Cut a glance at the back of the tent and grinned wider. Loudly: "Maybe he wants something a little more personal, yeah?"

She ignored Barkett, scooped her winnings into her palm. Made a show of counting them, as the shadows at the back of the tent rippled. Istel crossed the narrow space, fast and quiet, dodged the wet cloaks dangling off the center pole, and cuffed Barkett hard enough that the bigger man rocked on his stool.

"Shut it," Istel said quietly.

"Joke, Istel, shit!" Barkett swatted retaliation, missed completely as Istel smoked aside. "I think Dek's honor's safe enough without *you*—"

"Shut it," Teslin repeated, and Barkett's teeth clicked. Same sound the dice made as Teslin cast them onto the table. "Your own fault, Dek, that he's asking for you. Too damn *good*, yeah? Told you to fail once in a while, didn't I?"

"Mm. Be glad I didn't. It'd be you he wanted, then." Dekklis found her cloak among the others. Pulled it off the hook and shrugged into it. She didn't upset the makeshift dicing table, or the lamp. Managed, somehow and anyway, to flick a sodden hem across Barkett.

"Dek, rot it—"

"Owe you for that mouth. —What are *you* doing?"

Istel slung his cloak across his shoulders, with another rattail flick at Barkett. "Going with."

*Of course*. And *hell no*. "You stay. Don't need an escort. Rurik didn't ask for you, did he?"

"Rurik won't send one scout anywhere. Save you a walk back here if I come with you now."

"Rurik might want something else, yeah? And don't you say it, Barkett."

A friendly chat, maybe, with one of his senior scouts, during a snowstorm, during what had to be third watch by now. Rurik was such a socialite, sure.

Istel raised eyebrows at her. Pulled the tent flap aside and held it. "He hates to wait."

"Better go," Teslin echoed. "You're letting in all the toadshit cold, yeah?"

No, not all of it. Dekklis discovered there was plenty left outside. The optio hadn't waited for them. Probably ducked into shelter, dismissed for the night—last orders, dredge out Szanys Dekklis, then take some rest, thank you, Optio, that will be all. Trust any soldier here could find the commander's tent, especially his best pair of scouts.

That tent looked like all the others, squat and weather-stained goatskin, flap weighted against the weather. Grant Rurik that much: he didn't wear his rank like a title. There were some who did, in other cohorts: stories about officers who thought rank made them some kind of highborn, all pomp and title and ceremony. Those officers didn't get command of the Sixth, which was scouts and rangers and seasoned troopers. Mostly men, too, by design: a good place for senators' sons to make a career, if they had that luxury. The foremothers who passed the Reforms hadn't been stupid, oh no. Send the uncut and unmarried men into the legion and get those units far out of Illharek; send them to the borderlands among the Alviri. Keep the men and the Republic out of trouble in one stroke.

Hadn't worked for— "You remember his name, Istel? Rurik's brother?"

"Kenjak. Part of Salis's squad. She took a knife wound, up at the old temple. They found a couple people hiding up there. She killed one. The other ran, and Ollu and Kenjak went after her."

"How the hell do you know all that?"

Istel shrugged. "Men talk."

Kenjak. Dekklis tried to summon a face for the name. Couldn't. So fill in a new recruit, wide-eyed and too green for the Sixth, here on his brother's reputation and his mother's connections.

She hesitated at Rurik's tent flap. Boot-scuffs from the other side. Audible profanity that swelled and receded. Good guess that the First Spear was pacing, stalking. Impatient, famously, among his troops.

And waiting for her. Hell and damn. Rurik didn't mind running his soldiers on winter roads all the way to a town he couldn't save; damn sure he wouldn't mind sending a pair of scouts out into bad weather.

Dekklis glanced at Istel, and sighed, and peeled the flap aside. "First Spear? It's—"

"First Scout Dekklis, yes, about fucking *time*."

Terrified, that's what she was. Good thing no one was asking.

* * *

Awareness returned to Kenjak in stages.

He wasn't dead. That came first, with a small rush of pleasure. Then: heat on one side of him. Cold on the other. Wet all over. Sound tunneled in next. Hissing and spitting nearby. Flame-snap and pop. Thick silence just beyond those things, as if the whole world held its breath.

His toes were warm. He wiggled them. Pulled a lungful of wet air. Tasted burnt hair on the back of his tongue, burnt leather and charred wood and oil. Metallic stink under that, like old iron except it wasn't, he knew that, and knew he should remember why that was bad.

Davni had smelled like this, but this wasn't Davni. Wasn't anywhere near, he was certain, although he couldn't summon up reasons for that conviction. And that should scare him, but it didn't. He was in no danger here. Was warm enough, even with the snow

*denaelikk*

falling on his face.

Snowdenaelikk. Wait. Blue eyes, Alviri eyes, in a Dvergir face. Half-blood. The skraeling, tall and pale, furs and leather and the axe

*dull flash as it fell*

slapping his flesh so that the bones bent.

She must have

*saved my life*

drugged him. Must have

*saved my arm*

done something to him.

He realized, abruptly, what was burning. *Who* was.

He managed not, somehow, to vomit. Gagged and choked and coughed instead. He tried to sit up. Red and white fire lanced from wrist to shoulder so that he wished he might die right then.

He didn't, for the second time. This time he wasn't as happy with living. He opened his eyes, though, first a crack and then wider when his nausea stayed manageable. Bright flames, snow falling thick and constant, catching the light and sparkling before it melted. He turned his head, and yes, that was Ollu burning. Facedown, which was a mercy—except the shape of his body was wrong, somehow, the slope of shoulder to neck.

Oh. *Oh.*

His belly knotted again, and he looked somewhere else. There weren't many options. His choices were either

*Ollu*

the fire on his right, or the steep-sided bank on his left that he could barely see through the snowfall. He wouldn't be climbing it one-armed. Wouldn't risk a walk up or down the riverbed, either, until the snow stopped.

Wouldn't walk anywhere if he didn't sit up first. Rurik wouldn't lie flat like this, wouldn't be afraid of a little discomfort.

Kenjak held his breath and tried to sit up again. Succeeded and spent another forever blinking and swallowing bile. His arm hurt. But it was better now than it had been when freshly broken.

And yet. Kenjak picked at the knots and the binding around his right arm. Wiggled those fingers and—foremothers, that hurt, but not as bad as it might have. The line of the limb was straight. The half-blood wore Academy rings in her ears. The fat silver one meant Chirurgeon, First Class, master bonesetter and apothecary. He'd use the arm again. He might not have, if the skraeling had struck with the edge of his axe and not the flat.

So. Mercy from the skraeling, and healing from the half-blood, and neither one with a reason to help him. She'd spared him. Repaired him. *Wanted* him to remember her, yeah, and he would. Kenjak held his breath and looked at Ollu. Really looked. Ollu was charred bloodless now, as much smoke as fire, and still too much himself. Ollu was also in two pieces.

Motion at the riverbank caught his attention.

Kenjak snapped his head around. Strained for detail. Told himself it was nothing, *nothing*. A lump of snow on the riverbed where there hadn't been a moment ago.

A second lump of snow followed the first. A third. Kenjak glanced up, found a tree clinging to the edge of the bank, half-rooted and tipped almost horizontal. Another lump slid the length of a branch and fell.

A fox. A squirrel.

*And what animal's out in this weather?*

He willed himself calm. A soldier did not panic about falling snow. A soldier did not panic at all. He spotted his sword, sheathed and resting near the fire. He stretched for it, drew it one-handed and awkwardly into his left fist. When he got back to Cardik—when, not if—he would train with both hands. For now, he gripped the sword steady. Stood, very carefully. Angled so that the fire was behind him, lighting the shadows.

And then he saw—vaguely, barely—a silhouette on the bank that did not match tree or stump. Head, shoulders, a cloak over all of it. A shape, no details.

Kenjak's heart slammed into his ribs. The cloak might be a wet-darkened legionnaire red, but it might not be. "Ho!" he shouted. "Identify yourself!" and staggered to the firelight's limit. Jarred the broken arm, and this time he did retch.

When he recovered, the head and shoulders had vanished.

\* \* \*

Weak winter sunlight dribbled through clouds and branches and blasted the world all to white, except for the pole and

*K'Hess Kenjak*

the body impaled on it, and the spreading red below. He hadn't been dead all that long. The blood hadn't frozen yet. And he'd been alive when it happened, because that much blood did not come from a corpse.

Dekklis knelt beside the sad ruin of Rurik's younger brother. Gagged her breakfast into the snow. She had expected, when she joined the legion, that she might have to kill people. She had expected that she might be exposed to bodies hacked by sword strikes, or prickling with javelins and steel quarrels. She had prepared herself for blood, and shit-stink, and a body's insides on its outside. The reality had, over time, matched up well enough. There were only so many ways one person could kill another. This was new.

Dekklis settled back on her heels. Scooped a mouthful of clean snow and chewed it to liquid and spat it out again. The stake had entered between Kenjak's legs and exited through his mouth, jutting between his lips like an obscene tooth. Must've clipped his heart on the way through, *hope* that it had. His face, though, hell and damn, said the dying hadn't gone quick enough. Terror and pain and wide eyes gone gelid in the cold. At least the crows hadn't gotten him yet. At least he still had his motherless *head*.

Her stomach heaved again. She fastened desperate eyes on the— pyre, yeah, call it that, Ollu's pyre. A miserable thing, broken javelins and a few scraps of wood. Amazing it'd consumed as much of the man's corpse as it had. Almost as amazing as why someone would dismember and burn one soldier and stake the other still living.

"Dek." Istel didn't look much better than she felt. Wax-faced, grey where his skin stretched tight over bone. "Tracks, heading north up the riverbed. Two people. Looks like at least one dog, maybe two." He hesitated. Squatted beside her and poked a fingertip into the snow.

"What?"

"They look older. The tracks. Mostly full of snow. Like," he added when she said nothing, "like they left before the storm really got bad."

"I understand that."

He nodded. Stared bleakly at Kenjak, at the failed pyre. "You can get drifting, in a ravine like this. Strange wind patterns. So they could be fresher, too. He hasn't been dead that long."

"I understand that, too." She lurched to her feet. Ignored Istel's hand on her elbow, rot him anyway. "Anything else?"

"I don't see any matches to those tracks around here."

There *weren't* any tracks near the bodies, as happened, but the wind and the blizzard could account for that, too. It was harder to imagine that only two people could have done *this*. A band of Taliri, yeah, but bands of Taliri left tracks and *hell* if the blizzard could've erased that many people.

"Let's find them."

"Dek." Quietly, even for Istel.

Hell. He was going to argue with her. "What?"

Istel jerked his chin. "Who doctored Kenjak? That's a splint on his arm."

She kept a very narrow focus on his right arm from biceps to wrist. A broken arrow framed the forearm in two halves, tied in place with strips of a uniform sleeve. Black linen, red wool, a livid puckering of flesh in between. "Ollu must've treated the injury."

"If Ollu had this sort of skill, he never told anyone."

"Meaning?"

Istel's gaze skipped off hers, apologetic. Embarrassed, maybe, to see something she hadn't, to tell her what she should have noticed herself. Istel didn't like to do better, damn him anyway, because she was the

*woman*

senior of their partnership, leader and officer. He took the boy's hand gently, lifted the arm. "Meaning. This was a chirurgeon's work. Professional. Look at the splinting. It doesn't make sense that the ones who did *this* to him would've bothered with setting bones first."

It didn't, no. Dekklis stood up and gritted back another heave. "You're saying . . . what? That we shouldn't follow those tracks? They didn't do this?"

"I'm saying I don't recognize this fletching as Taliri, either, and the sky is clearing. There's not much wind. We've got time to report to the commander."

She closed her eyes. Let the watery sun glow red through her eyelids; let herself pretend it was warm. What was she going to tell Rurik, anyway? *Sorry, sir, your brother's dead, except in a way that makes Davni look like a midwinter festival?* Kenjak was fourth son of K'Hess. Word and details would get back to the Senate in Illharek—and then debates, again, about the provinces and how to handle the Taliri and how a senator's youngest son had died badly under her third son's command. And locally, in Cardik—hell and damn, when the praefecta heard about it, she'd strip Rurik back to mila and put him into the ranks just for spite.

*If,* whispered her grimmest self, *if the ones who did this don't get you, too, yeah?*

That chill had nothing to do with early morning, or the weak sunlight, or the exhaustion of a whole night's cold hunting. Had everything to do with patchy shadows among the trees, and the steep sides of the riverbed, and two bodies that said the last pair of soldiers here hadn't survived this patch of ground. Istel was right. Tell Rurik, collect a detail to bring Kenjak and Ollu back for proper burning. Collect Teslin and Barkett to follow those tracks. She'd rather she and Istel do it themselves, go another half day into wilderness and away from this—maybe catch up with the makers of those tracks and drag them back. Have something to show the commander, some report other than *sorry, sir, but your brother's dead.*

But Rurik needed to know about this, first priority. Needed to see it and realize what they had loose out here. Taliri raiders, same ones who did Davni. Except the Taliri were nomads who sent their spare men out raiding, and raiding meant bringing back goods and leaving people alive to make more for the next raiding season. There had been no stakes and dismembered bodies at Davni. All right. Report first, but she and Istel could get the kid down, at least. Cover him so that the crows didn't get him, or the foxes, or whatever else scavenged the dead. The legion took care of its own.

"We get him down," she told Istel. "Then we go back."

As if she knew how to start. The stake had been recently set—so reckon, with the ground frozen, it hadn't been set too deep. Wouldn't be hard to get it out. She locked her jaw against bile and a slowly rising anger. Reached for the base of the stake. Stopped.

Symbols, carved into the wood. Curves and lines, dots and geometrics. She followed them up the shaft. They stopped at Kenjak's body. No stains on the pole itself, when Kenjak's bowels and bladder had loosed. Only blood, and only in the carvings, as if it had run in channels.

Her lungs were too small, suddenly. The forest, too quiet.

"Istel."

He peered where she pointed. Shook his head. "What am I looking at?"

"I don't—" *Know*, except that wasn't quite true. Flash to childhood and Illharek's witchfire daylight; flash to a man in robes who parted the market crowds like water around a stone. He hadn't walked like men did, in child Dekklis's experience. Straight-backed, chin level, bold-eyed and fearless. He'd had a staff, and child Dekklis had wanted it, oh yes, because there was witchfire at the end, blue and bright, but when she tried to read the markings on that staff her head had ached and her eyes had watered and her stomach had gone all funny.

*Who*, she'd asked, and tugged Nurse Pasi's fingers. *Who is that?*

*Conjuror*, Nurse had hissed, and jerked Dekklis away. *Don't stare, Dominita. They're dangerous.*

Grown Dekklis could not have sworn that the symbols matched that remembered conjuror's staff, could not have sworn her stomach wasn't already fragile—but her head ached and her eyes watered, and that was proof enough.

"This is conjuring," she said grimly. "We go back to Rurik *now*."

\* \* \*

"Chrrip." Followed by a bump of a bone-hard muzzle in a harder-than-bone skull. "Chrrip?"

Snowdenaelikk knew better than to answer. Tugged the cloak a little tighter around herself, pushed her face a little deeper into the crook of her elbow. Not the most pleasant aroma, wool and leather and days of unwashed self, but preferable to a faceful of svartjagr and woodsmoke.

A sensation like knuckles on her skull, rap-rap. Like her first-year tutor come back to haunt her, minus the breathy, *Pay attention, Snowdenaelikk, and again—what is the formula for—*

"Chrrip."

Making a svartjagr vanish into smoke, yeah. *Wish* for something that useful.

The chill at her back said that Veiko was already awake, already moving. Damn sure he'd made breakfast, damn sure he'd shared some with Briel.

"You aren't hungry," she said into her elbow.

"Chrrip."

"Liar."

Another nudge. A hard, beaky muzzle needling under a fold in the cloak. Determined little motherless wretch.

Snow rolled away and sat up and pushed the cloak back onto her shoulders. Could have, in the next beat, dropped a dagger into her palm—if she'd *had* a dagger, that is. Had been a time she'd kept blades in her sleeves, yeah, when she'd *slept* with them. Now her daggers sat beside her seax. Laughing God. Getting complacent, that's what she was. Years in Cardik, on the northern frontier, with a garrison more worried about bandits than what the gangs did in the Warren.

Made a woman soft, that was what. Slowed her down.

Or not, if the dogs' expressions meant anything. Ruffs prickling, tails stiff, startled by her sudden burst upright. Helgi muttered disapproval and sat down. Logi whined. Veiko merely raised an eyebrow from his place across the fire. Veiko's face did most of his talking. A lot like his dogs, with their ears and tails and eyes. Of course he didn't have a tail, did he, had eyebrows and lips and all the same features she did. Had a voice, too, that he didn't use much. Didn't use it now, no, answered her like big grey Helgi might, with a slight narrowing of eyes. Logi, at least, made noise.

Briel crawled into the space she'd vacated, oozing satisfaction warm as wax. Little monster.

Laughing God, she was tired. And cold. And lost, still. She had no reliable notion of how far they'd come since the riverbed. She reckoned she should've died again when the storm got bad, with her feet soaked and numb and the wind chewing through wool and leather and flesh. With no fucking idea where she was, except following Veiko.

Who'd brought her here, to what Briel thought was safety. Shelter, anyway: a massive spruce, with branches that skirted out and left the space around the trunk needle-carpeted and snow-clear and reasonably warm with the tiny fire. Safety that really meant Veiko, with his axe and his bow and his dogs, with his spare blankets and his winter wisdom. Safety with *someone else*, rot it.

Someone else who was better with the cooking, too, who'd made use of her motherless iron pan. He plucked a flatcake out of it. Offered it to her. Golden on the edges, where hers would've been black as her skin.

She took it. "Thanks."

"They are not difficult to prepare." He prodded the pan around in the ashes. "It was more difficult to defend it until you awoke."

"Dogs?"

An almost-smile. "Briel."

"Of course." She poked the svartjagr—asleep now, or damn near— with a fingertip. "Toadshit."

Briel cracked an eye and hissed unconvincingly. Dragged a wing up over her head.

"She sleeps later than you do."

"Svartjagr are nocturnal."

Veiko's left eyebrow climbed toward his hairline.

"Nocturnal. Ah . . . means she likes the night better."

"Like an owl."

"Yeah. Like an owl."

Grunt, which might mean *oh* or *why not just say that*.

Snow carried the rest of her cake to the evergreen border and pushed the boughs aside. The sun stitched a path through a patchwork sky, blue and grey and occasional flurries.

"Storm's over, yeah?"

"Yes." Veiko squat-shuffled beside her. Put his face into fresh air and sniffed it, just like one of his dogs. "But there will be more snow by nightfall."

"And how do you know that?"

"It is the smell." He tipped his face into the breeze. "It is wet, and cold. It is *snow*," as if he'd described something simple and obvious.

"I was born in Illharek," she told him. "The city itself, I mean. That's the deep Below, yeah? No real weather there. Wind, sometimes, in the smaller caverns. But nothing like this. No snow. No rain. Everything smells wet, but it's a *cave* smell, yeah?"

The blank face said he didn't understand. Said he wasn't going to admit that, either. Right. She gave up. "So we're here another, what, night?"

He settled back near the fire. "Is there reason to leave sooner?"

"Sooner I'm back inside Cardik's walls, the safer I'll be. Then you can get back to your life."

He was busy, suddenly, prodding sparks out of the fire. "The city. It would seem safer to avoid that place. The soldiers will return."

"Soldiers don't go into the Warren. Not sober, anyway. And they won't find me, even if they do look. But they'll be all over the road, yeah? Between here and there. Have to dodge them."

"You are a healer. A chirurgeon." Veiko settled back on his heels. Looked at her now, steady witchfire stare and just as cold. "One wonders why it is that you have so much practice with evading soldiers."

She was suddenly, acutely aware of the axe beside him. She hesitated on a lie. Fuck yes, she was getting soft. Worse, getting *honest*. She settled on a half-truth. "I'm a conjuror, too, yeah?"

"Which you say is no crime."

"It isn't. But this far on the frontier—there's a bigger risk for backlash, yeah? Too much Wild out here. Not enough settlement. And people don't understand conjuring up here. Not like in Illharek. People get strange about things they don't understand. Soldiers are worse than most. Superstitious, yeah?" Which was true. Mostly.

"You are saying that your witchery is stronger in cities," in tones of deep skepticism.

"I'm saying conjuring *works* in cities. Outside, we take our chances with the Wild."

"I saw what you did to the creekbed. And the hillside."

"I intended the hillside." She grimaced. "The creek, though, that was backlash. That's *why* we don't conjure outside the walls very much."

"Is that because you have offended the spirits? The ancestors," he added. "The animals. The dead."

She blinked. Looked for the joke and, dear Laughing God, couldn't see it. "You're serious. Fuck and damn, Veiko, where *are* you from?"

"North," he said.

"Not a city."

"There are no cities. There are villages. Farmsteads."

"And your conjurors don't know what backlash is?"

"Our noidghe do not offend the spirits, if that is what you mean."

Guess what a noidghe was, clear enough. The rest made no sense. The Illhari had Purged their superstitions along with their gods. No ghosts. No angry dead. Conjuring, now, that was something else—bound to walls and roads, to Dvergiri creations, etched out in glyphs and gestures, confined to patterns. Limited to Dvergiri blood, too, the whys of which no one understood. Alviri, Taliri, skraeling outlanders—none of them could conjure. But anyone with a Dvergir parent could at least manipulate shadows, if they bothered to learn the trick. Oh, the Laughing God claimed credit for the shadow-weaving, but only his godsworn believed everything he said. Which she was not, being a woman and

*unwelcome*

too smart to take those oaths. The God wasn't fond of women. He'd made an exception for an Academy conjuror with no loyalty to Illhari rules, but that didn't mean he forgave her sex.

So, Veiko thought backlash was angry spirits. And why not? Just because she'd learned cant and gesture and runes and fucking conjuring *theory* didn't mean there weren't spirits behind the effects. If what Veiko said was true—and the man didn't strike her as a liar—then the Adepts back in the Academy might trade an eye for knowing how these noidghe avoided backlash. That might be worth something.

"Snowdenaelikk." His voice hooked her back to *now*, and a small fire under a tree's broad skirts, and a league of nothing out there except Wild, where her kind of spellwork was as likely to kill her as not. "Why did the soldiers pursue you?"

*This time?*

"Because I ran. Drasan threw a knife at one of them. My companion," she added. "Dead now, back at Davni."

"The burned village. I saw them on the road, running toward it."

"That's where they found us. We were supposed to meet someone there, yeah? A . . . courier. In the old temple ruins. But the legion found us first."

"Courier."

"Messenger. My friends in Cardik—we do business, sometimes, trade that the legion doesn't really approve of. Move goods. You know." Tsabrak would be pissed when she came back without the rasi, but he'd be less happy if the legion picked her up.

A slantwise glance. "Did you destroy the village?"

She remembered his expression at the pyre, when she'd coaxed light out of shadow, heat out of cold. His wasn't a civilized people. Spirits. Superstition. Angry dead. A serious question, from him. Did she burn Davni? Laughing God, to be insulted or flattered.

Honest, mostly, again and damn her. "No. Not our kind of business." She stabbed a hand in what she hoped was the right direction.

"We came from Cardik. Saw the smoke, yeah, but we didn't know what'd happened."

Grunt. Nod. An Illhari might've asked *what business,* and how it brought her into the Wild. Veiko didn't. His people did not, evidently, value that sort of curiosity. Or maybe it was just him. Other things he worried about, yeah, like,

"Do the soldiers believe you are responsible?"

*How bad do they want you?* in other words. *How much toadshit's following you?*

She scraped up a handful of spruce needles, fed them one by one into the flames. "They might. They're not famous for wits. Stupid people with weapons, traveling in groups."

"Yes," he said. "Better not to anger them in the first place."

"Yeah, well. I don't make it a habit."

"That is wise." A flash of blue, as he sailed a glance toward the branches overhead, and out toward the sky, and anywhere but her face. "An outlaw must be quick with wit and weapons, which you are. But an outlaw cannot forget her firestone in the winter."

No hint of a smile. A young man's face, and more grim than any young man she'd ever known except Tsabrak.

"Is that a joke?"

Still watching the sky, the shuffling clouds: "It is an accurate observation."

"So I'm an outlaw, am I?"

He would not look at her. "I cannot speak for *you.*"

Oh, Laughing God, it was time to trade truth. Not the one she'd expected to hear. She'd've named him a hunter, a trapper, wrapped up in some outlander's idea of honor that made him spare wounded enemies and help strangers and not, even once, hint at what she might do to repay him. Not a thief. Not a mercenary. And now he named himself outlaw.

"What did you do?"

Hesitation. And then, as if he trod on a twisted foot: "I killed a man. A thief. He stole takin." So calmly, so flatly, so *finally*. "And denied that he had."

Leave aside what a takin was—ask him that later, takin were valuable to his people, good enough—and focus on the action. "And the penalty for thieving among your people isn't death, then?"

He frowned at her. Narrowed his eyes until they looked like slivers of sky, bright and blinding. "It depends on what is stolen, and who steals it."

"So—"

He held up a palm. Stop. Peace. Don't distract me. The expression she'd learned meant *Veiko's about to say more than ten words, so listen.* "Takin are herd animals. Families rely on them to survive. To steal what another needs to live is a death-crime. But the thief was the chieftain's son."

"Oh dear Laughing God."

"I knew," Veiko said doggedly, "that there would be no fairness if I accused him. So I—"

"Made your own justice."

"Yes."

"Why not just hide the body? Pretend you don't know what happened?"

His eyes widened, shock and offense together. "I am not an assassin."

Best keep this one away from Tsabrak, with those attitudes. She said carefully, "No, you're honest. And you're a good man."

Another frown, and this one stuck. "I am a fool. And now I am an outlaw."

"Same thing, yeah? You're right. You're no assassin. An assassin won't put herself between a stranger and trouble. *You* did that. I'm glad you're a fool."

His eyes widened again. Pools now, not strips, of blue sky. Then he turned away. Grunted. Maybe that was Veiko for *you're welcome.*

Helgi raised his head and growled, then surged up and thrust his head past her. Sniffed, all the fur on his back ridged up, while Logi crowded Snow aside and mutter-whined under his breath. Briel hissed, suddenly awake. Click-scratch and whisper of displaced spruce needles, and then she was up the trunk, one more layer of darkness among the shadows.

Veiko raised a hand, unmistakable *shh*. Dropped that same hand in the next moment and took up his axe. Rocked into a crouch and edged his face into a gap between branches. A murmur, and the dogs ghosted out into the snow. One beat, two, ten, and then:

"Stay here," Veiko told her, and gathered his bow and quiver and followed them.

Fuck and damn. She drew her own weapon out of the folds of her blanket. Settled the belt round her hips and pulled the buckle one-handed. Pulled shadow with the other, from the skirt of trunk and limb and the gap between needles, and smeared the fire dark. Stretched that same shadow—wider now, so much thicker, over packs and blankets. An eye would slide over that shadow now, seeing only the dark space under a tree, not a campsite. But if someone came down the slope, if someone looked under the branches . . . Well. Snow might be safe, even then, unless that someone wondered why the shadows under this tree were so solid, and what might be hiding inside them.

Veiko had said stay, but he wasn't here. Was out there, with his bow and his dogs and his toadfucking axe. *Veiko* had room to run and maneuver.

*Because you did so well running last time, yeah?*

Snow tipped a glance up. Sent a tight-chested wish at the svartjagr. *Go.*

No sound at all from above, and no movement. No sign at all of Briel. *She* was hidden, and safe enough.

A dog barked. Helgi, from halfway up the hillside. A second bark. A third and fourth, echoing off trees and sky. Logi, this time, and he sounded closer to the top of the ridge.

Veiko's dogs didn't bark as a matter of habit. They had reason this time, a command from Veiko. Or Veiko'd gotten into trouble with whatever was out there. Whoever.

*Guess, yeah?*

No need. She'd expected legion efficiency, but this was truly impressive. Truly unlucky, too. Caught unprepared twice in a week. She'd deserve it if they caught her.

Sensation of cold wind on her skin, and a gut-hollow drop before the surety of wingbeats, of speed and escape, that sent her heart battering up in her throat. Almost a sending, and Briel's goddamned best advice. *Get away.*

Maybe she could. And maybe that would leave Veiko in trouble. But he could take care of himself. He'd got between her and the legion once already. Might not a second time. There might be a limit to what one stranger would do for another. What a good man would do for a woman who . . . wasn't. Consider that.

Except he wouldn't leave his gear. And his dogs wouldn't bark without reason. And he might've run into more than one inexperienced mila this time.

She eeled through the branches. Bright outside, blinding as any headache or any sending Briel might manage. Snow twitched the hood higher and put her feet in Veiko's tracks. He didn't leave many. She followed them to the next knot of trees before she lost him. Paused there, with her back against a spindly trunk, and guessed his likely path upslope. He'd step on the bare patches. On the rocks. She listened for more barking, or crashing, or some sign where he was. Got nothing back except wind through evergreens and her own breath, faint and rapid, pluming like smoke. A flour-fine snow began to sift down from a sky gone increasingly grey. She gathered the fast-fading shadows around her and hoped they'd be enough to blur her edges. Took a step, and two.

A creak. Wood bending in the cold. She froze, with one foot extended. Cast her eyes toward the noise which was

*please, Laughing God*

only a branch protesting the cold. And saw him, only just: an Illhari soldier. He wasn't wearing the usual legion black-and-red breastplate. All forest, this one, browns and greys and greens. Oh, tempting to peel the shadows away from him, to leave him vivid and visible. Tempting, and probably fatal. Maybe he hadn't noticed her yet. Maybe that toadshit bow of his was nocked and pointing at nothing.

"Hold," said the scout, menace-quiet.

Fickle motherless God.

# CHAPTER SIX

Dekklis was picking her way downslope, navigating a tumble of rock and ice and stubborn trees, when she noticed shadows moving where there shouldn't be. A trick of the light, she thought first, or an animal, and then, *No.* Too upright for any animal. Too deliberately irregular in its gait. Hooded, like a scout, but it wasn't Istel. She wouldn't have seen him at all.

Dekklis sank onto her haunches. Nocked an arrow. Measured wind and angle for a clear shot and drew breath to call out.

And heard Istel, invisible and unmistakable: "Hold."

Dekklis froze. The person in the hood—a woman, she thought, something about the glide and gait—froze, too. For a heartbeat Dekklis thought she might run. Coiled stillness, too controlled for panic. Mila Salis had reported a runner back at Davni, who'd fled into the forest rather than fight. Guess, then, that this was the same person.

The woman straightened, hands spread and visible. Said something that Dekklis couldn't make out.

No answer from Istel. But he whistled, two short and one long, *got one* not knowing where Dekklis was, maybe thinking Teslin and Barkett would hear it, too. Dekklis thought they wouldn't. *That* chase had moved over the ridge by now, a hunt for barking dogs and someone who crashed through the trees so loudly it had to be deliberate. *Her* hunch, to stay on this slope, closest to the smoke smell that had led them here.

Nice to be right on a hunch, nicer if the woman cooperated. Dekklis didn't want to drag a wounded prisoner all the way back to camp.

*Don't move,* Dekklis wished her. *Listen to Istel.*

A dog barked, distant now, and the woman's head snapped toward the sound. One beat, while Dekklis wished Istel to patience

*don't shoot her*

and abandoned her own cover. Made her own noise, rock-rattle, and straight-marched down the slope. Kept eyes on the woman as she did it, took her measure. Wire-gaunt. Nondescript clothing, leather and linen and wool. A short Illhari seax on her hip that looked like it belonged there. Hood pulled up and forward, hiding her features, until Dekklis came around front and looked up, into the woman's face.

That wasn't fear looking back at her, oh no. Measuring, appraising, and just the wrong side of hostile. Guess that for bravado, then, thin as the skin on boiled milk. It wouldn't last, never did, and only the guilty ever tried it. Blue eyes under pale brows, and escaped strands of fair hair instead of Dvergiri dark. Salis hadn't mentioned a half-blood. Hell.

Dekklis cleared her throat. "You have a name?"

"Yes. Do you?" Coolly, in an accent straight from Illharek's Suburba.

Try to be civil, see where it got her. Dekklis traded a look with Istel, past the woman's shoulder

*be ready*

and hooked fingers in the woman's collar. Tugged it past the jutting bones and blinked at the citizen's mark.

"You're freeborn."

The woman made a noise between nose and throat. "Expecting a collar, were you? Or a brand? Think I ran away?"

"Oh, I know you did. From Davni. And I know two milae chased you. What happened to them?"

"Bad storm, the other night. Maybe they got lost."

"Maybe. You're under arrest, half-blood. Hands."

Dek made a show of pulling the manacles out of her belt pouch, shaking them loose. Watched the half-blood's eyes dart and focus. Ah. So restraints got her attention, did they? And that wasn't an idle stare. Assessment, like an armorer with a new blade.

Dekklis reached for the nearest wrist. Stopped.

"Is that blood?" Knowing it was. Rust and copper on nondescript grey.

Blue eyes slid sidelong, landed on Dekklis, narrowed. "Yes."

"Whose?"

The half-blood's weight shifted, very slightly, onto the balls of her feet. Her hands remained where they were, spread and empty. Almost a smile on that knife-cut of a mouth, hard and insolent.

"Are you a hunter? A butcher?"

"Chirurgeon."

"That where the blood's from? Your last victim?"

"My last *patient* was alive when I left him, and I think you know that. Or did he tell you something else?"

Bile collected in Dek's throat. "He didn't tell us anything."

"He say who set his arm? Or do you think he did that himself?"

"He can't say, half-blood. Not skewered from crotch to crown."

"Laughing *God*."

Genuine, honest horror.

Call it intuition. Experience. But that wasn't a guilty woman's face staring at her. That wasn't feigned shock.

"Impaled. He was still alive when it happened." Dekklis choked on further elaboration. "Now give me. Your. *Hands*."

The half-blood stretched her fingers. Cracks in her composure now, a flinch as the cold metal touched flesh. A grimace as Dekklis clamped the metal tight to bone. And silence, so that Dekklis could hear the creak of Istel's bowstring in the cold, and the wind whining through evergreens.

She tugged hard on the chain, to signal to Istel he could ease off the draw. She expected a stumble. Expected some protest of innocence, a flood of panic and pleas. But the half-blood said nothing. Yielded to the pull, kept her footing. Only her hood slipped, puddling around her shoulders.

Hell and *damn.* "You're Academy."

Lazy smirk. "And you're legion. So?"

Istel frowned, having no idea. Cardik-born Istel wouldn't know what the topknot meant, or the close-cut sides, or the rings bristling at the top curve of the half-blood's right ear. The silver with the garnet, that meant a master chirurgeon. But the three gold, now, those meant:

"She's a conjuror," Dekklis said.

That, Istel understood. Softly, instantly, he stepped back and drew again: "Then break her fingers."

*That* was fear on the half-blood's face now, stark as winter, cracking sharp into the quiet. "We're in the *Wild,* yeah? What do you think I can do?"

Dekklis considered. She knew enough to read rank in those earrings, and three gold meant the half-blood was no Adept. She sat somewhere above apprentice, second-ranked in three disciplines, certainly dangerous—but Dekklis had the woman's wrists in shackles, didn't she, had a league of forest sprawled around her, and the woman hadn't resisted yet. Hadn't tried. So Dekklis waved *stand down* to Istel. Repeated the gesture when he didn't, and glared until his bowstring went straight.

"She can't conjure out here," Dek said. "We've got her. —So tell me your name, half-blood."

The woman drew breath, held it, spat it out. "Snow."

"That's your *name*?"

"That's the white stuff on the ground. *Yes*, that's my name."

"I don't think so. That's a shortname. Tell me what your mother called you."

For a heartbeat, Dekklis thought she'd refuse. She had that look. Then the half-blood shrugged and pulled on a smirk too cool by half, too controlled, to be anything but armor.

"Snowdenaelikk." She held her breath just a jot, between the first syllable and the rest.

It wasn't a Dvergir name. Sounded outlander. Alviri, maybe. Maybe even Taliri, or skraeling. The sort of name a freeborn Dvergir, Illhari daughter didn't get, as a rule.

Dekklis raised both brows. "Your *mother* chose that? Or your father?"

It was an insult, of exactly the sort Snow must've heard her whole life. Even Istel blinked. Snow grinned.

"And I'd thought you were highborn, from that accent. Maybe not."

Chiding *her* manners, now. Rightfully, too, Dekklis thought, which just irritated her further. She shrugged. "I'm a First Scout, Sixth Cohort. Just a soldier."

"Motherless hell you are. Family castoff? Exile? Too many sisters to buy you a seat in the Senate, but enough for a legion commission, yeah?"

Istel reached over, took the chain, and wrenched. "Civil tongue," he murmured. "*Yeah*, conjuror?"

That narrow jaw tightened. "Or you cut it out?"

"Something like."

Anger flickered. Defiance. "Safer if you break my hands, yeah? You don't learn anything if I'm mute."

"Leave *be*," Dekklis snapped. Glared at Istel, at Snow. "No one's cutting out tongues. Or breaking hands. We're just asking questions."

The half-blood rattled her manacles. "Persuasive."

"Precaution."

"*That's* what it's called."

"Answer some questions, maybe I'll take those off. Let you go."

"Toadshit. Your First Spear would have your head."

"Think he'd rather have yours. Might be more inclined to let you keep it if you cooperate."

That scored. Felt good, yeah, to see doubt flicker in dark, blue eyes. "Ask your questions."

"Long way from Cardik, aren't you?"

"*That's* what you're wondering? Yes. Clearly."

Maybe she should've let Istel break something. Teach a little respect. This Snow had no fear of consequences. "You want to say where your partner is?"

The half-blood's face closed tight as city gates against raiders. "You killed him, yeah? At least I think you did."

"You mean the boy in the tent back at Davni." Who hadn't seen twenty winters, when this woman was *her* age, more or less. Thirty winters and a bit. "I don't think so. There was another set of tracks, beside yours, in the riverbed. My people are chasing someone out there right now, with dogs."

A smile, sliver-sharp. "Must be a ghost. The angry dead can walk, yeah?"

Almost a full day awake now, on both sides of a blizzard, and Kenjak and Ollu waiting in the dark every time she blinked—and this half-blood Illhari *commoner* with her dry cloak and dry boots stood there baiting her. Dekklis uncurled a casual backfist that snapped Snow's head sideways and split skin. *That*, for consequences.

"I think you should worry about the angry living, yeah? My First Spear isn't patient. His interrogators aren't. That boy Kenjak was his brother. You savvy that?"

The conjuror probed at her lip with a deliberate tongue-tip. Spat afterward and left red in the snow. And said, cold and quiet: "You have to cut the head off the corpse. Did you cut off his head, Scout? No? Then I'd worry. The angry dead look for vengeance."

Decapitation. Angry dead. Ghosts. Dekklis raised her hand again, to strike that defiance *off* the half-blood's face, to beat some sense *into* her.

"Dek." Just that, from Istel, and the red haze burned away like fog at noon. She dropped her fist.

"Hold her," she said, disgusted, and turned sharply downslope. Stepped harder than scouts usually did, pounded her own tracks into the snow.

That hadn't gone well. That woman had a way of goading Dek out of her better sense. But she'd learned some things, too. Whatever her accent and parentage, Snowdenaelikk had been Academy trained. That took money, more than any Suburban mother might have. The highborn sent their extras into those walls: daughters and even sons, from the more liberal Houses. But the Academy took a measure of Suburban girl-brats on talent, who would owe allegiance to no House at all, and everything to the Academy. An unHoused citizen might get rank, recognition, respect, regardless of birth. But if that had been Snow's path, it begged asking why she'd left Illharek for life on the border, in Cardik, among the Alviri, who still thought that witches should burn. Had to be another reason. Another several. She must run with the gangs up in the Warren, which meant she was out here on cartel business. Smuggling, most likely. And she had sworn in the Laughing God's name, which made her a heretic twice over. Since the Purge, Illhari were supposed to swear by no gods at all. And the Laughing God was a man's order, no women among its godsworn. Maybe they'd raised standards in the two hundred years since the Purge.

Rurik wouldn't care this woman wasn't guilty of murdering Kenjak, wouldn't care she was a citizen, wouldn't hesitate at breaking bones to get answers. Say *ghosts* to Rurik, and this Illhari half-blood might find herself left with troopers who'd known the deceased and the rest of the camp gone suddenly deaf and blind. No one would notice another corpse in Davni. So best Dekklis find something, anything, to give him, besides Snowdenaelikk.

Focus on what *wasn't*. No campsite. No fire-circle, no curling smoke. Not enough gear on the half-blood's person for survival in a winter wilderness. There were boot tracks in the snow, partial and scattered, that might backtrail to a camp, but those tracks disappeared partway down the hill, where the wind had pushed up drifts and blasted the earth bare. There was nothing here but trees, a dense collection of wide-skirted spruce as old as Cardik. A swath of fresh snow with no marks on it. So the half-blood had flown, then. She and her ghost partner.

Dekklis pulled a lungful of cold air and held it. Blew it out in a plume that looked too much like smoke, like Davni, like Ollu's pyre. There'd be another storm later. There were already clouds invading the blue, grey and solid as shadow. No way she wanted to be out here for it, not with this hostile prisoner, and not with people who skewered the living and carved sorcery into the stake. Taliri might do the first. But the second—hell and damn. Conjuring didn't work in the Wild. If it did, she wouldn't have her prisoner. She and Istel would be twin smears of grease in the snow.

She turned her gaze upslope, where the trees cut a silhouette into the gathering clouds, where Istel waited, frown visible even from here—watching the half-blood, whose attention followed Dekklis, with the wind shredding her topknot and whipping strands across her face.

*You could ask her, Dek.*

Right. And expect any truth, any cooperation, from a woman with chains on her wrists and blood on her mouth.

But a village had burned, and someone had mutilated legion soldiers and maybe worked some kind of conjuring out in the Wild, and *that* was the real threat to Cardik. To all of the Illhari Republic. They had a new enemy out there in the forest, and this woman—whatever else she might be—wasn't that enemy. But maybe she could help them find out who. Maybe she would, if Dekklis could bargain with her, and protect her from Rurik afterward.

A whistle cut through the silence. One long blast, three short, another long, faint over the crest of the hill. Teslin and Barkett, coming back. The half-blood and Istel turned together and looked toward the sound. Dekklis heard the woman's voice, saw Istel stiffen. Guessed the content, the tone, but Istel didn't hit her. *Istel* could manage his temper.

All right. Then she could manage Teslin and Barkett. Dekklis pursed her own lips and whistled back

*acknowledged, we're coming*

and started upslope in the next breath. And she hoped, because the Illhari didn't pray anymore, that the half-blood would cooperate.

* * *

Snow decided that the sudden chorus of whistling was a good indicator that Veiko hadn't got caught. She glanced and added the scout Istel's face as confirmation: dismay on his features, and attention slivering downslope toward his partner.

Although if they *had* caught Veiko, well. Might make her life easier. Let them catch an outlander with a guilty axe, and they'd forget about her for a while. She only needed a scatter of minutes alone with the shackles. They were good steel, good locks—but nothing beyond her skill and practice. Nothing beyond her powers of improvisation, either. The scout had taken her blades, yeah, but she hadn't examined any seams. All Snow needed was a little time, a little distraction. Might get both, if they'd got Veiko after all.

*If.*

Sour knot in her belly that tasted like guilt. Veiko didn't deserve the legion, did he? He'd committed no crime, except helping her. Skraeling and half-blood—neither one all that rare, on the borders of Illharek's territory, but *together* would damn him.

*So be glad he's free.*

Sure. Glad. And be more glad the scout, this *Dekklis*, had given up her search for the campsite before she'd gotten another twenty fucking steps. Be thankful for a bounty of shadows tangled in between branches and trunk. Be thankful she'd managed a solid shadow-weaving.

Briel stirred in those shadows. A near-sending crowded Snow's vision to grey: a promise of wings and blood and fury. Briel would help. Briel would come *now*, would slash out of the sky and tear and cut and—

*No.*

Snow's chest ached with the force of both heartbeats. She imposed her own sending, gory and vivid imaginings of arrows and Briel's fragile wings. The svartjagr's presence shriveled like a cave-slug in sunlight. But she didn't disappear altogether. Clung to Snow's awareness like a bat to cave walls, which was brave for Briel.

*Find Veiko,* Snow wished her. *When I'm gone. Don't follow me. Find him.*

Shit, and then what? Lead him on another chase, to another rescue? Owe him again? And why should he help her a third time?

Pressure on her wrists, not gentle: Istel wanted her to move, neither leading nor following but pacing her, more or less, so he could see her hands. At least he didn't have an arrow nocked and drawn. The best threat he could manage now was the long knife in his belt, if she fought him. Long knife and two free hands, yeah, she'd look like Ollu when he finished.

Or Kenjak. Impaled, Laughing God. The sour in her belly curdled all the way to sick. Desecrating the dead was one thing, but *that* kind of murder—fuck and damn. Who would do that was one worry, and she had a few ideas. But the more pressing concern was what the legion would do to her if they thought she was responsible. She'd be lucky to die before sunset. Be lucky if the citizen's sigil on her skin mattered at all when they picked the punishment.

The scouts knew better. But bet on their mercy, yeah, sooner expect the sky to rain toads. At least the highborn woman looked unhappy, coming back up the slope. Doubt and distress as she fell in beside them. Irritation, too, when the next whistle came. She shifted into a jog, Istel with her, and Snow looped a fistful of slack in the chain and concentrated on keeping both footing and breath.

"You're good at that," said the woman. "Knowing where to step."

"Practice."

"In the snow? I wouldn't expect that from a native Illhari. Not a lot of uneven ground Below. You must've come to Cardik a long time ago."

Snow caught her wounded lip between her teeth and bit to fresh blood. Spat again. Her mouth hurt. Reminder, yeah, to watch that particular orifice. Keep it shut. Besides, she needed all her air for running in snow and uphill. Again. Twice in a week, fuck and damn, this wasn't a habit she wanted to keep.

*Might not become one if they kill you.*

There was a thought.

The scout tried again. "How many years did you spend in the Academy?"

Snow risked a full-faced stare and hoped she didn't ram herself into a tree. The scout was a small woman, no taller than Istel, safe from most branches. "You want to talk, we slow it down, yeah?"

Another gesture, and they dropped to a walk. "Listen, Snow. There's something I want you to see."

"Inside of a cell?"

"First Spear Rurik sent a detachment to retrieve the dead and secure the site. There's something there I think needs your expertise."

"You want a bone set, you'll have to unchain me."

A grimace. A glare. And still softly, patiently: "Whoever killed K'Hess Kenjak carved symbols into the stake. I want you to look at them. Tell me what they say."

"Whoever's probably Taliri, and last I heard we didn't manage to Purge them. Guess a prayer. A sacrifice. We Illhari used to make them, when we still had our gods."

"It's not prayer. It's some kind of conjuring."

"I thought you were just a soldier. Now you read glyphs, too? Is that legion-standard?"

"I'm fourth daughter Szanys Dekklis."

Laughing God. Szanys was as old a House as K'Hess. "Did Illharek export all its highborn, of a sudden?"

"Just look at the symbols. Tell me what they say."

"I don't read Taliri."

"So then you won't understand it, and it's not sorcery, and that answers my question."

"You let me go if I do."

"I can't do that."

"Then I can't read anything."

Istel jerked at her wrists, pulled the slack through her fingers. So *typically* male. Snow peeled a smile for him. "You think that'll help?"

"Istel," Dekklis said. Then, "Listen. I can't unlock you. But I can turn my back once you've done what I've asked. Say, oh, for the time it takes to sing 'Jukainnen's Lament.' That should be long enough, yeah?"

No simple scout, this one, no rebel daughter in disgrace. Smart woman. *Dangerous.* "Your word. Your *oath* as a Szanys, that you'll turn your back when I've looked at your sorcery and told you it's Taliri prayers. You, and the rest of the soldiers."

Hesitation, half a beat. Then a sharp nod. "My oath, on my House, on the blood of my foremothers."

Szanys had a reputation for honor in Illharek. This one might keep her word, yeah, even to a half-blood conjuring outlaw.

"Done." Tsabrak would call her a fool, but she'd have to live long enough to tell him the story.

"Dek," Istel murmured. "They're close."

They, yeah, guess who that was. The other half of the whistling chorus. More scouts, two, another male-female pairing. Big man, bigger woman, neither of whom looked as if they should emerge from trees and shadow without sound.

Dekklis's whole manner shifted. Straighter, suddenly, a small woman seeming much taller. Authority settled on her shoulders like a cloak.

"Teslin. Barkett."

The female pulled a deep breath. "I see *you* had luck, Dek."

"Toadshit luck." Dekklis shrugged. "We may've found her, but we couldn't find the campsite."

"Can't be far," said the man. "She's not dressed for travel. How hard can it—"

"You look," snapped Istel. "See how well you do."

"Hsst. Barkett. Shut up. If Dek says it's not down there, it's not." Teslin scowled. "The motherless toadfucker lost us on the other side of the ridge."

"Diversion," said Dekklis. "Trying to draw us off *her*."

"Maybe," said Teslin, and from Barkett, low-voiced: "What're you smiling about, half-blood?"

Snow shrugged. "Maybe you should worry. He's better at this than you are."

"That a threat?" Barkett took a step, and Istel ebbed between them. Threaten her fingers, yeah, he would, and her tongue. But he wouldn't let anyone else try it. Funny, on another day. But there was no humor at all on Istel's face, or on Barkett's. And on another day Snow would've appreciated that, too, two soldiers at odds over a prisoner. Less now, being that prisoner, with her hands locked together.

"*Him*, is it?" Teslin's gaze lingered past comfort. Hard eyes in a hard face, her mouth puckered tight and disgusted. Thank the God that this woman hadn't caught her. But she might wish *her* pair of scouts was a bit larger. Fuck if she hadn't got the runts on her side.

"I'm thinking," said Szanys Dekklis, "that Snow, here, is a conjuror out of Illharek. I'm thinking she should see Kenjak's pole. What's carved there. See if she can read it."

"She's a *what*?"

Dekklis shrugged. "She's a conjuror and a chirurgeon. Claims she's the one fixed Kenjak's arm. And that makes sense. She's Academy trained. See? Rings in her ears. The hair? That's the mark," the small woman added casually, as if that were a fact everyone knew. Everyone did, in Illharek.

But here, Teslin and Barkett did *not* know, clear enough. Laughing God. Surrounded by rustics, wasn't she, people who'd never seen witchfire daylight on Illharek's spires, except for fourth daughter Szanys Dekklis. Tsabrak wouldn't believe this, if she got back to report. But then, "Jukainnen's Lament" might give her enough time to get free of the shackles, maybe half a dozen steps. Dekklis hadn't promised time past that. Istel could still put an arrow in her back. Teslin and Barkett could run her down.

*Idiot, Snow, that's what you are.*

Kenjak had been the First Spear's brother. They wouldn't just let her go. They didn't dare. Her skin prickled, too cold for sweat. She'd get her opportunity, on the honor of Szanys. Wait for that, and use it, and hope.

*Dear Laughing God.*

Or pray, which was its own foolishness. Illhari law forbade it. Official Senate mandate, wrapped in cool reason, held that gods weren't reliable. True enough, on all counts. But her motives and the Laughing God's matched more often than not.

*What, it's his will that you're locked up right now, then?*

Or it amused him. Idiot, yeah, to trust in the God.

"I don't think she killed Kenjak," Dekklis was saying. "There's not enough blood on her."

"Maybe she's got two shirts."

"There's blood on *these* sleeves. And then why would she set the bone?"

Teslin thought about it. Snow imagined a grinding sound, and smoke curling on the edges. "All right."

But the man, Barkett, frowned. "Dek. I don't think it's wise."

"No one asked you—"

"Fuck *off,* Istel—"

"Fuck off, both of you. Dek's got rank, and I agree with her." Teslin pushed up close to Snow. Big woman, even among Dvergiri, almost as tall as an Alvir man. Pretty clear that she counted on her size to intimidate. Might've worked two days ago, yeah, before Veiko's towering, alien, axe-wielding presence.

"Where's your partner, half-blood?"

This again. Laughing God. No imagination in the legion. Then again, Teslin's casual backhand might break her jaw. Prudence. Sense. *Watch* her temper.

"You think the First Scout hasn't already asked that?"

"Mouth on that one," muttered Barkett.

Dekklis joined Istel, a casual touching of shoulders that hedged Teslin out of striking range, that added a two-body barrier between Snow and possible harm.

"She says," Dekklis said, deadpan, "that he's a ghost. Angry dead."

"Ghost." Teslin's eyes narrowed into amber slits. "Ghost's got boots? Ghost's got dogs?"

*Ghost's got away,* Snowdenaelikk thought, and managed not to say it. And wished that ghost: *Keep running.*

# CHAPTER SEVEN

The storm fell out of the sky at dusk. There had been flurries since midafternoon, and increasing grey, as Veiko worked his way back to the campsite. He meant to go faster. Had been, until a fear that wasn't his seized his chest and belly, left him sweating and reliant on a naked oak for support.

That was Briel's fear. Briel's anger came after, soon enough, clouded his vision red and forced another stop, this one crouched in a scatter of boulders. He gripped the rocks until his hands ached, that time, and willed her to stop, please. He shut her out, finally, or she gave up: a sudden blank, like the numb a wound feels after pain. Snowdenaelikk called it *sending*, said it was as natural to svartjagr as barking was to dogs.

*There's no witchery in it, Veiko. It's how the packs talk to each other. Wolves howl. Svartjagr send.*

But it was uncanny, nonetheless. Uncomfortable, to have an animal *but she isn't, quite, is she?*
intruding on his wits. At least Briel hadn't blinded him.

He had intended to lead the trouble away and return for Snowdenaelikk. Evidently something had gone wrong. Plans often did.

A fool trusted fate. A wise man relied on his wits. And a wise man did not, he was certain, share those wits with a bat-winged, snake-necked thief of flatcakes.

Dogs were more sensible companions. They confined their communication to honest noises, to ears and tail and things any man might see for himself. Solid, reliable creatures. And good use against wood-wise Illhari soldiers—Helgi and Logi's doing, and no room for his vanity, that he'd escaped so cleanly. Those scouts after him had been quick, faster than he'd expected. And quieter, and two of them to his one. He had been a hunter most of his life. Had been hunted, too. But never with quite this skill, or this determination. He might have thanked his ancestors, when the soldiers finally abandoned his trail. Might have, except for Briel's sending, which told him Snow was neither safe nor where he had left her.

So his ancestors had not yet forgiven him. Or Snow had made a mistake. Even so, she wasn't helpless. Carried one weapon openly, and several concealed, and was clearly accustomed to dangerous activities and their consequences. Briel's distress was no sure indication that she was hurt.

*Tell yourself that.*

He tried, instead and again, to tell himself nothing. Mind the snowfall, thicker now. Climb the last hill. Listen at the top for strange noises. Watch Helgi's ears, and Logi's tail, and gauge from their signals what waited on the other side. Two black noses worked the wind, but ears and tails stayed upright. So. Nothing worth their alarm.

But Briel had been frightened. Had been angry. So Veiko let himself think of her, fragile black wings and a narrow head very skilled at getting into packs and under blankets. Got back sullen nothing for his trouble, a blot of solid chill in his chest that said she could hear, but that she wasn't answering.

Contrary animal. Difficult. Snowdenaelikk's face swam up out of memory, the smile that pulled on one half of her mouth. Her voice, too, slipping like water over the edges of words.

Logi chuffed. Snowdenaelikk vanished. And Veiko found himself having traveled a good five paces without watching where he put his feet. Instinct might've kept him on rocks and bare patches. Not wits. Not sense. And he couldn't blame Briel for that lapse, either. The ache in his chest was his own this time.

Worry profited no one. What did: minding his surroundings, which meant Helgi, whose muzzle skimmed circles around a churned patch of snow. He growled when Veiko crouched beside him, which counted for Helgi's opinion on what he'd found.

There were tracks, the edges eroding with fresh snowfall. Veiko recognized Snowdenaelikk's narrow tread. Counted three others, maybe four, in the scuff and jumble. The trail led west again, toward the road and the riverbed where they'd left Kenjak.

Helgi whined and scratched at the snow. There, beside the trail: another mark in the snow, no footprint, and small as a fingertip, round and sunken. Liquid would do that in snow. Veiko's stomach knotted and sank. He could not be sure of the color, not in the storm-light, but Helgi's hackles and Helgi's flat ears warned him. Veiko touched a finger to the spot anyway, sniffed and tasted.

Blood. Of course it was. And it would be hers, too, sure as fire was hot. There was another spot of it, some several paces up the trail. And a third, farther on. Intervals, too uneven for coincidence.

So she was injured, then, and in custody, and leaving a trail for him. He wondered if they had dragged her from the campsite. If he'd lost his gear as well as his guest, his own survival became that much more of a challenge, and her retrieval much less likely.

*Retrieval now, is it?*

A man owed his guests safety, and he had failed badly in that. But a camp wasn't a hearthside. No one had taken Snow from his home.

*What home is that, Veiko?*

An outlaw had none, except his own fireside. And if by that reckoning Snowdenaelikk became part of his household, well, there were no elders here to protest his reasoning. The Illhari soldiers had taken Snowdenaelikk.

He would get her back.

Veiko squinted through the gloom. Storm-dusk now, all the colors washed grey. Snow falling thick and straight. He could just make out the spruce from here, a wide wedge among more slender trees. Helgi's rump poked out between the branches, pale smear against dark needles. That tail, he noted, was waving. The ache in his chest loosed a notch. Perhaps the soldiers had not found the campsite. Perhaps he might still have the rest of his gear. His arrows and bow.

A foolish hope. But he clung to it anyway and wondered if Briel would have allowed a looting, as she had so clearly allowed Snowdenaelikk's capture.

A single flash across his vision, lightning bright, and then the branches burst outward in a shower of white and sharp needles. Instinct kept him quiet, though he almost choked on the shout in his throat, and on his own heart slamming after it. He dropped and dodged and twisted, raised his axe to deflect

*Briel*

whatever came.

The svartjagr angled away at the last, a whistle of air across bone and membrane. She missed the axe blade. Keened as she reached open air, a damned-soul shriek that raised hair on his arms. She circled the tree once and landed on the branches above him.

Veiko lowered his axe slowly. Tremors all through his arm, his chest, his legs. Fear. Shock. His own anger, warm and growing hotter. Had Briel charged him like that the first time, he'd have shot her for certain.

This time he did stumble, at the raw wave of Briel in his head. An image of Briel broken and bleeding, with arrows in her wings. He could see every feather on the fletching, crimson and black stripes. Legion colors. Legion fletching. Veiko held his eyes wide against it. Made himself see the snow-dusted branches, white on twilight grey. Strangled out, "Briel, stop."

The image brightened, one last flash, and then Veiko's eyes were his own again. He braced for blindness, told himself it never lasted, Snowdenaelikk swore as much. But his vision cleared. Steadied. There was the tree in front of him and a pair of worried dogs. And when he looked up into the grey and snow-spit—a darker shape in the branches, red-eyed and watching.

"Chrrip." Plaintive. Terrified. Maybe apologetic.

"Did someone shoot at you?"

"Chrrip." She hopped lower, loosed another cascade of snow. Stretched her narrow head toward him, on that slender, fragile neck. Another sending ghosted his awareness, mostly impression, sensation. Warm and gentle hands. Smoke and spice. And over that, more fear and a seething frustration, pure Briel, a need to *do* and not to *wait*.

Worry, he understood. His anger smoked away. "We will go," he told her. "Soon."

Then Veiko readjusted his grip on the axe, moved the branches, and ducked under the tree. If it was twilight outside, then the inside of the tree was full night. No sign of the fire-ring, or the packs. The blackness pressed on him. Absolute, solid, and he was suddenly sure that he wasn't under the tree any longer, that if he took a single step he'd fall into a chasm with no bottom.

Panic crowded the air from his lungs. He lurched backward, flailed with the axe, and cut the branches wide. Grey light leaked through the gap and dissolved where it touched the unnatural, solid black.

This time his shiver had nothing to do with cold.

She had said any Dvergir could weave the shadows. Had shown him, around this very fire—pull and push, light for dark. A long-ago gift from the Laughing God, she'd said, forgotten deliberately, except within the Academy's walls. A child's trick, that simple. Not witchery.

Well. Children feared the dark. Men did not. Veiko gritted his teeth and braved the shadows again. He could smell the remnants of campfire, wet dog, the scent that was Snowdenaelikk. Could hear the chuff and rustle of the dogs outside, and the wind's push through the needles. He let his smile crawl onto his lips, where no one could see it. Held it like a shield while he found bow and pack and furs and fled back under the open sky. Another round of tremors as the darkness worked its way out of his bones, which made settling two packs on his shoulders that much more of a challenge. By the time he strung the bow, his hands were steady again.

"Can you find her?"

The dogs looked as he spoke, ears cupped and attentive. But they didn't understand him. Didn't answer. Couldn't, being dogs. But he wasn't talking to them, either.

"Chrrip." The svartjagr launched from the tree in a whisper of needles and fragile skin wings. In the twilight, through the falling snow, she was nearly invisible.

Veiko didn't need to see her to know where she was. Didn't need his dogs, this time, to follow Snow's tracks or her blood on the snow. He followed Briel into the forest, and the storm drew down over him like a blanket.

# CHAPTER EIGHT

Dekklis never saw the Taliri. Never heard them. One moment, she was dreaming supper, and the next—heard a gurgle from Barkett, as he twisted and flailed and fell. A fractured heartbeat as she marked the shaft poking out of his face, and saw the fletching, and understood what it meant.

Cloaked and hooded shapes spilled off the bank, half a dozen, then twice that. A blur of violence that left her disarmed and facedown in the snow, clinging to consciousness. She hadn't fought back when they chained her. Hadn't fought back when they jerked her back onto her feet and shuffle-marched everyone up the ridge. Toward, she realized muzzily, the legion patrol's campsite.

Pink and red licked off the cloud-layer, and smoke tangled with the charcoal stink of cooking meat. Too much light for a campfire, too bright and too big. It was, she realized, a bonfire. Realized in the next heartbeat that the roasting meat was not animal, no, nor edible, nor ever meant to be. Oh foremothers, those were *her people* burning.

There had been eighteen of them—the four scouts, the rest regular infantry—dispatched to retrieve Kenjak and Ollu. Dekklis tried to count bodies as their escort marched them past the fire. They'd been dead awhile. Fresh snow collected on faces, smearing the features. Dekklis hoped for Taliri among the dead and saw only legion armor and snow churned red. The carved pole presided, naked, over the clearing. Dekklis saw the half-blood looking at it as they passed.

She would ask Snow later what she saw on that pole. Because there *would* be a later. Believe that. For now: Keep her chin up, feet moving, eyes defocused. Pretend there weren't

*too many*

Taliri milling around the campsite, looting and sorting equipment belonging to people she knew. Pretend she couldn't see the smug expressions of their guards or hear the shouts they traded with their fellow raiders. The Taliri wanted a reaction out of her, well, they could go rot.

Foremothers knew Teslin was proving entertainment enough, running a bloody-mouthed litany of threats and helpless outrage. Istel, at least, kept his silence, but Istel had fought back hard and bled for it. They'd put him on the end of the chain, behind the half-blood, and Dekklis couldn't see how bad he was. Didn't dare turn and look and ask, with these motherless toadshits hovering. No telling what *they* understood. No way she would give them

*Istel*

a lever to use against her.

Their captors stopped, finally, at the far end of the camp. Huddled together in rapid and foreign conversation that spiked briefly loud. Then they peeled away, one after another, until only a single broad male remained. The Talir looped their chain around a stout, leafless oak and stepped out of range. Folded arms, hip cocked, his hand loose on the hilt of a stolen legion sword.

Take that as evidence, then, what threat they ranked. Eleven soldiers dead and burning already. Another damaged four posed no danger.

She could count herself lucky to be alive. She could count herself stupid, too, for having missed all the clues of ambush.

Complacence. Arrogance. Classic Illhari failings since the Republic's founding.

Well. Balance those faults against tenacity, ingenuity, training—

*What, this a motherless recruitment speech?*

It was luck she needed. Luck, and the rest of the Sixth.

*Or a lockpick.*

Legion shackles were two bracelets joined by a linked chain. The Taliri version had leather-wrapped bracelets connected by a rigid steel bar, welded to a ring with a chain running through it, stringing the prisoners along like beads. It was a smart system, if you didn't have to wear it yourself. Prisoners couldn't get their own hands together. Couldn't move, either, without rattling the whole business and dragging on everyone's wrists. So it was bad enough when the half-blood slithered over to Istel. Rattle, clank, and the guard's narrow-eyed stare. Dekklis reckoned he couldn't see much through the snowfall. Reckoned, when he didn't move, that he didn't much care what one prisoner did to another. But then Teslin heaved herself up and began pacing, staggering, the length and limit of the chain. The snow swirled around her, eddied and clumped in strange patterns.

That was nervous energy, and anger, and grief. Teslin had a temper. Had a certain lack of sense, too, under some kinds of stress.

So Dekklis let Teslin pace. Tried to ignore the rattle and the guard's stare. Winced every time Teslin ran out of slack, jerked around, and started back. Dekklis knew there was something wrong with her ribs, yeah, knives every time she drew breath. Bruises, she hoped. Not broken. But Istel. Dekklis caught glimpses, between Teslin's pacings. He slumped in the snow like a sack of meal. The half-blood had both hands on him, doing—hell. Whatever chirurgeons did.

It was more in line with the half-blood's self-interest to let Istel bleed out, to Dekklis's reckoning. But there she was, her gloves stripped and crumpled like skin in the snow, her hands slick and wet. Her breath steamed grey, mingling with Istel's where their heads almost touched.

Dekklis couldn't hear what she said—might be murmuring comfort or something more arcane. Or profane, if she'd got to praying. Dekklis stared hard at Snow's gloves and tried to remember if the God's cult had been much for healing. Thieving, extortion, smuggling, murder, yes, those she recalled. A man's god, a criminal god, whose cult had been subject to persecution even before the Purge. Dekklis recalled her nurse's voice and wrinkled face, Pasi's fair Alviri skin gone pallid as mushrooms in sunless Illharek.

*Their punishment fit their worship, Dominita. The cult was savage. Lawless.*

Child Dekklis had been horrified, fascinated, driven to nightmares of imagination. Adult Dekklis, chained and prisoner to Taliri who'd impaled a living K'Hess Kenjak, decided, dry-eyed and awake, she did not care if the half-blood worshipped toadshit and snails, so long as she saved Istel's life. Let her eat Alviri babies later and swear by whatever gods she liked, so long as Istel didn't die here.

But that pole. The letters carved into it. *Taliri prayers,* Snow had predicted, and maybe that was true. The Taliri had never been easy neighbors, superstitious and violent, a collection of tribes held together by common language and common hatred of all things Illhari. They had been allies of the Alviri thegns long ago, murdering any Dvergir fool enough to set foot Above. But then the Dvergiri legion emerged from Illharek, wielding both godmagic and conjuring. They smashed the thegns and scattered the Taliri mercenaries who fought with them. Forged the Illhari Republic across what had been Alvir territory. Offered citizenship to its defeated enemies, which the Alviri took, more or less. But the Taliri had rejected the offer. Taken up raiding instead, and they didn't discriminate between old allies and new enemies. But their gods had never demanded living sacrifice before, either.

Dekklis rocked onto her hip. Pitched her voice beneath Teslin's clank and snarl. "Snow. You get a look at that pole? I saw you looking before, when we passed it. Is it prayers?"

The half-blood flicked a narrow stare at her. "Couldn't tell."

"Prayers mean gods."

"Your tutors teach you that, Szanys?" Snow clamped both hands around Istel's arm. Squeezed hard enough that he gasped. "Need some of his sleeve. Or yours. Long strips."

Dekklis blinked. "What?"

"I can't tear them myself, yeah?"

Hell. Dekklis couldn't reach her own sleeves, either. Twisted and crabbed closer to Istel and tugged at his undamaged wrist. Wet wool, and silk under that. Nothing that wanted to rip.

Teslin slouched past them. Eclipsed the guard behind broad shoulders.

"My boot," hissed Snow, and thrust out her left leg. "In the cuff. *Hurry.*"

Dekklis fumbled, double-handed, at the leather. Wet, heavy, oiled and scuffed and stiff under cold fingers. But she found the tiny pocket folded into the seam. Plucked the narrow blade out and tucked it into her palm.

Wicked thing. Sharp.

"How many of these you hiding, half-blood?"

"As if I'll tell you. Just cut me bandages, yeah? Fast."

"Cutting. You want the guard to see?" But Dekklis sawed at the wool. Good-quality weave, hell and damn. First time she wished second best on the legion. Third best. Motherless *beggar's* robes, right now, if it meant easy cutting.

Teslin fetched up hard at the end of the chain. Dekklis braced against the sudden drag, feet slipping in the snow and mud. Held the tiny knife, didn't drop it. Held her breath, too, behind gritted teeth, until Teslin swung a half circle and started back.

Clink and rattle, louder than the curse Dekklis kept under her breath.

"Got it," she told Snow. "How many strips you need? How big?"

"Two strips. Three, if you can man—" And then the half-blood locked up, corpse-stiff. Squeezed her eyes shut. A muscle knotted in her narrow jaw. She greyed as pale as Istel and hissed something under her breath.

A name, sounded like. Or a curse. *Briel*, whatever that meant. Maybe another name for her Laughing God. Maybe a lover. Dekklis was half a breath from asking *are you all right?* when Snow shook her head hard, as if to clear it. Squeezed her eyes shut and held them like that.

"What is it?" Dekklis asked, low-voiced.

The eyes cracked. Blue gleamed through pale lashes. "Nothing."

"Toadshit. You hurt? Take a headshot?"

"No and no." Snow shook her head again. Her eyes flashed in the fireglow. "Guard's watching us close, Scout. You want to tell your friend to sit down before she brings him over here?"

Dekklis cleared her throat. "Teslin. Sit. You're getting attention. If he comes over here, we've got trouble."

"If? What the fuck we in now, Dek, you tell me that?" Teslin's voice climbed. Peaked and broke.

"We're still alive."

Stark fear in Teslin's eyes, and grief, and all of it tinder awaiting a spark. "Barkett's not. Neither's Kenjak or Ollu. Whole fucking *camp's* dead, yeah? We're next."

"We're in no shape to run."

"There's one of him. We can take him."

Dekklis closed her eyes and counted five and opened them again. "Teslin. Sit. Down. *Now.* Order, savvy?"

Teslin stared at her. Sat, sudden and hard. She hung her head between her knees, coughed, and spat a rope of blood and slime.

Dekklis took a slow, shallow breath. Held it. Twinges all up and down, and a deep pain in her side like a knife. She let the breath out, thin and careful.

The half-blood shot her a narrow look, white brows crowding the bridge of that proud nose. "Your ribs," she said. "I'll have a look soon, Szanys."

"Worry about Istel."

"Oh. I am."

She didn't like the look on Snow's face, that tight-lipped frown. She sidled closer. "How is he?"

"Awake." Istel cracked an eye at her. Stretched a smile. "Fine."

Right. Skin washed grey, where it stretched over bone. He hadn't complained. Wouldn't, being Istel. "Toadshit. Snow?"

The half-blood knotted another strip of Istel's former sleeve around the wound.

"Won't die," Snow said. "Wish I had thread and a needle. He moves, he bleeds."

"So he won't move."

"He will." Snow's eyes gleamed flat and bleak and blue. "They'll break camp tonight. Move us or kill us, something will happen."

"It's snowing. It's *night*."

"They can't wait. Your First Spear comes up here looking for you, they're outnumbered. All they've got is surprise."

"And arrows," snapped Teslin.

"Arrows will work on a camp bedded down and mostly out of armor. That's how they got your friends here. But on marching infantry, snow coming down, arrows won't do much. And in this riverbed, they're rats trapped in an alley, yeah? They're worried."

"Worried. *How* do you know this?"

Tight smile, no teeth. "Heard them talking, yeah?"

"Thought you didn't understand Taliri."

"Said I didn't *read* it. And I lied." The half-blood thrust her hands into the snow and scrubbed until it turned pink. Pulled her hands out and grimaced. "All right, Szanys. Let me see your ribs."

"Bruises."

"Listen. We get half a chance, we're leaving, yeah? Not going to let you slow me down."

"Thought we can't run in the chains."

"We can't. So they'll come off. Istel's already unlocked."

Hell and damn. Dekklis stared at her. Teslin did. Istel blinked and twisted his wrist. Blinked again. "Oh."

"Laughing God, stay still. Give it away now, we're all dead." Snow's expression never changed. "Now. Dekklis."

"You're going to help us."

Snow shrugged. "Not going to leave you to die."

"Why not?"

"You want truth? Sure. I won't cry if you die here. But you see this bar between the cuffs, Szanys-daughter? Makes it tough for me to get my fingers around to my own locks. I'm stuck. But I can pick *you* loose. And Teslin."

"No." Dekklis cast her own bleak stare toward the fire. Their weapons had marched *that* way, with the rest of their escort. "We won't last unarmed."

"In a pitched battle, no. But"—Snow flicked a glance at Teslin— "only one of them on us, yeah? We can take him."

"Heh," said Teslin. The unswollen half of her mouth lumped into a smile. "Like how you think, half-blood."

"I don't," said Dekklis. "I count fifteen of them by the fire. They killed more than that many of us already."

"They surprised your soldiers," Snow said. "Like they surprised you. This time, we surprise them."

"And fight them with snowballs? No."

Teslin coughed. Spat. Said, fluid-thick: "Rather die in a fight, Dek. Like Barkett."

"Didn't ask your opinion."

"I agree with Teslin," said Istel faintly. He winced when she looked at him. "Sorry, Dek."

She glared at the half-blood. "Insubordination's contagious."

A smile spasmed on Snow's lips. "Yeah. Maybe. But I think we're better off dying fast than what I think they'll do to us."

Hard to argue with that. Dekklis nodded at Snow. Didn't flinch when the half-blood slid a hand under her armor. Ground her teeth together and let breath hiss between them. Hell and damn, that hurt. Sent sparks across her vision, tunneled grey on the edges.

Snow's breath warmed her cheek. "Cracked."

"I'll manage."

"You'll have to." Snow angled herself between Dekklis and their guard and dropped her hands to the shackles. Metal flickered between her fingers. Chirurgeon. Conjuror. Motherless thief, too.

"What stops us from leaving you to the Taliri, once we're free?"

Click. Thunk. Snow slid the pick out of the lock, rolled the slim steel between her fingers. "Your honor, Szanys."

"You're not that stupid."

"You saying that's a mistake, trusting you?"

"I'm saying it's a risk."

"I might be that desperate."

"Hell you are. *Truth*, half-blood. You've got a plan."

"Truth." Challenge in those blue eyes. And not a bit of doubt, or fear, or any sensible, predictable emotion. "I do have a plan. But it works on my timing, yeah? You move too early, we all die."

"Wait for what?"

Snow angled a glance from the corners of her eyes. Crouched there, with only the steam from her nose to say living, not statue. Snowmelt beaded on her cheeks. Dripped down.

"Well?"

"We need a distraction, yeah? Well. It's almost here."

Teslin got it first. "Your partner's coming."

Flat smile, no teeth, that looked like it hurt. "Call him that, sure."

Dekklis choked on a dry laugh. "One man. *One* man, against twenty—"

"One man, armed. Three of you. One of me. Shadows solid as I can weave them around that fire, so we get a little darkness. Surprise on our side." She laughed soundlessly. "Since I bet you're too orthodox to pray, Szanys . . . hope that's enough, yeah? Or we end up like Kenjak."

* * *

A man waited at the bend in the riverbed, an armored silhouette that said Illhari legion. A sentry, Veiko thought, and stopped.

Then he noticed the faint glow limning the soldier. Noticed that Helgi and Logi, reliable sentries themselves—had not yet smelled a man standing downwind. And Veiko realized, as he noticed no breath pluming out of the man's face, that he wasn't looking at anyone living.

*Run* was his first thought. A child's instinct, to flee for light and the safety of walls. But there was no place he might go—no lodge, no tent, no shelter—that a ghost could not find him. And so Veiko shifted the bow on his shoulder, set his hand on the axe, tried to remember the lore. Could a living man wound a ghost? Some of the walking dead wore their own skins, could be hurt—but this one wore only the memory of flesh. Perhaps it would not notice him, or the dogs, and he could double back and try another route—

Briel swooped low over his head, whisper-wings and the damned-soul *shee-oop* that Snow said was a svartjagr hunting cry. The dogs paused in midstep to look at her, muzzles pointed like fingers. Helgi whined. Logi waved his tail. Briel circled back to Veiko, braked, and caught her claws in his cloak. She settled her length across his shoulders. *Chrripped* as she settled.

Unafraid. Willing him to be unafraid.

The ghost looked and began walking toward him. Now the dogs noticed. Even Helgi clamped his tail and retreated, ears flat and fur spiked.

Wise animals, dogs. One could not say as much for svartjagr. Small wonder Snowdenaelikk required much practice with escape and evasion. She had Briel for company.

*Skraeling,* said the ghost. A young man's voice. A young man's uncertainty. *Can you hear me?*

Veiko closed his eyes. Clamped his lips hard together. One did not speak to wandering spirits. One offered the dead no anchors on the world of the living. One did *not.*

*Skraeling.* The voice grew no louder. But when Veiko cracked his eyelids, he saw the ghost a mere arm's length away. Now he recognized its features, and the cold in his belly grew teeth. *Skraeling, I remember who helped me.*

"Chrrip." Briel's hard little head butted his cheek. Smooth hide, warm as coals. Her wings flared as she stretched her neck forward. He felt, rather than heard, the warning hiss.

The ghost stopped as if he'd struck a barrier. Looked at the svartjagr with something like fear. Looked at Veiko with something like desperation.

*Skraeling, please.*

Fool.

"K'Hess Kenjak," Veiko said, in his clearest Dvergiri. "I hear you."

Ghosts did not feel relief, surely, but this one's face sagged into a smile. *I hoped you would.*

Hoped. The dead should not hope. The dead should be dead. And this boy-man should not be dead at all.

"We left you alive," Veiko said carefully.

A ripple across translucent features. *The Taliri came.* Another ripple. For a moment its eyes gleamed bright as Briel's. *They killed all of us.*

"All."

*All but three troopers. And your half-blood.* The ghost looked over its shoulder. Frowned. *But one of them will not survive.*

Do not ask, Veiko told himself, how he knows that. Do not ask who will die. Ask useful things, like:

"How many Taliri?"

*Ten. Fifteen.*

"There is a difference."

*Too many,* said the ghost, and Veiko did not like its smile. *Too many for one man. But I can help you, skraeling.*

Fools talked to ghosts. Fools gave hospitality to half-blood Illhari outlaws. Fools cleaved the chieftain's son's skull, too. But to leave Snow now—that was dishonor and cowardice, and his ancestors would remember it. He would, all the rest of his life.

Veiko worked his tongue around until he'd gathered enough spit to speak. A fool he might be, but he had listened to the noidghe's winter-night tales.

"For what price?"

The ghost's smile changed then and scrubbed away any resemblance to the boy he remembered.

*Revenge.*

# CHAPTER NINE

Snowdenaelikk examined the fluttering ache in her throat. Named it *hope* and *stupid* and tried to swallow it smooth. Dekklis was right. *Hell* of a risk, big as all the fucking sky, to trust highborn honor. But there was no one else *to* trust. Teslin would leave her to die. Istel might not, left to his own, but he'd follow his commander's orders. Do what Dekklis told him, and hell with his own honor. Dekklis herself had two hands free now. She might lose patience. Might decide Snow would be distraction enough, left chained, while she and Teslin and Istel escaped.

Except they wouldn't. Their best hope, their only hope, was a man and two dogs and Briel. But if Veiko walked into this, he'd get killed.

Her chest ached, gut to throat. She closed her eyes and sent

*wait*

clear and hard as she could. Let Briel listen, for once. Please, Laughing God.

An uncivilized people, the Taliri, known for cruelty, for hating the Dvergiri only a little more than they hated Alviri. They raided and took things that belonged to other people, in a way that the gangs and the cartels didn't. In a way that Veiko might understand and condemn.

*The people need takin to live, do you see?*

Well, say the Taliri stole everyone's takin. Say the Taliri hunted and killed what they caught. Two-legged wolves, yeah, and worse than wolves.

And that was the problem, wasn't it? Taliri would've burned Davni, murdered everyone—but they'd have looted it first.

Unless.

*Prayers mean gods.*

Say the Taliri had offered a sacrifice. Say something had answered. Or someone. Prayers meant gods, yeah, and the scratching on that pole—fuck and damn, no conjuring she recognized, not ward or spell. But she had known the shapes, even so. Glyphs that flashed her back to hundreds of candlemarks spent in the Academy archives, reading the histories. The Purge had been about choices: Dvergiri changing their reliance on godmagic to conjuring, trusting their own wits more than the gods. When the foremothers who conducted the Purge had destroyed temples and executed the godsworn, they'd assumed that meant the gods had died, too. The Laughing God hadn't. And clearly, neither had Tal'Shik.

Snowdenaelikk shivered, hard.

"What?" Teslin tried to turn her damn head, to see Snow with her one working eye. "You see something?"

"Nothing," she snapped. "Thinking, that's all. Hold still."

There wasn't much she could do for Teslin's eye, or the right side of her face, or the tooth cracked to gumline. The nose, yeah, that she could fix. Straighten it, anyway, for another rush of blood and Teslin's explosive profanity. And in that distraction, slip the pick into the lock, twist and work metal on metal, and pray

*Laughing God*

the blood didn't make her hands slip.

"Hsst." Warning from Dekklis, all she had before:

"Illhari." Their guard, with an accent thicker than Veiko's, yeah, slurred and impossible. Closing on them, rot him anyway. "Illhari."

She thought he meant Dekklis, or Teslin, or Istel. Took her a moment and the Talir's impatient boot to figure otherwise. "Illhari," the guard said, and jerked the chain. *Get up* didn't need translation.

Snow slipped, in rising, and palm-planted and pressed the pick into the snow. Put a boot on it in the next motion. Please, Laughing God, Dekklis noticed. Please, she picked it up before the guard did. Ugly motherless toadshit, scowling with his blunt Taliri features. A solid people, the Taliri, stone-hard. This one had agate eyes, flecked gold, buried in deep sockets.

Fuck and damn, she'd seen more wit from Logi.

The Talir produced his own key and rattled her back to freedom. Instinct, to rub the liberated flesh. Her fingers were cold as the metal had been. He let her shackles drop. Gestured, chin and shoulder, toward the fire, and when she didn't move, shoved her, one-handed.

"Go," he said. "She waits."

*Who?* she thought of asking. Didn't, as Dekklis saved her, murmured "Snow" and "Over there, left, look" in a tolerable approximation of Illhari street-cant.

So Snow turned, with what she hoped was appropriate nonchalance. And there, the who: a woman, striding away from the bonfire. Shadows dripped from the folds of her cloak, eddied around her feet like living ink. Hair long and unbound, reddish and warm in the fireglow. Honey-gold eyes stared out of wide Taliri cheekbones and past a proud, definitely Dvergiri nose. Another half-blood.

Who stopped, halfway between fire and trees. "Snowdenaelikk." Her Dvergiri was less precise than Veiko's. Stiffer. "I am pleased to have found you. I worried when I saw the legion come to Davni."

Hear a feather drop in that silence. Feel three pairs of eyes—hell, no, two and a half—scorching the back of her head. Only one way this woman would know her name. Tsabrak's motherless courier, right there, Tsabrak's toadshit orders ringing clear in her head.

*Wait for the courier . . . She'll find you.*

But he hadn't warned her about another half-blood. Some of that was Tsabrak, who liked to keep his own counsel. Make his own plans. Keep secrets, even from her. Probably thought it was a great joke to surprise her.

Manipulative, motherless, *honorless—*

"Half-blood," said Dekklis. Curious flatness to her voice, which Snow took for *you motherless toadshit* and *you traitor* combined.

Three easy steps to the forest, yeah, just fucking *run.* She let the guard guide her forward. This new half-blood was tallish, curved like an oil lamp under cloak and Talir tunic. She pulled Snow's sword out from under her cloak. Offered it sheathed and balanced between her palms. The ends of the belt dangled like limp arms, a scant fingerlength from the snow.

"My apologies for your rough treatment. My people did not recognize you among the soldiers."

Snow nodded, in what she hoped was a good approximation of mollified offense. Looped and settled the belt on her hips, under the cloak, and wondered if she dared ask for the rest of her knives. Damn Dekklis anyway, for her diligence. She felt naked.

"My thanks," she said in unlovely Taliri. "But I don't think we've met."

"You may call me Ehkla." The half-blood offered a bow. "You are unharmed?"

A polite people, the Taliri, when they weren't burning towns and impaling the wounded. "More or less."

"Good." A nod, grave and slow, as if Snow's health were the most important matter. "And your companion?"

"Dead."

A second bow. "We regret the loss."

"Don't. He was an idiot. I'm here for whatever you've got. Let's get to that."

Snow held her right hand up then, palm out, and tilted it toward the firelight. The Laughing God's glyph wasn't easy to see, black ink on black skin.

*Shadows of a shadow,* Tsabrak said. *Just like we are.*

Tsabrak liked his drama. More

*honest*

accurate if they called themselves thieves and assassins. Or better, *merchants,* just the sort who dodged tariffs and taxes and Senate inspections and did business in the alleys. Call them those things, along with *heretic,* for honoring

*serving, Snowdenaelikk, we serve*

"The Laughing God," Ehkla murmured. "Unusual, to find a woman in his service."

"I don't serve him," Snow snapped. Tsabrak had allowed the godmark on a woman's flesh, but not the oaths. She wasn't sure she'd have taken them, anyway. *Serve* didn't suit her. "I *work* with the God. Like you do."

"I?" Ehkla laughed and opened her own palm. "I do not work with *the God.*"

And it was not the Laughing God's jagged black mark there, no. Round series of loops, this mark, bloodslick red and gleaming. It made Snow's head ache to look at it, made her skin prickle like parchment too close to a flame. Sweat carved a channel down her ribs, chilled where the wind sliced down to skin. *This* was Tsabrak's idea of ally, was it? Better off without, if he'd asked her. Which he fucking hadn't.

Ehkla smiled. Nodded. "You recognize her mark."

Tsabrak's eyes lit like that, too, when he had a new audience. Fanatic gleam that Snow had mistaken once for attractive. She liked it even less on Ehkla's face.

"No. Sorry. Should I?"

"Tal'Shik led the Illhari out of the darkness. Tal'Shik—"

"Told the highborn godsworn to burn the God's temples. Yeah. Now I remember. Heard a lecture on her once, 'Why the Senate Conducted the Purge.' Listen. I'm here for whatever you've got for Tsabrak, yeah? Let's get to that."

Ehkla looked at her. Her breath smoked out in a long, slow exhale. "The Senate betrayed Tal'Shik. Her daughters—"

"She might've had allies if she hadn't killed everyone else. *Delivery.*"

Another long breath, in and out. Watch the shift in Ehkla's eyes and consider that picking fights with Tal'Shik's

*motherless half-blood Talir*

godsworn wasn't the wisest choice, no, not if Tsabrak wanted an alliance.

*Fuck the alliance. You want to walk out of here, yeah? Be polite.*

Snow was on the teetering brink of apology, excuses clotting against the back of her teeth, when Ehkla jerked out a tiny nod.

"No delivery. A message. Davni."

"What's it mean, *hey, Taliri raided here?*"

"Your master understands."

Master. Right. Razor-cut subtle, this one. Snow peeled her own smile. "I should get back, then, and tell him. Don't want him to get mad, yeah? He might beat me."

Ehkla floated a glance past her shoulder, at Dekklis and Teslin and Istel. "You should wait. There is an Illhari cohort on the road."

"I'll get past them."

"It's not safe."

Damn right it wasn't, and the legion the least of her worries. Riverbed full of Taliri, yeah, motherless forest full of them. Rather face the storm naked, except she wouldn't have to with Veiko out there. If she hurried

*wait, Briel*

she might catch him before he

*died*

tried a rescue that she didn't need.

*Tell him to run, yeah? Do that, Briel, and I'll let you have all the flatcakes.*

"We will provide you an escort when the storm breaks."

"I'll leave *now*. And alone. Master's orders, yeah?"

Ehkla's smile made another appearance. Lingered this time, like a nightmare on waking. Shadows spilled from her cloak and pooled around Snowdenaelikk's boots like

*blood*

water from a cracked bucket. Began to rise on the leather. The shadows stopped when Snow glared at them, but they did not recede.

"It's a Dvergir skill," Ehkla said, in the same tone Tsabrak might say *highborn* or *female*. "It can be useful. Do you know it?"

A Dvergir trick, simple as breathing, except the Dvergir version didn't bring a cold with it that soaked all the way into bone. If this was simple shadow-weaving, then Briel was a dragon. This was godmagic, which didn't rely on gestures and formulas and syllables uttered just so. An older kind of conjuring that the Academy didn't teach anymore. Call it prayer, and remember the runes on the pole. Ehkla wasn't worried about backlash. All the advantage was on her side.

Snow looked up. Damn near impaled herself on Ehkla's smirk. Ehkla's godmagic shadows surged over Snow's boots. Felt like a carpet of teeth, digging for purchase in the leather. Crawling up her leg, fuck and damn.

Wisdom said shake off the shadows, turn her back on this woman, and walk out of here. Conjuring in the Wild was begging for backlash, *begging* for another rearrangement of trees and turf. Last time she'd made this riverbed. This time she might end up bones and buried.

Wisdom could go eat toadshit.

Snow held out her hand. Witchfire collected in her palm, blue and cold and swirled out of nothing. This, too, was a Dvergir trick, simple as breathing, for those who'd learned how. *This* that passed for natural light

Below, that lit Illharek's windows and towers. But the conjuring wasn't trivial now, surrounded by forest and snow and open sky. Discomfort spread from her chest to her belly and into her bones. Pressed up against real pain and stopped. Ebbed away, as the Wild chose to ignore her trespass.

Or the God loved her after all. Maybe that.

*Focus.*

Snow closed her fist around the witchfire. Tipped her palm and slow-spilled it, like wax from a candle. The blue flames struck the shadows, spread and flared and burned. Tiny bonfire in the snow, heatless, smokeless, that still raised sweat on her skin. It devoured Ehkla's shadows. Chased them back to Ehkla's boots and stopped. And slowly, as Snow willed it, the witchfire sank back into nothing.

Her former teachers would have been pleased with her effort. Tsabrak might have been impressed. Veiko, hell, Veiko would probably look a lot like Ehkla did, flat lips and narrow-eyed disapproval.

And then a man shouted from the far side of the bonfire. Warning, terror—and silence, suddenly and abruptly.

*Fuck and damn, Briel, I said wait.*

Except this wasn't Veiko's attack that sent the Talir scout hurtling off the steep bank. Certainly not Veiko's arrows sprouting out of his back, red-and-black fletched.

All of that in a heartbeat, before Snow's gaze tangled with Ehkla's, twinned shock and horror making a pair of them. Then Ehkla spun toward the disturbance and raised a palm and said

*a name*

something that hurt all the way to bone. Power that wasn't conjuring built on the wrong side of Snow's skin, white and hot and lethal.

She didn't think. Struck, knuckles to the side of Ehkla's head, and Ehkla's godmagic curdled into a recognizable sentiment.

Taliri or Dvergiri, *motherless toadfucker* had the same venom behind it.

"Snow!" Dekklis shouted.

Snow curled a shoulder and dove. Harder than it looked, that half-frozen mud. Slicker, too. She skidded sidelong, ended up on hip and elbow instead of neatly back on her feet. An arrow punched into the dirt in front of her. For a suspended second, she saw every bristle on the red-and-black fletching.

Then the arrow dissolved like salt in water. One second, solid, and then gone, as if it had turned to falling snow.

Losing her mind, maybe, except there were still screams and shouts and chaos all around her. The Taliri thought the attack was real enough. And there was a hole in the snow where that arrow had been. Damn good bet there'd've been a hole in her flesh, too, had it hit her.

So there was a third conjuror out there, too, with an Adept's talent and no sense, throwing that kind of power around out here.

*You should criticize, yeah?*

Except witchfire was minor. This, *this*—

Whump, and a second burst of snow and dirt, close enough that the clods peppered her cheek.

—this was something to think about later, from a very long and safe distance.

She rolled onto one knee, got the second foot under her. Sucked a breath and pointed herself up the riverbed. Sprinted, in a ragged line, and wished the arrows elsewhere.

An Illhari trooper appeared then, swirled out of snow and wind. Nothing and *there*, that fast, blood-vivid. He drew his sword and lunged at a passing Talir, cutting him down in a silent, bright spray. And then the trooper looked at her and flashed white teeth in a familiar Dvergir face.

*The angry dead can walk.*

Oh Laughing *God.* And climb down from poles, too, apparently.

*Run, half-blood,* said K'Hess Kenjak.

Damn good suggestion.

Snow pulled shadows from between roots, and grooves in the bark, and the narrow places between evergreen needles. All of the dark, drawn out of the places where the fire had cornered it, every scrap of it she could hold in mind and skill.

And then, with shaking hands, she pulled the bonfire black.

\* \* \*

The soldiers blurred out of the storm and became solid, much as any man might. Veiko heard the clink and creak of their gear, and their muttered, rapid Dvergiri. But Helgi swerved to avoid one, with an un-Helgi yip, and Logi pressed up against his knee hard enough to threaten his balance. And it was then that Veiko noticed the cold, beyond the storm's doing. There was rime on the dogs' fur and on his cloak. And when he looked down, he saw fog swirling around his ankles.

He understood where he was then, and how K'Hess Kenjak meant to sneak among the Taliri. Understood who these soldiers must be, and shivered.

"Chrrip."

Veiko rolled his eyes sideways. Briel rode on his left shoulder, claws dug through wool and leather and into the flesh underneath. She rapped her chin on his skull, exactly as his mother had, when he was a child.

*Don't be an idiot, Veiko.*

Far too late for that. Living men should not walk the ghost roads. Living men should not bargain with the dead, either, but he'd done that, and of his own volition. He was gathering a great many such *should nots* of late, for a hunter and a crofter's son.

"Skraeling." Kenjak angled in front of him, solid in the ghost road. Muddy boots, hair slipping its queue, a scrape on one cheek that still oozed. He had a sword in his hand, and his arm was unbroken. "We are here."

By no means could Veiko confirm that. There might be trees an arm's length away. There might be nothing at all.

Kenjak watched him. Smiled slowly, and Veiko thought about cats and cornered rabbits.

Briel hissed, and Kenjak's smile vanished. "Our bargain, skraeling."

Unwise, like so many other things, and a gamble—short-term stupidity against greater gain. "I remember it. You will attack first."

"We will."

"And you will find her."

"We will."

"Then you," Veiko told Briel, "will lead her clear, and find me."

Briel hissed again, first at him, then at Kenjak. She launched off his shoulder. For a moment Veiko thought her wings covered all the sky, and then he realized that there *was* a sky. Grey, and full of snow, and close enough he might touch it. The snow felt warm on his skin. The fog wisped away, and the soldiers vanished with it. Briel did, too, soundlessly.

He was alone in the riverbed, except for Helgi and Logi and the ghost of K'Hess Kenjak. Trees, dark against the snow, striped the bank above him. Faint orange glow ahead of him, faint smell of smoke. The first screams.

*Skraeling. We've begun.*

Veiko pulled a deep breath.

"Stay," he told the dogs. He took a step closer to Kenjak. Held out his right arm. Waited. Did not close his eyes. It was not a great price to pay for the ghost-legion's help.

And so Veiko watched as Kenjak drew his sword and slapped it down, flat first. The sword passed through his flesh like a net through water. Numb in its wake, and then cold, and then pain that smeared his vision black.

And then—cold spot on his cheek, warm breath. He blinked and found a blurry Helgi at eye level. Realized then that there was cold and wet soaking through the knees of his breeches. That his left hand was knotted in dog fur, that his axe was—there, head down in the snow, dropped by his numb right hand.

His face burned. Men fought through worse wounding and did not drop their weapons or fall to their knees or forget that they had done either. Be grateful there was no one to witness it, except the dogs. Except a dead man, who—

Wasn't there, either, when Veiko looked for him. Having collected his payment, Kenjak had gone to keep his side of the bargain. Kill the Taliri. Draw them off. Free Snowdenaelikk.

And so, without any witnesses that mattered, Veiko pulled his right arm to his chest. Imagined that he could feel his fingers curling into a fist. Imagined he could feel anything at all, from fingers to shoulder. He pushed the useless hand into his belt. Worry for it later, and hope that Snowdenaelikk's skills extended to ghost-wounds.

If she survived. Which he was supposed to be helping to ensure.

He spat one of the words Snow had taught him in their time together under the tree, and used an uncomplaining Helgi to lever himself upright. Staggered and risked balance again, to retrieve the axe. He hefted it, left-handed and awkward. The fireglow had given way to grey and snow. Almost full dark now, with snowfall getting heavier and coming sideways when the wind gusted. A mountain storm that killed men caught in it.

Veiko thought it more likely that a sword would get him first, or an arrow. Men might fight with greater hurts than his, but men also died of lesser, and those men all had more experience in battle than he did.

*Bad time to think of that, yeah?*

If his better sense spoke in Snowdenaelikk's voice now, he might welcome the blizzard.

He hefted the axe and started toward the battle noises. Fog swirled, and snow did, and he wondered if he'd managed to slip into the ghost roads again by mistake. He lost sight of the dogs. Hoped they were having better luck, finding her. Hoped Briel was.

And there—ahead, like a summoning answered. A blade-slim darkness in the fog and snow. Her little seax had broken, he saw, slivered off into a spike of itself. Pity for *that* man, then. At least Kenjak had kept his word. Got her loose.

Veiko drew a lungful of spirit fog and honest cold. Shouted, "Snowdenaelikk!"

And realized his error, in the next moment. Wished he could take back the shout, the name, as the woman spun toward him. Not Snowdenaelikk. Clearly not, and more clear still as the fog and snow dissolved into details. Shorter than Snow, wild-haired, with golden eyes the same shade as a rock leopard's, and as pitiless. His skin tightened. Prickled. He would be safer with a dozen rock leopards than in this woman's company. Veiko took a careful step backward. Lifted the axe, dual warning and warding.

The woman raised her right hand. Fire writhed and flashed on her palm, yellow and hot and in a pattern that made his head ache, his gut seize and burn at the back of his throat. Veiko cut sideways, turned to sprint for the trees. Got two steps before all the world froze solid: breath in his lungs, heart in his chest, every muscle he owned.

She drew near enough he could smell her, woodsmoke and oiled leather and old blood. The wet tips of her hair struck his cheek, *that* close to him. They might have been the only people alive in all the world, trapped in a pocket of

*hell*

calm. Too quiet here, only her breath and his. He squirmed against her witchery, helpless as a scruffed puppy.

The woman said something in a language he did not know. And then, in bruised Dvergiri, "You are looking for Snowdenaelikk. Tell me why."

*I am a fool.* That was a truth. *She is my guest.* That was another. And this woman, with her cat-yellow eyes, would have neither one. He clamped his lips tight together.

She frowned. And again, in Dvergiri: "You summoned the dead. Tell me how."

Veiko stared at her, and shook his head a second time, while anger and fear tangled and burned in the back of his throat. Witch-woman, the sort who might poison wells or steal children or drink blood in the dark of the moon.

She smiled faintly, cold-eyed. "The Taliri are like you. So stubborn. Dvergiri men are wiser. They do as they are told. But I don't know you. Who are you? Who are your people?"

Veiko shook his head as far as her witchery permitted. A wise man would stay silent. A wise man would not be here. He answered her in his own language, forced between teeth: "I have no people."

She put her hand on his chest, as if to feel his heartbeat through bone and leather. Paused there while snow melted on his cheeks and ran down like tears.

Gathering herself, he thought, like a rock leopard before leaping.

"It seems," she said, "that I must take the answers from you."

Veiko licked his lip. Collected enough wet, between saliva and snowmelt, to spit. He missed her. Barely.

She nodded. Then she said a word, and a razored net dredged his skull, slicing bone and brain and making him glad he had no breath for screaming.

Horrified, he heard himself answer. How he knew Snowdenaelikk. His name. His bargain with the dead. He would have collapsed after, except her witchery would not let him. Held him upright while his legs shook as if he'd been running.

She stood very still and looked at him. Then the anger drained out of her eyes, and something else took its place.

She showed him her weapon: no broken sword, he saw, but a spike, bone-colored and slightly curved. It looked like the tip on old Kaari Mykkanen's spear that Kaari swore was a wurm's tooth. Veiko was suddenly very glad that he had not asked Kenjak how he had died. If he did not know what was coming, he might still meet it bravely.

The woman knelt at his feet like a lover. Drove the spike into his thigh and dragged it downward. It sliced easily through breeches and flesh and muscle, stopped hard at bone, while Veiko struggled with a hundred boyhood lessons that said a man did not cry out, did not show an enemy weakness, did not—

*Let himself be trapped by a witch-woman, involve himself in another's battles, strike down a chieftain's son one spring morning.*

He managed the first, at least. Only just. He stared hard at the spike sticking out of his leg and told himself he could bear this. Men fought through such wounding.

She turned the blade once, in the wound. Pulled it out. Heat followed, and wet. She waited a heartbeat and stabbed it into him again. Carved a second line through his flesh.

Veiko thought about the great flat expanses of ice that a man could not look at in sunlight without going blind. Imagined himself staring until his vision turned white. Let her cut him into carrion. He would *not*—

Scream, yes, he would, when she stabbed him a third time. He caught it behind his teeth, strained it out into a sound that would shame him all the short way to his dying.

He wished for a stray arrow. Wished for his dogs, for a distraction, wished for one chance to strike and to see how this witch handled an axe in her skull.

Logi barked from very nearby. The witch-woman's head snapped up. But it was Helgi who leapt at her, soundless, from the other side. The big grey dog struck her shoulder, sent her sprawling, tearing the spike out of Veiko's leg as she fell.

But she was quick, this witch-woman. Got her knees under her and crouched, unmoving, as Helgi skidded around for another charge. Veiko could not see the spike in her hand, but he saw the shape of her shoulders. A man would know that meant a weapon raised and ready. But a dog would not.

*Wait.*

Veiko's fingers convulsed on his axe handle.

Helgi gathered himself and leapt. The witch-woman twisted, drove the spike deep into the dog's ribs. Rolled aside as Helgi squealed and spun, midair, to snap at the wound.

Veiko dragged the axe upward, one-handed. Too slow.

Helgi staggered a tight, panicked circle. Ears flat, teeth bared. Foam collected on his lips. Dripped as he snapped and whined. He collapsed. Churned snow and dirt and stopped.

The witch-woman stood slowly. Reached for the spike where it thrust out of Helgi's side. Not looking at Veiko, because he was held and helpless, left him caught up in her spells, which she counted solid. Which she had not checked. Which had unraveled like poor knitting.

*Fool.*

He brought the axe down with all his force and fury. Missed her skull as his leg betrayed him, and cleaved her shoulder instead. Bone snapped, and flesh split, and red sprayed out into the snow. Her mouth rounded wide as her eyes. Stretched around a sound that was neither scream nor cry. His bones hurt again, and the inside of his skin.

He fell hard, crumpled backward across packs and gear and the hard line of his bow. Ice closed over his head, water seeping through his lips and filling his lungs. He strained against it until he couldn't anymore, and then he sank. The light retreated, but it wasn't dark: grey, like falling into solid, frozen fog. Roaring in his ears, a hundred waterfalls, a thousand rockslides.

*Dying.*

And then a palm slammed into the center of his chest—

"Fuck and damn, Veiko, don't you die."

—and with it came Snowdenaelikk's stone-and-spice smell, and hands he took on faith were hers, rolling him onto his side in fresh snow while he coughed himself back to living. Hot breath on his face, and more wet: Logi whined and licked his ear, and clawed as if he meant to crawl into Veiko's shirt like a puppy.

"Idiot." Snowdenaelikk elbowed Logi aside. Peered into his face from blurry too-close. Familiar planes and angles, eyes that would be blue with any light at all. "Veiko? You all right?"

*Yes,* but she'd moved on already. Ran hands over him, brisk and efficient and unconcerned for his modesty. She stopped at his leg. Stared down with something like horror. "*Fuck and damn.* That's Tal'Shik's mark."

"The witch-woman." He blinked focus past Snowdenaelikk. Flurries whited the world into smooth edges, blurred boundaries. "She cut me. She made me—" He clamped teeth together over that shame.

"That's godmagic, yeah? You're lucky you're breathing." Snow clamped hard on the wound. "I'm sorry, I'll look at it later, but we have to go, yeah? Now. There might be Taliri, still. Or Ehkla. Or *Dekklis.*"

He caught her wrist, stopped touch and talk together. "Helgi."

Two beats silence, this time. She pulled loose, very gently. Shook her head. "No."

He swallowed hard. Foolish, to hurt so much for a dog whose life had bought his own. More foolish to have asked at all and hoped for any other answer. And *stupid,* entirely, to feel guilt for that death. It had been luck that brought Helgi out of the storm at that moment, not his wishes. Not his need. A man could not wish such things.

*But a noidghe might.*

His right arm was still cold, but the fingers worked when he tried them. He made a fist of that hand. "Did Kenjak find you?"

A frown. She helped him sit up. Kept her arm across his shoulders. "Yeah. He did. Twice. Told me to run the first time. Second time, he told me where you were. Said I should tell you his debt to you is clear. You know what that means?"

"Yes." Veiko dragged his good knee under him. Drove the axe shaft-first into the snow and leaned hard on the head. Ground his teeth against sudden nausea. Something wrong in the wound. Cold deep inside it, and burning.

Snow grabbed a fistful of sleeve and shirt. Steadied him when he might've fallen again. "You need to walk, Veiko."

"I have two legs."

"Yeah? I see one and a half."

"I will walk slowly."

"Right." She slipped an arm around his ribs. "Just don't fall on me, yeah? Never get you up twice."

# CHAPTER TEN

Snow could—and did—haul Veiko up a second time. And a third, then a fourth. His blood had soaked through her trousers, where their legs touched. Should have begun to clot, yeah, and hadn't, and—

"Got to stop, Veiko."

A grunt that she felt through his ribs, a momentary grip on her shoulder that she took for *all right*. She angled against a pine, let him shift his own weight to the tree. Laughing God, all she could do to keep *herself* steady. He was taller, broader, and the sort of heavy that meant a person sliding in and out of consciousness. Sweat soaked her shirt, which was both exertion and death sentence in this weather. The wind was coming crosswise now, blizzard getting thicker, storm-twilight that would only get darker when the sun set. They needed shelter *now*.

And she had no idea where they were, except out of the riverbed. She looked back, as if she might see if ghosts and Taliri still fought. As if her motherless svartjagr would appear just for wishing.

*Find your own food from now on if we die. Hear me, Briel?*

Veiko kept saying, "Go up." Might mean a delirious man thinking of home, the land above the tree line, all snow and ice and wide skies.

Might be following some sending of Briel's that Snow herself hadn't gotten.

And he might just be dying. That was her worry. She knelt in the snow at his feet. Risked her flesh to frostbite and peeled her gloves off. Risked backlash and called up a witchfire, candle-sized. She balanced the flame in her left hand. Snowflakes fell through it and collected on her skin and melted.

"Is that wise?" At least he sounded like Veiko, and not a man one step from dying.

"Witchfires are cold. You won't burn."

"That is not what I meant."

"Then no. But I need to see. *Not* you." She nudged Logi back with an elbow. "Sit, yeah? Don't need your help."

She peeled the edges of his trousers back—leather, and wool under that, and all of it soaked. Found a pale strip that might've been skin, might've been bone, amid the wet and gore. The wounds weren't wide. Precise, very deep, clean on the edges, except the one that ran to the edge of his leg, as if a scribe had dragged her stylus sideways off the parchment. But the cuts were nowhere near the big veins. He shouldn't be bleeding like this. And the wounds shouldn't be swollen on the edges, either, shouldn't be hard and hot.

Snow dipped a bare fingertip into the wound, touched it to her tongue. Salt and metal, bitter under that. She made a slow fist. Counted five. Crossed stares with Logi, who'd defied orders again and crowded in close.

"Poison," she told him, under her breath. "Killing him. You get that? You lick it, you're next. Get back and *sit*."

Logi sat. Flattened his ears. Whined and watched her as she scrubbed her hands clean in the snow and forced them, still wet, into her gloves.

"It burns," Veiko said quietly. Calmly. Asking, without asking.

She glanced up at him. Kenjak's ghost had looked healthier. "It's poison."

He nodded, unsurprised.

"What'd she use on you? Knife?"

"A spike. Curved." He tried to sketch out the shape of it, one-handed. "Like a wurm's tooth. The spike. Kaari has one on his spear."

Delirious, definitely. No motherless idea who Kaari was, and, "Worms don't have teeth."

"Not worm." He frowned at her, Veiko-earnest. "Wurm. Like Briel, only larger."

Just like Briel. Yeah. Big fucking cousin. "Dragon, yeah? That's the Dvergiri word."

There'd been a whole shelf labeled "Dragon" in the Academy, vials and jars and bits. But never whole teeth. Never whole claws. Never the tail-spike, which was the more likely source of Ehkla's carving tool because that's where the poison was.

Ask where that toadfucker had got herself bits of a dragon. Ask how. That was Tal'Shik's beast. Tal'Shik's favorite *shape*.

Snow tugged at her belt with stiff fingers. She could carry her blade. She looped the leather twice around Veiko's thigh, once across the worst of the wounding, and once above it. Pulled it tight and buckled it. Please, that the bleeding stopped now. Slowed down. Something, until she could help him.

Logi whined. Nudged her, this time, and licked her cheek. Snow stood up fast. Slapped the snow off her knees hard enough to sting. "Should've kept running, Veiko. You were clear."

"A poor way to treat my guest."

"Your what?"

"Guest. At my fire. I am responsible for you."

Laughing God, conversations with this man were like exploring deep caves without a candle. Think you have a path, yeah, and then slip right over the edge.

"It was only a campsite, Veiko. Not a homestead."

"That is all that I have." He seemed to think that was funny. Delirious. Dying. Poisoned and laughing himself off the tree. He caught himself on her shoulder. Hung there while she sidled against his ribs and held on.

"Well. We need to find another one, yeah? Briel give you any idea where we're going?"

*Shee-oop* answered, and then Briel burst into her awareness. Showed her a narrow slit between boulders near the ridgeline that might be wide enough for two people, for a dog, for a svartjagr tired of the cold. Showed her something else, too: a pair of figures on the trail behind them.

Snow stopped. Closed her eyes, because they were useless, and carefully did not think about roasting Briel on a spit.

"Veiko."

"Yes?"

"Briel's found us a safe place. A cave. Up the hill. Problem is—"

"You cannot see."

"That's the first, yes."

"And the second?"

She told him.

* * *

Dekklis took a certain pride in her tracking skills, finding the merest trace of an animal, or a person. Broken twig, displaced leaf. Tracks in winter layered in the dirt and the snow until the next storm wiped a trail clean.

Which this storm was well in the process of doing. Down to an arm length's visibility now, Istel only a smudged suggestion at her shoulder. But she could have followed this trail with one eye, in the dark, by smell alone. Fresh bloodstink that would bring every predator for a league.

Dark splotches on the snow. The ragged tracks, already half-full, that told her two people together, the bigger of whom limped and leaned hard on the other. One dog that walked mostly on three paws.

She'd found the other dog already. Looked at it and considered that she had no idea what could do that. Decided that she should find the half-blood and ask.

She tried not to think—as the snow got deeper, thicker, in the air and on the ground—whether or not Snowdenaelikk might know how the big dog had died. She just walked and listened to battle sounds receding. Followed the tracks as they snaked up the riverbed, then up the bank itself. Didn't think about the storm getting worse, or the sun going down, or the cold that already made her lungs ache. Didn't think about dying out here. Patrols disappeared in winter sometimes and thawed to bones and rust.

She left that thinking to her partner.

"Dek. Where're we going?"

"Blood goes this way."

"Yeah. See that. But base camp's the other way."

"You cold, Istel?"

"Yes. Not the point. Dek. Rurik needs to hear about what happened."

"Which part? You want to tell him you saw his brother's ghost killing Taliri? Or that those same Taliri killed a whole patrol?"

"How about, there's a Taliri warband in the forest and they've got a conjuror?"

"So did we for a while. Funny how the Taliri's conjuror knew Snow. I'm curious about that."

"All we saw tonight, *that's* what you're wondering?"

"I'm not sure what I saw."

"Dek." All Istel's objection, condensed to one syllable.

"A little further. Look at that blood. Her friend's bleeding out. They can't keep going."

"Neither can we."

She remembered then that he was hurt. That he'd probably taken more damage in the escape. Guilt roughed her voice, turned honest query into accusation. "You need to stop?"

"No, First Scout."

Good and pissed at her, which meant yes, he needed a rest. Dekklis tucked into the lee of a big pine. Crouched and pretended to study the tracks while Istel leaned on the trunk and made no attempt to pretend that he cared about much of anything besides staying upright. She snuck a glance sidelong. Couldn't tell if he'd started bleeding again. He'd take her head off, justifiably, if she asked.

She'd kill her own man, she kept this up. But, "The trail keeps going. They can't be that much ahead of us."

"Might be laying an ambush."

"That much blood? More likely we'll find a body than a fight."

"Haven't found one yet. She's a chirurgeon, Dek."

"So what, her partner can't die? Look. Istel. That motherless Talir half-blood knew Snow's name. I want to know why."

"And you think she'll tell you?"

"I think she gets away, we can't ask."

"Dek." Wearily. Resigned.

"Give me to the top of the hill. We don't find them, we turn around."

"Dek." He sounded *bad* now, breathless.

"All right. We'll turn—"

His knee knobbed into her shoulder blade as he lurched forward. Whisper and creak of cold leather as he reached for his weapon. Grunt as he wrenched it out of its sheath. She stayed down, because that was the smart thing, with naked steel overhead.

But she didn't hear anything except wind sifting through branches. Nothing but quiet, deep and oppressive as any she'd heard in the caves.

Snow falling thick enough she couldn't see more than five paces, and then only trees, dark stripes in the otherwise white.

"What," she began to ask Istel, and then a *shee-oop* cut the quiet.

Dek folded backward. Hit Istel in the knees and took him down, damn near cut her own throat on his sword. The svartjagr whipped overhead, wingslice through the snow, sounding exactly like an arrow.

"The fuck is that?" Tight-voiced, pain or panic. Istel was Cardik-born, had never been Below.

"Svartjagr," she told him. "Pack hunters. Keep your head down. There's always more than one. They'll go after people, if they're desperate."

Which they must be, to hunt in a storm. She rolled off Istel, went flat on her belly. Instant coldseep through leather and flesh, instant chill that turned to hard shivers. She gritted her teeth against chattering. Twisted and one-eyed the branches. No sign of the svartjagr or its nestmates. She'd never seen them this far north. Never thought there *were* any.

"Long as we're low, we're okay. They need altitude to fly. They get on the ground, they're in trouble."

"Right." Heard him panting now, close and shallow. Bet he was bleeding again. Bet that damn animal smelled it. She glanced toward Istel. Impossible to tell blood from shadow in the fold of sleeve and coat.

And then she could see, suddenly, because a

*witchfire*

blue light spilled and spread through the darkness. Dim to twilight in three seconds, showing Dekklis the half-blood and another big dog in the middle of the trail. The witchfire bobbed in Snow's right palm, gentle glow that smoothed her features and gleamed blue off the naked edge of the seax in her left.

"You're lucky," Snow said, "that Briel's not that hungry."

"The svartjagr's yours?"

A shrug. "More or less. What are you doing up here, First Scout Szanys?"

Dekklis pulled her knees under her. Stood warily. "Followed the trail you left. Lot of blood. It's not yours."

Snort. "You worried it was? Well, I'm fine."

"Whose is it?"

"No one you know."

"Teslin's dead" slipped out before she caught it. Hung there while she forced the grief back down her throat.

Snow shook her head. "Sorry for that. I can't bring her back."

"You can tell me why she died. Start with that Talir half-blood back there."

"Her name is Ehkla. And you were right." Snow's eyes gleamed in the witchfire glow. "It was prayers on that pole. To Tal'Shik."

The back of Dekklis's neck prickled, sweat and chill and sweat again. "How do you know that?"

"She told me. And I saw the mark on her hand. That's what you're dealing with. Godsworn, yeah?"

"She knew your name. How?"

"Sorry, Szanys. That's all you get."

"Hell it is. That woman is dangerous—"

"Oh, you reckon?"

"—and I need to know how she knows you." Dekklis put a hand on the hilt of her weapon.

The dog growled and took a stiff-legged step. Snow grimaced. "Logi. Sit, idiot. —Need? No. What you *need* is shelter. Istel *needs* a chirurgeon's care. You want him to die out here? Keep arguing. Or come with me now."

"Go with *you*?"

"Istel's looking bad, yeah? I don't think he'll make it, you try and go back."

"All compassion now, are you?"

"No. Practical. My partner's bleeding out. So's yours. We can do something about that, you and I, or they can both die."

Dekklis had sworn oaths to Illharek. Serve, uphold, and defend, with life and honor. So ask what honor Snow understood. Smuggler and probable heretic, with that godmark on her hand. And she had patched Istel once already, picked locks for them, hadn't betrayed them to Ehkla. Hadn't attacked them here, either. A hundred maybes to answer the why, but it was clear enough she didn't want a fight. Clear enough, too, that she knew more than she'd say, and Dekklis couldn't force a confession. Not with Istel hurt this bad, against that dog and Snow's conjuring and that svartjagr, wherever it had gone.

Dekklis had sworn oaths to Illharek. And dying out here wouldn't serve those oaths.

She sheathed her sword. Locked stares with the blue-eyed half-blood. There was no point in asking *can I trust you,* so Dekklis didn't. "Let's go."

\* \* \*

The cave looked like two rocks propped together, a narrow V that might, at its center, let a woman stand upright. Snowdenaelikk hadn't tried it. Her exploration had stopped at getting Veiko inside, and

*please, Laughing God*

hoping he survived until she got back. She'd left him slumped over a small collection of wet brush, one-handing his flint and promising fire when she returned, like she only meant to go out for more wood. She came back now to warm yellow spilling out of the cave, and to Veiko propped against the exterior, eyes half-shut like a man dozing at guard duty.

*Dead,* she thought on a punch of panic, and then *No,* because Briel sat sentry on the rock beside him. Cold Briel. Miserable, wings and tail wrapped tight. She would've been warmer on Veiko, hell, Snow could see his fever from here. Faintest pink under colorless skin now, and sweat beading like rain.

She let Logi go on ahead. Held her breath and pretended to wait for Dekklis, who was coming at Istel's pace. Watched as Logi nudged Veiko's left hand and licked bare fingers that might've twitched at the contact. Let her breath out when those witchfire eyes opened wide and found her.

"Didn't we say you'd stay inside?"

"We did not." He skinned a smile. Shook his head. Snowmelt sluiced off his braids. "I heard voices."

"Fever dreams."

His eyes slid past her. "Fever dreams in armor." Which meant, then, he wouldn't show weakness, not

*in front of the enemy*

for first impressions. She could blame his pride, sure, blame his honor, and pretend her shoulder blades didn't itch with armor creaking behind her. She felt better with him watching her back, even if he shouldn't be.

"The woman's Dekklis. The man's Istel."

Veiko nodded. Winter peace, he'd called it, where enemies might share a fire and shelter and set a quarrel aside. But what happened when the storm ended—yeah, just guess, they'd be right back where they'd started. And maybe not. Maybe she'd work another deal with Dekklis. Get the legion after Ehkla, let them hunt her down.

*Let them die, yeah?*

Not her problem. She had Veiko to worry about.

*And after?*

Tsabrak. Ehkla. Godmagic and Tal'Shik. All of that would wait for later. For now: inside, all of them. Snow held out an arm for Briel. Collected a chilled svartjagr across her shoulders, and a wide-eyed stare from Istel.

But Dekklis had eyes only for Veiko. Narrow, thoughtful eyes that Snow didn't like at all, that lingered too long on wounds and weapons and scraped the length of him.

"You're the one Teslin and Barkett couldn't catch. The ghost."

"I am no ghost." Veiko drew up straight and returned her stare, in a way that Dvergiri men simply didn't.

The surprise on Dekklis's face would've been funny without the anger that came with it. Expect an oathsworn defender of all things Illhari to distrust what she didn't know, yeah, whole histories full of that; the Purge hadn't cured it. But it was Dekklis's temper that worried Snow, the spear-thrust—

"Where are you from?"

—as if Veiko was a man in her household, or her prisoner.

"Little settlement north of the border," Snow said quickly. "Very north. Takin herders, yeah?"

Dekklis ignored her. "What did you say your name was?"

"I did not say."

"Veiko," Snow said, to settle it. She put her hand on Veiko's chest, as much to hold him back as hold him up. Fuck and damn, he was hot. "Can we move this inside?"

He grunted, which was Veiko for *no*. She put her face close to his, so that he had to look at her. Red lines all through the whites of his eyes now, red on the rims. "Got them handled. Trust me, yeah?"

Another grunt. But he let her push him backward until he had to duck and fold himself into the cave, trailing Logi and a fresh smear of blood. She listened for the hollow thump of a falling body. Let her breath out when she didn't hear one. Maybe he'd managed a quiet collapse. More likely he was still standing, axe raised, waiting for battle.

Stubborn. No shortage of that. She rounded on Dekklis, fast enough that Briel flared for balance. Istel flinched back, caught himself on the rock, and hung there. He did not, she noted, reach for his weapon.

Dekklis did. Stopped, halfway. "Do we have a problem?"

"We might, you go after Veiko again."

Dekklis looked like a woman who'd had one surprise too many in a day full of bad ones. Looked like she had a mouthful of vinegar, too, and still, "My apologies."

Snow wished badly for a stick of jenja, for walls and a roof and a city's stink around her. For familiar and safe and no one bleeding. Bet Dekklis didn't wish for something like that, too. Dekklis was at the end of her patience, more than a little bit scared. Tempers frayed under those conditions.

Laughing God, getting soft, if she felt sympathy for this soldier.

"He might not remember when that fever breaks. *If* it does. Need your help, Scout. I owe him. Life debt, yeah? And *she* did this to him. Savvy that?"

Another blink. Szanys Dekklis came back, hard-eyed and hard-jawed and focused. The soldier, wanting orders. Wanting *order*. "I savvy. Tell me what you need."

# CHAPTER ELEVEN

Warmth. Women's hands and women's smell. Women's voices, that swelled and murmured and buzzed. His mother and sister, he thought sometimes, going about women's business, which embarrassed and distressed him. He was a man now. He shouldn't be in the women's house. Other times, he recognized Snowdenaelikk by touch and scent and sharp Dvergiri syllables. There was another woman with her, and he would panic until he remembered

*Dekklis*

who she was, and where he was, and what had happened.

Sometimes he burned, and sometimes he shivered so hard that he forgot the other pains. And sometimes he could see, and hear, and speak. Rasped out yes and no to whatever Snow asked him and wished he could ask her how he was, truly—because she would not tell him, in front of soldiers, if she thought he would die.

He thought he might. He smelled vomit, sweat, and sour skin, and he knew they were his. And there was pain

*almost*

worse than any he'd known. It had its center in his thigh, but it had traveled to all his limbs now. Lodged in his chest and crushed him, so that he took bites of breath and saw white and blue on the back of his eyelids. Bright blue, like the witchfire, except on the edges, where it matched the bruise-midnight dark of Snow's eyes.

That was part of his awareness.

The rest of it he spent on the twilight expanse of the glacier one day's walk from his village, with a winter sky like metal and a sun that offered no warmth and hung, pale and sullen, near the horizon. He sat on the ice while the wind sang and whistled through the cracks and crevasses that a man could fall into if he was careless.

He was not cold, although he should be. He flexed bare hands that should be stiff and numb, took deep lungfuls of air that should burn and make him cough and that felt warm and smoky in his lungs instead.

"—more wood, Istel—"

The wind lifted the ends of his braids, and he turned his face into it. He was completely alone, except for the takin: his eldest brother's herd, with the one-horned billy who had broken his leg seven winters ago and become a rug and several sweaters, jerky and bone needles and gut-thread. Had become a carving, too, palm-sized, that Veiko had given to Kaari's eldest daughter, whose name was—

"Snow, listen—"

No. That wasn't her name. Snow was Illhari, the half-blood Dvergir, whose hair was fair as Kaari's daughter's, but Kaari's daughter had been round breasted and round rumped and dimpled when she smiled.

It bothered him that he couldn't remember her name.

Helgi looked at him, slant-eyed, and put his head on his paws. Sighed, like Helgi did, gut-deep heave and groan as if all the sky pressed down on him. Veiko trailed his fingers through his

*dead*

dog's fur, and watched the

"—what are—"

takin

"—don't know, yeah, but—"

wander the edge of the glacier. There was short grass, which there shouldn't be in winter, and the takin snatched mouthfuls as they moved.

"—like a goat—"

Like a goat, yes, except larger, split-hooved and hulking, that children and women might ride. Thick tawny fleece that women could spin into thread. Veiko tried to explain, but the sky and the ice swallowed whatever he said, so that he couldn't hear his own voice. Only his heartbeat, too loud, in his chest.

Veiko stood up and walked along the edge of the glacier. His leg did not hurt here. He rubbed the place where the witch-woman had cut him. It felt smooth through the breeches, unwounded. He scuffed his boots across the ice. Helgi trotted beside him, his tail curved over his back like

*a wurm's tooth*

a crescent moon. The takin ignored them, except the one-horned billy, who lifted his head and eyed them suspiciously. Foul-tempered animal, to Veiko's recollection. No tears shed for its dying.

But Helgi, now,

"—who is—"

had been a good dog. A fine hunter. Smart where Logi was merely clever. Brave, if one might call

"—a dog—"

him that. Men were brave, and men were heroes. Dogs were dogs. And Helgi

"—saved his life—"

was a ghost now.

Veiko's heartbeat thumped, too loud and too steady. Sounded less like flesh now, and more like a drum, one of the noidghe instruments, rough-cured hide and crude painted symbols. He found himself walking in rhythm, while Helgi's paws beat a counterpoint.

The glacier stretched on forever, and Veiko might have walked forever, except he rounded a curve and returned to the place where he'd started: the one-horned billy, the herd, the metal sky, and endless ice and wind. He stopped. Helgi did.

He thought about striking off across the glacier, if only to see where it ended. But only a fool would cross the glacier alone, and he was not a fool. Men died if they tried it.

But he had Helgi, didn't he? And Briel, too, gliding circles against the iron sky. He wondered how he had not noticed her sooner, in this empty place. A svartjagr wasn't a subtle creature, and Briel least of all.

*Only a fool.*

He called her name, and this time the sound carried. Echoed

*iel, iel, iel*

off the ice and the rocks while his heart throbbed a counterbeat. She turned on a wingtip. Saw him and began her descent. Her wings spread across the sky like spilled ink, churned the clouds into fog and sent them swirling groundward.

His

*drum*

heart pounded harder, louder, painful against the bones of his chest. He gasped like a man drowning. Put his hand under his shirt, peeled the cloth aside. Symbols moved across his skin: noidghe symbols, and one that looked like Ehkla's palm tattoo.

He rubbed at his skin, hard enough to sting. Pulled back red fingers and saw a hole where flesh and bone had been. His heart beat raw and naked and steady in the gap. He drew it out. Held it, twitching and throbbing, in his cupped hands.

Blur and flash, and Helgi leapt at him. Grabbed the heart from his fingers and sprang onto the ice. Stood there, tail waving and ears tilted back, with Veiko's heart beating in his jaws. A game he might have played with a piece of antler or bone.

"No," Veiko said, and, "Helgi, come here," but he could not shout past Briel's wingbeats, which boomed and gusted in time to the heart, the drum, because now it seemed to be both.

Helgi turned and trotted away, brush tail curved over his back like a
*wurm's tooth*
moon, silver against the dull-grey ice, against Briel's descending
darkness—

No. Not Briel. A wurm, the sort that a
*fool*
hero might battle, finger-long fangs and gaping jaws and bloodstink
breath. Almost upon him, only moments, and no place to run.

The ice.

He
*always*
hesitated. The wurm
*always*
struck. Claws long and black as Snow's sword punched through
armor and bone. And it hurt, oh ancestors, as bad as
*exactly like*
what Ehkla had done.

"—Veiko—"

And then he came back to the familiar ache and agony of his body.
To Briel, curled over his heart, against flesh and under blankets. To
Snowdenaelikk's bruise-blue eyes.

"Veiko," gently, as if he were a child. "Easy, yeah, you're fine."

*No,* he thought. But she knew that. He was dying. Burning and
freezing by turns. Poisoned and fevered, despite her every effort turned
to saving him. *You're fine* was a lie as much for her sake as his.

"Fever dreams," he croaked, as he always did. It was the second
lie. The glacier was no dream. Too real for that, too regular and too
stubborn. It hovered now on the boundary of his awareness. If he
blinked, he might fall into it.

He had none of a noidghe's training, but he understood that hearts
did not become spirit drums in mere fever dreams. The ghost roads
wanted him. Well. They might wait until he died, then. Today, or

tomorrow, or twenty years from today, they would wait. Only a fool went to meet them.

A fool, or a noidghe.

*Which are you?*

Neither. Both. Frightened, though he would not admit it. He had never felt this weak, so that he did not mind that he lay naked and helpless among women not his relatives. No, he was happy for it. Naked and helpless meant he was not on the glacier, not spirit-walking, which only noidghe should do. Which only noidghe could do. Which he had been doing, more and more frequently, as the fever grew worse.

*I am no noidghe.*

*Tell yourself that.*

"Veiko," Snow said again, magic third time to bind him into his flesh. He wondered if her Illhari conjuring taught such things. Should ask her, yes, but not now. All he could do to keep the glacier at bay, staring at her.

Now she should say *here* and *drink this* and offer him a cloth-teat soaked in melted snow. But she did not. Stared, and her expression frightened him as badly as the glacier and the drum-heart together.

"I am dying," he said, because she would not.

She touched him, cool fingers tracing his brow, and he slammed back into his own flesh. She wouldn't quite look at him, no, staring hard anywhere but at his eyes. The firelight snagged in her hair, turned fair to white and silver, like Helgi. Winter-colored Helgi, waiting for him on the glacier. The spirit world pressed closer. He thought he felt wind on his face. Thought he saw the glacier's wide stretch. Cross, and he'd leave flesh behind. Might become lost in the spirit world. Noidghe did.

*I am not.*

Yet. He had almost died once, and Snowdenaelikk had drawn him back. She held him living now, while Helgi's nose pressed his palm.

"Yes," said Snow, and Helgi became a blanket clutched in his fist. "Got one thing left, yeah? But it could kill you."

Veiko blinked between glacier and firelight on cave walls. "Better your doing than hers."

Snow chipped out a smile. "Glad you feel that way."

It hurt to look at her face, as naked as his own flesh. He found something simpler. Stared at Logi's red-brown shoulder, curled against his left hip, and Logi's warm brown eyes. A dog did not grieve for what *might* be. Did not know enough to despair.

A woman did. Snow had her back to him now, so that he could see the hard knobs of her spine above her sweater's fraying hem, the curve and ridge of her ribs. Not a comfortable woman, Snowdenaelikk. Hard, he might have named her once, brisk and biting as first frost, until a storm spent under the spruce sharing stories, sharing blankets and the dogs for warmth. It seemed now that he could see past the bone and armor, past leather and wit, to the core of her, all steel and bright fire.

Couldn't hear it in her voice. That was cool, steady. "Hand me that pouch, will you?"

Metal rattled, then glass. Veiko smelled damp earth, and rot, and flowers all at once. The other woman, the soldier, coughed like a cat. "What the hell is that?"

"Red Lady."

"Red Lady?"

"Fuck and damn, Szanys. It won't jump out of the pouch at you. Don't eat it, you're fine. Don't knock it into the soup, either."

"You can't give him—"

"Can. Have to. Now sit him up, yeah? Or do I need to ask Istel?"

"No." Dekklis slid between Veiko's face and the cave roof. Tight-jawed, hard-eyed woman. A polished stone, that one, smooth and brittle and sharp where she cracked. She twitched back the blanket. Flinched when the svartjagr hissed.

"Briel," Veiko said, all the voice he had left, which didn't creep far past his lips. Briel stopped, wings half-spread, and *chrripped*. Then she retreated, slither and slide, into a black puddle beside him. Propped her head on his belly and watched Dekklis.

Who muttered words Veiko had learned from Snowdenaelikk and edged within Briel's strike range. She peered into his face.

"You know what she's trying to give you?"

Close enough, and, "Yes."

"And you want to drink it."

"Yes."

That was the look his father had worn when Veiko told him what became of the chieftain's thieving son.

*Fool.*

Dekklis shoved her arm under Veiko's shoulders, heaved him sitting. She steadied him, neither rough nor gentle. "You want to die that bad, skraeling, I won't stop you."

"I will not," he began, and stopped. The glacier wind lifted his braids, carved channels across his cheeks, through the several days' stubble. Poured down his throat and burned him with its chill, so that he coughed.

"C'mon, Dek." The man's

*Istel*

voice, rare and low and soft. "Ease up."

Veiko did not hear Istel often. Saw him even less. But there he was now, on the far side of the fire, a blanket and two red legion cloaks around his bare shoulders. Half a smile when he saw Veiko looking. And, more quietly, "Hope it works."

The well-wish surprised him. Scattered what was left of his wits, so that he blinked and stared like a child. And then it was too late to recover, as Snow moved between them. She had a small glass vessel cupped in her palm. A dark liquid clung to the inside like blood.

Snow cradled the back of his skull. Held the glass to his lips. Effort to swallow, oh yes, and more still to keep it down. He'd thought he was too weak for more vomiting. Damn near proved himself wrong. The women steadied him, one on each side, as his belly knotted him double.

"Got him," said Snow, and then there was only one woman holding him, all bone and steel and bright fire, ward against the glacier and the wind.

"Listen to me, Veiko," murmured against his ear. "Don't you fucking die."

"Do not let me," he said, and then he was falling backward while his skin burned from the inside. His vision failed, or his eyes melted. His tongue and teeth turned to ash and blew away in a blizzard wind.

And then.

He stood beside the glacier again. Dull metal sky, dying sun, a herd of takin snipping grass from the tundra.

Helgi put two paws on the ice. Looked back expectantly.

Veiko stepped after him.

* * *

Istel, Laughing God bless him, had jenja. Four sticks, in varying conditions of damaged, stuffed in a pouch on his hip. He pulled them out and tried to straighten them, one-handed, against his thigh.

"Bad habit, yeah," he muttered when he caught Snow staring. "But damn, I want one."

"You and me both."

He blinked at her. Offered the least damaged, and a crooked smile. "Thanks."

She squatted beside him and stared into the snowfall. Sucked on the jenja and willed her hands to stop shaking. Blame exhaustion for that. Blame Veiko, who hadn't died yet, against all expectations. Don't let him die, he'd said. Fuck and damn, she had no intention, but she'd reached her limit. Nothing else she could do, yeah, out of tricks.

*Please, Laughing God.*

Down to prayers. Down to superstition.

"How's he doing?" Istel sounded sincere.

"I don't know. Fever's down. But."

"That's happened before."

Several times, in the recent forever, and every time it had come back. "Yeah."

"Mm. Will it work, that Red Lady?"

"Hope so. Don't know."

A quiet man, Istel. But the look he cast sidelong damn near shouted.

"Truth, Istel. I don't want to kill him."

"Huh. Don't have to convince me," soft as snowfall.

No. Not him. Dekklis, ever and always. Winter peace meant Dekklis did the bulk of wood gathering and fire tending and cooking. Cool, efficient Dekklis, who'd held flesh together for stitching, who'd mopped puke and swabbed blood without protest, who'd balked only when she'd seen Red Lady in the pouch.

So. Bet that winter peace was about to end. They were two days into it so far, and the snow was still falling—sideways, when the wind gusted—and piling deep outside. There was nowhere else to go, and the cave wasn't a big place. Dekklis had arranged and rearranged her gear and Istel's a dozen times, prodded the fire. Now she was scraping spoon against pot until the soup itself must be bruised. Those were the sounds of a woman thinking too much. Of a woman bothered. Of a woman checking for certain ingredients in the supper, maybe.

And then, suddenly—no sound at all. A patch of cold spread on Snow's back as Dekklis came between her and the fire, and oh yes, that was a north-wind disapproval raising hair on the back of her neck. Snow turned sideways and fit her spine against the stone at the cave mouth. Propped her forearms across her knees. Winced as muscle and bone popped and settled. Looked up at Dekklis, finally.

"Something on your mind, First Scout?"

Dekklis stared down over cheekbones that said highborn, well bred, blue blood running under that smooth black skin. She folded her arms under her breasts. "Few things, yeah."

"Let me guess. You don't like jenja smoke."

Not a blink. Not a twitch. Laughing God, the woman didn't smile. "I don't, but that isn't what I want to discuss."

"Huh. Well. That's a surprise."

Istel sighed, audibly. "Truce. Remember?"

Sliver scowl, flicker-fast, at Istel. "Do I have a weapon?"

He ducked her irritation. Flicked the butt of his jenja into the storm. Rocked onto his heels and straightened slowly, as far as the cave mouth allowed.

"Just the one in your mouth. Look, Dek. I'd be dead without her. If that matters." And then he retreated, no other word for it, back into the cave, around the fire and back to his bedroll. He wasn't out of earshot—impossible here—but he'd taken himself out of the conversation. Let the women work it out, yeah, because that's what Dvergiri women did, and Dvergiri men lived with the decisions.

Not Tsabrak. No, Tsabrak would've knifed Dekklis already, and Istel with her, and hell with winter peace. Defiant, angry Tsabrak would've been dead three times by now, too, by legion hands or Taliri. At least he understood when to send women. Consort with Tal'Shik's godsworn, no, not him. He sent Snowdenaelikk, who had a little more patience, a little more woods-wits. A pair of tits, however small, to give her some legitimacy.

And tits or not, wits or not, she'd've died, too, again three times over, but for Veiko, who had also not known when to retreat. She had an eyeful of him at this angle, blanket mound and Briel and Logi's furry lump. White face above that, tight flesh and fever-slick skin. It hadn't been conjuring that had let Ehkla hold him still for cutting without ropes or chains. That was godmagic, Purged magic. The Academy didn't teach it. Snow didn't understand it. But Veiko did. Somehow.

Superstitious, *what-is-that-witchfire* and *do-not-interfere-with-spirits* Veiko had brought Kenjak and a squad of dead soldiers with him to save her. Veiko had gotten himself loose from Ehkla's godmagic, which he shouldn't've been able to do. And now he told her not to let him die, as if she had that power.

Snow closed her eyes. Pressed the heel of one hand against the sockets, one after another, so that she saw colors. So that she didn't have to look at Dekklis, still waiting, fuck and damn, still standing.

"You have a smart partner," Snow said. "Listen to him. Leave me alone."

"Can't." A little gust of fire-heat, woman-smell, as Dekklis moved into Istel's place across the cave mouth. Creak and pop as she settled, and a breathless little sigh. "Don't think I'm not grateful."

Snow cracked her eyes. Stared from under the lids. "Oh no. Never think that."

"It's not what you did. It's that you knew how to do it at all. Chirurgeon, sure, I'll believe that. I've seen you work on Istel. And courier, smuggler, I'll believe, too. But what you did today with the Red Lady—that's assassin's work."

Snow took another mouthful of jenja and held it. A little stale, a little sour, a little burn in the back of her throat. "Only if he dies. Before that, it's medicine, yeah?"

"Medicine. Right. So you learned this at the Academy, is that it? Red Lady's common treatment there?"

"Common? No. But I've got this." Snow tapped the silver ring, high on the curve of her ear. "And we keep archives, for the advanced students."

"Illegal archives, then. Those records were Purged. Senate decree. Red Lady is a proscribed substance."

"Only because Tal'Shik's godsworn loved it so much. But it's because those godsworn got so good at killing each other we've got all these medicines and antidotes. You think the Senate doesn't fucking well know the Academy keeps those archives? Sure they do. That's the point of the Academy. Record keeping. Lore. Knowledge locked up in the library, not running around the taverns. Besides. Never know when you'll have a plague. Or need a rival's death to look like bad fish."

Dekklis looked at her. "They teach heresy at the Academy, too, or did you learn that somewhere else?"

"I thought I was an assassin. Now I'm a heretic?"

"I think you can be both. I think you are both. I saw you flashing palm-marks at Ehkla. And I don't think you learned to be godsworn at the Academy. So where did you learn it?"

Snow laughed. Not a happy sound, nothing funny—violent laughter that clawed like a badger on the way out. Made her eyes sting, her throat hurt. Fuck, she was tired, too tired, and Dekklis too smart and too relentless, and yeah, maybe Tsabrak would've been right to gut her and Istel both and leave them for the crows.

"What's so funny?"

"You. Motherless storm out there, motherless Taliri warband burning towns and sacrificing soldiers, and you're worried about my orthodoxy?"

"Yeah. I am."

"All right. Then don't worry. I'm not godsworn. Just"—she studied her palm, where the godmark was—"associated. Allied. But not godsworn."

"That makes it all clear. Thanks." Dekklis took her breath. Held it. Then: "You're in the middle of all of this. Start at Davni. You ran, and both of those men died. But Kenjak's not your fault, no, he's killed—"

"Sacrificed."

"—by a woman who happens to know your name—"

"Been over that, yeah?"

"—who you say worships Tal'Shik, who you say carved up your partner."

Snow's laughter dried up so fast that it hurt. Dry-voiced now, dry-eyed: "Look at Veiko. Look at his toadfucking leg."

"I did. I helped you stitch it, remember?"

"That's Tal'Shik's sigil. Or part of it."

"So why would this Ehkla try to kill your friend?"

"Because she's a motherless—" Swallow. Stop. Think. Not for retaliation, no, because, "She couldn't've known who he was. I didn't know him before Davni. But he brought the ghosts, yeah? So my guess is, that scares her."

Dek's eyebrows climbed. "The ghosts were Veiko's doing? I thought you—"

"No. Not me. And don't ask me how he did it, because I don't know."

"So he summoned ghosts and picked a fight with Taliri for someone he's known what, all of four days? Five? Damned altruistic of him."

Altruism, hell. Blame Briel for it. Svartjagr lived in groups, and Briel wasn't picky about how many feet her groupmates had. Briel liked Veiko, and she liked Snowdenaelikk, and she even liked Logi, and she was probably poking herself into Logi's head as much as she did to Snow's and Veiko's. She had her pack. But Snow didn't want to explain that to Dekklis, no, didn't need to toss oil on that particular fire. Try part of the truth first—

"Said he had responsibility for his guest, yeah? That's what he called me."

"Guest. That's a new word for it."

—and when truth didn't work, then let Dekklis smirk and imagine something else.

"You like *lovers* better? Fine. Call us that. Ask him, if you want to know why he does anything, and good luck getting an answer that makes sense. But what doesn't change is I didn't know him before. He's not part of any of this. Ehkla didn't know who he was. He's an accident, yeah? Swear that, on my mother's honor."

Dekklis offered no opinions on the honor of a half-blood's mother. Offered nothing except an unblinking stare that reminded Snow of Briel in poor temper. "So Veiko's an accident. Ehkla's a mistake. Davni's no fault of yours, either. You're damned unlucky, Snowdenaelikk, that your life is so full of coincidence."

"Right. Look." Snow stared at the jenja's burning tip. Blew a slow tangle of smoke. "You want to arrest me after this, fine. Just let Veiko go."

"And what would stop him from leading an army of ghosts after us?"

"You could ask him."

"I might. But I think I already know the answer." Slow headshake, and a deeper frown that slid into thoughtful. "All right. Say I believe you. Then what do the Taliri want with Tal'Shik?"

"You're thinking the wrong direction. Ask your grandmother, if she's still alive, what Tal'Shik wanted with her grandmother."

"That was before the Purge. We don't—"

"What, talk about it? You highborn. One civil war, and you want to pretend history never happened. You think the Republic's safer that way?"

"It's because of history that we want that knowledge destroyed. Tal'Shik gave us nothing but grief."

"Oh, toadshit. Tal'Shik gave us the Republic. Before her, Illharek was just one city, and Dvergiri were targets for every Alvir toadshit with a sword. Don't look at me that way, yeah? You know it. We don't talk about Tal'Shik because of highborn politics. Listen. Your grandmother's grandmother was godsworn to Tal'Shik, like every other highborn woman who aspired to a Senate career. She marched to temple on the holy days. She prayed for the same things as every other woman. Power. Prosperity. Healthy daughters. Death to the enemies of the House. Not an imaginative lot, our foremothers. But if everyone's praying for the same thing, now how does Tal'Shik decide whose prayers to grant?"

"Sacrifice. I know that."

"Good. Then you must know who and what. Dogs. Goats. Svartjagr, sometimes. And if a godsworn really, really wanted her prayers answered, she'd use a man. A slave, maybe, but if it was something too important, she'd use a Dvergir. An Illhari citizen. An uncut boy, or the father of one of her daughters. Her extra sons. Kids like Kenjak, yeah? Sacrificed to Tal'Shik for the fortunes of her House."

"This is the history of the Purge, Snow, and the foundation for the Reforms. I did have lessons."

"Right. Well. Bet your lessons didn't cover this. Godmagic's not conjuring. It comes straight from the god. Tal'Shik or the Laughing God. Alviri and Taliri gods, too, I imagine. It's what they give us for all that sacrifice, all the worship. We give them power, they give back. Tal'Shik used to have the whole Republic on their knees to her. You think she might not be a little pissed off that those sacrifices are gone?"

Dekklis thought about that, honest thought that came with silence and scowling. Finally, low-voiced, "So this attack is the beginning of some kind of revenge on Illharek and the Dvergiri. Tal'Shik's got new Taliri friends to pray to her. All right. Then how's your Laughing God fit into it? Because I have read my histories, and his cult hates hers."

Tsabrak's face on the back of her eyelids, beautiful and cold and angry, always angry. Snow imagined an alliance between Tsabrak and Ehkla, fanatics together. She shivered and pretended that cold was the reason.

"I don't know. But." Snow dragged a last lungful of jenja. A little stale, a little sour. "Listen to me, Szanys Dekklis. I'm not sorry for the Purge. I don't want the temples back. Any of them."

"Then why ally with the God at all?"

"Best offer I had at the time." And Tsabrak had been asking. Beautiful, angry Tsabrak.

"Hard to believe that. You're Academy trained. You've got a master's ring."

"In chirurgery, yeah? Not conjuring." Only gold rings for that. Second rank. Never Adept, not enough talent for it, and hell if she'd tell Dekklis that. "And I'm half-blood."

"Ah. All right. Then I understand."

"Do you, Szanys-daughter?"

Dekklis's gaze slipped for the first time. "I'm highborn, but I'm not blind. The Reforms didn't change who's in power. The Academy wouldn't give you a post, would they? So you came out here."

"Close enough." Snow flicked her butt after Istel's. Flare and hiss as it hit the snow. "There're more freeborn Alviri in Cardik. No one looks twice at a half-blood."

"Even a half-blood with an Academy topknot."

"Well. Not many know what that means, out here."

"Your friends understand?"

"Some of them. The ones who appreciate what I can do."

"Heretic friends? Huh. Right. The Laughing God doesn't love women, Snow. Ever think of finding different friends? There's always work for chirurgeons in the legion."

Snow laughed, sharp enough Logi looked up and whined. "Just when I think I could like you, you say something like that."

"Well. That's the problem. I do like you, and I'd hate to end up killing you someday. Or drinking Red Lady by accident."

"You're safe from me. And I won't mention your name to my friends. But look to your own, yeah? What will you tell your First Spear?"

Dekklis shrugged. "Nothing about you. I say we found shelter and outwaited the storm."

"Istel's wound?"

"Dekklis stitched it," said Istel abruptly from inside the cave. Shrugged when two pairs of eyes landed on him. "Not that different from mending a shirt, is it?"

"Corrupting my partner," Dekklis muttered. "See that, half-blood?"

"Not sorry for it. What about Ehkla?"

Dekklis grimaced. "*Godsworn* isn't a word I can use without proof."

"What, then? Talir bandit? Rogue conjuror?"

"Something like. You're the one who knows what she is. You're the one who's got experience with gods."

It took Snow a moment, eyelocked with Dekklis, to understand. "Oh no. I'm not going back with you."

"We can arrest you. Protect you."

"From my friends? No. I don't owe you that much. The legion is your problem. You make them listen."

"And what will you do?"

"Make sure my friends haven't made a mistake. Make sure they're not making really bad friends themselves."

"And if they have? If they are?"

"Then maybe they stop being my friends."

Dekklis said nothing, very loudly. Waited until there was only fire-snap to compete with Veiko's rapid, ragged breaths. Sounded like he was running, or fighting.

*Dying, yeah? That's what he's doing.*

Not her fault. She hadn't asked for his help, had she? He'd offered it to her. His people's customs, his skraeling notions of honor had got him this far. But it wasn't unpaid debt that made her stomach hurt, no, wasn't obligation making her wish for that little twist his mouth got that passed for a smile, and his clear witchfire eyes.

"If Veiko dies," Snow said slowly, "then I'll have business with Ehkla. And maybe even if he doesn't."

Blink and sudden stillness on that highborn face. Calculation. A careful, "Do you think you can kill her?"

"Don't know. Depends whether you're right about all the things I am."

A smile, dark, fleeting, dry as summer winds. "I'm right."

"Then I can. And I will."

Believe that, yeah.
*Please, Laughing God.*

# CHAPTER TWELVE

The glacier went on forever.

Veiko was not cold, despite the wind that should have sliced through leather and wool and did not. His hands did not ache, although he had no gloves. The chill soaked up through the soles of his boots and did not, somehow, sink into his flesh. He did not slip, not once, on the ice.

He walked, following Helgi's crescent tail and grey haunches. The takin had long since vanished. Only ice on the horizon, chunked and broken and jagged as teeth.

He had his axe with him. His bow, a quiver of arrows, the long-bladed knife in his boot. No flint or meat-knife or blanket. No gear besides weapons, as if he were going to war.

It had been his wish, as a boy, to do that very thing. Dreams of axes and spears and battle. Taliri raiders, Alviri rangers, Illhari soldiers in their banded steel. Child Veiko had slain them all, sent them to the spirit world and their ancestors.

But a crofter's son did not go raiding. A crofter's son—the third and youngest, not counting his sisters—might look forward to his own herd of takin someday. His own household, too, if he married well. He might, maybe, defend his home from bandits, but that was as close as a man got to battle in this age of peace.

His village's noidghe had said only a fool would seek violence. Then he'd spoken instead about how a hunter might appease an animal's spirit after killing it. How a man honored his ancestors and bound restless ghosts to their graves. Those were practical things that every man must know, whatever his station.

Veiko did not remember the noidghe mentioning endless glaciers in his stories, or what a man should do if he found himself walking the spirit world. Child Veiko might've asked, because the noidghe loved to tell tales, but child Veiko had cared only about fighting. Besides. A crofter's son did not become a noidghe. Noidghe chose their apprentices from better-born sons and daughters, unless there was an obvious talent. Which Veiko hadn't had back then. What the old noidghe would make of Veiko *now* was another matter.

What Veiko was sure of: a crofter's son turned outlaw might need to learn what a noidghe knew, and quickly. His body would not live forever with him wandering, no matter Snowdenaelikk's skills. Best he figured out what he was supposed to do. Follow Helgi, who seemed to know where they were going.

Who slewed a sudden crossways and stopped, stiff-legged and stiff-ruffed. Helgi growled and stared at a crack in the endless ice that had not been there a moment before. The crack widened, soundless, while the ice underfoot remained steady. A river, Veiko thought, black and deep and so smooth that it seemed frozen, except for the tepid sunlight shattering on wavelets and ripples. Deceptive, fast-moving water, solid darkness. And wide, yes, farther than a man might jump.

Veiko stepped around Helgi and knelt on the bank. The ice fell away in a steep and smooth-sided slide into the river. He stretched flat on his belly and crawled, knees and elbows, until he could look down into the water. He could not see the bottom. Saw himself instead, in the mirrored black. A young man just past twenty wearing hunter's braids, slant-boned and pale-eyed and perfectly unremarkable. A young man who showed no signs of

*foolishness*

having murdered a chieftain's son, or fought a witch-woman, or bargained with dead soldiers. Who did not look at all like he was dying.

Veiko leaned closer. Held a hand over the water, as if he might reach down and pull himself out. A newer self, stronger. Whole. Wiser, maybe. A simple enough gesture, to reach down and touch that reflection, to draw it into himself. Noidghe could do such things, he thought.

Helgi growled warning. Veiko hesitated. It seemed to him now that the reflection wasn't quite his own face. Perhaps a little more gaunt. A little older.

And still moving, he realized, still reaching for him. Its fingertips broke the water's clear black. And then, only then, did Veiko notice the other faces in the water. Eyeless sockets, gaping mouths, cheeks nibbled raw by fishes, rising up from the darkness. He jerked backward. Too fast, too sudden: he skidded on the ice. A hand colder than Kenjak's seized his wrist and pulled.

Helgi lunged and bit hard, just above Veiko's elbow. His claws furrowed the ice. At the same time, Veiko twisted and reached and tore his axe loose from its lacings, short swing and chop. The blade bit, and Veiko held hard to the handle. Stopped his slide into the river. He strained backward, all his strength and Helgi's together. Won a fingerwidth before ghoul fingers ground into the bones of his wrist and stopped him.

It wasn't a victory. He could not remain strung between river and glacier forever. Already the strain shivered through shoulders and belly and thighs. Spirit flesh would weaken. Exhaustion would win eventually, and so would that ghoul. He would be dead in that river, dead forever, beyond the reach of his ancestors.

Helgi snarled around his mouthful of Veiko's sleeve and arm.

Veiko's fear fled then, left a cool anger behind. He thought he might manage—if he moved quickly and did not slip—to rip the axe loose, to cut himself free. Sever his own wrist, yes, but a spirit-self would not bleed to death. The maiming would not follow him back to his body.

And if it did, well, a man could survive the loss of a hand.

Veiko held his breath. Gathered wits and will and wrenched at the axe. The blade rocked. His body did, just a little. And his river-self seized that moment to wrench at him. Veiko felt his clothes tear on Helgi's teeth, felt his flesh rip beneath that. And then he was loose, slinging sideways around the pivot of the axe. His head and one shoulder slewed out over the river. And then Helgi grabbed his leg, and Veiko drove his knees and boots into the ice. Stopped and damn near tore himself into three pieces, but he kept his grip, and the axe did not come loose.

And so he hung there, pulled between the river-ghost and Helgi and an axe blade only one fingerspan deep in ice. If it broke loose, he would die, because Helgi would not be able to hold him. He was already halfway over the river, looking down into his river-self's open mouth and hollow eyes. It smiled, and Veiko wondered how he had ever mistaken that thing for his reflection.

*Fool.*

No. Spirit-world trickery. A lesson, if he lived to remember it. Things were not what they seemed.

At least the dead thing in the water was not much for strategy. It relied on brute force and patience. Maintained a steady drag on his wrist to wear him down and moved only in reaction to his movements.

So. Like a puppy, then. And there were ways to outwit a puppy. Please, oh ancestors, the ghoul was more Logi than Helgi.

Veiko strained backward. And then he relaxed and let himself slip half a fingerlength farther toward the black river. The river-ghoul's grip loosened on his wrist in the unexpected slack. Then Veiko wrenched backward with all that was in him. The ghost lunged to keep its grip.

Veiko granted it that small victory, borrowed its momentum, rolled onto his shoulder and used his weight to jerk the axe free.

The steel glittered in a last thread of sunlight. Hung there, for a small eternity, like a ribbon caught in a breeze. Then it fell and cut cleanly through the ghoul's wrist, with only a brief hitch on dead bone.

The ghost-hand slipped off his wrist and sank into the river. The faces sank with it, all of them, dropping like stones into the depths. The river itself stiffened, as Veiko stared at it, into smooth solidity.

A man might walk across that frozen river if he trusted that surface.

A man might well lay on its bank, too, and shake for a very long time, before he sat up and examined the damage—because Helgi was not a small dog, nor weak, and he'd played his own game of tug with Veiko. He found rips in the leather and wool over his calf and elbow, no great matter. Bruises underneath that, certainly, and blood, but his ankle moved well enough. His knee flexed and held him when he stood. His elbow bent.

"Good dog," he told Helgi. It seemed wholly inadequate for thanks, but Helgi flattened his ears and grinned.

He tried a few practice swings with the axe and grimaced. His dog-gnawed leg twinged. His ghost-wrenched wrist and shoulder ached. Best if he avoided a fight, yes, best if he walked for another forever before he trusted that damned river. He squinted across its width.

And blinked. There were trees, suddenly, on the far bank. A whole forest sprung up from nothing, mixed evergreen and naked white birch. There was a trail on the other side, winding away from the river, which had suddenly shrunk to a narrow trickle.

Helgi bounded across it, with more enthusiasm than Helgi needed, and darted into the brush. Veiko followed more carefully, half expecting the river to spread again, midstride, and swallow him. But it didn't, and the bare earth on the far side felt steadier under his boots than the glacier had been. The wind disappeared, too, as if someone had slammed a door on it. Damp-rot chill to the air that collected in the back of his throat when he breathed. Ink-spot shadows, darker under these trees than the watery sun should create.

Then he noticed that Helgi had not returned and that he did not hear any dog-in-the-underbrush noises. Fear threaded cold through his chest.

"Helgi!"

That might be a bark in the far distance, much too far for a dog to have run in so short a time. Veiko hesitated, one foot on the trail, while the forest brooded around him. He had never feared a forest, but he was afraid of this one. Safer to stay on the trail. Helgi would find him again. Helgi always did.

He walked alone for what might've been an afternoon or two days, with only an awful silence for company. The trail widened from deer track to a hardpack and then to sunbaked bricks. An Illhari road, like the one he had crossed near Davni, wide enough for soldiers to run four abreast. Veiko drifted close to its shoulder, where the stones scuffed less loudly.

He did not see the woman until he was almost on top of her. She stood a little off to the side of the road, where the shadows gathered around the skirts of evergreen trees, tall and pale as one of his own people. And close. Very close. He *should* have noticed her.

Veiko stopped and put his hand on his axe.

"You have no need of that weapon." Soft-voiced, a little rough, like fingernails on the back of his neck.

"Perhaps not," Veiko agreed, but he did not let go of the axe. He must not trust appearances in this place. The ghoul had taught him that. And still. Her voice was not unpleasant. He wished she would say something else.

She smiled, and it seemed as if the sky went a little dimmer. Twilight now over the treetops, purpling like a bruise. She reminded him of Kaari's daughter, and a summer night when the sky had rippled green and pink and gold. Reminded him of other things, too, that did nothing at all for his wits.

"I have no business with you," he said. She was no woman. Some spirit. Some trick.

"I hope we can change that," she said. Then she stepped onto the path, and he saw she wore nothing but shadows. They lapped her hips and breasts like waves on a lakeshore, and Veiko found himself wishing they might recede just a finger's width. Heat pooled and spread south from his belly.

"Stop," he croaked.

The spirit-woman did, which surprised him. She widened eyes gone dark in the twilight. Offered her hands, just as Kaari's daughter had on that summer night.

"Come with me," she murmured, and his skin ached. All he had to do was take those hands, and then she would lead him

*up onto the tundra*

into the forest

*under the summer sky*

into the twilight.

*No.*

Eat his soul, more likely, and bury his bones beside the trail.

"No," he told her. And, a second time, "I have no business with you."

He walked around her. Pointed his eyes at the Illhari road and thought very hard about snowbanks and wet socks and stepping through ice into cold water. Anything except women's curves and women's smell.

"Ah, but I have business with you." Her voice changed into something cooler and harder. "Veiko Nyrikki. Stop."

His leg, the one Ehkla had cut, buckled and cramped. Veiko caught himself on a convenient tree. Leaned on it, panting, and traced the heat throbbing up from his thigh. Another lesson: that witchery left marks deeper than muscle and bone. If Ehkla's marks on him responded to this spirit's voice, then he knew who she was, and how she knew his name.

He drew a deep breath. "Tal'Shik," he named her in return. "What do you want?"

"Only what is mine." The shadows sank into her flesh, dyed her skin and hair as dark as any Dvergir. Left her naked, too, and he was glad of the tree behind him. Not at all sure of his knees or the steadiness of his hands.

"I am not yours."

"No?" Tal'Shik crossed the short space between them. Ran her fingers across his thigh, and the pain melted into something else entirely. "This says otherwise. That is *my* mark, Veiko Nyrikki, put there by *my* godsworn."

"It is unfinished." Snow had told him that. He held to that certainty.

"A small matter." She put her hand on his chest and stroked the place over his heart. Her breath chilled his cheek, damp-rot and old iron. "You could resist, but you will lose. Yield now, and save yourself the effort. I am not a cruel mistress."

"That is not my understanding."

Effort, now, to look at her face, like climbing uphill on ice. Hard to breathe with her so close, damp-rot and woman-smell clotted in his throat and all his limbs shaking. It had been a long time since Kaari's daughter. Months of Alviri women who refused his eyes and whispered *skraeling* when he passed. And very recent nights spent near a woman who met his eyes and his wits without any fear. He summoned up her memory like a shield, imagined her exasperation

*for the Laughing God's sake, Veiko*

with his foolishness.

Tal'Shik frowned at him. Veiko met her gaze and stared back, defiant. He would not flinch. Would not show her weakness. Did both when her features blurred and ran together and became Snow looking back at him. Snow's midnight eyes, and Snow's jagged smile, and Snow's flawed voice:

"Who is this woman, so large in your mind? Is her shape more to your liking? I can assume it, if you like."

Witchery. Trickery. And anger, oh yes, that slipped past his wits and escaped. "Do not try. You make a poor copy."

Tal'Shik hissed, and Snow's features melted and ran into a terrible, offended beauty. She trailed her finger along his jaw until it rested in the hollow of his throat.

"You lack manners," she mused, and stroked the place where his life beat under the skin. "I will have to teach you. I will enjoy teaching you."

"No," because that was all he could manage. Ehkla had left him no choice at all, with her witchery. Tal'Shik offered the illusion of refusal, but she would wear him away like a river over stones. Take him eventually but make him yield first. He made fists instead. Bit his lip through to bleeding. Wished he had drowned, wished he had died in the snow, wished—

"Do not touch me," squeezed through teeth clenched to cracking. "Ehkla did not finish her sacrifice. I do not belong to you. Go."

Her eyes turned the color of fresh blood. "Not without what is mine."

Patterns swirled under her skin like embers in charcoal, shapes that he did not know, which made his gut knot and pushed bitter into his throat. A whirling, violent dark spilled out of her, liquid storm clouds that shredded the twilight and spread around her like a cloak.

Or like wings. Very large wings. His chest constricted to a breathless white heat.

*Dragon, yeah? That's the Dvergiri word.*

Veiko threw himself sideways. Gasped and flopped and writhed until he fetched up against another tree and squirmed onto his one working knee.

"Where are you going?" Tal'Shik asked. Then she shook off her woman shape utterly. She grew larger, her limbs melting together and twisting into new shapes: wings, claws. Her eyes glowed like a bonfire burned down to ashes.

Veiko worked the bow loose from its ties. Braced the end and slid the string up over the tip, there, fitted it into the notch. Fumbled for an arrow, fitted it to the string, and drew it back, steady as he could. It was not a good angle, a worse position.

Tal'Shik made a sound between thunder and laughter that shivered all the way to his bones. "You cannot intend—" she began, and he shot her.

Not a good shot, no, but lucky. The arrow caught her high in what had been a woman's thigh a moment before, what looked like tail and haunches now, and buried itself to the fletching.

Tal'Shik's rage was all the more awful for its silence, and for the efficiency with which she reached down and snapped the arrow off in the wound. The look on her face—no longer a woman's now, something terrible—said that Veiko's own end would not be as quick, or as final.

Veiko pulled a second arrow, nocked, and drew. And saw, from the corner of his eye, a grey dog running through the trees. At him, and then past him, charging straight for Tal'Shik.

Veiko loosed the arrow. Made a one-armed grab for Helgi as he bounded past. The dog slipped through his fingers like water.

"Helgi!" Might as well call the sun from the heavens. Might as well ready himself to watch Helgi die a second time, and probably only a handful of seconds before Veiko himself, and all Snow's *don't you fucking dies* would not bring him back. He wondered if his body would linger, or if it would simply stop. If Snow would think she had killed him.

But Helgi snapped at Tal'Shik and dodged away, circled back, and came at her flank. She struck, and he danced out of reach, flickered back and nipped at a hand gone halfway to talons. He gleamed like old steel in moonlight, except there was no moon. Almost full dark, now—not night, because night had stars, night had shape and sense to it. This was nothing, pure and empty and aggressive. Tal'Shik's doing, and part of Tal'Shik herself, that devoured the trees and ate all the sky.

Her eyes blazed, the only sure lights in this place, like signal fires.

Veiko drew a third arrow. Nocked and sighted and held it until his arm burned.

His second shot had gone wide. This one did not. One of Tal'Shik's eyes went dark.

She vanished in a thunderclap and a gust that shattered the bow in his hands and flung him aside. Veiko struck the same convenient tree, much higher on its trunk, hard enough to white his vision. Struck the ground in the next beat, and all his breath gusted out. The color came back in slow stages—twilight greys and blues. Misty grey. And Helgi's winter eyes, on the other end of Helgi's very black nose.

He sat up slowly. Touched the side of his head, expecting blood, and was pleasantly surprised. Checked all the rest of him, too. The leg Ehkla had marked still hurt, but it responded. His bow, however, was beyond help. He gathered the pieces and put them into the quiver. He borrowed the tree for balance and pulled himself to standing.

His whole body hurt, chill and ache in his joints that had nothing to do with bruises or trees or hard landings. The path had vanished, along with Tal'Shik. There was only forest around him, no trail—no sign of the river, or any indication which way he'd come.

So. That had been Tal'Shik's trickery. Show the fool a convenient path. Let him lose himself in the forest. Time was uncertain here. Noidghe who went walking too long died, sometimes, if their bodies failed them. And his had not been healthy at all when he'd left it. He needed to find the path out.

Helgi had led him this far, but Helgi sat at his feet now and sniffed, narrow-eyed, and looked doubtful. Veiko took an experimental step in one direction. Helgi did not move. Veiko tried another, and Helgi stood up. Took a pair of stiff-legged steps and stopped. Growled, more warning than menace, staring hard past Veiko's left hip.

Guess, then, that it was not a moose-spirit Helgi saw, or a bear-spirit, or any kind of animal. Some new encounter to delay him, some new threat from which he could learn a great deal if it did not kill him first.

This new experience wore a man's shape, Dvergir and unarmed, with flames in the sockets where eyes should be. He leaned hip-shot against a sapling that did not seem to notice his weight. Not a man at all, no, and Veiko could guess who he was, too. Snow swore by him often enough.

A man could trip over the Dvergiri gods, for how often they seemed to appear. As well try to avoid Briel when she wanted a flatcake.

"Laughing God," Veiko said sourly. "Why are you here?"

The God laughed. The trees slumped like candles too close to fire. "Such a welcome. I suppose I can't blame you, can I? After Tal'Shik."

"What do you want?"

"From you? Nothing. I'm here as a favor to Snowdenaelikk."

"Snowdenaelikk."

"Surely you remember her. Tall woman, features as sharp as her tongue? Ah. I see that you do. Peace, skraeling. I know she inspires men to violence. But." The flame-eyed man grinned and showed empty hands. "Most times she's the target."

"Snow would not ask your help. She does not know about this place."

"She knows you're dying. And you are, by the way. She also thinks it's her fault."

"It is not."

"I know that. But she asked for my help, and I'm here. So. Shall we go?" The Laughing God held out a hand.

Favors meant obligation. Meant debts and entanglements. And Snow had asked favors for his sake, which was worse. "What does she owe for this asking?"

"What does that matter to you, skraeling?"

"I will pay it."

"You. What can *you* offer me?" The God tipped his head, so that the smile spilled into one corner of his lips. "Do you know where you are? Or how to get back to where you want to be?"

"No."

"And do you know why Tal'Shik didn't rape you?"

He flushed. "No."

"Or rip out your heart and eat it?"

"No."

The God grinned, a little unkindly. "Well, then. Maybe you don't know so much, yeah? Maybe you've got nothing I want. Maybe you should be glad of what help you're offered and take it."

That was truth. He was only crofter's son turned hunter turned outlaw, who thought he could be a noidghe now because he'd spoken twice to ghosts and because he had his dead dog to guide him. See how that had turned out. He'd almost fed a river-ghoul. Almost given himself to Tal'Shik. Almost lost Helgi a second time.

*Toadshit, yeah?* He imagined Snow's half-twist smile, that angry one that would not reach her eyes. *Lot of almosts, Veiko, but you're still here.*

True enough. He'd escaped the river. Refused Tal'Shik and hurt her and driven her away. But he was certainly lost now, in the middle of a spirit forest, no path and no idea where he should go, Helgi crouched and confused at his feet, and the Laughing God offering help for a price not yet named. He was out of luck, out of skill.

*Not out of brains, yeah?*

Veiko stared very hard at nothing. Thought about trickery and witchery and half-truths.

"Do you know why Tal'Shik did not rape me, or why she did not eat my heart?"

"I told you."

"No. You asked me if I knew. That is not the same thing."

The God's eyes banked back to embers. Smoke curled from deep in the sockets. "No. It isn't."

Veiko should have felt satisfaction, hearing that. Felt only a grim relief instead, that he'd got something right at last. Noidghe walked the spirit world, and they bargained with spirits, and they crossed death like men crossed rivers. Noidghe could also lose themselves in the spirit world if they were unwise, and oh, he had been that.

"You are no noidghe," said the God. "You're just a crofter's son. You're an outlaw. You are lost, and you need help. So take it."

Veiko regarded the God's outstretched hand. A noidghe knew the way home, but he wasn't noidghe. The God was right about that.

*Toadshit, Veiko. What else would you be?*

Truth in that, too. He was a *poor* noidghe. Untaught. Knowledge he'd never wanted. Never sought. A crofter's son did not need to know those things.

But he wasn't a crofter's son anymore. He was an outlaw, dead to his family and his tribe. Dying now, and trying to get back from that. If he managed that, he'd be noidghe by definition, however badly prepared. And if not, he'd be dead, that was all.

He didn't want to die.

Or he could accept the God's help and pay the God's price. He had made deals before, with Kenjak, and the price had not been too terrible. But Kenjak was not the Laughing God. A god's help might cost more than a numbed arm. The God's price might not be his to pay at all if the debt became Snow's. A man might make such a deal to save himself, but a man did not betray his

*only*

friend and drag her into his debts.

"Well?"

That sounded like Snow's voice, and Veiko looked up sharply. For a single heartbeat he saw Snow's face in the God's razor-bones. Then she faded, and it was only the God again, whose eyes smoked like wet wood.

Like the fire in the cave had. Veiko remembered the sting, when he opened his eyes, and the constant itch in his throat. Remembered Snow's tired

*Wood's too wet, yeah? Look at that smoke.*

and Dekklis's *You can go get it next time.* Which Snow hadn't, no. She'd stayed with him, fingers wound through his.

*Don't you fucking die.*

*Do not let me.*

He might not be worth much as a noidghe, but he was a good hunter, and he had his dog to help him. Veiko knelt and took Helgi's face in his hands. Looked hard into winter-pale eyes and remembered midnight-blue eyes and the strength in her hands. Remembered the smell of her as she leaned over him. Remembered the steel and bright fire core of her.

"Go," he told Helgi. "Find Snowdenaelikk."

Helgi sniffed, narrow-eyed, and turned a stiff-legged circle. Stopped and raised his muzzle and whined, as Helgi did when he'd caught a scent. Veiko patted his ribs, *go,* and Helgi went, tail curled and gleaming like old steel.

The God laughed, and this time the trees melted utterly. "Oh, I see why she likes you. Clever. Proud. Well, then. Good luck, skraeling."

"I will not need it." Veiko drew a deep breath. Held it and turned his back on the God. "I know the way."

# PART TWO

PART TWO

# CHAPTER THIRTEEN

Cardik had been an Alvir city, several wars and another name ago. Some petty thegn's local seat to which the tatters of the allied Alviri tribes had retreated when it became clear that the Illhari Republic would not be stopped farther south. The city squatted on both sides of a ribbon of water that only counted as a river during spring snowmelt, when it spread out of its banks and smeared mud across most of the valley. The Alviri had counted on that spring flood to save them, to sweep the Illhari back into the Below and drown what their artillery could not crush. They had trusted their walls, and their vats of hot oil, and their godsworn, who said that the Illhari would not prevail against the righteous.

But it had been Illhari engineering in the end, and Illhari conjuring, that had cracked Cardik's walls from root to crest. Illhari determination and Illhari discipline that had waged war through the winter. Illhari vengeance that had shattered most of the city, dismantled the keep and the temples, and razed the whole Hill. Illhari pride that rebuilt it in Illharek's image, except for the red mountain sediment that even conjuring could not change.

The conquerors had built roads, too, out of imported Illhari stone and still more red mountain brick. Roads were more efficient than tunnels, and faster to build, and—most important to the Senate— more affordable. Cardik had two. One, the wider, ran south along the mountains toward the distant city of Illharek, threading together the conquered Alviri settlements like beads on a string. The second jumped the river and trailed east and lost itself in the sunrise and the plains. Dekklis had traveled both, and their packed-dirt cousins, with the Sixth. But this homecoming, she marched overland and through the forest, as the first legion soldiers had done, following the Wild's convolutions at a pace far slower than the most burdened soldier managed on pavement.

She and Istel could have returned on the road much more quickly. Should have, by every regulation and rule. But her companions could not, and Dekklis wasn't certain if her niggling guilt was because she'd stayed with Snow and Veiko, or because she had considered no other option. The half-blood was healthy enough. But the skrae— Veiko, Dekklis self-corrected—Veiko wasn't. He'd woken up with the stormwind screaming outside two days ago. Just sat up, fever broken. But he was not well, no, still weak and limping badly. He couldn't outrun a lame rabbit, whatever *I am fine* and *I can walk* and *I will manage* he insisted. As if everyone couldn't see the wounds in his leg, as if the cave hadn't stunk of vomit and shit and sick sweat. As if the fever hadn't melted flesh off him—that, obvious even to Dekklis, who had not known him before.

"Toadshit," Snow had said mildly, and shared a smirk with Istel— who still had a gash grinning across his arm and chest—before she'd looked at Dekklis and raised both eyebrows. And so it was Dekklis who'd said *We'll go back together* and *We'll stay off the road* as if there'd never been any plans to the contrary.

It wasn't a bad idea. Dekklis could admit, to herself anyway, that her own cracked ribs made her glad enough for Veiko's hitching limp and Istel's need for frequent rests. Snow was the only one healthy, and she spent most of her energy propping up Veiko—who'd protested the help exactly once, until he hit his first deep snow, and then got thin-lipped and quiet.

So, going by forest, at Veiko's best pace—two whole days of travel, so that they came to Cardik just past sunset. The city threw a warm glow up against clouds pregnant with more snow to make a second, weak twilight. Another storm on the way, in a week that had seen three already. Not unheard of this close behind midwinter, but not typical weather, either.

Blame Tal'Shik's pet Talir half-blood, maybe. Blame bad luck. Dekklis wanted, bad as she'd wanted anything lately, four walls and a roof, a bed and a fire and warm toes. Tired and cold, and, in the privacy of her own head, more than a little bit scared. Dek understood the dangers of weather and edged steel. It was Tal'Shik and ghosts that bothered her, and Red Lady, and Veiko's cool *Ehkla is not dead* conviction.

There had been no signs of Ehkla or any surviving Taliri. No signs of Rurik and the Sixth, either. The road out of the forest was all untouched snow and the occasional scattered footprint, and none of the pounded-half-to-ice hardpack that troopers made on a march.

"He can't still be out there," she muttered. "We took provisions for five days. It's been that, and more."

"Half rations," Istel said, the first thing Istel had said since midday. "Wouldn't be the first time he's done that."

"Huh." Dekklis liked the quiet less and less, those silent farmsteads with their windows cutting little squares and shapes into the dark. There should be sentries in the watchtowers. Should be patrols in the fields, among the farmsteads through the lattice of stone walls and snow-buried cart-tracks. "Still. Rurik should've sent a runner back after Davni."

Istel's gear creaked, only proof that Istel was in that particular patch of shadow. "We might've beaten a runner."

"At our pace? Only if he sent one of the cooks and broke her leg first."

"Maybe the Taliri got her, then."

"Maybe the Taliri got *all* of them."

"Why're we waiting?" Snow eased down beside her, on the side Istel wasn't.

"Looking for patrols."

"Briel doesn't see anything down there."

"Well, all right. As long as Briel says so, then I guess we don't need to worry."

"You sound like someone I knew once. He's dead now."

"That a threat?" Knowing better, but tired and cold and worried now about what was left of her cohort, and the first flakes of snow coming down.

Whatever Snow might've answered—and she would have, no chance otherwise—disappeared under a *shee-oop* and wingflap, right overhead. Dekklis made fists and did not, would not, flinch. Would not look, either, and couldn't quite *not*, as the svartjagr crawled up Snow's arm and settled across her shoulders.

And then, because that half-blood could not leave a silence: "Briel's on your side, yeah? Won't bite you or hunt you down in the dark."

Dekklis ignored the jab. "There *should* be patrols out there. Fires in the towers. Some sign of sentries."

"Better for us if there aren't."

"You sound like Teslin." Who would've been calling her too cautious by now, would've marched up to Cardik's gates and talked herself past the nightwatch. Who was dead because of that impatience. Dekklis imagined Teslin's ghost coming back, or Barkett's, and wished even harder for fire and bunk and Rurik's ill humor.

"Listen," she said, one last try. "If Rurik's not back yet, then something's wrong. He hasn't sent anyone back yet, means he can't. Guess I can't ask you to care about that, can I?" Bitterly, which was more a product of cold and tired than real grievance. As soon ask the sun to shine blue as a heretic half-blood to care about Cardik's legion.

"Guess you can't." A sigh, faint, that reminded Dekklis she wasn't the only one tired, that Snow might have more reason to stay outside than go in. "We can't help your First Spear anyway, yeah? Not against Ehkla. So go report Davni to the praefecta and get your patrols out. Just get us inside first."

"Yeah. Sure." Dekklis straightened gingerly. Took a shallow breath against the ache in her ribs. "You got a plan for the gates? Because it's after sundown, and there will be the nightwatch. Or were you planning some other way in?"

Snow chuckled and stood, much more easily. Stretched, and Dekklis heard her spine crack. "What, secret doors? No."

"No, there're no secret doors, or no, that isn't your plan?"

"Both. And none of us are up to climbing walls, so can you talk your way past the nightwatch?"

"Yes. My way, and Istel's. Yours? Maybe. *His?* Not likely. Not unless you're prisoners, and that makes a whole new problem for us, because they'll want—"

"No," said Veiko firmly.

"No," Snow echoed. She circled back to Veiko, where he slouched against a tree. Slipped her arm around his ribs and steadied him upright. "No need for elaborate acts. Get the gate open, that's all I need."

"And what, they won't notice you?"

"No. They won't."

No one sighted could miss either of them. Add the dog and the svartjagr and you might as well wrap them in witchfire—oh. Comprehension sank in like a javelin. "You're going to conjure. Spellwork."

"What did you think? I'd poison my way past the guards?"

"You've noticed we're not that far from the Wild, right?"

"Won't be any backlash," Snow said blithely, coolly, which Dekklis didn't believe for an eyeblink. Always a risk for a conjuror outside of a city, even this close. Illhari-born would know it. Snow surely did and knew that Dekklis would, too.

Announcing that danger wouldn't change its necessity. Dekklis bit down on an argument, having no better ideas. Trust that Snow knew a half dozen ways into a city that didn't involve gates, guards, or conjuring. Bet that this wasn't her first choice. But Veiko was the problem, and would be, no matter who was on the gates or what time of day was involved. He might pass for Alvir in coloring, sure, but not with the braids and the axe and the dog. Man like that would draw notice.

"And once we're in? Then what? You have a plan?"

"I know a place . . ." Snow trailed off, half a question, half a statement, and a pause for punctuation. She looked at Veiko, who nodded, tight and terse and grudging. Snow nodded. "Yeah. Got a plan."

Dekklis let go the air she'd held warm in her lungs. "Do I want to know where you'll be?"

"Probably you do. Better if you don't."

"Then I need some way to find you. Because damn sure you won't come up to the barracks."

"*Find* me? Our peace is over at the gates, yeah?"

"So we make a new peace. Davni is ashes. Veiko is godmarked. Kenjak's dead, and *you* pissed *her* off. I say we've got several common problems, and we need to solve them."

"And what about your commander? Last I recall, he sent you to find me. You think he's forgotten that? Think he can tell one half-blood from another?"

"I won't turn you over. Swear that, Snowdenaelikk. On my House and my honor. But you're the one saying Tal'Shik's back. You're the one saying we've got a half-blood godsworn in the forest, and she's friends with *your* friends in Cardik."

"And I will handle them. I told you that."

"Ehkla's starting a war. That's legion business. I can tell you what the patrols find. You tell me what your friends are doing."

Snow said nothing for a few steps, then, "The Street of Silk Curtains. You know where it is?"

Every soldier did. "Yes."

"Go to Still Waters bathhouse. Ask for Aneki."

"Bathhouse? You mean brothel."

"Don't tell me you're a prude, Szanys."

"I'm not. I just thought you'd name some place in the Warren."

"Figure we stay on the near side of the Bridge, you visiting won't stick out so bad. And that might keep you from trying to look for my *other* friends, who *will* be in the Warren. Remember, Szanys. They're *my* problem, not yours. You handle the raiders."

Dekklis shook her head hard. "Aneki. Still Waters. All right. And then? How long do I wait?"

"You leave a message."

"How long?"

Snow chuckled. "Take Aneki's advice on the wait. If she says more than a few hours, you go and come back later. Or you find something to do in the meantime. Still Waters has a variety of options."

"What says Aneki doesn't just kill me?"

"Bad for business, yeah? She won't. Besides." Snow smirked, audibly. "Half the garrison's down on the Street any given night. No one will notice one more soldier. Or two."

Truth. Dekklis sighed. "Fine. So I'm safe. What about you?"

"Lots of half-bloods down there. Aneki is, too, yeah? Looks like her mother. *She* was a bondie out of Illharek. No high Houses, though, just—"

"Snow."

A sigh. "Do me a favor, Szanys. If I don't meet you, or if Aneki says I can't come—get Veiko out of Cardik."

As if he wasn't leaning on her shoulder, listening. As if Dekklis had a matchstick's chance in a bonfire of *making* that man do anything.

"No," said Veiko.

Which engendered an eyelock between partners that ended with Snow's quiet, "Debts are clear, if I'm dead. Yeah?"

"Yes," grudgingly. And more quietly: "But there will be new debts if you die."

"Then pay them back from *outside* the walls. You, too, Dek. Istel." Snow pinned them both with a stare Dekklis felt through the dark. "If something goes wrong, get out."

"Something's already wrong. You turning up dead will be one more thing."

They were past the fields now and winding around the last farmstead, where the cart-tracks joined up to the road. A lop-eared dog came partway into the yard and barked, and Dekklis thought hard about shooting it, *rot* that animal. At least Logi didn't answer it. Didn't charge into the yard and kill it, either. But the barking got more frantic until the door cracked and spilled a wedge of light onto mud and snow. A woman's shape moved in the doorway. A woman's voice called out, "Who's there?" and "Shut *up*, dog!"

The dog yipped to quiet. The woman came out a few steps. Metal gleamed in one hand. An axe, Dekklis thought, some little wood-splitting hatchet. No match for a trooper's sword, or Veiko's broad-bladed monster.

Or Taliri spears, or godmagic. *Where* were the patrols? Dekklis angled across the lane, so that the light snagged on gear and armor. Trusted Istel to follow her, trusted Snow to get out of sight.

"Scouts," she called. "Just back from the forest. Peace, citizen. Apologies for the disturbance."

"No matter." The farmer waved. Grabbed the dog by the scruff and dragged it backward and watched from the safety of her doorway.

"Near thing," Dekklis muttered. Turned and damn near bumped Istel, close on her hip. Only empty lane beyond him. Nothing. Shadows. Two sets of footprints, hers and Istel's. No dog tracks, even.

Her scalp prickled tight. "Hell and damn."

"Shit," said Istel.

The shadows melted at the side of the road, spilling away two tall, fair-headed people and one wolf-sized dog.

"It's a simple enough trick." Snow wasn't smiling now. Thin-lipped, and a muscle tight in her jaw. "Any Dvergir can do it. Children. Even half-bloods. Want me to teach you?"

There were laws against teaching shadow-weaving outside the Academy, which this woman wouldn't care about, which Dekklis wouldn't waste her own breath reciting. "Is *that* how you're getting through the gate?"

"No. I'm going to conjure us through." Snow slid her arm loose, so that Veiko limped on his own. Spread her palms and cupped them, as if she held a bowl only she could see.

Then she vanished with Veiko and Logi and Briel.

Dekklis felt as if she'd missed a step in a long series, sick lurch and drop. A chill settled under her skin and sank straight to bone.

"Snow?"

"Go, Szanys," from nowhere and everywhere. A laugh, low and quiet. "Told you there wouldn't be any backlash."

\* \* \*

The conjuring was simple enough. A third-rank spell, one of the first she'd learned. Call up the light, whisper it smooth, shape it in your hands, and then push it outward, so that casual eyes slid away. It was like making mirrors, her teachers had told her. Let the conjuring reflect what people expected to see. That was easy enough when walking through a gate with space for two people and a dog to pass without touching anyone. Much harder inside Cardik's walls, where illusions strained under jostling and startled glances. At least no one trod on Logi. Hell if she thought she could hold a conjuring against yelps and snarls.

The crowds were thin this near the gate, with most of the shops closed. The streets wouldn't be this empty or quiet where they were going. At least the Street of Silk Curtains wasn't quite in the Warren. It sat just this side of the Market Bridge. Snow could see those lights from here, bob and flicker of lanterns and torches spanning the river. The merchants on the Bridge never shut shop.

Dekklis and Istel turned and wound their way up toward the barracks. Snow counted ten, then angled Veiko toward a wall and a web of shadows in varying greys, where window lanterns and Cardik's street lamps overlapped. Big houses up here, large shops. A lot of money, to pay for all the oil. A lot of shadows, too, where the light didn't reach.

"Going to drop the conjure," she murmured.

Veiko grunted, which meant *yes*, probably, and *what choice do I have?* Might mean *we're going to die now, what matter?*

She spread her fingers. Let the conjuring go like breath, like the warmth when tight muscles relaxed. None of the passersby noticed them, shuffling with their heads down against new snowfall. Snow gathered up shadows anyway and dragged the darkness across them.

"Where are we going?" He hadn't asked before now. Had leaned on her and trusted and followed. Balked now, in woven shadows. Scared, oh yes, leaving bruises on her shoulder where his fingers gripped. He'd never been in a town with walls. Never walked on pavement. Never seen this many people in one place, on one street, or heard so much noise. Witchfire eyes wide as she'd ever seen them, the Veiko equivalent of Logi's tucked tail and flat ears.

"Safe place," she said, which was enough to get him moving again. Limp and hitch along the wall, looking for the nearest northbound alley. "Still Waters."

"The—bathhouse. Brothel," rolled out carefully, with more accent than Veiko usually had. A new word, bet on that. And, "That is exactly what you told Dekklis."

"You thought I'd lie."

Dryly: "It had occurred to me."

"Me, too. But she's kept her side of things so far, yeah? Besides. Still Waters is safe," she added, because he wouldn't ask it. "You won't be noticed."

His ribs vibrated. "There are so many outlaws here?"

"Lots of private rooms with locks. And Alviri. And baths," she added, because Laughing God knew he needed one. She did. *Logi* did. "The whole area sits on a hot spring. Here." She turned them into an alley that stank worse than any of them. "This way's faster."

"I do not mind faster," which was as close as he came to complaining. Tired, yeah, all drag and weight on her.

"How's the leg?"

"Hurts," he said. They'd moved past *fine* and *no matter*. "But it is not bleeding."

The wound had been redder this morning than she liked. Healing, yeah, but not well. She needed more herbs and oils. She'd taken enough for emergencies. Hadn't figured on two storms and three woundings and a godsworn-carved *rune*.

Hadn't figured on bringing someone back to Cardik, either, who'd never been inside a city, who needed her help, and *when* had she ever been anyone's guardian?

Since he'd opened those damned witchfire eyes after the fever broke the last time, and his fingers had clenched around hers. She owed him a turn as her guest now. A turn at her protection.

Snow hitched a breath and a better grip on Veiko's ribs. Guided them both from one alley to another, leaving the wealthier neighborhoods and descending toward the S'Ranna River and the little lattice of streets before Market Bridge. The Street of Silk Curtains was actually several streets, a whole, tiny neighborhood just far enough from the Hill that no highborn had to see it, and just on the right side of Market Bridge so no highborn had to cross into the Warren to visit its charms. Tanners, butchers, dyers—all banished to the far side of Market because bondies and servants could walk that distance, but the brothels had to be convenient. Which was fortunate, because Veiko wouldn't manage the Bridge limping like this. Fall down in the middle of it, yeah, and she'd never get him up again.

Here, finally. A wider alley, studded by gates into courtyards, and by balconies on the brickwork walls. The silk curtains that gave this neighborhood its name weren't in evidence in the alleys. These were flat-fronted facades, narrow and deep, where the only windows might face the courtyard, or the alley, and relied on shutters instead of curtains and glass. Shutters that were, at this time of evening, all closed, leaking light on the edges.

Just as well, Snow reckoned. Didn't need any extra attention, with a wounded man hanging on her shoulder and no easy reach for her weapon. Most of the locals knew better than to bother anyone in the alleys, but there was always the chance of an amateur or an idiot.

She dipped her shoulder and shrugged Briel off, twist and snap she'd thought were gentle, which still startled Veiko and damn near dumped them both into Laughing God alone knew what on the pavement.

"Sorry," she muttered. "Thought Briel should scout for us. Her eyes are better at night."

"She is nocturnal," Veiko agreed.

Too tired to laugh, no air left for it. She kept to the edge, with Veiko between her and the wall, with Logi damn near tripping them both, through another pair of intersections, until she got them to Aneki's courtyard gate. Wrought iron, solid oak, a respectable lock that wouldn't keep Snow out for more than a dozen breaths.

Half a mind to pick it, yeah. She opted for the honest bell cord instead. Eased herself clear of Veiko and settled him into the shadows beside the gate while Briel clung to the rough bricks and poked her head between the bars on the gate.

"Chrrip," she chided when the back door finally opened. A lantern swung into the courtyard, on the end of a skinny Alvir's arm. Its glow landed on Briel. On Snow, too, as she pulled her hood back and thrust her face forward.

"Oh," said a boy's voice. The lantern changed altitude fast enough the flame guttered. Clattered onto the steps as the boy set it down and bolted back inside.

Veiko's hand dropped to his axe.

"Easy," Snow told him, and took hold of his wrist. "Boy's new, that's all. Doesn't know me. It's not trouble."

*Please, Laughing God.*

"Well," said a voice from the doorway. The lantern glow caught on the orange silk hem of a skirt not meant for outdoors. Traveled back up, glinting off embroidered skirts, to a waist laced as narrow as leather and bone could make it. And farther north: long curls, bleached moon-white, dangling between breasts that protested the shock of the cold. A face that was still pretty enough above that, despite lines around eyes and mouth. Skin just a little darker than Alviri milk-pale, garnet-dark Dvergiri eyes. The smell of incense and perfume, sweeter than jenja.

"Well," Aneki repeated. "Snowdenaelikk. Can't say I expected to see you at my back gate."

"Aneki. Let us in, yeah?" Snow wrapped her fingers through the bars. Put her face next to Briel and looked pointedly at Aneki's blouse. "We can all see it's cold out here."

"Ha. Funny, aren't you? Why don't you open it yourself? Easy lock for your skills, I should think." Aneki was already stepping out into the yard, dragging her orange hem into ruin. She hiked the lantern higher, so that Briel hissed and hopped back onto Snow's shoulder. "We, is it? —Hush, Briel. Who—oh. You've brought me a present."

"His name's Veiko. I need a place to put him, yeah? So the whole Warren's not talking."

"See why." Metal rattled. The gate started to swing open and stopped, with Aneki's hand on the bars. "That's a dog."

"Yeah. That's Logi." Snow shoved the gate, once and again, when Aneki wouldn't yield. "And he's better mannered than most of the soldiers you let in the front door."

"The dog, or the skraeling? All right, Snow. It's a joke." Aneki swung the gate open. "But if it destroys anything—"

Veiko stopped, with his hand on the lintel for balance, and looked at Aneki with that unnerving, un-Dvergiri directness. "I will pay for any damages."

"Toadshit you will."

"Now, Snow. Let him talk." Aneki shifted her stare to Veiko. Sucked her lip thoughtfully. "I could ask how you'll pay, couldn't I? What you can offer?"

*"Aneki."*

"But I think Snow will gut me." A smile, which collapsed as Veiko took his first unassisted step. This time her stare was all for Snowdenaelikk, cool and measured and worried, yes, because Aneki wasn't half as cold as she played. "Tsabrak do this to him?"

"No. *No.* Just a bad wound, yeah? Poison and fever."

Aneki cocked her head. "That hardly disqualifies Tsabrak." But she let them through the gate, swept around them, and beat them back to the door. Held it wide as Veiko struck out in a hobble that helped neither wound nor pain. That was pride, fuck and damn, and he'd bleed for it if he tore out his stitches.

Snow crossed stares with Aneki past Veiko's shoulder. Then Aneki took his elbow as he came up the steps, as if she helped filthy outlanders into her back door every day. Didn't blink as Briel oozed onto his shoulder, no, reached up and scratched Briel's chin, and Snow watched Veiko's spine loosen a little bit.

"I have just the room," Aneki told him, and tucked in tight against his side. "It's a short way up this hall. Very nice." She drew him off with a professional's grace while Snow coaxed Logi into the hallway. The dog's nose worked madly, eyes wide, ears flat, all the fur on his shoulders ruffed and stiff. He startled as she reached around him. Yipped and spun toward the door as she kicked it shut.

"Logi." Snow crouched. Took a handful of hair and skin and dragged him close and stroked him calm again, one arm hooked around his neck.

Laughing God knew where the new boy had gone. Up the side corridor, probably, fled with tales of skraelings and half-bloods in the garden.

"Domina?"

Or lurking in the shadows and surprising her and Logi, who lunged and snarled and reminded her that he'd only seemed small beside Helgi.

"Logi!" which made him stop, and "Idiot!" for the boy. Snow called up a witchfire. Raised it up so she could see his face. The blue flame snagged in the fine silver links of his collar. Laughing God, he was young. Alvir, because Aneki bought nothing else, and male. Well. Illhari troops were mixed sex, and tastes varied, and Aneki was too smart to specialize for one side or the other. One thing Aneki relied on was that Dvergiri didn't mind fucking Alviri, even if they paid for it, so long as they washed it off after. Call that an old grudge. Call it justice, maybe, for the Ten Thousand. Aneki called it lucrative. She might even let the boy buy his freedom in another dozen years.

"Have a name, or should I call you dogmeat?"

The boy's eyes rolled white. "Esa, Domina."

"Esa. I'm Snow. This is Logi. Do you think you can find him something to eat, or shall I set him loose?"

"I—yes, Domina."

"Smart boy. Bring it"—she jerked her chin down the hall, where Aneki's chatter floated thick as the smoke from the braziers—"wherever she's going. Can you manage?"

"Yes, Domina." Esa fled, a patter of thin house shoes and the rattle of fine chains.

Domina. Fuck and damn. Only in Still Waters would a half-blood rate that title. Aneki had been born to the collar, the daughter of an Alvir slave sold and traded out of Illharek. Bought her freedom here in Cardik by serving the same troops who made her fortune now. Proud woman, Aneki, of her business and her freedom and the pale scars on her throat she flaunted like jewelry. Damn right she'd insist on domina from the staff.

And for a woman in orange silk and too much perfume, she'd vanished far too easily. The corridor was silent, except for Logi's panting. Maybe Aneki'd discovered how heavy a tall man could be, leaning on her, and given up on her chatter. Maybe Veiko had fallen and dragged them both down. Snow imagined that for a moment—tangled silk and leather and Briel flapping free and indignant—and smiled. And then she stood and moved fast, because Veiko alone with Aneki was as safe as a flatcake with Briel.

But she found Aneki alone around a bend in the hallway, and Veiko nowhere in evidence. Behind the partly open door, presumably, that Aneki guarded with a ring of keys in her fist. She twitched her skirt aside as Logi darted past her. Frowned at the wet pawprints on her tiles.

"Sent your friend inside," she said, no trace of chatter or chirp. This was business-Aneki, who knew trouble when it limped through her door. "I'm afraid for my linens."

"Bath's next."

"And I'm sure you don't want the public chamber."

"His people are modest."

"Mm. Right. I'll clear a private room. Pick the one with the open curtain, yeah?"

"Thanks." Snow brushed a kiss on her cheek. "Owe you."

"I'm protecting my linens."

"Speaking of. We'll need something to wear, too, while our things are drying."

"His size? You don't want much. What else?"

"Privacy. Food. For the dog, more than anything. I asked Esa already."

"Esa." Aneki sniffed. "Boy's a gossip. I'll send someone else, after you're done polluting my baths."

"Discretion, Aneki."

"Reckoned that. Who's after him?"

"No one. Yet. But there might be a soldier who comes looking for me, or a pair. The woman is First Scout Dekklis. Smallish, highborn, accent straight out of Illharek's Tiers. Pretty face. The man's Istel. They're all right. I'll want to talk to them."

Aneki's eyebrows climbed. "Strange company. I'll send a messenger, then. You'll be at your flat?"

"I'll stay with Veiko," which she hadn't intended, until the words slipped. "My responsibility, all right? Whatever he does."

Aneki laughed, without sound or humor. "How long do I have you both, then?"

"I don't know."

"Better and better. And Tsabrak?"

"Doesn't know I'm here. Or about Veiko. I'll go see him when this storm's over." At least a day's grace, there. Maybe more. Time enough to collect her wits and her temper and figure what the hell she'd say.

"Oh, he won't like it, you staying here. He really won't like Veiko."

"Since when do you care for Tsabrak's opinions?"

"I don't. You do. Or you did." Aneki tossed her hair. Tipped her chin back, so that the old collar scars gleamed like silver around the long column of her throat. "Is this going to bring trouble?"

"For me? Maybe. For you? No."

"I'll hold you to that." The keys chimed as Aneki fingered through them. She unhooked one half of a pair, heavy and brass and notched. "As if my locks could stop you. Still. This will be simpler. Here."

"You're sure?"

"No. Take it anyway." She took Snow's hand and pressed the key into her palm. Folded her fingers over them and squeezed. "Anything changes—if there *is* trouble—you tell me, yeah?"

"Yeah. Swear it."

"Mm. You're going to owe me for this." A pause that wasn't at all accidental. "Is he yours?"

Which took Snow a wit-scattered moment to figure, staring at Aneki's merchanter eyes. She hadn't thought she'd the energy left for that kind of anger, which she squeezed down to ice and civility:

"Veiko's not anyone's, yeah? And he won't be."

Aneki looked less certain now. "Just a question, that's all. The man's hurt, nothing says you didn't pull him out of slavers' hands—"

"I didn't. Long story, yeah? Not the time for it." The anger disappeared like smoke in a draft. "Thanks, Aneki," she said, and brushed past, before she lost any more temper. She eeled through the door and kicked it shut and leaned against it.

Much warmer in here, with a fresh-kindled firedog and the hot springs' heat throbbing up through the stone. Veiko hadn't sat, whatever Aneki had told him. Standing in the middle of the room, as if bench and bed might attack him. Close enough to the door for listening, too, and his scowl had a new shape to it. Snow pretended not to notice. Looked at Briel instead, who'd abandoned Veiko's shoulder for the firedog's hearth. The svartjagr had her wings stretched to soak the heat, a living curtain. Veins spidered through the membranes, crosscut by quicksilver scars. Neat lines made with a fine-edged, sharp knife, knit by fine, small stitches, that wouldn't show at all without the fire's backlight. Snow remembered a much smaller Briel, victim of a highborn student who'd thought he could build wings like a svartjagr's if only he could see how those wings worked from the inside. She'd spent a good chunk of her life stitching wounded things back together. Veiko was just the latest. At least *he* wouldn't bite.

She sighed. "You can take your gear off. Aneki's clearing us a bath. She'll bring us something so we don't have to walk around naked. Not that *this* place would notice."

He didn't move.

"Veiko, for the Laughing God's *sake*. If there's some kind of taboo about sharing, get past it. It's not as if I haven't seen you—"

"That is not it."

"No? Then what?"

His mouth leveled, pulled tight by the knot in his jaw. "I do not want you bearing my debt."

"There's no debt. Aneki and I trade services, yeah? Soldiers get rough with the bondies. Women get pregnant. Sometimes there's babies, sometimes there aren't, and either way, I help. This place sits over the hot springs. Best baths in Cardik, unless you're up in the governor's villa."

"I will pay whatever's owed," dogged, stubborn. "I heard her say you would owe her."

"Shouldn't listen at doors, yeah? Didn't your mother teach you?"

Anger flickered in those witchfire eyes, which made her remember what he'd done to outlaw himself. Anger, and a wounded, tattered pride. "I am not a child."

"Yeah? Couldn't tell, the way you're bleating. Sit down."

He stiffened. Sank into a silence as cool as the wind and turned and limped to the bench, oh so carefully, and lowered himself onto it. Graceless thump when the bad leg gave out. He said a word in his own language, whose meaning she guessed. Then he got to work stripping harness and gear and axe, sharp efficiency that left no doubt of his anger.

Snow took herself on a circuit of the chamber. One large space, all open, with a narrow, shuttered window. That, for Briel's sake, another of

Aneki's kindnesses. Except there was a draft coming through the cracks, and a ribbon of melted snow on the sill. That was why this room had been so conveniently vacant. At least there were blankets on the bed, on top of Aneki's precious linens. Room for at least three people in that mattress, too. Snow perched on the edge of it. Leaned her elbows on her knees and watched Veiko peel the boot off his good leg. Dropped it, so that the slap of wet leather on tile made Logi jump.

Ask if she'd hurt his feelings, and expect no honest answer. She had Briel to confirm that she *had*, all muttered *chrripps* from the hearth and a cool disapproval that stung almost as badly as watching him reach for bootlaces on the end of a leg that would not bend far at the knee, that had swollen since midday and strained his leather pants shiny. Sweat gleamed on his cheekbones, above beard scruff and dirt and sunken eyes. Pain there, and pride, and *hell*, he made her chest hurt.

Snow levered off the bed and went and knelt in front of him. Did not look at him, did not cross the stare she knew he was drilling into the top of her skull. "Look. I'm sorry. Shouldn't have said that."

"No need," very quietly.

"Listen, Veiko, there's no—"

*Shame*, she almost said, and changed her mind. There was, and that was exactly the problem. Not the first time she'd undressed him, was it? Just like a child. Ask if the man had any pride left as he winced and looked somewhere else as she worked the boot off his foot. She touched his good knee as she stood, as if she needed the balance. Kept her hand on him until he looked at her, weary and wary and more naked than she'd ever seen him.

She turned away, for both their sakes. Peeled out of her own gear and draped herself in a blanket before he'd worked himself free of shirt and sweater and breeches. She watched him sidelong. Offered a blanket when he was done, and a hand to help him up. He took both without comment. Stood and wrapped himself decent and took the hand back on the second offering. Leaned on it, and her, the whole slow trip from bedchamber to bath.

# CHAPTER FOURTEEN

The Sixth's remainder limped into Cardik the morning the snow stopped. Dekklis found out when a mila whose name she couldn't remember burst through the barracks door and almost got Istel's javelin through the gut for his efforts.

"The fuck," Istel snarled as the mila gasped, "The Sixth," and sagged against the door. "Thought you'd"—gasp—"want to know."

"Thanks," Dekklis said on the way past, at a jog her ribs wouldn't forgive. They hadn't reported any injury to the garrison's chirurgeon, who would not have believed Istel's neat stitches were Dekklis's work. Claimed fatigue, that was all, and she'd treated Istel's wound the way Snow had showed her, and masked her cracked ribs with slow movements.

She ran now, and rot the ribs, down corridors and steps slick with snowmelt. Dodged a line of wounded incoming, litters and limping and bandaged. Hell and damn, there were a lot of them. And worse, in the courtyard: stacks of canvas, body shaped, in the slush and mud. She did a fast count. Fully a third lost. Her throat ached. Her stomach did.

"Shit," said Istel, and then, softly: "Alviri."

She'd thought he meant among the bodies. And then she saw them, a huddled knot by the gate. Rurik and an optio stood with them. One of the Alviri had a fistful of Rurik's sleeve.

"Who the hell are they? Davni's survivors?"

Hell and damn. "Davni had no survivors. The Taliri must've hit other villages."

"Think that's why he stayed out? Collecting refugees?"

"And corpses," Dek said grimly. "Praefecta's going to *eat* him."

Praefecta Stratka might. She'd already taken report from Dekklis and Istel, sat behind her desk and stared through laced fingers and asked about Davni and the estimated size of the Taliri raiding party. She hadn't looked at all convinced, but she'd sent patrols out and lit the watchtowers anyway. Good bet she'd believe in raiders now, with all these bodies.

*Or she'll flog Rurik for incompetence.*

Conservative family, Stratka. Even after the Purge, they had voted against the Reforms. It was a mark of the praefecta's waning familial influence that she'd ended up posted at Cardik. And there were old blood feuds between Stratka and K'Hess, from before and after the Purge. The legion was above that, the Republic's good before Houses, oaths to that effect and still. Dekklis had no doubt at all that Stratka's seventh daughter would strike at K'Hess's third son if she had both opportunity and legality behind her.

And if she caught the youngest Szanys-daughter in that same strike, well, all the better. No love between Houses Stratka and Szanys, either.

Dekklis angled for Rurik, Istel behind her.

"First Spear!"

He wheeled. Saw her and Istel and aimed for them while the optio beside him waved and talked to empty air for another five paces. Grief and exhaustion and horror hollowed his eyes above his customary scowl. But he still managed that K'Hess Rurik wide-shouldered, squared-up challenge Dekklis associated with uncut highborn males who'd managed any rank and wanted everyone to notice.

"Where—" he began before he'd even stopped moving. Dekklis risked career and skin and interrupted.

"Listen, sir. Before you talk to Praefecta Stratka. Want you to know what *we* saw, and what we didn't tell her," low-voiced, while Istel intercepted Stratka's optio and sent him on another errand, with an un-Istel "Move, idiot" and an even more un-Istel shove.

Rurik settled into that cold stare that he must've learned from his mother. "You say you lied to the praefecta, First Scout?"

"Omitted some details. Sir."

"Omitted."

"The praefecta." Dekklis wasted a gesture, waved a hand at sky and walls and milling bodies. "She might misunderstand the significance of all this. You wouldn't. You won't. So I'm telling you first." Treading close to insubordination, yes, and to the limits of an uncertain temper.

Rurik said nothing for too many heartbeats, jaw clamped, while his breath steamed out his nose. Looked like the man was boiling. Like he might burst. Dekklis held attention against aching ribs and waited. But it was *Istel* Rurik looked at, long and hard. Istel, who stood at her shoulder and didn't flinch from Rurik's stare.

"I sent you out after Kenjak's killers. You didn't come back. Where were you?"

"Storm caught us, sir," she said, which was true. And then, what she hadn't told Stratka: "After the Taliri did."

Rurik forgot to scowl. Raised eyebrows instead. "You were captives?"

"Not long, sir. Escaped." Swallow and fast, before her nerve cracked: "Lost Second Scouts Teslin and Barkett."

"We found them. And the rest of the patrol." Rurik bit the words off. His gaze drifted inward for a heartbeat, took his shoulders and chin along with it. A smaller Rurik, worn down by memory. Then he snapped back to now. Drilled his eyes into Dekklis. "How did you survive?"

She told him, low-voiced: about ambush and chains and ghosts, and a half-blood—

"Godsworn," she said, "of Tal'Shik. Leading the Taliri. They called her Ehkla."

The wind pulled hard at the black strands of Rurik's queue. He blinked, finally, when one of them lodged in an eyelash. Shook his head and rubbed an unsteady hand across his face. "I saw the pole. And the marks carved into it. I thought it was Taliri barbarism, and you're saying sacrifice? To." It was bad luck for a man to say her name. Rurik grimaced and spat. "To Tal'Shik?"

"Yes, sir."

"And that it was ghosts of *our* soldiers who killed those Taliri."

"Yes, sir."

K'Hess Rurik stared at her. Shouts all around them, in the courtyard, and no sound at all in this small circle, as quiet as one of Snow's conjurings. Then his face closed like Cardik's gates at dusk. "Did you run from battle, First Scout? Is *that* what you don't want to tell me? Is that why these fantastic tales?"

Dekklis ignored the jab. Ignored the heat crawling up her skin and the cold-punch fury in her chest. Losing temper with this man wouldn't help. "I'm a First Scout. You report these things to the praefecta on my say-so, she'll call you an idiot. I report it to her around you, and she'll think you can't hold a command. In either case, she'll say what you just did: that I ran, and I'm lying to cover. But you know me, sir."

"Mm." Rurik glanced at Istel a second time. Twisted out a grim little smile and brought his stare back to her. "All right. Is there more?"

"Yes." Carefully, hell, as if she had glass in her mouth: "I think that the Taliri have allies among the Illhari. Here, in Cardik."

"Allies."

"Heretics. People who might regret the Purge. In this city. In Illharek, too. I think Davni was a message to those people. And I don't think the praefecta's going to believe that."

"And I will?"

"You saw what happened to Davni. What kind of raiders torch a town and leave the loot? They took nothing, First Spear. *You'll* ask why. I don't think the praefecta will."

"A message. A sacrifice. So *you* say."

"And the survivors? What do *they* say?"

Foremothers, that was too much. Rurik snapped rigid, eyes blazing hot. Drew breath to blast her insubordination. Stopped, his mouth partway open. Steam leaked from between his teeth. Then he clipped them shut. His nostrils pinched. The blaze in his eyes banked back to embers. "Nothing that the praefecta will believe. As you say, First Scout."

She blew a breath out. "Yes, sir."

"You say we have traitors in Cardik. Heretics. We need to find them."

"*Yes*, sir. I have a contact in the Warren who can help."

"A contact." Suspicious, imagining vice and indiscretion. "Who?"

Hell and damn, treading close to another oath, more lately sworn and no less binding, because it, like her first, served Illharek's interests. Give up Snow to this man, she'd lose any hope of finding how far the conspiracy went.

Istel saved her. Angled his shoulder in front of her and said, "Mine, sir. A friend from childhood. Dek can't say who because I haven't told her."

Istel's voice stayed steady. His gaze did, as Rurik looked at him. Unblinking, chin high, eyes locked on his commander's face like they would never dare lock on to Praefecta Stratka's.

*Or on to mine.*

Rurik's scowl relaxed into something closer to neutral. "All right. See your friend. Find out what you can, and report to me. I'll deal with the praefecta."

That was dismissal. Rurik spun and resumed his cross-yard stomp, spattering mud and snowmelt.

"Told you," Istel said, damn near breathless. "*Told* you, Dek, to let me talk to him."

"Yeah. You did."

UnHoused Istel, Cardik-born, who'd never seen Illharek's vaults and spires, who spoke his Dvergiri with a border accent. He had nothing in common with Rurik except being male, and *that* was enough to win trust where rank and blood and reputation wouldn't. Dekklis stared hard at the empty air past Rurik's shoulder. Would not show her irritation, no, would not scowl at the Snowdenaelikk in her head, who smirked and whispered,

*See now, Szanys. Highborn daughter, this is how the Laughing God succeeds.*

"He's a stubborn, motherless—"

"Dek." Istel shrugged. "His mother's exactly his problem. And yours. And Stratka's."

"Meaning what?"

Istel pretended not to hear.

\* \* \*

Snow managed to avoid Tsabrak for nearly a week. Poor luck, *surely*, that every time she tried Janne's tavern, he wasn't there. She knew his patterns, but a man could change those. So she checked, every time. More than once she'd ducked back across Market Bridge, prowling among the stalls, until she was sure Tsabrak had moved on. Then she'd soft-foot up the tavern's back stairs, examine the traps and locks on her flat's door. Collect a few belongings. Slink back down again, bundle in hand, and make a public show of looking for Tsabrak. Then she'd leave another message with Janne.

And collect gossip, too, because she was a good tenant, and Janne liked her better than the rest of Tsabrak's tame rats. Shipments in his storeroom, he told her, crates that were too heavy for Tsabrak's usual contraband. *Weapons,* he whispered, and put his beery face next to hers. Tsabrak was sharing his plans with no one—did *she* know what he was doing?

She didn't, but she could guess. Citizens had a right to bear arms in the city, but *citizen* meant Dvergiri and the rare Alvir who'd taken the oaths and inked proof of allegiance into her skin. Rare, because those oaths weren't cheap. Most residents couldn't afford them. But weapons, now. Those *were* affordable.

But for Janne: wide eyes and *I don't know what he's onto, yeah? You think he tells me?* before she skulked away, pretending disappointment and irritation. *You see him, you tell him I'm looking, yeah?*

She'd gotten most of her belongings down to Still Waters that way, one and two bundles at a time. The herbs and drugs first, because Veiko's leg was still grinning unpleasantly through its stitches. Clothes next, and her scrolls. The pair of leather-bound books she'd taken on permanent, secret loan from the Academy's shelves. This would be her last run: for a pair of pots she hadn't yet missed, having the run of Aneki's kitchens. *That* would change, though, and soon. She couldn't stay in that room with Veiko forever, however much Aneki hinted otherwise. That was a favor that could turn permanent. Already Aneki had Veiko repairing pots and cracked shutters and doors that hung ajar. Cutting wood, too, or hauling it, when Snow wasn't there to stop it. Ask where he'd gotten the splinters in his hands, yeah, and test his honesty.

Or pretend she didn't notice, not splinters or the soaked leather of his boots. Pretend, and pack more moss into the wound, and let him feel as if he wasn't living on kindness, mostly, which was worse for Veiko than any wound rot.

No, she had to see about settling them somewhere else, somewhere other than Aneki's charity. A flat, maybe, in Still Waters, if she could negotiate a price with Aneki, if Veiko would agree to it. Two levels of unpredictable right there, fuck and damn, a woman needed a plan to deal with that, needed to think two and three moves ahead.

So Snow wasn't paying attention, not entirely, as she climbed the weatherworn staircase. Didn't smell the jenja smoke until she got to the top. Her scalp tightened. Prickled counterpoint to the ice-fingers on her spine. Someone was inside her flat—no, not just any someone. Tsabrak, because anyone else would've left marks on door and lock and latch. Tsabrak had a toadfucking key.

And still. She hadn't hit one of the loose boards on the steps. She could turn around and go back the way she'd come, trot across Market and delay a conversation she did not want.

*Coward.*

Tsabrak wasn't a danger to her.

*Sure of that?*

No. She flexed her fingers. She had no proof he'd sided with Ehkla. All he'd asked was a delivery brought back to him from a new courier who just happened to be half-Talir and godsworn. Ehkla'd been the one who wanted a message delivered. Ruined Davni might mean *no deal*, or *we'll destroy Illharek without you.*

Snow had her own messages. Dek had appeared at Still Waters' door with Istel at her shoulder and a report of another ruined village, another column of smoke stabbing into the winter sky. But this time the destruction hadn't been total. A trickle of uncitizen, homeless Alviri had come through Cardik's gates, across Market Bridge and into the Warren, where there was a sudden new crop of contraband weapons.

Dekklis hadn't stopped with bad news, no. *There are new rumors, Snow. Some say there's a dragon setting the fires. Dvergiri witchery.*

The Alviri didn't need encouragement to see superstition. The Republic might have imposed its Purge on them, broken their temples and forbidden their festivals, but it took more than a citizen's sigil to make an Illhari. And most of the Alviri in villages hadn't bothered with citizenship. Held to their old ways, best they could, and hated the Republic. It wasn't hard to see why those refugees might want weapons. It was what they'd *do* with the weapons that worried her. Not likely they'd go marching out and make war on the Taliri. Not with a city full of Illhari right here, and all those old grudges.

She could tell Tsabrak *that* and check his reaction. She didn't think he could lie to her. Knew him too well for that, every twitch and tell he owned. Except she hadn't seen an alliance with Tal'Shik coming.

And he hadn't fucking told her, either.

Laughing God, she wished for Briel, but Briel was back with Veiko, a warm spot of satisfaction in the corner of Snow's skull. Briel liked a roof between her and the weather, liked fires in the hearths. Liked Veiko, let's be honest.

And that was another issue Snow might have with Tsabrak. Veiko had told his own ugly stories, hushed in the bath's hissing steam. Recounted his spirit-walking, yeah, and scared her cold.

*I saw the God in the spirit world. I saw Tal'Shik.*

She didn't like that the God had his attention on Veiko, when Tal'Shik was threat enough. But what Tsabrak would think, what he'd *do*, if he knew that the God was talking to Veiko, she couldn't guess.

*Ask him, yeah? He's in there.*

She summoned witchfire. Spilled it onto the landing and willed it to flow into the cracks around the door, up the frame, around latch and lock. Then she borrowed the shadows it made, and wrapped herself damn near opaque, and tried the handle.

The door swung on oiled silence, trailing witchfire on its edges. Dark, more shadows and a square of dirty grey as the fading afternoon oozed past the open shutter and through the oiled canvas panes. She drew the witchfire back into her palm and raised it like a lantern. Tsabrak sprawled across her ancient couch like a decadent highborn.

Hair loose. Limbs draped *just so,* so that his hands were never far from his knives. He watched her, unmoving, while she shut the door and latched it.

"I wasn't sure you'd survived." Slowly, quietly, as if he'd asked for more wine.

"I left messages. Janne should've told you."

"Janne did. I was beginning to think he was either drunk or lying, how many times he said I'd just missed you."

"He tell you I've got the legion on me?"

"He did. I thought you might hole up somewhere else for a while. But." Tsabrak waved a hand at mostly bare cupboards and an absence of clutter. "I thought you meant to come back."

She shrugged. "So did I. Changed my mind."

She'd taught Tsabrak shadow-weaving in their early days. He was good at it. The shadows dripped and draped and swirled like velvet as he flowed off the couch and glided toward her. Hard to see the man, even with the witchfire cupped and cool in her palm. "I was worried."

"You know me. Hard to kill." She shouldered past him, sent his shadows swirling out of her path. Crossed the room to the cold hearth and crouched beside it. She spilled the witchfire onto cold embers and willed it to a blaze. Bright, but cold. Seemed fitting. She took a lungful of dust and cold ash. "You haven't asked if I found the courier. I'm guessing that means you already know the answer. And I'm guessing that answer has something to do with the crates in Janne's storeroom. Since when do we steal from the legion? You think no one's going to notice a crate of swords gone missing?"

"You're angry."

Snow stared into the witchfire. Thought about Veiko's eyes, and, "You sent me out with an idiot. Drasan damn near got me killed, yeah? The Sixth caught us at Davni, and he wanted to fight. They got him, and now there are soldiers who know what I look like. And your motherless courier was *late,* and she was *sloppy.*" She bit off a mouthful of air. "And then I find you moving on new markets that you haven't told me about. So yes, I'm angry."

"Snow." The old board by the hearth creaked. Tsabrak crouched beside her. Flattened his hand against her back. His thumb stroked a line along her shoulder blade. Moved to the back of her neck. He worked at the thong holding her topknot until her hair slipped loose, fell over ears and neck and his hand. He combed his fingers through it. Took a fistful of her hair and pulled, gently, until her face came around to his. The witchfire limned his features, picking out the fine bones, casting the large eyes into shadow. Easy to get lost in that beauty, yeah, to fall in and drown.

"Tell me about Ehkla, Tsabrak."

He trailed his eyes over her face like fingers. Brow. Nose. Lips. Back to her eyes. "You're not jealous?"

"Tell me."

"You are." Soft laughter. "I didn't think you'd mind."

"Which part? That she burns villages? Or that she's godsworn to Tal'Shik?"

He took his hands off her. "I know what Ehkla is."

"She spiked the First Spear's brother. Carved the pole. Sacrificed him to Tal'Shik in the old ways, Tsabrak, like the Purge never happened. The God approves of that toadshit? *You* do?"

"Don't ask me to mourn for a highborn."

"A fourth son, yeah? You think he has much more choice than you did, what his life's like?"

"Highborn is what *she* required."

"Now you do what *Tal'Shik* says? You switch gods when I wasn't looking?"

His face settled into stillness, darkness, as deep as any cave. "Enough."

Pride, anger, swallow them now. Smooth her voice, soften it. Dekklis would sneer at her for it, playing gentle for a man. But Dekklis wasn't here. Dekklis wouldn't understand you had to come at Tsabrak some way other than headfirst.

"Tsabrak. What *is* all this?"

"The God's plan."

Tsabrak's first and last reason for everything, *the God*. And if she pressed, she'd get *the God spoke to me* or *the God asked it*.

"There's talk among the soldiers that other villages have burned now. That there's a dragon doing it. The God didn't do *that*."

He didn't answer. Didn't have to. *I know* in his eyes and the set of his shoulders. So there was her answer.

Smart to get up and walk out, yeah, collect Veiko and go—fuck and damn, anywhere. *Away*, before whatever connivance Tsabrak was playing at burst like glass in a fire. Except she'd never been smart enough to walk away from Tsabrak, not once, not since he'd staggered out of an alley in Illharek's Suburba and collapsed at her feet. The first of her wounded things.

Ask if she regretted that now.

"You want a sycophant, fine, I'll find you one. But I'm not. You didn't see what she did to that boy. Don't ask me to like this new friend you've got."

"So you've moved across the Bridge and out of the Warren and over to the Street of Silk Curtains in protest."

"You got a tail on me?" That she hadn't noticed, fuck and damn, that Briel hadn't seen either, getting careless and soft and—

"No," he said, and her stomach dropped back where it should be. "A guess."

"So I just told you."

"So you did." A breath, hissed between clenched teeth and back out again. "Still Waters, yeah? Aneki."

Tsabrak would eat live coals before he'd admit fear of any woman. Say what he felt for Aneki was loathing, of the sort cats had for water.

She shrugged. "Yeah. It's safer."

"Than what? No one's followed you into the Warren. No one's followed you across Market the several times you've crossed it. The legion doesn't know where you are. So say what your real reason is."

It occurred to her then that Tsabrak might've had someone down at Still Waters already, whatever he claimed. He knew her habits and haunts as well as she knew his. Could've guessed where she'd bolt. Could've known where she was this whole time, and about Veiko, and waiting to see if she'd lie.

She met his stare and held it. "All right. Besides the soldiers—I brought someone back with me."

"Someone." He forgot his shadows. They dripped away, stripped his face back to bone and skin and beauty. "Who?"

So he hadn't known. Fuck and damn. "Skraeling." She damn near choked on the word. "Barely speaks Dvergiri, yeah? He's the reason I survived out there after Drasan's spectacular error in judgment. I owe him."

"You owe." His left eyebrow quirked. That side of his mouth went with it. "What is this, *you owe?*"

"He got between me and a legion sword. Say they know him now, too, yeah? I let him go, they pick him up, and he dies. And before that, he'll give me up. So."

"So you brought him back to Still Waters. That's clever. Aren't any soldiers down there, yeah?"

"Aneki can hide him. What's one more toadbelly in that place? Besides. This isn't sentiment. You know me." Mix truth with lies, see if it held. Eyes locked and unblinking: "I saw him call up a whole army of ghosts. Command them like a First Spear. We can use that kind of power, if I can get him to teach me."

"Ghosts." Tsabrak leaned forward. Whole new gleam in his garnet-black eyes. "Will he? Can you learn it?"

"It's just conjuring, wrapped up in his people's toadshit superstitions. Got to convince him I believe in it first. The rest will be easy."

"So bring him across into the Warren. I'll find him a safe place."

"I barely got him into Cardik." She shrugged. "He's skittish."

"What is he, a feral cat? Fine." Tsabrak scythed an impatient hand. "Stay with that toadfucking slaver, then, learn what you can from your skraeling." Sly smile, half malice. "Enjoy yourself."

"Big man, this skraeling. Won't be a problem."

He snorted. "Save some energy, yeah? I have work for you. There's new blood in the city. New markets."

"Yeah. About that. Awfully rustic for you, aren't they? And short of silver. And the metal you've got for sale isn't cheap."

"We can make deals. Besides. I think they're angry. And I think there's going to be more of them, very soon."

Fuck and damn. "Yeah? The God tell you that?"

"As a matter—" Tsabrak began. Stopped. His tongue moved slickly behind his lips. Should've been words to go with them, should've been sound, and there was nothing, except her own heartbeat too loud in her ears. Slow build of power over her skin, her scalp, prickling and stinging like the threat of backlash, like the tension before lightning. An echo of power that filled up the room until her skin hurt, until her eyes ached in her skull.

"As a matter of fact, I did," said Tsabrak's mouth, syllables drawn and dropped like pebbles. Not Tsabrak's voice. Not Tsabrak's eyes, licking fire from the sockets.

*Oh Laughing God.*

"Speechless, Snowdenaelikk? That's not like you." The God rearranged Tsabrak's features, eyebrows raised over flame-filled sockets. "I won't hurt him, if that's your worry. And if I did, he'd call it a blessing. A gift. Which is what he will say when he finds out I've been here."

"Will he remember this?"

"What was said and done? No. He isn't here." The God tapped Tsabrak's temple. "You and me, Snowdenaelikk, all alone."

She cut a glance sidelong, measured the distance between hearth and door. That was a habit Tsabrak had taught her early on. Know your exits. Never get too far away from one. Hell of a time to forget that. But then, not like she could stop the God if he chose to burn Tsabrak into ashes or melt her where she sat.

And the God knew it. Smirked with Tsabrak's mouth, tight and feral. "I won't take much of your time."

Mocking her, yeah. Enjoying her fear. That was the God she knew. Mercurial. A little cruel. Not inclined to social calls.

"What do you want, then?"

The God laughed. Tiny blisters sprang up on Tsabrak's cheeks. Burst and ran like tears. "Your skraeling asked that same thing, in much the same tone. I am pleased that he found his way back to you."

"So am I."

"He refused my help. I might call that ungrateful. But then." Tsabrak's eyelids drooped red and glowing, so that Snow could count the veins. "It wasn't his prayer I answered, finding him. It was yours."

Fuck and damn, she saw the way this river ran: straight over a cliff onto rocks. "I'm grateful."

"Good. I trust that you are. Tell me about your Veiko. What he can do."

"I already told Tsabrak—"

"I heard what you said." The God tapped Tsabrak's temple again. "He believes you. Trusts you. Relies on you, yeah?"

"I know."

"He hates you for that. You know that, too?"

"Guessed it." Tsabrak had never been safe. Not his friendship, not his temper. Certainly not his affection. "So what?"

"So if he finds out you lied to him, he might be disappointed. I don't think you have any intention of learning how to command ghosts. I don't think you can. I think you already know that."

"I can handle Tsabrak's disappointment."

The God nodded. "Maybe. Still. I find myself needing your skraeling's skills. I need them directly. I need them reliably."

Ask why, and look into firepit eyes, and have a heartbeat's pity for the God's enemies. "And you're coming to me for what, exactly? Veiko already told you no."

The God thrust his hand out, faster than Tsabrak could have moved. Clamped fingers around her wrist. Somewhere in the back of her skull, Briel thrashed and panicked. And then didn't, suddenly. Silence inside and out, and only the God for company.

Flames licked between Tsabrak's eyelids. "Be wise," he said softly.

She rolled her wrist in the God's grip. She might beat Tsabrak in a fight. But the God *in* Tsabrak's skin, she'd end up grease and ashes. She licked her lip. "Veiko works on debt. You've got nothing he needs, so he won't bargain with you."

Embers now, in the sockets. Discomfort now, where he touched her, spiraling to pain. "Perhaps I can find something he wants, then."

Snow made a fist of her trapped hand. Met that eyeless stare. "Threaten me, hurt me—that won't get you what you want. It's not like that between us. You may've found Veiko, on my asking. But you didn't bring him back. He thinks I did. *My* skills. So maybe Veiko owes me for his life, and I owe you for finding him, and that's how we work this out. Yeah?"

A smile slashed across Tsabrak's lips, sly and feral. Snow smelled her own skin now, heard the sizzle.

"All right, Snowdenaelikk. Let's hear your terms."

# CHAPTER FIFTEEN

Veiko tipped his face skyward. Fitful flakes scraped out of frigid clouds stung where they struck him. It should be luminous grey overhead, snow-dim twilight. But there were witchfires on the Street of Silk Curtains, throwing bruise-colored shadows. Lanterns in the alley, their glow oozing across slick-dark cobbles. An extravagance of candles in Still Waters, melting in their sconces and leaking light around the edge of door and window and curtain, cutting a bright wedge from the open back door. Aneki's shadow stretched long on the margin. The lightspill made an uneven shape on the snow, spangled by snowfall.

He reckoned the snow wouldn't last. The clouds would split, around moonrise, and the air would turn bitter. Not a night for outdoors. Not a night to

*limp*

pace the perimeter of Still Waters' courtyard, Logi beside him, waiting for a woman who—

"—won't thank you for this," Aneki said. "She's fine, yeah? No cutpurse would touch her. You get sick out here, or start yourself bleeding, she'll—"

"No," he said, only that. He did not want to say why there was a good chance Snowdenaelikk was not all right. Did not know if Aneki would understand why it mattered that Briel had thrown herself at the latched window just past dusk. She had flapped and clawed and keened until he opened it. And then he'd retched and dry-heaved after, echoes of the svartjagr's fear.

And now the spirit world lurked at the borders of his awareness like a starving wolf. He blinked and saw glacier on the back of his eyelids instead of honest black. That was not right, either. It had started after Briel's panic. As Snow would say, fuck and damn if that was coincidence.

Veiko paused, for the twentieth time, at the gate. Looked back at Aneki's cross-armed silhouette in the doorway.

"This Tsabrak."

"Him. Motherless toadfucker. Skin his own sister if the God told him to. If she's with him, you're wearing a path in the garden for nothing."

It was a recurring thing, Veiko decided. Half-blood Dvergiri said a great deal, very quickly, and only a very little bit made any sense. He traced the iron bars, sharp with frost. Thought about his axe, back in the room. About the stretch of corridor between here and there. About the cobbles outside, and endless buildings, and no landmarks he understood.

"Can you take me there?"

"To Tsabrak? Oh no." Aneki made a noise in her throat. Her hair, in the lamplight, was the color of old teeth. "He'd gut you."

Her certainty rankled. He was grateful for the cold and the darkness. Imagined the snow hissing to steam on his skin. "He would have no reason to attack me."

"He doesn't need a reason. He's Tsabrak."

"Will he hurt her?"

"Snow? He might try. Doubt he'd get far." A snort. "She can care for herself, Veiko."

Clearest memory: Snow slicing at him with that seax, the thud of black metal into the handle of his axe. He hadn't understood Briel's sending, had only seen a woman blind and, therefore, he had thought, helpless. But he had seen how fast she could move, and where she might've cut him, sighted or not, if he hadn't been ready.

Laughter ricocheted off his skull, off the flat walls, off the glacier and the sky. He saw a man's face, flames where his eyes should be.

*Think she owes you for her life, skraeling? Think she'll ever pay you back?*

Aneki moved in the doorway. Came two steps out into the snow. "Veiko? You all right?"

He was not. He was slipping. Holding tight to the gate and the bars. He would not ask what the God wanted with him, would not acknowledge, would not invite. A noidghe never allowed himself to be summoned.

*You are no noidghe.*

"I am," he said, under his breath. And louder, to Aneki: "Fine. I will wait." *Here,* he added, to the God and the glacier. *Here. In my flesh.*

Aneki said something that was lost beneath another hiss of laughter.

"—listening to me?"

"No," to her and the God. But the God left him then. The glacier slipped away.

Left a new wide bar of light in the yard, and no silhouette, and, "Well, that's honest," a sudden arm's length off his shoulder.

He spun, too fast for his leg. Almost toppled into the snow. Caught himself on the gate and hung there while Aneki tucked a hand under his elbow. She leaned close, so that the curve of her breast pressed his arm.

"I said come back inside. Wait in the kitchen. I'll have Esa watch for her. No sense in freezing out here yourself, yeah?"

He knew what *brothel* meant now, and what it was that Aneki sold here. What she was offering now. Her fingers were warm. Her perfume tasted like sweet oil in the back of his throat.

"I will wait here."

"Veiko." Mixed impatience and sympathy spilled out of her. "They go way back, her and Tsabrak. Came out of Illharek together, them and some others. Built the cartel here, between them; she's his right hand and more besides. She'll be *late*, she's with him. You savvy?"

"Yes. And I will wait here." The word did not wholly describe the tapestry of debt and loyalty and little kindnesses between them, but, "She is my partner."

Sudden hardness in Aneki's voice. "That what she calls you? Partner?"

He blinked at the force, and the anger. "It is what we are."

"Listen. Tsabrak's an old—not friend, I don't think he knows what that word means—habit with her. He says *jump*, she does it. He says *kill*, she does it. And they're lovers, Veiko. You won't get between them, whatever she says about partners."

He looked at her. She was Snowdenaelikk's associate, yes, and his host, *yes*, and those things alone made him reclaim his arm with some degree of civility. "She is my partner," he repeated. "And I will wait."

Aneki let him keep the last word, which he had not expected. Crackling quiet, in the look she gave him. Then she turned and left him at the gate. The door thumped and took the light with it. Silence pooled in the courtyard, and darkness, and cold.

Logi *oofed* and leaned against his thigh. Veiko trailed his fingers through the winter-stiff fur. He had not seen Helgi on the glacier. *That* was a sign. Only a fool wandered that place with no guide. He'd learned that much. Learned not to doubt Snowdenaelikk, either, whatever Aneki thought. Sooner doubt the sun's rising, or winter's cold.

*Idiot, yeah?* Exactly what she'd say to him, wielding that half-twist smile. His own mouth hitched at the corner. Hung there, like thread caught on a nail. She could care for herself. Aneki had been right about that much. About Tsabrak, well. Veiko did not know the man. Thought maybe it was best that he didn't.

Another *oof.* Logi cocked his ears and straightened. Veiko saw her then, gliding through the alley, caught in the crevice between pavement and buildings. Heard her when he held his breath. Just a whisper, boots and cloak, just the faintest *chink* of metal.

Witchfire flared and wrapped like a vine around the bars. It picked out the edges of nose and cheekbone. Caught the gleam of her eyes and settled there, bright blue on darker.

"The motherless hell are you doing out here." Not even a question, no, too weary for that.

"It is a good night for walking." He unlatched the gate. Stepped aside and let her through while Logi danced his paws and whined a greeting and did not, miracle of discipline, leap at her.

"Toadshit." She fumbled the latch, gloveless and awkward with the sack across her shoulders. She dumped it onto the cobbles. Rattle and clink as it landed. Pots, Veiko recalled. She'd gone back for cooking pots.

"Briel," he said as she tugged at the latch.

"She's hunting."

"Toadshit," he said clearly.

That won a grim little smile from her. "It's where she is now, yeah? She'll be back. She's all right. I'm all right."

"Tsabrak," he began, and stopped when she looked at him. Eyes cold and empty as caves. Angry, he realized. No. Furious.

"What about him?"

*Did he hurt you* shriveled on his tongue. He did not want to insult her. She did not need his protection. Whatever had upset Briel, Snow was alive on this end of it. That was obvious.

"Aneki," she said to his silence. "Motherless gossip. What did she say?"

"That you are lovers. That he would not hurt you. That he would gut me."

"She's wrong." Silent about which. She scooped up the strap again. Slung it onto her shoulder and settled it and hissed, sudden and sharp. Made a fist of that hand and dropped the sack and sent Logi skittering sideways. Abused metal echoed off the walls.

Veiko ignored the sack and the strap. Took her hand instead, far more carefully. Turned it over. There were finger-shaped burns on her wrist, livid even in the lamplight and witchfire. Whitish blisters torn red and oozing.

"What is this?"

She hitched him a smile's poor cousin. "Inside, yeah? You and me. Need to talk."

She didn't wait for his answer. Flexed her hand loose and reached for the sack. Scooped it up and shouldered past to the door. Left it open behind her, so that he must pause to latch and lock it as snow collected in swirls on the lintel.

He followed her back to their room. He shut their door behind her, too, and rested a moment after, forehead and his palms flat on the wood. The ghost roads' glacier spread out behind his eyes. Invitation. Temptation, to find the God and

*get yourself killed, yeah?*

ask questions.

He turned his back on it. Sank into the dark instead, into the ache and breath of his body. Listened. A dog's paws on stone, and the thump as Logi settled. Muffled scraping of boots across the small woven rug. A rush of heat against his back as she opened the firedog's hatch. Wet dog smell, wet wool. The murmur of clothes coming off: slap and squeak of wet boots. Leather whisper, linen sigh.

He opened his eyes again. She'd abandoned the sack just past the threshold. The canvas had settled around its contents like hide over the bones of a strange animal. Blackened iron peeked out, ate the light, and spat it back dull and blue. The pots.

Splashing from the basin, and Snow's brisk, "How long were you out there? Since Briel?"

"Yes."

"How bad is the leg?"

"It is no worse than usual." Sharp herbal smell now, to keep company with smoke and wet dog, and the quiet grind of a mortar and pestle. He did not need a poultice. Turned around to tell her so, with a hand on the door for balance. Heat crawled up his face that had nothing to do with the hearth or the blood pricking under chilled skin.

She was sitting on the hearth, naked to her hips. The pestle's white stone glowed pink in the firelight. There was a puddle of grey and sharp shadow beside her boots, where the light didn't quite reach. Her shirt, he guessed, and her undershift, and the sweater she wore over the shaped leather vest. Her seax lay propped on the hearth, belt and scabbard.

She had the blade's same hard, narrow grace. He'd stared, the first time he saw her naked, before he'd made his grim peace with Illhari modesty. She hadn't laughed when she caught him, although he thought she had wanted to.

*Laughing God, Veiko, am I that different than any other woman?*

Yes, though he had not said it. Not in shape, but in her utter unconcern in her nakedness, as if she was unaware what a

*skraeling*

*outlaw*

stranger might do to her.

*She can care for herself, yeah?*

Except. His eyes caught on the ruin of her wrist. There was another burn on her shoulder, the size and shape of a mouth. A handprint, blisters that were still solid bubbles, on her ribs. Veiko found himself staring again, and this time the ache in his belly had nothing to do with a naked woman.

Snow cut him a smile that tried and failed at casual. "Need some help with bandaging, yeah? You mind?"

He walked over and sat carefully on the hearth, where the firedog's heat was almost painful after the soaked cold of his waiting. She set the mortar between them. Pale pulp in it, mixed with chunks of dark green and a distinct minty bite.

She twisted her wrist. Offered it to him. "Start with this."

"How?"

"Put a little on your fingers, and—"

"Tell me."

She sighed. "It wasn't Tsabrak."

"Who, then?"

"The God. He borrowed Tsabrak's skin. It's a blessing, yeah? A sign of the God's favor, that he chooses you."

Veiko frowned at her. Some noidghe could sing a spirit into their own bodies, so that their mouths spoke in the spirit's voice. But spirits did not take bodies unbidden, by any stories Veiko knew. Unless those spirits were Illhari gods. Unsettling.

"Would he have agreed to *this*?"

"No. I don't know." Deep, shuddering breaths that had to hurt, stretching raw skin. "He bolted when the God left him. When he saw." She stopped. Swallowed. "Just get on with it, yeah? It's all right. You're not going to hurt me any more than's already done."

He nodded. Took a grim lock on her forearm and dipped his fingers into the paste. Cool, thick, yellowy brown. He smeared it on. Braced against her recoil and got only a shiver. She held still while he moved on to her shoulder, where the burn wept clear fluid. He traced the edges of it. Imagined what the God had done to make the wound, and then wished he hadn't.

Better to know, if she would tell him. "What happened?"

She stared hard at the stones on the hearth. "We—Tsabrak and I—were talking about you, yeah? And the God decided he had something to say. You got his attention, yeah? Impressed him."

"How?"

"Avoided rape and murder."

He had not told her all those details. Flushed now, imagining the God's account. "I was fortunate."

"Luck doesn't turn Tal'Shik. How did you do it?"

"I am a noidghe." It felt like fraud to say it, with everything he didn't know: the songs and the true names of things, how to take himself to the grey world by will and choice, how to beat the spirit drum to send another across. Noidghe wasn't something he'd ever wanted. But *want* didn't govern a man's life. Choices did. And his choices had brought him here, sharing a hearth in an Illhari brothel with the woman

*partner*

who'd called him back from death.

"Noidghe." She tried out the unfamiliar word. "That why you can talk to ghosts? Make deals with them?"

"Yes."

"Well. That's what the God wants from you. You can be *his* noidghe."

"Why does he not ask me, then?"

"I talked him out of it. Said you wouldn't deal with him. And he thinks I owe him. The Illhari never bargained with their gods, yeah? They prayed. The God's followers *still* pray. We *ask*. And we're supposed to be damn grateful whenever our prayers are answered. You're alive."

"That is not his doing."

"I know. He knows. But the God *found* you, and that's half what I asked. So I owe him."

"I told him I would pay your debt."

Headshake, so that the rings in her ear flashed and clicked. "You need to watch what you say, yeah?"

Which stung, coming from her. He opened his mouth to tell her so. Clipped it shut again.

"He could try and claim that debt from me."

"He will if I don't pay it." She hissed. Braced her arm against the hearth, which exposed a long chain of blisters that wrapped farther down and around her than he had thought, all the way to the hollow under her ribs, and the soft skin above her hipbone. He wondered how far the burns went. Asked instead,

"And this is his idea of persuasion?"

"This is punishment." Her mouth knotted up at the corner. "I argued with him. Besides. He reckons hurting me will make you jump the way he wants. He's got a different idea what's between us, yeah?"

"What idea?"

"Lovers."

"Ah." He had been, with Kaari's daughter. He wondered how she might've answered had he asked her to go with him into outlawry. He hadn't thought to ask. They had not been partners. "How would doing *this* to you inspire my cooperation?"

"Because if I—we—don't do what he wants, he'll do it again. Maybe worse, next time. Wait, stop." She shuddered away from him as he reached for a blister at the top of her hip. Took his wrist. Her hand shook, tremors he could see working up her arm and all through her. "That's good," she said hoarsely. "That's enough. Thank you."

Veiko made a fist of his empty hand. "What does he want?"

"For me to kill Ehkla. For you to kill Tal'Shik." She let him go, squared to face him. "How much you know about Illhari history?"

"That your people are very efficient at building roads."

Whole lakes would freeze at that look. "Tal'Shik's godsworn don't die easy. Archives are full of stories. She doesn't like to lose, yeah? But if you slow Tal'Shik down, you hurt her, you buy me space to kill Ehkla. So then Tal'Shik will kill you, but that's *fine*, yeah? The God won't mind that. He doesn't expect you to win." Snow leveled a blind stare into the fire. "Here's my advice: you take Logi and get out of Cardik. Safer out there in the forest, even with Ehkla roaming around."

Safer, perhaps. But the life of an outlaw meant solitude and exile. Meant the company of dogs, so that sometimes he forgot to speak for days at a time. Meant loneliness, which ached worse than a week of poor hunting in his belly. He wouldn't go back to that. Would not leave *her*, however short that might make his life, because,

"If I leave, then the God will kill you."

"More than likely, whether or not you stay."

"I have only one dog now," he said. "It would be difficult to hunt enough surplus to trade. It will be *more* difficult, if the villages are worrying about raiders, for me to trade at all. Nor am I certain I am strong enough—"

"It's not a toadfucking *joke*, Veiko."

"I know that." Ancestors, did he know. He remembered

*dying*

the wurm's tooth deep in his leg, and the marks carved on him. The power that had held him, helpless. The power that had forced answers from him. He had thought then that it was witchery, Ehkla's own strength. But perhaps she had borrowed it from Tal'Shik. He rubbed his thigh where she'd cut him, traced the familiar pattern.

Snow hissed like a boiled cat and swatted his hand away. "*Don't.* Let me tell you something else. Conjuring's about changing things, yeah? Working with what's already there. It's about patterns. Taking one thing and *making* it something else. The shapes your hands make, when you're conjuring. The patterns of the glyphs you cut to make wards so the power stays in the shape. Like this." She showed him the godmark on her palm. "Like the mark Ehkla's got, too. But for godmagic, real godmagic, the power's in cutting the pattern, not in the mark left behind. So every time you trace that, you carve its pattern—its power—into you. Leave it alone."

Veiko eyed his leg warily. Power in *symbols*. Symbols that meant names. Noidghe—real noidghe, not accidental noidghe whose knowledge came from fireside tales—had songs to describe the essence of things. Animals. Plants. *Patterns*, maybe, in the way Snow described them. But no gestures. No shapes any fool with a knife could duplicate. The Alviri and the Dvergiri put so much stock in symbols. In writing. A dozen Ehklas, all armed with knives and carving symbols—what chaos could *they* cause? Small wonder there had been witch-wars.

But still. To meddle with a Dvergir god, a man had to use Dvergiri weapons. Those symbols, those *prayers*, would be a way to call Tal'Shik. But he would need to learn them. To see them. No *living* person he knew bore those marks whole and complete. He would have to learn them using the only noidghe skill he had, which was bargaining with the dead. Which meant he had to get back to the ghost roads and find a particular ghost and ask favors.

"Veiko." Snow was looking at him, narrow-eyed. "You're thinking. Do I want to know what?"

"I am considering how to kill a god."

"Fuck and damn. *Can* you? Is it even possible?"

"If it is, I will do it." Almost an oath, that. Certainly a promise. And then a second, because the smells of sweat and medicine and pain in this room were hers, and not his: "And if one god can die, then so can another."

She winced. "Fool, Veiko. That's what you are."

"So my father said."

"And your mother?"

He almost smiled. "She was too wise to argue with him."

* * *

Snow took a breath, held it, slid hip deep into the water. The tub's stone rim pressed a line across her back, unpleasant on the knobs of her spine, agony on her burns. Veiko wouldn't thank her for undoing some of his handiwork, but she needed the bath. Needed to wash away what had happened, as much as water could. She closed her eyes and emptied her lungs, very slowly, as the hot water cooked the ache between her legs to numb. Raw flesh there, but not burned. The God had wanted to hurt and humiliate, not kill.

Maybe smarter if he had. He'd reckoned to teach Veiko a lesson. Do what you're told, or she suffers. Veiko, being Veiko, had learned something else entirely.

*If one god can die, then so can another.*

She'd left him back in their room, eyes flat and distant. Same look he'd worn before he went off to play decoy for Teslin and Barkett out in the forest, before he'd damn near got himself killed. That was a man making plans. So now Veiko would try to kill Tal'Shik for her sake, and die over in the ghost roads where Snow couldn't get him back, before he ever got a chance to go after the Laughing God.

And meanwhile she would kill Ehkla or die trying, and Tsabrak would—fuck and damn if she knew. Tsabrak had gotten his body back while it was still inside hers. Pulled out like *she'd* scalded *him* and retreated, first across the couch, then the room. Shock on his face, maybe horror. He hadn't said anything. Not *I'm sorry* or *the God has his reasons* or *it's the God's will.* He'd just left her there, to gather the shreds of her composure. To limp back here, all the way across the motherless Bridge, because where else could she go now, except back to Veiko.

The hot rock in her belly kept getting bigger, until her ribs and chest hurt with it. Until her eyes stung and smarted and she had to close them. Tsabrak met her on the backside of closed lids. She pressed the pads of her fingers against her eyes until he dissolved in sparks and flashes.

Always knew where his allegiance sat, hadn't she? Godsworn fanatic, however cool he played when he did business. Smuggling was one thing, yeah, but *heretic* set a man against all of Illharek, highborn and Senate and legion. And *heretic* sounded just fine to a woman who already knew that she didn't have the talent to make up for blue eyes and fair hair, who shared his hatred for all things highborn. They weren't friends, weren't partners, however often they fucked—but she'd assumed some thread of loyalty from him.

*Fool, yeah? Not Veiko. You.*

Aneki had warned her. Fuck and damn, even Dekklis had known better. Tsabrak was the God's, first and finally, and the God did not love women.

The God still had use for her, clearly, and use for Veiko, but useful and valued weren't the same thing. She could've stayed in the Academy and been *useful*. Ground powders and distilled potions and mopped blood and boiled scalpels for someone whose mother had a House name, whose mother *didn't* run an apothecary in Illharek's Suburba.

She wasn't done with Tsabrak, or the God. That was the toadshit part of it. She couldn't be. Had to play along with the game. Wait. Slide herself back into the cartel, into whatever plans Tsabrak had for those crates of weapons. Veiko needed time to heal. She did. Give it a month. That should get Veiko walking. Give her time to figure out what she was going to do about Ehkla. And then, after that, she would—

Fuck and damn, what, put a knife through Tsabrak's eye?

A draft stirred the curtain, smelling faintly of familiar incense. Snow gathered the room's shadows around her, covered the burns and the slick shine of salve. She didn't want conversation. Didn't want company.

Aneki wasn't asking. She tugged the curtain aside. Steam rolled off the bath like fog off the river. Settled again as Aneki twitched the curtain shut. No paint on her face, this time of morning, and every line showing.

Anger, Snow noted with some surprise, real anger that squeezed down to a near-svartjagr hiss. "What are you playing at, Snow?"

Snow slapped a spray of water over the shadows, drops glittering like snowflakes in lamplight. The shadows swallowed their descent. Plink and splash as they landed, invisible.

"Soaking my feet. Got a little cold on the walk back. Might have a hole in one of my boots."

Another hiss. "I mean with Veiko."

"Veiko?"

"You know. Tall, fair, skraeling? Paced around the courtyard all night waiting for you?"

"Aneki," softly and all edges. "What's this about?"

"You might want to tell him what *partner* means. Translate it into skraeling. I think he's got the wrong idea."

"The wrong idea? What the—oh. I *see*. He wouldn't bed you." Snow's aggravation misted away in the steam. "Listen. That's not my doing. His people have different customs. He calls it modesty—"

"He asked about Tsabrak."

The anger came back, hot and too big for her lungs. "I know. Do I need to ask what you told him? Or can I guess?"

"Truth."

"Ah. Truth. So, you have Tsabrak eating babies yet? Or just kittens? Or did you stop at saying I fuck him, and figure jealousy would get Veiko in your bed?"

"Tsabrak's a—"

"I know what Tsabrak is. Better than you, yeah?"

Snow pushed her hand under the skin of the water. Let Aneki see. Let her understand. Snow banished the shadows to the corners of the room, to the space under the bench. Banished them under the water, turning it mirror black, so that her own face rippled up back at her through the steam. So that she didn't have to see Aneki react when the lantern spilled across her bare torso.

Heard her, though: another hiss, this one all shock, and a chain of profanity that ended with, "Did Tsabrak do that?"

"No. You think I'd let him?"

Aneki's face said she thought exactly that. Aneki's mouth, for once, was wise enough to stay closed. She came around the tub in a swirl of silk and incense. Touched Snow's shoulder almost as gently as Veiko had.

"You want to say what happened?"

Snow's throat sealed up. She shook her head. Gagged and choked and pushed Aneki's hands away. "It was the God."

Utter quiet from Aneki, for long enough Snow cranked her neck around to look at her. The moment Snow's gaze touched hers, Aneki blurted, "But why?"

"Veiko asked the same thing. Say it's the price for disobedience."

Aneki squatted beside her. Her skirt dusted the water's surface. Darkened and sank, while Aneki didn't appear to notice. "I had a mistress like that once. Thing was, I wore a collar."

"Meaning?"

"Meaning, you're freeborn. And you're not godsworn. You can walk away."

"*Can* I?"

"You're a master chirurgeon, yeah? You're Academy."

"You think that's worth shit? Listen. You know why I left Illharek? Not because Tsabrak asked me to go. Because of Briel. Some third son of some toadshit senator carved her up for a project. See what makes her wings work, he said. She was, oh, *this* big. He did it because he could, yeah? Because she had less power than he did, and he'd been shat on his whole life by his sisters, and his mother, and everyone. So I get this mutilated hatchling, and I make her *my* project, yeah? He had her flayed to fucking bone, and I got her back flying." Snow gathered her hair into a topknot and twisted it up, so that Aneki could see her ear. "I got the master's ring. But you want to guess who got the honors? Who got the motherless *teaching post*? Not the Suburban half-blood."

Aneki grimaced. "Snow. I get why you linked up with Tsabrak. I do. But there are other ways to hit back at the highborn besides *him* and his toadshit God."

"Yeah. I know. And you picked the best way to do it. I know that, too."

"Not the best. Just the best one available to me." Aneki shrugged. Scrunched into a crouch at the edge of the bath, arms around her knees. "Best would've been to walk away from it. Open a tavern, maybe, near the garrison. Water the ale, scorch the flatcakes, serve the chicken bloody."

"Be a toadshit tavern, then."

"Yes. Instead I run a good brothel. Now they pay for what they used to take. But you've got more options than I do."

"Had."

"Toadshit. Walk out the gates, yeah? Take Veiko and leave. The Republic's got other cities. There's always work for what you do."

Echoes of what she'd said to Veiko. Echoes of his answer. The irony tasted like blood. "I walk out now, they'll come after me. All the Tsabraks and Drasans. The God will make it his business to find me, and he has a lot of fingers."

"Mm." A feather touch on her shoulder. "You're not afraid for your sake."

"I'm not—listen. Veiko's people. They bargain with spirits, yeah? That's what the gods are to him. Spirits. Just like, ghosts and animals and whatever else. Veiko made some half-assed promise to the God that the God will happily collect, until and unless I do what the God wants. Don't even ask what, yeah?"

"Think I can't guess? I know you." A pause. A breath. "You could let him have Veiko."

"You come in here spitting mad about partners, and you say that?"

"I've known you a long time."

"*Thanks.*"

"Snow. You just met him how many weeks ago? Partners? What does that even mean?"

"He could have let me die out there, and he didn't. Got between me and the legion. Came back for me when the Taliri got me. That's how he got cut, yeah? That's how he almost died. And just now I told him *go*, and he won't."

"So he's loyal. You want that, you have Briel."

"It's not just that. He's—" The only person she knew who didn't see half-blood, or woman, or not-quite-good-enough when he looked at her. He only saw *her*. Whatever she meant to him. Whatever made a man take on Taliri and bargain with ghosts. Unique in all her experience, Veiko Nyrikki, and precious because of it.

Stop. Swallow. Try again. "He's my partner, yeah?"

Aneki grimaced. "So what will you do?"

"Hope I think of something clever before some godsworn kills me. Ask you for another favor. Maybe two. First one, the big one: we need somewhere else to stay. I know you've had Veiko crippling himself going up and down the stairs to repair the second-floor shutters. I know there's an empty flat. Let us have that."

"Right." Aneki sighed. "For how long?"

"Until he's healed. Until I figure what Tsabrak's doing over there in the Warren. Until that highborn soldier and I figure out what to do about it."

"And then what? You stop Tsabrak? Or the God? Or *both* of them?" Aneki shook her head. "You go off and get killed, how will you pay me back?"

"Ask Veiko. He talks to ghosts."

# PART THREE

# CHAPTER SIXTEEN

Snow was still out when Veiko returned from the grey world. He knew that from the silence in the room, and the peculiar empty of the flat without her. A man grew accustomed to that. She spent most afternoons out on the God's business. On *Tsabrak's* business, as if the burns hadn't happened, as if there weren't scars on her skin and deeper, too, that woke her up in the night. Whenever she had to see Tsabrak himself and talk to him. Then she dreamed.

A man might ignore that, for her pride's sake. A partner could not. A *partner* got up and went to her when she woke and touched her as much as she could tolerate, so that she knew she was not alone. And he asked, every time:

*How long will you do this?*

And every time, she told him:

*Until you're healed. Until we're ready for Tal'Shik. Until Ehkla gets to Cardik.*

He was healed enough, anyway. Most of a month since Ehkla had marked him. He had only needles in his thigh now. A tightness in his knee beneath the bone. No great matter, and until today, the only progress they could mark. They still did not know Ehkla's whereabouts, though Dekklis and Istel brought regular word from the garrison. Another village burned. Another flux of dispossessed Alviri through city gates. Getting closer, Dekklis said. The toadshit Taliri, working their way to Cardik's gates one gutted village at a time. The praefecta wouldn't authorize more patrols. A few villages was the price of raiding season.

Veiko sat up and blinked at the sunlight knifing through the dust. Aneki had, the morning after the God's attack, moved them up here to the residents' wing, onto wooden floors that creaked and groaned when he limped across them. The windows had shutters that did little to keep out wind or chill or svartjagr.

*They might if you closed them, yeah?*

Which he would not. He claimed it was for Briel's sake, but it was as much for his own. He needed the open air. The wind coming off the mountains. The illusion, if he only looked up, that there weren't walls around him.

Veiko levered upright, scooping one hand out to retrieve the cup on the floor beside the pallet. Stared at his knuckles while his body remembered how to wear bone and skin. A noidghe must loosen his grip on his own flesh to walk with the spirits. Easy enough if a body were weak or sick, if there were an apprentice to beat a spirit drum. Veiko had neither apprentice nor drum, weakness nor sickness. But there were other ways to loosen his spirit's hold on his flesh, and his partner knew herbcraft.

*Call it poison, yeah? Dekklis does.*

The remainder of Snow's potion clung to the sides and pooled at the bottom of the cup, skinned over and curling up at the edges. The smell made his stomach knot up in protest. They had tried more than a dozen before settling on this one. Its advantage was digestibility, which made the headache afterward a small price. The rest of Snow's attempts had come out either as fast as they'd gone down, or later and with greater vengeance.

*Going to kill you one of these tries,* Snow had said grimly.

*You will not.* And once, only once: *And if you do, you can call me back. You have that power.*

He had hoped for that crooked smile. He'd gotten a scowl instead, the whole width of her lips drawn up and tight. *You want to say why it's so damn important you keep getting back to the ghost roads? What's worth this risk?*

*Your life,* he had not said, which was one truth. He gave her another: *The ghosts have advice about Tal'Shik. I am learning.*

And he was ready, now and finally.

Veiko crossed to the window and braced both arms on the sill. Closed his eyes and reached and found Briel half-blind in the glare off the snow. Higher than she liked to be

*exposed*

above the streets. Circling on the perpetual breeze cutting down off the mountains, over the S'Ranna as it ran through Cardik. It looked more like a ribbon from Briel's vantage, one more source of silverglare in the sunlight. Patches of tile and thatch below her that Veiko knew were rooftops. Bright paint on the walls in designs that must be pleasing to the Illhari and looked garish to him. More people than Veiko had seen his whole life, making noise and stench that would shame all the herds of takin in the world. And the Bridge, *the* Bridge, the one wide as an Illhari road, arched stone and lipped with wooden planks. It might've been another street, except for the river cutting under it. Tents and kiosks lined its edges, vendors selling cooked meat that Briel wanted, badly. Her gaze kept snapping back toward it, dizzying shift that took his stomach with her every time.

A svartjagr's vantage was nothing like a man's, but it was better than Aneki's descriptions of Cardik, or Snow's idea of maps.

*The S'Ranna divides Cardik,* she said as she arranged cutlery and fruit on the table. *That's this knife. This, here, this spoon: that's Market Bridge. It connects both halves of Cardik. On* this *side, we've got the governor's mansion up here, and the garrison right under that. Down by*

*Market—this pip—that's Still Waters. The brothels stay on this side of the river. On the other side—*and here she set an apple on one side of the knife—*we've got the Warren. That's where the tanneries and the abattoirs are, things that offend highborn noses. And that's where people who can't afford the Hill, or don't want highborn neighbors, live. So, Alviri. Cartels. Refugees. And me once.*

But not all refugees. There had been a sudden surge of Alviri in Aneki's halls, all whispers and weeping. Bright new collars. Eyes pale as his own staring back out of faces nearly as white. Winter-gaunt and flinching at shadows, all of them, women and girls and boys. *Refugee* meant *desperation*, Veiko decided.

Briel changed angles. Leveled her wings and dove, dizzy-fast, so that Veiko held his breath and locked his teeth. She dipped low over tile and thatch until she found a ledge and beat her wings and stopped. And crawled, after, up the wall and onto a sloped tile roof. Warm on her belly, rough under claw and foot. She wedged herself under the eaves and snaked her neck around and settled. Satisfaction, warm as the tiles, when she got into the shadow.

Veiko took his eyes back and looked down into the courtyard. A man's legs would break if he fell from this height. A dog would not survive. He did not like it, that he could not get out of this place except through the door, and down the stairs, and across that patch of grass and gravel. But it was no worse than a tiny cave, was it, and larger than any other space he'd shared with Snow so far. She had the bed, and he had a pallet, with the firedog and hearth between them. And Snow had put her own locks on the door and given him one of two keys that he wore on a thong now around his neck, beneath his clothes where Aneki would not see it. Snow had traced glowing shapes on the steel, too, that faded like cooling embers.

*Wards, yeah? Someone tries to force the door, they'll regret it.*

He reckoned that a possibility in this place. In a crofter's hut, there were brothers and their wives and parents in residence, and only curtains between them. A man learned to ignore what wasn't his business. But Aneki's residents had no such restraint. Stares and whispers whenever he passed through the halls, and this woman or that man or any combination of them might happen to want their bath the same time that he did, in the same chamber and pool.

*They're curious,* Aneki told him. *No harm, yeah?*

He hadn't understood at first, until Snow explained. *Curious, sure. And they're making an offer.* And added, unsmiling, *It's safe enough, if you want it. Your choice, Veiko.*

Safe, perhaps, but not wise. It was one thing to take a girl out onto the tundra and know that she and her sisters would whisper about it later. It was quite another to have the entire village discussing his technique and measuring his worth accordingly. Aneki had made no further advances, but her people had. Any indulgence of curiosity would be in her ears by morning, and all over Still Waters by breakfast.

Logi watched him, chin on paws. Flattened his ears when he saw Veiko's eyes on him, and sighed.

"Yes," Veiko told him. A man could grow soft spending all his time in the ghost roads. He could grow weak watching Cardik through a svartjagr's eyes, seeing brick all around him, tiled roofs and twisting streets. And he could go a little bit mad worrying after his partner.

Veiko crossed the room, crossed his own shadow, black as any Dvergir, where it stretched across floor and table. The room seemed dim after the bright of outside, all the color smeared to ash and dust. Grey as the scars the God had left on Snowdenaelikk.

He'd caught her scrubbing them in the bath once. Blood spidering through her fingers, where the scars had bled along the seams. He'd taken her hands and held them while she swore a stream of gutter Dvergiri and shook.

Tal'Shik, he promised himself, would be only the first god he killed.

*Brave words,* in his father's voice. *But a man wants more than pretty speeches. A man wants deeds. A man must act.*

It would have been better, maybe, if his father had told him, *a man wants thought before action.* He had done little but think, and heal, and drink poison, for the past month. Best he remind himself what acting felt like.

He would not think Tal'Shik to death, and Snowdenaelikk thought enough for both of them.

\* \* \*

The tavern door banged open, which was common enough. But this time the man—Alvir, dirty hair in a tail, in clothes more filthy still—paused in the doorway. Squinted inside, against the raw almost-spring afternoon leaking in from behind. His shadow sprawled large and dark on the smooth dirt-pack floor. His eyes roamed the room. Settled on Snow, finally, where she sat. Then he squared up and stalked inside, beelining for her with all the subtlety of a rutting bull.

So. Tsabrak's contact was here. Finally.

Snow leaned back. Propped one boot on the edge of the table and tipped the chair onto its back legs. She'd practiced during her wait. Gouged the chair legs into the dirt until she knew it would hold if she had to kick the table. Hell of an embarrassment if the chair skidded. End up on her ass, on her back. Probably dead if this Alvir brought friends.

Which he had, and more than the woman slouching in his wake. Briel was certain of it. Snow dipped her eyelids and sorted Briel's pepper-sharp impressions. Precise numbers were tricky with svartjagr. Briel knew *pair* well enough, but the feeling Snow got now was *many*, which could mean three or a dozen. She glanced around the tavern's guts. Too full for midday, yeah, too many Alviri, even for this part of the Warren. Could be any of them, or all of them, or none.

*Many.*

Dirty-hair stopped beside her table. This man had aristo bones, and that tip-tilt cast to his eyes that reminded her of Veiko. Uncertainty in his face, hostility. A doubling of each when he got a look at her face. Alvir accent, thick as cold vomit: "You awake, half-blood?"

"Marl," she said. "That's you, yeah? Sit." She kicked a chair at him under the table. Kicked a second at his companion, after a long moment's consideration. "Exactly how many friends did you bring, when we told you come alone?"

Cold-burned cheeks turned redder, and cold-raw knuckles paled considerably where they gripped the table's edge. He stayed standing. "Just Isla."

"Don't lie to me. Bad way to start a relationship, yeah?"

He closed his mouth. First sign he had any intelligence. Second sign, that he looked a little worried now, wondering how she knew. Damn certain this Marl didn't know what her topknot meant. All he saw was Dvergir half-blood and—

"Didn't expect to meet a woman," he admitted. "I heard—"

"I know what you heard." She flipped her hand. Flashed her palm and the godmark. Both Alviri looked at it. "I speak for Tsabrak."

Marl grunted. Nodded. Sat, deliberately.

Briel prickled through her awareness. *Many*, getting up and walking out the tavern's door. *Many*, melting away into shadow and street. A dizzy heartbeat, and the smudge and blur of a svartjagr's vision. Would've blinded her once, but not since Veiko'd come back from the dead. That was a mystery and a blessing and still a half measure. The sendings still left a crater in her skull.

"How many friends?" she repeated as a draft snatched at the candles and the lamps.

"None."

"Because they just walked out. Listen. Half a mind to tell Tsabrak you're trouble, yeah? Tell him you're too stupid to do business with us if you can't count to one."

The Alviri had different customs. Even now, even after the Purge, they had certain expectations. She'd disappointed this one in a half dozen ways, yeah, see that clear enough. Aristo eyes, aristo bones. Some watered-down highborn, this Marl, some descendent of thegns who'd never forgiven the Illhari legion, the

*women*

Dvergiri for being better soldiers, better strategists, for smashing his birthright from thegn to village headman. He puffed up like rising bread. Looked down that long nose.

"Maybe I take my business elsewhere if all I get are insults."

Empty threat. She knew it. Smiled to show him she did. "Maybe you don't try and threaten me, toadshit. Maybe you listen when you're told come alone. Or maybe you send just *her* next time, yeah? She seems smart enough to follow instructions. Don't," as Marl started to get up. "You're not in whatever motherless village anymore. You're in Cardik. You're toadshit nothing here. So why don't you tell me what you want. Stop wasting my time."

Another reddening of Marl's fair skin. Snow glanced past him. Got her first glimpse of Isla's eyes, grey as winter skies and startled round. Alviri women did not sit with men and deal for anything more dangerous than cook pots, and here this one was. Guess her merit, then. Confirmed when she laid a hand on Marl's arm.

"Please," she said, to one or both of them.

Marl settled. His chair squeaked and skidded on the smooth dirt. He reached into the fold of his shirt and plunked a fist-sized sack on the table.

"We want weapons." And when Snow only stared at him: "The legion took ours at the gate. This city is not safe, do you understand? There are thieves. Killers. We need to defend ourselves."

"Don't see Illhari ink on you. There're rules on the borders, yeah? No metal without ink."

"I didn't think you cared about legal."

"I don't. But it's not me the governor will hang. It's you. Damn sure she'll ask questions, first, about where you got it. And if you tell her, then I get worse than hanging."

He leaned over and spat onto the floor. "Fuck the legion. Fuck the governor. Fuck the whole Republic."

"That's a safer choice than you're making." Aneki'd had half a dozen new arrivals at her back gate just this week, offering themselves for sale, wearing bruises and desperation. Asking to sell themselves and serve those same troops, just like Aneki had.

*And eat. And live.*

And wear a collar. It was either that, or buy weapons from the local cartel that happened to belong to the Laughing God. Risk a rope instead of a collar's certain safety.

Ask Isla which she'd rather have round her neck, sitting across the table in a man's too-big shirt and breeches.

Snow didn't mind making trouble for the legion, or for Illharek. She'd done it more than half her life, yeah, had the godmark proof inked into her palm. Smuggling. Stealing. Murder, too, oh yes. She hadn't flinched from that.

But there was making trouble, and there was *this.* These Alviri who'd never bought citizenship to Illharek and taken the mark, who'd never lived long inside walls with working sewers and the governor's bread in long winters. These Alviri with grudges and pride and too much frustration, without collar or tattoo to mark them and nothing left to lose.

Weapons, oh yes. There were weapons for sale here today. Most of them walked on two feet. Marl, Isla, many. Tsabrak's army of convenience. As likely to turn on their wielder as cut down their enemies. Like loosing a mad dog into the market and hoping it killed only cutpurses.

Snow drummed her fingers on the table. Pretended to consider while Marl fidgeted and Isla watched her sidelong. "Say I can get you what you want. You think you'll have more luck against thieves than you did the Taliri?"

Sorry the moment she said it. Thought he'd come over the table, or simply burst, like a cold bottle dropped in boiling water.

"Witch," he said. "They had a *witch*. Cursed magic, filthy half-blood—"Choked silent when his companion put her hand on his arm and squeezed.

"Who are you talking to, Marl? Who am I?"

He blinked. Turned the color of oatmeal. "You're. I mean. You're not her."

Fuck and damn. If Tsabrak armed these people, she'd have to watch her back. Everyone would. Tsabrak wanted the legion tangled in civil disorder; Tsabrak wanted blood and fire. And if Tsabrak wanted it, the Laughing God did. But until now, the God had survived the persecutions and the Purge because he stayed to the shadows.

*Tell me why we're doing this, yeah?*

*Have faith, Snow.*

The foremothers had learned the dangers of faith, hadn't they? Damn certain she had. Snow measured *faith* in the scars on her wrist, her shoulders, her back. Measured it out in nightmares and cold sweat.

And meanwhile Ehkla's motherless Taliri burned their way toward Cardik's gates and choked the city with refugees and kept the legion inside the walls keeping order. It had been more than a month since Davni. At this rate, Snow reckoned the city would burst before the spring snowmelt.

"Please," said Isla a second time, neither highborn nor Illhari. A woman doing what a man would not among her people. Begging.

Which Dvergiri women didn't, ever.

Snow dropped her chair back onto four legs. Scooped the sack into her palm.

"All right," she said. "Let's talk business."

* * *

Veiko stripped his sweater off and dropped it on his blankets. Left his shirt on for decency, although the people here would probably prefer if he went outside bare as birth. Aneki would sell space at the windows overlooking the courtyard. See the naked skraeling doing axework in the snow, two marks.

Veiko waited a moment, with his ear near the door. There were no voices. Logi crowded his knees and *oofed*, faint and impatient. Veiko cracked the door and let him through the gap. Followed more slowly, remembering which boards creaked. There was no one in the hall, by some fortune, but not all of the doors were closed. Aneki's voice smoked out of the one closest the stairs, thick as incense.

". . . that's the way, right, oh yes, see how she likes it—*no*, Tomi, too fast, that's better . . ." A woman cried out, and Aneki said, "Good. *Good.*"

His ears burned. Not at all like a crofter's hut, no, *nothing* like. A whole village under one roof, and no curtains, and no modesty. Veiko held his breath and ghosted past that doorway. He thought someone saw him, a flicker of fair skin and bright hair as he passed. But no one called after him, thank the ancestors, and no one followed.

Veiko took the stairs less softly, one hand on the wall for balance, and ached by the bottom. At least it was warmer in the courtyard. The sun baked off the bricks and left treacherous footing, mud and grass and gravel under snow. A man could slip easily, even with two good legs. Logi had no problems. Galloped the perimeter on four sure paws, snapping mouthfuls of snow. Veiko chose a spot near the center. Rolled his shoulders and shook his arms out, one after the other. He had known this dance since boyhood, when his father had put a hatchet in his hands and taken him onto the tundra.

*A man should be able to defend his herd and hearth.*

Not his father's intention, no, not by any imagining, what shape his youngest son's herd and hearth would take.

One cut, one step. Step and turn, swing and dodge. As a boy he had imagined raiders from the neighboring clans falling under his blade like grass before a sickle. Had not imagined the truth of it: spraying blood and grey brains and tiny shards of bone. The drag of steel through flesh. The effort after, to wrench his blade loose again and see what he had done.

Step and cut, turn and swing. Mind the angle of the blade, so that his weight stayed behind it, and his limbs, too. Remember Ehkla's face, yellow-eyed and beautiful. She should have died from the wound he gave her and had not, because Tal'Shik would not allow it.

*Hard to kill the godsworn, yeah?*

Harder still to kill a god. A hunter could not do it trapped in his own flesh. A noidghe might, with the right allies, the right bargains. He wasn't good enough as a noidghe, but he was a very good hunter, and his axe would do its work in either world.

Step and turn, duck and swing. Ehkla had left a mark in him, half-drawn and ragged. A glyph. A prayer, because Illhari asked their gods for help and did not bargain. So he had been a gift, but only partway. But there were rules. And whatever the Illhari thought, the gods were spirits and must abide by those rules. Snow had believed him when he told her that. She had used that knowledge with the God and wore the scars of her bargaining.

Spin and cut, reverse the blade and chop again. That was watery almost-spring sunlight warming him. Raw spring wind lifting his braids. And a cold kiss on the back of his neck, a damp gust out of place in the warmth. There were clouds smudging the ridgeline. Another storm by nightfall, dropping heavy spring snows. This one might wait for Snow and Briel to get back, if Snow's business did not keep them late.

Turn and slice, chop and step. Again. Again, until his muscles burned, until his mind relaxed into habit. Step, turn, cut.

Slip.

Ice, he thought first. Drove his heel into the mud and stopped the skid. Pain skewered him from knee to hip, red and white and blinding. His knee buckled. He twisted with it, *mind* the blade, rolled without cutting off his own foot. Came up neatly enough, on bad knee and good foot and the axe nowhere near either. Clapped a hand over his thigh and pressed hard on the throb and ache. A strain, that was all. Too much exertion. Not an arrow, or a spear, or a

*wurm's tooth*

dagger. Only smooth, unmarked leather under his palm. But there was a spreading wetness, too. He thought it must be water at first, until he felt the warmth. Turned his palm and saw a red dampness soaked through the leather.

That wound should not bleed—had been, this morning, a livid, smooth channel carved in his flesh. Dry, yes, *healed.* There had not been a scab for fifteen days, and he had been diligent with salves and oils.

He gulped air. Held it and fended off Logi's wet, black concern. Flexed his knee. Grimaced. Men fought through worse. He had once and walked away after.

*With help, yeah?*

He borrowed a handful of Logi's ruff for balance. Let the good leg lift his weight. Swore, very softly, as snowmelt ran down the back of his neck. Took a step and swore again. Fresh pain backed up in his throat. He pressed his whole hand over his leg, and clenched his teeth as he found the whole cut reopened, split wide under the undamaged leather.

A ritual. A prayer. Ehkla's witchery, which Snow would call godmagic. And something was making it work now. Someone. Ehkla must be doing this, here and now. Must be here in Cardik.

Snow needed to know that, right now. He tilted his face into the sunlight. Closed his eyes and reached through the red on his eyelids.

*Briel.*

Nothing. Quiet dark where Briel should be. Briel, who crowded into his skull whenever he stubbed his toe, demanding assurance that he was all right. Now, with blood running into his boot, she didn't notice. Perhaps she'd found a cat on the rooftops. Briel liked cats.

*Tell yourself that.*

*Briel,* more insistent. Got a flutter of alarm from her this time, a phantom heartbeat too fast in his chest. Got a sending, in gashes of blue and stone and thatch, Briel flying. Then a sudden stillness that meant she'd landed again. And then, there: a man's face, Dvergir and fine boned. Veiko rode the echoes of Briel's recognition.

*Tsabrak.*

Red heat and hazed vision, cold punch in his chest and skin gone tight and hot. He got another pair of steps on that anger. Found himself with his hand on the gate's latch before better sense caught him.

Better sense, and Aneki, whose voice uncoiled and snapped across the courtyard and stopped his hand, midlift on the latch. "The hell you going, Veiko?"

His fingers stretched. Curled. "Out," he said. Then, "Nowhere," as the pain caught up with him again. He blinked through the greyness. Swallowed bitter and nausea together.

Shuffle-slap as she crossed the yard. The low murmur of profane disapproval of mud and Logi's paws.

"Don't you come inside with those feet, dog. You'll track all over— ah." And silence for the beat it took Veiko to realize that he'd left his axe in the snow and she'd found it, before, "You dropped this, yeah?"

He turned. Rested his back on the gate and his hand on his thigh because it hurt and because, oh ancestors, he did not want to explain the blood. He took the axe and one-handed it into its sling.

"I fell."

"I guessed that much." Aneki came closer now, so that he smelled the cloud of incense that followed her like a shadow. Her eyes scraped his face. Narrowed. "You all right?"

"Yes."

"Toadshit." Her gaze darted down. "You're bleeding again. Did you tear it open?"

"It is—"

*Nothing,* he told Briel, *nothing.* Felt her attention glance off him like sunlight on snow. Yes, distracted. Worried. Focused, which Briel rarely was. So reckon that Snow had her own problems just now and did not need his distraction.

*She can care for herself, yeah?*

And water was wet. This witchery was Ehkla's doing, which meant Tal'Shik. And *she* was his problem. He had promised his partner.

"—nothing." He licked his lip. Looked past Aneki, at the doorway, and did not feign his dismay at the width of the courtyard.

Aneki sighed. "You hurt yourself, Snow'll be mad, yeah? At both of us. Come on. I'll help you back."

"Yes," said Veiko, and let her take his arm.

# CHAPTER SEVENTEEN

There were Alviri behind her. *Two*, by Briel's reckoning, which might really be three or seven or *many*. Street gangs weren't unusual in the Warren. One per several blocks, usually, and they'd learned to leave the God's people alone. Sad day, yeah, when *she* had to worry about a new crop of thugs and delinquents who didn't know the rules. This lot must be new to the Warren and Cardik. Bet they were carrying more steel than was legal.

*Bet we didn't smuggle what they're carrying through the gates. Bet we didn't sell it to them.*

So. Time for a lesson in professional courtesy. In city geography, too. Snow knew the Warren's streets and alleys by the tilt under her feet, by the smell and the pattern of shadows. She knew the best places to fight and where to leave bodies. And best, smartest: how to shake pursuit. There were two ways onto the Market Bridge from the Warren, and only this, Broad Street, was wide enough for handcarts. She was counting on the clots and snarls, where foot traffic met wheeled and everyone claimed right-of-way. She threaded through, ducked and doubled back into one of the cross streets and flattened into a doorway.

Pulled the shadows after. Counted to thirty while people passed and did not so much as glance her way.

She waited another thirty to be certain. Turned back toward Market Bridge again. Hoped for no more tails. Trusted Briel to warn her if there were.

Flicker, as the shadows peeled back and Tsabrak stepped out of the nothing-space between buildings and reached for her.

He damn near lost the hand when she drew and cut, one motion. Damn near lost both eyes when Briel keened and arrowed, tail hissing like a whip. He ducked and rolled and came up a graceful pace and a half farther away than he'd started. He'd lost his shadows. The daylight showed her Tsabrak in city drab, rumpled now and smudged with alley muck. He had a knife in one hand, she noted, and another hilt visible in his boot.

"Fuck and damn, Snowdenaelikk." He peered up, where Briel had gone.

Snow slid her own blade back into its sheath. "The hell are you skulking out here?"

His teeth flashed white. Smile or snarl, she couldn't tell. "Next time I'll shout my name first, yeah? That better?"

Her own heartbeat had almost settled. She watched, unsmiling, as he brushed at sleeves and trousers. "Might be, yeah. Or meet me where we agreed, yeah? Janne's tavern. Tomorrow."

"Was a time you'd be glad to see me."

"You, fine. The God wearing your skin, not fine. Which are you?"

His mouth slashed downward. He spread empty hands. "Just me. Snow. Come with me. There's something I want you to see."

"What, right now?"

"Yes, now." He made a show of looking left and right. "Are you busy?"

"Say I've got plans, yeah."

"Fuck your plans." Honest affront on his face, honest surprise, both eyebrows hitched high. "You forget how this works, Snowdenaelikk? You're my right hand. You do my business."

She strangled the laugh. "I've been doing your business all afternoon. That idiot Marl. Just got done at Janne's. And now I'm going home."

"Plans changed. Got more work for you."

She squinted at the thin strip of sky. The sun had to be crawling up on the ninth hour. "Smarter to let me move at night, you know that. Briel doesn't look like a crow."

"Most people don't look up to notice her. And the Alviri mistrust the dark. You know that."

"Superstitious toadshit, yeah, I know. Can't wait to see them stage a daylight raid on the garrison. You planning to run a betting pool? Because I think we could make—"

"Snow." The God's own smile on his face, and only dark Dvergiri eyes to prove him still Tsabrak. "I'm losing patience."

"Right. Fine. Just." She drew out two sticks of jenja. Pinched them between her fingers. "You want me good for anything, I need a smoke first. You want one?"

He poked his tongue between lip and teeth. Sucked and spat. "Yeah. Thanks."

She let her eyes close. Sank awareness into Cardik itself. There were patterns in the stones, as predictable as Illhari architecture. Patterns in everything. A conjuror knew them. A second-rank conjuror who'd earned her gold knew how to change one to the other.

Flower and flesh, tree and root: those things are fickle. Fire, water, constant stone: those are best. What is shaped once can be reshaped.

A simple thing

*fuck it is*

to borrow stone's strength. To hold that strength in your fist, with your fingers curved just so, the patterns the Adepts had taught you. Call it conjuring, yeah, like you made something from nothing; but know, in your bones, that it was borrowing and shaping, and dangerous as dancing on spring ice. Cardik was not Illharek, which was Dvergir to its core, all its patterns mapped and known. Cardik was stone walls and cobbled streets, Illhari order raised on Alviri ruins. One set of patterns on a different set. That was one wrinkle for conjuring. More urgent, more dangerous: the Wild was not so far away here. Forest on the other side of patchy fields. The S'Ranna ripping white down the canyon. The Wild didn't appreciate Dvergiri conjuring. Veiko said that was because conjuring offended the spirits. Maybe. But—

*Focus.*

She opened her eyes. Tightened her hand into a fist and extended her forefinger straight. Exhaled. And there: a hair-slim coil of smoke rose from the end of the jenja. The glow followed. Then flame, finally, that flared and spat as it caught. Tsabrak flinched and scowled hard when he saw that she'd noticed. Eyed her as the smoke curled between them, as if he'd just remembered what that topknot meant, and the rings in her ears.

Good. Let him. She handed him one of the sticks.

"All right. Show me what's so important."

\* \* \*

Rare sunlight this afternoon, brass-bright past the clouds caught on the peaks. It cut stripes along the cobbles, bounced blinding off the ice congealed in the gutters. The Street of Silk Curtains looked better in shadow, Dekklis thought, with lamplight and witchfire to scrub away old paint and cracked shutters. Legitimate business didn't happen on this street with the sun up. Soldiers didn't come here before dark, not in uniform.

But Dekklis didn't look like a soldier just now. Neither did Istel. Civilian clothing, civilian slouch that Istel did better

*hunch, Dek, and stop looking at everyone*

than she did. Just two Illhari going about whatever business happened in daylight. Not much on this street. Daylight commerce happened on the Market Bridge, or on Broad Street, or in one of the squares on the Hill. The Street wouldn't open its doors for business until sundown.

But here they were, in daylight, on Rurik's errands, which had more to do with what happened in the Warren and in the dark, and was not business at all.

"There have been fights, one beating, and three murders in the last week," Rurik had said just this morning as the dawn bled through the windows. "All in the Warren. All Illhari, you savvy?"

She did, oh yes. A double handful of villages burned since Davni, the survivors arriving in clumps and clots and trickling away into the Warren. Alviri, all of them, and not a one with a citizen's ink. Snow had told her about the new residents up in the Warren, a patchwork of men and boys and women.

*Scared people, Szanys. Angry people.*

*And your friends? What do they say about it?*

"Ask your friend something for me," said Rurik, and Dekklis had blinked and stared at him.

"Sir?"

"You understand that I am generally confined to the garrison. I don't hear what happens in the Warren. But your friend, unless he lives under a rock, must know about this."

And Rurik had scooped a legionnaire's sword, short and thick-bladed and notched, off the riot of his desk and held it out like an offering. "We took this off an Alvir on the Hill tonight, Szanys. The motherless Hill. No ink on him, you savvy? You want to tell me how destitute, homeless Alviri come to buy weapons?"

Looking at her when he said it, not Istel. But Istel had answered, even-voiced: "My friend knows godsworn, sir. Not Alviri rabble."

Rurik's stare had burned like sparks on bare skin. "If I remember my lessons, Scout, there's a long and glorious tradition of rabble and certain godsworn going together. So maybe your friend knows something."

No, not a stupid man. Not a fool. The same shape and shade of angry he'd been the night Kenjak had gone missing, when he'd paced and cursed and sent her and Istel out into the storm. Same leashed fury in his voice:

"The governor's one step from ordering us into the Warren to keep order. But those Alviri aren't soldiers. I don't care what they're carrying. We go down there, we'll butcher them, and what do you think happens then?"

Revolution. Blood and fire.

"You're thinking again," Istel said, just louder than his footfalls on the cobbles.

"Of course I am. The Warren's coming apart, you noticed? Her friends behind it."

"Alviri behind it," Istel said patiently. "Homeless, hungry, frightened refugees. That's the Taliri's fault."

"Armed Alviri." Killing citizens now, and each other. The second no one really minded. But the first, hell and damn. "I warned her, yeah? What would happen if this didn't stop. I told her. We'll have blood in the streets."

"And you think Snow wants that?"

"I don't know what she wants."

Istel scowled. "Trust her, or don't. But if you don't, then we turn around now."

Sour taste in her mouth, thinking that. "Who's this we? You don't meet with her. You go down into the baths and . . . do what, exactly?"

Flatly: "What you told me to do. Give us excuse to be there. Be seen."

"Great hardship, is it?"

Istel rolled his eyes. Lucky he didn't pop them out, send them bouncing down the street. Anything but turn his head, anything but look right at her. Typical Istel. She found herself thinking of Veiko's unblinking stare. Found herself getting angry.

"Armed Alviri," she repeated. "You wonder where they're getting those weapons? I don't. Her friends."

"Smugglers," he said mildly. "The God's people, probably. That's what I told Rurik."

"She's the God's people. She couldn't mention they're selling weapons?"

"What would you do if she had? Tell Rurik, and then he would what, send a detachment down there to arrest people? How much do you think she'd be worth after that?"

As much as any corpse in the river. Dekklis ground her teeth together.

"So we bring her in. Protect her. Get names out of her. Stop this now, and settle the Alviri before the legion does."

"Bring her in? Didn't you promise her otherwise?"

Dekklis did not appreciate that look from

*a man*

Istel, no, that thin-lipped disapproval just like her mother's. Didn't like the tone of her own voice, pitched high and defensive. "Rurik needs something for the praefecta."

"Snow can't be that something. And even if you got the ones selling weapons—even if she gave you names—it won't solve a damned thing, Dek. This fight has been coming since the Purge."

"Oh, has it? When did you become an expert on Illhari history?"

"I'm not. But I know Cardik. I know the people."

A mixed population, he meant. The Illhari had not butchered the Alviri natives when they'd breached the walls. Razed the temples, reduced the streets to piles of brick, yes, but they'd spared the residents. Sold them citizenship if they wanted it and let them stay with their homes and their businesses, such as the war left. The Republic had showed more mercy than the Alviri thegns ever had shown the Dvergiri.

*Tell yourself that, Szanys. How many Alviri you think can afford Illhari ink? And how many stayed, doing shit work, with no ink?*

"You sound like Snow," Dekklis snapped. "This is why the Alviri are angry, this is why the Illhari are unfair, this is why what the heretics do is justified. You change sides when I wasn't looking?"

"You seem to think so. That's why you tell me to stay in the baths," so softly she thought she'd imagined it. Wind, surely, a stray voice from a courtyard.

"What?"

"You don't trust me," quiet as only Istel could be.

Teach her to push him, wouldn't it. Teach her to probe and poke and trust he'd never push back. And he wouldn't have before. She wouldn't have doubted him before.

*You're poison, Snowdenaelikk.*

"All right," she said. "All right." To what, hell if she knew. Nothing all right in the look he gave her, Istel-calm and Istel-still. "Come up with me this time, then. I'm not saying we'll do more than talk to her—"

But he wasn't looking at her anymore. Chin up, pointed into the wind, narrow-eyed and sniffing like Veiko's big, wolfish dog. She turned her face the same direction. Smoke wasn't unusual in a city. But this smoke burned nose and throat.

"Feh. Smells like the tannery."

"No. My mother's a tanner. That's something else." Istel angled out into the crossroads and squinted, while she wondered how it was she'd never known what his mother did, or that he had a mother still living.

*Never asked, did you? Highborn.*

"Fire, Dek."

She looked up. No smudge across the blue yet, nothing visible, which meant only the flames weren't that high. "The Warren?"

"Or the Bridge." He rocked onto his toes. "Might be nothing. Maybe someone kicked over a firedog."

"Might be riot, too." Imagine a mob of ragged Alviri with torches. Hell and damn. At least the city was snow-soaked. She cut a look at the sky again. Another storm coming, piling up grey and bruised on the peaks. That would stop fire, too.

"I can find out. Run up there, meet you here after." He was looking at her now, waiting permission, exactly like a good

*male*

soldier.

*Yes* on her lips, and she clipped it off. "No."

She should send him back to Rurik, to warn him there was a fire in the Warren. And then the legion would come, armed and angry. If it were a shop fire, then she'd start slaughter for nothing.

*And if it's not?*

If it weren't, then the garrison would notice the smoke and come anyway.

She could see Still Waters from here, grey wedge with cobalt curtains shivering in the late afternoon. Trust Snow. Trust Istel.

"Scouts work in pairs, yeah? Come with me," she said. "Let's hear what our friend has to say."

\* \* \*

The streets were steeper and narrower here in the Warren's top half. The S'Ranna was louder, too, where it tumbled out of the canyon, tearing itself white on the rocks. Too loud for highborn Dvergiri ears, who preferred the other side of the Hill. The Warren was too dry and too high, with no springs beneath it. The public wells were few and far. And it was darker, too, pinched so close to canyon sides. The sunset came earlier here, and the winds were constant. Only a breeze at the moment, but biting damp.

Laughing God, Snow knew that smell, and the chill that crawled between skin and clothing. Witch-weather, the Alviri called it. It had been a witch-winter, with endless storms rolling east over the mountains, sunlight to snowfall in a handful of heartbeats. It would be a witch-spring, too, no doubt, when all the snow melted. Turn the twig-slender river into a torrent, yeah, wash away half the farms in the valley. And then there'd be witches everywhere, behind every shrub and shadow.

Witches had been the Alviri's best excuse, once, to murder Dvergiri. The Ten Thousand had burned, men and women, across the Nine Realms when the last high thegn's favorite priest decreed it. Tal'Shik had risen from the ashes of that grief and outrage. Her godsworn took the Senate elections, swearing vengeance. The Houses set aside their blood feuds and birthed the Republic. The legion marched out under Illharek's banner and Tal'Shik's spirit.

And they won, against Alviri troops and their Taliri mercenaries. The Nine Realms had fractured into ten, and then a dozen, when the high thegn fell. Tal'Shik kept her promises. The Alviri kept their hatred of witches and precious little else. The Illhari had allowed them to stay in the Republic, oh yes, but only in the places the Illhari did not want.

The top of the Warren was one of those places, oldest Cardik, that the Illhari had not bothered to renovate. Squat and graceless houses huddled together like toads on a log. Timber walls instead of brick. Thatch instead of tile. Slivered wood and bark on the streets instead of cobbles, which smelled of rot and squished unpleasantly under Snow's boots. A trio of matted Alviri clumped at the crotch of three streets. Men, all three, with sullen eyes and hidden hands.

They didn't challenge Tsabrak. Scowled at her, though, and one of them spat "Half-blood" and phlegm as she passed.

"Wonder where he learned to hate half-bloods?" she asked cheerfully. "Wait. Bet I know. Bet he saw one burn his village, murder his wife, eat his children—"

"Ehkla does not eat children."

"Right. Skewers them, then, before a slow roast. Unless she carves them first."

Tsabrak eyed her. "You're worried about a rat's opinion?"

"When that rat's got a knife. You noticed the rats are getting pretty fucking brave lately, yeah? Sad day, Tsabrak, when I don't know all the thieves in Cardik. Sad day when I have to worry about my back."

"You have Briel," he said dryly. Brushed at the stains on his sleeve. "She's watching."

"You think she's much good in a fight?" Another jag, another slope. Her chest ached. Her calves did. She frowned. Precious little this far up except Alviri houses and the Finger. It had been Cardik's shortest bridge, connecting the Hill and the top side of the Warren, before an Illhari ballista ended its career. Now it was just a narrow stone ruin, totally exposed. Beautiful view of the city, too, looking east, if you didn't mind the climb or the smell of raw sewage. The Alviri had never quite understood the technology of Illhari plumbing, preferring their shit running free in the streets.

Or clogged in the gutters. She stepped over a particularly noxious puddle and onto the Finger's base. Followed Tsabrak up onto its curve, chest tight and heart beating too hard and nothing to do with the climb.

"Whatever you have up here better be good."

Tsabrak cut her a strange look, crossbred smirk and scowl. She didn't like it. Liked it even less paired to a perfectly civil, "How is your skraeling? Veiko, isn't it?"

"Huh. What do your spies say?"

"That he keeps to Still Waters. That he works in the courtyard some afternoons, with his axe. That he limps when he walks. That he keeps a toadfucking dog. I should congratulate you and that Alvir slaver. Her bondies will spread ass or legs for legion coin, but they'll keep the lips on their face closed tight against mine."

"Aneki's a half-blood, not an Alvir."

"Even more reason she should gut soldiers, not fuck them."

"Her choice, what she does with her freedom. She bought it."

"As I bought mine." His face convulsed with old anger. "One hundred seventeen silver marks and ten years of my life. A brand out of it."

A tiny silver scar burned beside a citizen's sigil, which meant indentured, contract paid. The law said a male citizen could only sell his service once. But a legal distinction had let Tsabrak's mother sell her son's youth to a proconsul who liked pretty boys. The grown Tsabrak still counted the debt unpaid, even past the proconsul's death.

Ask how that proconsul had died. Who'd done it.

*Bad fish.*

Damn sure Tsabrak remembered that favor, which bought her the space to argue. "You made your choice, yeah? Aneki made a different one."

"Toadfucking coward, she is." Tsabrak sucked his temper back through his teeth. "And you defend her."

"I understand her. I might've made that choice if I'd been in her place. I think she might've done better than I did." Dekklis's words then, falling out of her mouth like stones. "The God doesn't love women. Got my own brands to prove that, yeah?"

Tsabrak flinched. Walked a little farther and stopped, four paces from the Finger's jagged tip. The wind snapped and tore long strands of his hair loose, sent them waving around his head like black flames. He was beautiful enough to rip breath out of her. Was a time she'd have done anything for him.

"Come here," he said without looking back. "Want you to see this."

And that time was over. "Been on the Finger before, Tsabrak."

Now he did look. "You haven't seen this. Come here."

She did, minding her distance. Stopped out of arm's reach and looked. The city sprawled below them, crawled up again on both sides of the S'Ranna. On the Hill side, where the Illhari had rebuilt, the architecture changed with altitude. The Street of Silk Curtains at the bottom, butting up to the merchants' houses nearest the east gate, all in plain Illhari stonework. The higher you looked, that plain stone gave way to conjured walls and rooflines, elaborate shapes and figures. Highborn vanity, highborn wealth, which met its zenith in the governor's villa. Beside it, the plain, practical garrison looked like a river stone among diamonds, almost directly across from them here, and a ballista's range distant. Below them, more directly down—there was Market Bridge, monument to Illhari engineering and Illhari conjuring.

A monument with smoke coming off it, coiled up thick and brown all along the Bridge's length. Too much smoke for meat vendors. Snow blinked.

*Briel.*

The svartjagr circled back. Skimmed over the smoke on the Bridge. Not meat cooking, no. Cloth. Leather. Wood. Oil. Flames, too, big enough that Briel saw them. People massed and clotting in the streets. Screams and pushing and the wet slip of bodies off the edge.

"Fuck and damn, Tsabrak. What is that?"

"Revolution," said Tsabrak, dreamy-quiet.

"It'll be slaughter when the legion shows up."

"They don't have to last long. They just have to start it."

"They. The refugees. You tell them who they're dying for? They know it's Ehkla calling orders? They know it's Tal'Shik behind her?"

"No. And they won't find out. As you say. It will be slaughter when the legion comes. And the ones who pick up the fight after, they'll only see Illharek."

Cold knot in her belly, metallic bitter in the back of her throat. "Are we done? I want to get back across that bridge before your revolution makes it too hot for me to get home."

"Time was, the Warren was your home. You mean, you want to get back to your skraeling." He tipped a glance at her. "What is he to you, this Veiko Nyrikki?"

*No one* and *nothing* dried up on her tongue. Lied enough, hadn't she? "My partner."

"Partner." Tsabrak tasted the word, rolled it around in his mouth. Spat, finally, over the Finger. "Pretty way to say *we fuck*, isn't it?"

"We don't, as it happens. You jealous? Because if that's—"

"Kill him."

"What?"

His gaze slithered sideways. "You heard me."

"Is that you talking, or Ehkla? Because I told you what she wanted with him."

"I know what you told me. And now I'm telling you. It doesn't matter what he can do with spirits. What power he has. Kill him."

"The God approves?"

"My orders, Snow."

"No."

Gentle headshake. "So. You're refusing?"

"I am."

He nodded. "She said you would."

Then Snow understood, fuck and damn, blind not to see it sooner. Sweat prickled up. Chilled on her skin and sank into bone. "Ehkla's here, isn't she? Now. Already. In the city. That's why your revolution's happening on the Bridge."

Tsabrak showed her a blank face for his answer, as good as a yes.

"So what, you brought me up here to kill me?"

"No." He should have been angry. Wasn't, dear Laughing God. Hurt, which she'd never expected, and no act. "Was a time you didn't argue with orders, Snowdenaelikk. Was a time you knew who your friends were."

*We were never.*

"Check a mirror, yeah? I'm not the one in bed with Tal'Shik. What's she promising you, Tsabrak? Revenge on the highborn? Bring down Illharek? Converts?"

Nothing coming off him now but cold, deep as the dark Below. Shadows she couldn't unravel. "Don't fight. You won't get lucky enough to die."

He dipped his chin and flicked his gaze past her. She knew what she'd see when she looked. The street gang, no surprises, gathered around the base of the Finger. Half a dozen matches to her sword down there, badly hung off hips and shoulders. Ask if any of them could use the blade for more than graceless hacking. Ask if it would matter, that many to her one.

Briel felt her panic. Began to circle back, sick wheel and bank that kicked hard in Snow's guts. *Go,* she wished Briel, with the memory of Veiko's witchfire eyes and all the urgency she could manage. Briel wasn't good for complex messages. Trust Veiko's natural paranoia. Trust her conjuring on the locks. Trust Dekklis to keep her promise and get him out of Cardik.

Which Briel didn't want. Sent back images of ruined Ollu with Tsabrak's face overlaid, flavored with a courage that tasted too much like Veiko. Snow countered with her own worst imaginings. Briel broken. Veiko pale and dead. She shut Briel out hard, on a final

*just go, yeah?*

and blinked past the white spike of pain. Watched a shape that looked nothing at all like a bird dive into Cardik's rooflines.

Tsabrak watched the svartjagr's convolutions. "Sent her straight back to him, yeah?"

"He'll be out the gates by sunset."

Tsabrak smiled. "You don't believe that."

Snow glanced at the Finger's edge. Flexed her fingers. Stone underfoot. Water, wind, and sky. She might bring down the Finger if she tried, by conjuring. Take the decision out of Veiko's hands.

And damn him, too. The God would come to collect on his bargain, without her there to pay it.

Snow tied down her panic. Took a breath, held it, let go. She wasn't going to fight. Tsabrak wasn't going to kill her. He was going to take her to Ehkla. And Snow'd made a bargain with the God, hadn't she, burned and branded into her skin. She needed to settle that first.

Tsabrak was still watching. Waiting, with that smirk going stiff on the edges. He jabbed his chin at her hips, where the seax hung. "You going to give me that? Or are you going to fight?"

She draped the sword belt across his palm and let that be her answer.

# CHAPTER EIGHTEEN

Dekklis arrived at Still Waters, Istel behind her, in no good humor. Imagination, that was all, that the air seemed thicker. Imagination that she could hear screams and shouts from the Bridge. Call the haze overhead mist on the edge of a spring storm, yeah, except it smelled like Davni's memory.

*Shop fire, hell.*

She paused in front of the steel-and-wood door to gather her temper and her wits. Pulled the bell cord gently and fisted her hands at her side. One of Aneki's boys opened up. Little scrap of an Alvir, eyes blue as summer sky, which rounded when he saw her and Istel.

"Domina," he choked out, "Dominus, it is a—" before she cut him quiet.

"Snowdenaelikk."

His throat moved, nervous gulp beneath the collar. "No."

"No?"

He blinked. Accent thick as paint, made no clearer by nerves. "She is not here. Domina. I am sorry."

Dekklis stared at him. Traded a look with Istel.

*She's flipped on us.*

*Something happened.*

*Going to kill her.*

*Wait, Dek.*

Istel said, more gently: "Veiko, then."

"Dominus." The boy had no orders against it. That, plain as daylight on his face. But he didn't want to. Hesitated while Dekklis drew off her gloves and slapped them into her palms. One, two. He flinched both times.

"Now?" she suggested.

"Domina. He is—" He glanced over his shoulder.

"In the baths?" One thing for her to strip and sit with Snow in the hot water and whisper through the steam. Quite another to imagine herself that near Veiko. He wouldn't appreciate it. She wouldn't. Istel would laugh at them both.

"No," said the boy. He pointed. "Upstairs."

"Take us to him," Dek said. "You understand?"

"Yes, Domina." Turned and scuttled, that was the only word for it, head ducked and fast glances over his shoulder.

The stairs were steep things, smooth wood and dubious railings. Dekklis stopped. Peered up into the shadows and thought about traps and traitors.

"No. This isn't the right way."

"Yes." The boy gestured up. Bowed. Wouldn't look at her, no, kept his eyes fixed on the flagstones. "Up."

There were other people on the second floor, open doors and voices raised and people propped on the railing. Collared, all of them, mix of male and female. Laughter that she had no reason to think was at her, but she couldn't tell. She spoke an academic Alviri. This was local dialect, fast and impossible.

A cream-skinned woman leaned out over the railing. Fox-colored hair spilled over her shoulders, collected in the valley between her breasts. She smiled wide recognition.

"Istel!"

Embarrassment rolled off Istel like steam from a boiling pot. "Fridis."

"I didn't expect you today." Fridis's Dvergiri was flawless. She came down the stairs now as the remaining pale faces turned toward them. "Let me get my—"

"We're here for Veiko," Dekklis snapped. "Both of us."

"Both?" Fridis paused partway down the steps. Frowned. Bounced a look between the boy and Istel and settled a hard-eyed stare on Dekklis. "On what business?"

"Ours and his."

Hell and damn. Dek counted a half dozen unarmed, collared Alviri arranged on the landing, all gone silent and staring.

"No harm, yeah?" Quiet, as only Istel could be. "You know me, Fridis."

"Your coin's good. I know that. Illhari." Fridis drew her lips together. "We will be waiting right here. All of us. And the walls are thin."

"Come on," Dekklis muttered. "You think we're here to hurt him?"

Fridis's face said that was exactly what she thought.

Dekklis followed the boy up through the cloud of perfume, and the more oppressive weight of Fridis's anger. Dekklis was not gentle, carving out space for herself on the steps. Soft-bodied Fridis grunted when Dekklis put an elbow into her ribs, and still would not yield a fingerspan.

Snow hadn't been stupid, choosing this place. Collared or not, Aneki's people weren't cowards. Ask if she and Istel would walk out of here when they'd finished. Ask if Aneki's slaves might not trap her up here and—

*What, kill you?*

Not likely. That was one of Snow's skills. But Snow wouldn't bother with stairs and ambush and other hands doing her work. From her it would be a knife in the dark and the whisper of svartjagr wings. Or bad fish.

Doors open all along the hall, glimpses of rumpled beds and scattered clothes and people's lives. Dekklis tried not to look. Tried to ignore the whispers that sprang up in her wake. She should've waited in the baths. Made Veiko come to her. Except he might not have, being Veiko, and unlikely to answer her summons.

The bondie boy stopped in front of the very last door in the corridor, solidly shut. Shadows clustered around it like cobwebs. Snow's doing, damn sure. Ask what other conjuring she'd done, what spells she might've laid on lock and latch.

Dekklis flexed her hands. Hesitated, with her knuckles a hairsbreadth from the wood. "You're certain he's inside."

"Yes, Domina." Earnest blue eyes. Oh, this one was pretty. Being trained, wasn't he, by those women. By collared Fridis and freed Aneki, who made their lives flattering soldiers. Ask if he didn't know how to lie.

"You can go," she told him. Waited until he'd slunk back to the stairs before she rapped hard on the door. Once. Twice. Veiko's dog snarled on the second knock, from close on the other side.

"Logi," in Veiko's low tones, and then louder, "I do not require any help. I told you."

"It's Dekklis. And Istel."

Feel that silence, bowstring tight. Dek jerked her hand off the latch as it moved. Made a guilty fist of it as Veiko opened the door just wide enough for his face. Steam puffed through the open gap, the smell of hot water and herbs. Blame skraeling custom, or skraeling prudery, which would ask for water and a tub brought upstairs with the hot springs below. She'd've guessed Veiko a eunuch, or disfigured, if she hadn't seen otherwise. Not an ugly man, well made, if you didn't mind skin pale as a cave-toad.

"Snowdenaelikk is not here."

"Yeah. The kid said as much. You'll do for what I need."

Tall man. Broad shoulders. Solid in the door gap. He looked down at her. His braids slithered against each other. Water beaded and dripped off the ends. "And what is that?"

Wish for her armor and the rest of her kit. Wish for a legion sword. Just a knife in her belt, not even as long as Snow's black seax. Effort to keep her arms loose, her voice steady. "You want to discuss that in the hallway? No? Then let us in."

He grunted. Showed her a bare shoulder, and then a naked back. He wore trousers, at least, loose Illhari silk that stuck and clung to still-damp skin and gave Dekklis a fine idea what lay beneath.

Not exactly a welcome, no, but she'd take it. Stepped into the narrow entry with Istel behind her. A fringe of beads hung between it and the rest of the room. They clicked and swung as Veiko pushed through them. One big room beyond the beads, a dining couch and a table stacked with scrolls, jars, bowls. A rumpled bed on one side of the wide hearth, a pallet on the other, neatly arranged with Veiko's pack and gear beside it. Pots lined the hearth, stacked by size. A copper tub, big enough for two Dvergiri or one tall skraeling, steamed in front of the firedog, with a shirt and a pair of breeches draped over the edge. The afternoon spilled through the open shutter, panels of light and a breeze just on the wrong side of cool. The dog sat near the hearth, triangle ears up. A lingering smell of jenja clung to everything.

Veiko lowered himself carefully to the edge of the hearth, between axe and dog. Straightened his leg and kneaded his thigh. The silk was darker there, and not with water. He pulled a slow breath through his nose. Let it out the same way. "What do you want?"

She eyed the dark patch of silk. "You're bleeding."

He cut her a look of pure exasperation. "Yes."

"How'd it happen?"

The laugh came out like a man kicked in the belly, gust and grunt. "Witchery. Ehkla is here."

"What? In Cardik? Now?" Dek's priorities heaved and shifted. "How the hell do you know that? Snow been back here?"

"No." Flash of a blue eye in the sunlight's reflection, the other half of his face thrown shadow-black as any Dvergir. "I bleed because of Ehkla's witchery. Tsabrak has Snowdenaelikk. He is taking her to Ehkla."

She knew the name, having dragged it out of Snow—

*You tell Rurik that name, Szanys, deal's off.*

—as a gesture of good faith. Heretic, godsworn, head and heart of whatever illegal business ran in Cardik.

*Runs the gangs, yeah? The whole Warren.*

Trouble, oh yes, this Tsabrak.

"Shit," said Istel. "She's all right?"

"If Tsabrak's made her, she's dead," Dekklis said before Veiko could draw a whole breath. "What matters now is how much she spills before—"

"She is not dead."

"She's mortal. She bleeds. And if he takes her to Ehkla—"

"Briel knows she's alive."

"Briel—" Dekklis began, and then Veiko turned the full weight of that glare on her. Didn't look like a grief-stricken partner, no. Cold as midwinter moonrise.

"Svartjagr hunt in packs."

"I know that. I grew up in Illharek."

"Then you know that they send to each other. We are her pack, Snow and Logi and me." She could hear Snow's Illhari lilt behind the skraeling's words. "Snow is not dead, or Briel would know it, and so would I."

Unease scrabbled in her belly. "Sure. Whatever you want to believe. Istel, we've—"

"Where is she? Does Briel know?" Istel said, like some credulous Alvir who still left gifts in the old temple ruins.

Veiko's eyes slid out of focus, reminding her of his fever, and what she'd thought was a dying man's stare. Paler. Greyer. His voice thinned to smoke and gravel. "Briel shows." Veiko planed his hand. Tilted it. "Up. Near the walls. Old buildings."

"The Warren." Istel's eyes gleamed as madly as Veiko's. "That's where she is. That's where we go, Dek."

"What? No. We go back to the garrison. Report to Rurik."

"And what, tell Rurik his brother's killer is up in the Warren? What will that do?"

"Rurik," she repeated. "Figure that fire's no accident. You smell a trap? Because I do. You looked at the mountain? See those clouds? There's a storm coming tonight. I think the Taliri will walk right up to the walls under its cover. Rurik's got to keep the legion out of the Warren, down near the walls, for when that happens."

"The praefecta will order troops to Market Bridge if there's a serious fire. We can't stop that. Rurik can't, no matter what we tell him. And if there are troops on Market, we won't get across, either. We got to go now, Dek." Istel yielded a half step, put the long bar of sunlight between them. "I remember my oath. Snow dead won't make Illharek safer. Ehkla dead will. Put her head on the gates. See if the Taliri stop then."

Sense to that, a bloody-minded Illhari logic. Dekklis hesitated. Imagined the Sixth arrayed on the Bridge, lines of armor and javelins and crossbows. Hold Market. Keep the Warren contained on the far side of the river while the Taliri—how many did Ehkla have with her?— came at the outer gates.

The sunlight smeared to water, then to heatless grey. The clouds had arrived and taken the warmth with them. Istel's face bleached back into focus as the brightness bled out.

"We'd both be dead now, except for Snow. We owe her. It's honor, Dek."

Honor was something that governed Illharek, that ran in highborn veins. Grow up breathing it in a House with busts of all the foremothers lining the halls. Soak in it, like silk in a dyepot. Warren-born, Cardik-bred Istel. He didn't have a House sigil inked in his skin. Only the citizen's mark, and the jagged glyph that meant legion under that. His honor was simpler than hers.

*Or maybe yours is too complicated.*

"Listen, Dek." This was an Istel she didn't recognize, chin up and arms crossed. "Do what you want, but I'm—"

She pinned him quiet with a fingertip. "Not going to say anything stupid. You mutiny on me, I'll kill you right here. I'm thinking, rot your guts."

"While you argue," said Veiko, "Snowdenaelikk gets farther away."

She rounded on him. "So what are you doing, then? Taking a bath? Doing a little laundry?"

"Bleeding," he said shortly. "I could not walk that far. And if I did, I would do her no good when I arrived."

"You could." *Try,* she almost said, and gulped it back when she crossed Veiko's stare. Rage in those pale eyes, and frustration, and the first hint of something that might have been fear.

That shook her. Dried her voice up in her mouth and left her tasting dust. Snowdenaelikk in Ehkla's hands, think about that. About what Ehkla did to her captives. Poles and carving, yeah, and long, slow death. Veiko knew it. He had a partner now. Likely wouldn't by sunrise, whether or not she and Istel went looking.

Dekklis made fists. Ground her knuckles into her thighs. Snow was hardly helpless. But she was only one woman, at day's end, against—

"How many others up there, Veiko? Briel tell you that?"

His mouth quirked. "Many."

"You noticed there's only two of us?" She clawed for eyelock with Istel again and dragged another breath. "We need better than *she's up near the walls* if we're going to find her. You got more than that?"

"I do not. Briel does."

"And Briel is where?" Knew the answer, guessed it, even before Veiko's head turned. Leather flap and rattle of claws on the window ledge. The svartjagr looked at Dekklis and flexed her wings and draped that barbed tail over the sill.

Dekklis made her hands relax. Hoped her voice sounded steadier than it felt, creeping and hitching out of her throat.

"Dramatic. You plan that entrance? Circling around out there, waiting for your cue? Veiko call you in?"

"I did not have to," said Veiko. "She saw you arrive."

There was a thought to make skin creep. Dek glared at the svartjagr, who stretched her neck toward Dekklis and opened her mouth. Needle white teeth in plum-colored gums, a tongue more blue than black. A hiss that Dekklis felt more than heard.

"She says hurry. She says the fire is spreading, and soon you will not get across the Bridge. She says the legion are moving down from the Hill."

"She say who set the fire? No? Pity." Shallow breath that tasted like smoke, which Dekklis held until her throat hurt. She let it out and made herself look at the svartjagr. Disconcerting to look into those hot coal eyes and imagine Snow on the far side. "Big risk you're taking, yeah? Trusting me."

The svartjagr's head dipped. "Chrrip."

Imagine an echo of Snow's barbed grin, and her dry *maybe I'm just that desperate.*

Oh yes, bet she was. And bet she had some plan, too. Believe that she did.

The wind picked that moment to change direction. Straight out of the north now, whistling over the sill, dragging flat grey and chill with it. Smelled like dead things, which only meant it was coming over the butchers' quarter first. Didn't mean ghosts, or the sudden horrible certainty K'Hess Kenjak was in the room, in the shadows behind Veiko's naked shoulder.

"That storm that's coming. Yours, or Ehkla's?"

"It is not mine."

"Too bad. Be nice to have a little help up there."

Veiko cocked his head. Poured a grim smile into the corner of his mouth that did not reassure her at all.

"You will."

# CHAPTER NINETEEN

The storm started as rain. Fat drops from fatter clouds that had already swallowed the sun. It would turn to a thick spring snow later, slick the streets foul. Make it hard to run, yeah, harder still if she got herself lost. Snowdenaelikk counted the alleys, left and right. They were up near the walls, a long way from Market Bridge. The overcast meant no convenient shadows, either. Everything flat and grey and smeared on the edges, and half an afternoon before sunset.

"Maybe you should put this toadshit off another day, yeah? Try to burn Market Bridge again tomorrow?"

Tsabrak ignored her. Hooded and hunched up like a wet crow, he took point. She came second. One man behind her, and one on each side. The rest, she reckoned, trailed out behind them, like a hem unraveling. Might figure to stop her if she ran. Might figure to hack her to pieces, too. Too many hands too close on their hilts for her liking.

She leaned sideways. Controlled the smirk as her left-side escort veered away. Afraid of her. Very flattering. She tried on her brightest smile.

"I'm not your enemy, yeah?" Spread her hands as far as the ropes would permit. "See? Not even dangerous. Got no weapons."

Tsabrak had seen to that. Picks and daggers, all collected in a none-too-gentle search of her person. He'd bound her hands after. Mere rope, which she figured for arrogance, so certain he was that he'd got all her metal. He'd handed one end of the rope to her right-side escort and the other to Left Side, who wrapped it once round his wrist and kept his other hand on his blade. Who eyed her now, well out of strike range, as if she were a dragon on the other end of a leash.

The rain picked up. Pelting now, like tiny hailstones. Beading on her hair and soaking through, so that it ran cold down her scalp and into her collar.

She dipped her shoulder and reached for her hood, hands bound and awkward, fingers waving like baby birds after worms.

"If you could just grab that, yeah? Help me out," she said, peering under the crook of her arm.

Left Side said nothing. Right Side, however, snapped, "Shut up and move, bitch."

"Bitch. *Bitch.* That's such an Alvir insult." She succeeded, finally, in catching the edge of her hood. Straightened and turned all the way round to face him, with her hood clutched in her fists. "We Illhari like to say *motherless.* Can you manage that one? Moth. Er. Less. Oh come on, the accent's not hard—"

She relaxed as he hit her hard and square between her breasts, mostly the broad heel of his palm. Pretended to stagger and checked her footing while she did it. Yeah, slick enough underfoot, even though it was only rain. Blame a lack of plumbing. At least the shit didn't stink so much now. Not as much as Right Side's breath, in a face close enough she could bite it. Features she wouldn't forget

*carve your fucking heart out, feed it to Briel*

gathered into a scowl. "I said shut up."

"Yes, I heard you. But I'd like to get my hood up, yeah? Motherless rain."

He struck at her again, and she bent out of his way. A step closer to the Left Side, another loop of slack in the rope. She dropped both hood and hands. Gathered the rope between her palms.

"Enough!"

Tsabrak glided into her periphery. Snow watched Right Side flinch at what he saw in Tsabrak's face. Let her own lips crack into a grin.

"See now? You've slowed us all down. Got the boss's attention."

Tsabrak didn't shout. Chip of ice and darkness, and no sign of his hands in the cloak. Soft voice, razor tone. "What're you playing, Snow?"

"Trying not to get wet. These toadbellies here wouldn't help with the hood. I asked."

"Mm." Tsabrak made a show of pulling her hood up, of settling it over her topknot and smoothing the loose strands out of her face. His breath was sweet and warm on her cheek. "Enough out of you, yeah?"

"Sure. I'm no trouble. You know it."

He jerked hard at the rope. Pulled the extra out of her hands hard enough to sting. Took up all the excess and delivered it first to Right Side, then Left. Told them both: "You keep this tight, yeah? And keep her close. She's killed more people than you've ever met. Get careless, it'll be you."

"Flattery," she murmured. "And lies, yeah? I haven't killed that many. Real trouble's where we're going. You should tell them what Ehkla does to Alvir—"

"Shut up." She knew the tone well enough. At the end of his patience. Violence next, if she pushed him.

She didn't. Dropped her chin again and counted steps to the crossroads. Fifteen steps, left. Angle north, left.

They'd run short of city, they kept this direction. Tsabrak would walk them right into the walls.

Pressure on her wrists. Right Side and Left, pulling carefully, as if she were a particularly aggressive goat. She pretended not to notice. Tilted her face up until the hood threatened to fall back again. Mark that cornice and that roofline. That angle where the streets joined, which looked like a dog's leg, and the alley slanting off and down. A trail that a svartjagr would recognize, coming in from above.

Veiko might understand what'd happened by now. Had a gift for understanding Briel, yeah, like she never had. Please, Laughing God,

*if you want my help, you listen*

he packed his gear and left before the storm.

*He won't, yeah? You know that.*

No. He wouldn't. Responsibility for his guest had turned into something else.

Partner.

She couldn't think about his chance against Tal'Shik, no. Had to worry about her own chances. She could hope for Dekklis to come. Hope for Istel. She had to hope for someone, or she'd lose nerve. Though none of them would do much against Ehkla.

*Not their problem, is she? Yours.*

Snow planted her feet. Stopped. Waited until Rear Guard found his courage and shoved her, mostly knuckles on her spine. She yielded this time, fell hard, and twisted on her way down. She wrenched Left Side off his balance, earned a burst of profanity, Right and Left snarling at Rear. She landed on aching knees in the

*Laughing God, what is this sludge?*

street while Right and Left and Rear snapped among themselves.

And then Tsabrak was on her. Took her arm and wrenched her upright. "Next time I'll have them break a finger. You walk."

She gave his own smirk back to him. "You tell them no pushing, yeah? Hard to keep balance, with hands tied together. Or you could let me go."

"No."

She shrugged. Let him steer her into motion. Made an obvious look at his cloak where it broke on the line of her sword.

Tsabrak followed her gaze. Snorted. "Too late for that," he said, and laid a hand across the scabbard anyway. "You wanted a fight, you should've tried on the Finger. I'm still not sure why you didn't."

She showed him teeth. "For you, yeah? Way I reckon it, you drag me in all beat up, she won't have as much fun killing me, and then she might take it out on you."

"She isn't going to kill you."

"No?"

"No." Gently, as if he were telling a child not to believe in monsters. "Give her what she wants, she won't hurt you at all."

"Toadshit. If you think she's going to leave me alive, you're smoking something stronger than jenja. Bets how long it takes me to die?"

He made a strangled noise. Squeezed her elbow hard enough to numb her fingers and held on for a pair of hissed-through-teeth breaths. Pushed her away then and stalked back to the front. Maybe she'd hit a nerve somewhere. Wouldn't call it a conscience. Maybe the remnants of old affection, old loyalty.

Snow closed fingers over her palm. The God's mark felt warm.

This time she let Left and Right pull her along. Rear crowded up on her heels and muttered unintelligible threats at the back of her head, punctuated with the occasional fingertip shove. She ignored him. Kept count of streets and steps and realized that Tsabrak wasn't leading them anywhere. Walking around, knotting through the same streets and alleys, pausing and looking up sometimes and doubling back. Trying to get her lost, maybe, for what good it would do him. She had been born in the labyrinth of Illharek's Suburba. Made the Warren look like neat rows of grain. If he wanted to get her lost, he should've hooded her first. Gouged out her eyes and dragged her blind.

*There's a thought. Why don't you keep it to yourself, yeah? Give him ideas.*

Third time past the same ruined, ancient frieze on the same cracked wall, Tsabrak called a halt. He jagged alone into the alley and tapped a pattern onto the door. It snicked back less than a finger's width. Someone's breath plumed out hot, or jenja-laced, or both, too far to hear the conversation.

Snow shifted one miserable foot to the other. Raked a cynical stare across the frieze. It was cheap work, old, pre-Republic. Predictable subject: a golden-haired Alvir man—some thegn, probably, some forgotten hero—with his sword hilt deep in a

*wurm*

very small, very unconvincing black dragon, pinned halfway out of a cave and dribbling fire from its dying jaws. Painted sunlight blazed off the mirror-steel of the thegn's breastplate. It was a common enough theme, yeah, see some version of it in half the village taverns. Didn't take an Academy scholar to understand it: some defeat of the Dvergiri, who crawled out of the earth only to die on bright Alviri blades. Guess whose fault, that dragon and Dvergiri were linked in Alviri minds. Something else the Republic owed to Tal'Shik. She wondered if it had been Tsabrak's idea, or the God's, to hide Ehkla inside this building, someone's idea of irony. Either way: the frieze made an easy landmark for Briel.

So she stared hard at it.

"You know," she muttered, "whoever he is, that man, he's killing a svartjagr. You ever seen a real dragon, toadbelly? Bet you haven't, living up here. They're a lot bigger. No way one soldier can kill one. Especially not some toadbelly man."

Right Side growled. "Shut up, you b—"

"Bitch, yes, I know. And that armor. Your people stopped wearing all that metal when we killed your horses and you had to march for yourselves. You can thank Tal'Shik's godsworn for that. That was serious godmagic. Surprised there's any of you left at all. All that rotting meat, the plagues. Too bad all your fighting skill relied on riding animals. You aren't much without them."

Predictably back-knuckled clout to the side of her head. She let her neck roll with the blow. "Way the chronicles tell it, the Taliri were real pissed about the horses. Herded them, didn't they? Nomads. And there they were, foot-bound and angry. No great wonder they turned on you lot. You know what they say about mercenaries. One day they're fighting beside you. Next day they're burning your village and putting people on stakes."

This time Right Side punched her hard enough to send sparks across her vision. She squeezed her eyes against reflexive tears. Chuckled out loud. Kept the grin when Tsabrak doubled back and snagged the rope for himself.

"I'll take her from here," he said. And added, conversationally, "If Ehkla doesn't kill you, Snow, I might."

Better sense said shut up, but better sense could fuck itself. She smiled a promise at him.

"Likewise."

His anger bled into an unkind amusement. Another crank on the rope, and he pulled her face down and level with his. "I'd be kinder than what he'll do, yeah?"

Snow flicked a glance past Tsabrak's shoulder. There was a Talir standing square in the alley, in front of the now-open door. He wore patchwork legion armor, leather and metal stitched over his vital bits. Taller than she was and broad as her and Tsabrak together.

He looked at her like something he'd found floating in the gutter. "Snowdenaelikk."

"Sorry," she said brightly. "I don't think we've met. Mind if I call you toadfucker? Because it looks like your mother might have been."

The Talir skinned his lips back tight against his teeth. "I will rape you to death for what you did."

Tsabrak snapped out a fist and popped the Talir in his stolen breastplate, squarely on the Illharek seal. The tension on her rope and wrists never wavered. "No," he said gently. "You won't."

Ask what the Talir saw in Tsabrak's face. Snow could guess it. Could muster a twinge of reluctant sympathy, as the man crumpled like parchment in a fire, folded sideways, and shuffled aside. Left the doorway behind him gaping and uncontested.

Snow dropped her chin to Tsabrak's shoulder. Breathed a lungful of oiled, wet wool and old jenja and murmured, "The fuck did I do to him?"

"Not to him. To Ehkla." Tsabrak turned a profile, mouth twisted weary and tight. "And not you. Your partner."

"Right. So what did Veiko do?"

"Patience." Tsabrak pulled her through the doorway, where the shadows seemed unnaturally solid. "You'll see soon enough."

* * *

Veiko squatted at the edge of the black river and watched his reflection ripple and change. A boy's face one moment, all the angles rubbed soft. A middle-aged man's the next, weathered and gaunt. An old man, finally, one-eyed, his braids gone to ropes of grizzled hair. Then a copy of his own face, the one he'd seen this morning in Snow's silver-glass, winter-pale. Blood bubbled out his mouth, ran out his nose, pooled red on the underside of the water.

Take that as warning or prediction. He might live to be an old man. He might die today.

*Guess which, yeah?*

"Go," he bade the reflection. "I don't want you."

The river rippled hard, and his face sank back into the depths. Other faces crowded up, washed and rolled like weeds against each other.

Helgi paced impatience into the river's soft banks, sniffing and growling under his breath. He yipped and laid his ears back when Veiko drew his knife.

"Wait," Veiko told him. Rubbed his palm down hip and thigh to dry it. Flexed and curled the fingers.

Noidghe bargained. The stories were full of examples: asking the spirits for advice, for power, for help or harm or healing. And always, in the stories, the noidghe gave the spirits back something of equal value. A wolf-spirit might want a rabbit left tethered in the bushes. An elk might ask for a rock leopard's paw. But he already knew what the river-dead wanted. On this side or that, blood was a ghost's preferred currency.

He drew the blade across the meat of his hand. Quick and shallow cut that welled up red. He clenched his fist over the river. When the first red struck the black, he spoke.

"K'Hess Kenjak."

A second drop.

"K'Hess Kenjak."

Whose face appeared before the third drop fell and caught the drop on open lips. His eyes were cloudy, a corpse's stare, blind and hungry.

Another drop, and Veiko said, "I call you, K'Hess Kenjak, by blood and your name."

Blink, and the boy's eyes cleared. He frowned recognition. Puffed his cheeks round and pushed through the river's surface. Black water streamed off him, thick as ink. He dragged himself out, hands and knees. Coughed as if he still had lungs, until Veiko thought the ghost might choke himself to a second death.

Veiko offered him no help. Cleaned his knife and sheathed it. He drew his knees up, rested wrists and forearms across them. Waited as Kenjak found whatever breath a dead man needed.

"Skraeling. I thought we were finished. There's no more I can teach you. You know everything I do about the glyphs on the pole. You can summon her when you're ready."

"That is not why I am here."

"Then why? Wait." The dead Illhari's eyes raked over him. "I smell Ehkla on you."

Unsettling. Veiko resisted the urge to rub his leg. Put his hand on Helgi's ruff instead. "Yes. That is why I require your—"

*Help,* he'd meant to say. Changed his mind midbreath. "Your advice again. She is in Cardik. She has Snowdenaelikk."

Kenjak made a face. Took a fistful of his hair and squeezed. The water dripped and ran into nothing before it ever struck the bank. "You want to know how she'll kill the half-blood? I'll tell you that for free. So will half this river."

"I do not intend to let her kill my partner."

Long stare, river cold. "And you think my advice will prevent it?"

"Perhaps you are right." Veiko opened his hand again. Cracked the fragile scab, so that fresh red welled up, bright against the half-dry smears. "You can go back to your river, K'Hess Kenjak."

It seemed to Veiko that the river was rising. Lapping much closer to his boots while Helgi nipped at his sleeve. He retreated, knowing better than to argue with the dog. Definitely rising, yes, the river reaching fingers up the bank to drag back what belonged to it.

Kenjak jumped as the river touched him, and Veiko saw the boy again beneath the ghost. "Wait. Wait, skraeling. You might want more than advice."

"I might." Veiko closed his fist again and tried not to notice the way Kenjak watched him. Like Logi watched scraps. "But let us begin with that."

\* \* \*

It was dark inside the building, in this narrow corridor, except for the ghost-glow off plaster walls that might've been white once. Dust sifted down from the ceiling. Snow blinked and coughed and blinked again, until she could breathe. Until she could see, too, for what good it did her. The passage ended some ten steps ahead, took a sharp right into a wash of faint light.

And quiet. A long time since Snow had felt real silence, that tangible weight pushing in on her, counterpressure to straining lungs and heart. Hungry quiet that devoured any whisper of boots or breathing. The dust hazed into a backspill of peatfire smoke that suggested a partly blocked chimney nearby. Candles, too, a lot of them, throwing tallow and perfume into the cold, humid air. Under all of it, almost buried, a sweet rot any chirurgeon through her apprenticeship would recognize.

Laughing God, please there wasn't a corpse already spiked and waiting. Snow had a sudden, irrational conviction that it was Veiko dead around that corner, that Ehkla had breached Still Waters and dragged him up here and killed him.

And Briel didn't notice? Not likely.

Dekklis, then. Or Istel. Aneki, yeah, Tsabrak would see some amusement in that.

*Focus, yeah? No imagining.*

Snow locked her jaw against asking. Patience. See soon enough, wouldn't she?

Tsabrak stopped in front of her, so suddenly she almost stepped on him.

"This is where I stop."

"And I what, just keep going? On my honor?"

"Oh, let's not call it honor." Too dark to see his face, shadows pulled to solid in his hood. His voice hissed like rain on coals. "You'll go because you have no choice."

"Always a choice."

"Always a price." Imagine fire where his eyes should be. Imagine the God's serrated smile. "The only question is, who pays if you don't?"

"Toadfucker. Surprised you don't want to watch, yeah? See her take me apart."

"I wasn't invited." He jerked the rope. Trapped her left hand and laced his fingers through hers. Gripped hard, so that the joints creaked. "I warned her. Told her"—hissed mixture of stale jenja and nervous sour—"what you can do. But she insists she sees you alone."

That was new information. Snow's thoughts burst down a half dozen paths, running like thieves from the legion. A woman could choke on hope.

No. A woman could get stupid.

Snow made herself look at Tsabrak. Focus on now, on here, on prodding that smirk off his face. "And you do what she tells you. How very proper of you, Tsabrak. Guess the old habits die slowly, yeah?"

"Sometimes I do what she says," he whispered. "Sometimes not."

He wrenched his wrist around and down and twisted. Snow had enough time to recognize what he intended, dropped her shoulder and elbow and turned with the movement. Mostly success, mostly, and still not enough: she twisted four of her fingers loose, curled them to safety in her palm, but her smallest finger remained trapped in Tsabrak's grip. She had a stretched moment to prepare for the inevitable. Held her breath and clenched her jaw.

Audible crack. White flash across her eyes, and then tunneling grey. Briel's wings beat the borders of her consciousness. Cold flooded in after, glacial stillness, which felt like Veiko. Imagine that, sure, and cling to it, to him, long enough to keep the acid contents of her belly behind her teeth. She swallowed the burn and bitter.

"That wasn't orders," said Tsabrak from a very far distance. "That was my idea."

Then she heard him draw a knife. Felt the sudden slackness in her arms as he cut her loose from her tether and left her wrists bound. Then a swirl of air that said Tsabrak had left her. She leaned against the wall and listened to the retreating murmur of the footfalls on the floorboards through the whole swarm of bees in her head.

Istel had threatened to break her fingers once, but Tsabrak knew better than Istel what that meant to a conjuror, who needed hands to make gestures, to hold power just so. And Tsabrak also knew her left hand was her strong one, not the right. She should be thankful he hadn't broken more than the littlest finger, that he hadn't pulled all five out of their sockets or cut off whole joints.

*Thankful, yeah. Sure. Thanks, Laughing God. You want me to fail, is that it?*

There was a thought, cold splash through the shake and nausea. If she failed here, the God could come collect from Veiko. And maybe that's what he wanted all along. Fuck and damn, hands were shaking, both of them. It was just a little fucking bone, nothing lethal. Nothing permanent. There were ways to kill Ehkla that weren't conjuring.

From the sweet-stink and tallow-bright room, right on cue: "Snowdenaelikk," soft and slurred and lazy. "Snowdenaelikk, come here."

Motherless toadfucker was probably flat on a couch, nibbling cheese, smirking fit to split her pretty face. Ehkla should be worried about letting Snow into her presence without guards and steel shackles and a whole handful of broken bones. So ask why she wasn't, and Laughing God, hate the answer.

*Because she thinks I can't hurt her, with or without broken fingers. Because she's Tal'Shik's godsworn. Because I'm going to die in there, soon as she gets what she wants out of me.*

Whatever that something was, Snow meant to sell it dearly.

She pulled herself straight and stalked the last handful of steps to the corner.

And stopped.

She had not believed, until then, that Ehkla would really meet her alone. Expected a roomful of Taliri, and chains, and a spike sunk into a hole in the floorboard. Expected rough hands at the least, and maybe a first round of gang rape while Ehkla watched and smiled.

But there was only a single chair near the smoky hearth, and a single shape sitting in it, robed and hooded in Taliri browns and greys. Ehkla's left hand claw-clenched at her throat, holding the hood up. Her right hand lay across her lap like a dead bug, Tal'Shik's sigil gleaming blood-dark on the palm. A rope of braided hair coiled out of the hood's cavern-dark. It looked, Snow thought, like a rat had crawled in there and died.

"Snowdenaelikk," said Ehkla. "Come here." And then, after a moment, "Please."

"All right," Snow said, as if she had any choice. One step. Another. The rot was much stronger now. Choking. Gagging, fuck and damn, there weren't enough candles in Cardik to mask that stench. Snow coughed. Flinched as her eyes stung and watered.

"What's dead? You hiding another sacrifice in here?"

Ehkla cackled, sounding like dice and dust. Her left hand crept sideways and plucked at the edge of the hood. The wool slipped once, twice, before she scraped it back. "Nothing dead. Not yet."

Ehkla's face still had that crystal-carved beauty as the hood puddled down around her shoulders. But one of her eyes was cloudy blue now, fogged and blind. Sweat gleamed on her forehead, beaded the top of her lip. Pain and fever shivered through her like wind through branches. She rocked sideways on the chair, so that its legs thumped and scraped. Writhed and squirmed and worked the cloak off one shoulder without moving her right arm at all.

Snow had seen wound rot, yeah, all stages. A chirurgeon either got used to blood and bone on the wrong side of skin, got used to pus and maggots, or she found different work. But she'd never seen a wound this far gone on a body still upright and lucid. Pus green as grass, the jagged ends of a collarbone jutting up like snow-covered peaks out of muscle as much grey as pink.

Snow remembered Veiko hunched on the hearthstones, firelight casting him orange as he honed his axe smooth.

*I hit her shoulder. She wore no armor. The blade drove in true, through bone.*

The eye, though—that had been his wound to Tal'Shik, an arrow in the spirit world. A wound that had transferred to Tal'Shik's godsworn, apparently.

"You're a mess," she said. "What's wrong? Tal'Shik can't fix you?"

"She can."

"Then why won't she? You're her favorite, yeah? Or have you pissed her off?"

Blind strike, a javelin thrown in the dark. Saw it stick, in Ehkla's sudden stiffness. The single yellow eye drooped and dipped away. Circled the floor, intent on nothing. "You are not here to ask questions."

"Then what am I here for? Bait? You think Veiko's coming to save my ass, you're wrong. Told Tsabrak that. And even if he could lift whatever curse is on you, he won't. Promise you that on my mother's—"

"No." Ehkla peered out of her remaining eye. Narrow, golden, glittering with fever or fury or both. "Haven't you guessed, Snowdenaelikk? I want you to kill me."

# CHAPTER TWENTY

The half-blood Aneki was waiting for them in the hallway, crossed arms and one hip hitched against the wall. She straightened as Dekklis came through the door. Skipped a glance past Dekklis's shoulder, once and twice.

Dekklis sighed. "We didn't touch Veiko, yeah? He's fine."

Aneki's gaze settled, hard and clear. "Of course he is. You're no danger to him."

"Your bondies thought otherwise."

"You're highborn," Aneki said, and shrugged. "And legion. What else should they think?"

A woman could get tired of being the enemy in her own city. Dekklis shouldered past Aneki with a little more force than she needed. Choke on the woman's perfume, that was one thing, but that skirt had folds enough to hide a dozen knives. "Sorry. Have some place to be, savvy?"

"Oh, savvy." Aneki kept pace with her. "But you'll want better weapons than you have, if you're going into the Warren."

Dekklis snapped a look, closed her mouth. Through teeth: "And I suppose you happen to keep some on hand."

"And armor."

"And armor. Well. That's lucky."

"Not luck." Aneki's lips creased. "Might not be the best fit, but it's something between you and angry people."

\* \* \*

Aneki proved correct: the armor wasn't a good fit. Wasn't scout's armor, either: a heavier set, meant for the Sixth's infantry and a man's frame, which meant gaps at the waist and neck, and bands of black steel around her chest, across her shoulders, weight a scout didn't carry. Teslin wouldn't have noticed; then again, Teslin wouldn't have gotten the hooks together across chest and back, wouldn't have gotten the straps buckled at all. But the sword belt fit fine over Dek's shoulder, and the blade was pure legion-standard, and she knew how to run with both.

The gear bore the tribune's stamp, destined for the legion, and here it was, in a brothel in the Street of Silk Curtains. So yes, this was part of the contraband moving in Cardik, part of the God's smuggling. Bet she and Istel ran into people wearing part of the same shipment before sunset, on the wrong side of that riot.

If they got there in time. That meant running faster. Never thought she'd thank Rurik for the drills, for his insistence on running every-damn-where.

"Snow," she said to Istel, who ran beside her. "Thinks of everything, doesn't she? Storing gear for us with Aneki. So thoughtful."

"She knew this was coming, Dek. She told us as much. You surprised she thought of it, or surprised that she'd rather we live through a street fight?"

Istel had fared better with his gear, Istel being closer to the shape the smith had intended during forging. He jogged beside her, breathing easily, with no need to keep tugging the armor square over his hips. Sleet slashed down, muffling footfalls and the creak of new leather and metal still sharp on the edges and smearing the remnants of the day into an early twilight. The lanterns flickered uncertainly.

It would be full dark by the time they got up near the walls, except for whatever light the Bridge fire gave them. Assuming it managed to keep burning through the storm. Assuming they got across Market at all, which they wouldn't if the praefecta's troops beat them there.

"Faster," she snapped. And hell with that lingering twinge in her ribs, which did not like cold or wet or extra armor.

"Feel like a green again," Istel said cheerfully. "You ever infantry, Dek?"

"First Legion, Second Cohort," clipped short. The rain stung like gravel where it hit her face. "Where is that animal?"

"Not like we need her yet. We know where the Bridge is." Reasonable Istel, now that he'd gotten his way. Off on a rescue now, following the half-blood's tame svartjagr and her less-than-tame partner's directions.

Be lucky if they didn't run straight into ambush, up in the Warren's dark. Be lucky if Briel didn't lead them right into one—

*Shee-oop*, diving out of rain, skimming close over her head. Dekklis saw herself, for a dizzy moment, through Briel's eyes. Saw, in the next moment, the wet gleam off Illhari steel, helmets bobbing four abreast through a street rinsed in lantern light from glass windows. Signs jutted out of the wall, most of them paint and pictures, all of them crisp-edged and unchipped. A tankard, a loaf of bread, a weaver's wheel and spindle. The perspective tightened, vision sharper than Dekklis's own. Red-and-black livery under the armor, and the Sixth's crest on the helmets.

And then she was alone in her own head, her vision blurred by rain and dark. She staggered and picked up her stride again and pretended she didn't need Istel's hand on her elbow for balance. Pretended her heart wasn't banging panic off breastbone and throat. Veiko had warned her, hadn't he, about Briel's sendings.

*Snowdenaelikk used to lose her sight afterward.*

*Used to. And now?*

*Now she does not. But she says that it is still unpleasant.*

It was, hell and damn. A blinding headache, so that Dekklis felt every cobble on the street vibrate up her spine.

"The Sixth," she gasped. "Just passed the main square."

"Shit." Istel's grin wasn't cheerful now. More like a dog's bare-toothed warning. "It'll be a near thing if we beat them."

In the end it was *too* close and just on the wrong side of victory. Dekklis had a moment's elation, skidding out onto Market Street from the alley and seeing rain-slick empty between them and the Bridge. And in the next heartbeat,

"Hoy! You there," from upslope and behind. "Stop! Identify yourselves!"

Dekklis spun partway. Jogged sideways, with the Bridge's faint pinkish-orange glow like a sunset on the limits of her vision. There was a line of legion up the street, coming this way.

"Keep going," she told Istel, and louder, "First Scout Szanys Dekklis, Second Legion, Sixth Cohort, *on orders!*"

"I said *stop!*" A woman's voice, *that* woman: front and center and pulling away from the line. Rough-cut features, not highborn, a face Dekklis knew. Dekklis slowed to a trot, squared her back to the Bridge. Listened to Istel's splash and clank, and the dull thud as he stepped onto wood. Put her arms out, fingers spread and empty, and stopped.

"Haantu, hoy, it's me."

Second Spear R'Haina Haantu raised her fist and kept coming. Stopped beside Dekklis as the ranks broke and streamed around them. Her breath steamed through her teeth like jenja smoke.

"What you doing down here, Dek? And the fuck is your uniform? That infantry kit you've got?"

"Told you. Orders. This armor's part of it."

"That's Istel with you, then?"

"That's right."

Haantu grimaced. "Sorry. Got my own orders. No one crosses. Call him back."

"Can't do that."

"Huh." Haantu grabbed a passing legionnaire. "Jari. Get that man on the bridge, yeah? One of ours. Be gentle."

"Haantu, listen, First Spear K'Hess is aware of our mission."

"Didn't mention it to *me*." Haantu looked past her. Bellowed: "*Take your positions.* —Sorry, Dek. I'll send a runner. Your story checks, you're on your way."

Hell and damn. Haantu had a reputation for sticking at details. Made her a good commander, exactly the right woman to hold the Market Bridge against whatever came out of the Warren. Exactly the wrong woman to argue with, too.

So Dekklis didn't. She turned to check Istel's progress. He was a third of the way across now, dodging hard around tipped carts and panicked chickens, Jari coming up fast in his wake. Most of the Bridge was deserted. At least one kiosk had burned utterly, gone to black sticks and smoke, the ones on either side of it sputtering. A clot of confusion at the far side, where a mob pressed up against—what, Dekklis couldn't see. She stretched onto her toes. A barricade, looked like, debris and a couple of handcarts piled together and blocking the Warren side of the Bridge. Istel hit the back fringe of the crowd and disappeared, one more dark Dvergir head among dozens. Jari was easier to spot, in the legion helmet, in the bright red and black. And then Dekklis saw the Alviri: pale heads studding the top of the barricade and more on the ground on this side of it. Foremothers defend, there was a whole wedge of them already *on* the Bridge, coming over the barricade and forcing their way upstream through the crowd. Legion weapons in their hands, mostly swords, a few spears.

*Revolution. Blood and fire. Damn you, Snow.*

"The fuck?" Haantu shouldered past Dekklis, hand on her sword. "What are *they* doing over there? Are they *armed*? Eiri, Jako, get the crossbows up here—"

Dekklis ran. Fast, driving steps as Haantu shouted something at her, brushing past startled shoulders just setting a line across the Bridge. And then it was a long stretch of empty ahead, wood booming hollow under her boots

*too loud*

and a burning in her throat, exertion and smoke together. Grinning as she ran, lips peeled back and rain pelting cold on her teeth. She dragged her sword out of its sheath. Shouted Istel's name as Briel shrieked overhead.

And impact as she hit a crumbling wall of civilians. She battered through them, shoulder first, elbows scything. Like swimming a river in snowmelt, debris and currents and best she could do to hold on to the sword and avoid cutting anyone. Half chant, half shout:

"Get out of my way, clear, *clear*!"

Until she met an Alvir, who mirrored her grin and raised his right arm. She punched, pommel first into his face, slashed down and across and shoved him sideways.

She knew the feel of metal parting flesh, knew a mortal wound from the scaling shriek that followed. Knew that it would draw others like wolves. Chop and cut, don't stop. She kept an eyeline on Jari, cornered and half-mooned inside a ragged perimeter, howling like one of Veiko's angry dead.

A bolt whistled past Dekklis. Thumped home into someone.

*Legion's firing into the crowd. Here's your riot, Snow.*

A scream, then another, then dozens, swelling to some fresh panic. The crowd reversed its surge, carrying her back across the Bridge, away from the Warren and Snow and Ehkla.

And behind her: "The Sixth! The Sixth!" growing closer as the legion charged.

So much for orders, then, or Haantu had lost control of her troops. Dekklis drove her heels down, bent knees and braced and *there*, carved her own path.

She caught an elbow in the side of her head, dull thump that spread white and hot and blinding. She stabbed that way, pure reflex. Felt the sword sink into flesh and stick there. Held on, twist and pull—

And staggered free, off balance, one eye blurred and streaming. Water, blood, tears. Sword in her hand, rain stripping it back to clean steel. She spun.

Eyeblink: the dull gleam of a steel bolt. The realization that it was going to hit her. And then falling, twisting, as her chest exploded.

A hand seized her arm. Wrenched as her vision sparked and flickered. Kept her upright, more or less, dragged her into the lee of an upended handcart and pulled her down again.

*Don't be in such a damn hurry, Dek*, from a distance. Dying, wasn't she. Must be, to think she saw Teslin hovering over her. Teslin, who had died in front of her, cut down by Taliri in a winter forest. Fresh blood on filthy snow. *That* was Teslin, not this

*angry dead*

woman made of mist, whose flesh was no barrier to the slashing rain. Hell and damn, that was *Barkett* with her, no arrows bristling out of him, both eyes whole and wide and worried. She could see the handcart's outline past—no, *through*—his shoulders and torso.

Dekklis hid in the black behind her eyelids and wondered how long it would take her to finish dying.

"Dek. You okay?" That was Istel, who seemed solid enough. Whose hands were warm on her cheek.

She put her hand on her chest. Expected a hole, expected blood, and found neither. She stared at her fingers, wet only with rain. Fog drifted across her vision, company to the chill settling into her bones. She shivered.

"Yeah. Somehow."

Istel probed along the seams of the armor. He was, she realized, no longer wearing his own. Down to plain wet wool and leather, his hair plastered in strings to his face.

"Bolt glanced off," Istel said. "You were lucky. Sixth's on the Bridge, savvy that? All of them, coming across." He touched her cheek carefully, winced at the face she made. "It's starting."

Riot. Revolution. Snow's blood and fire.

Dekklis pushed herself a little more upright. Craned her neck and peered around the cart. There was a body on the Bridge an arm's length away, young Dvergir sprawled on her belly. The rain had rinsed the surrounding wood to a thin pink froth.

Dekklis stared at the woman's dead eyes. "You see what happened to Jari?"

"Down," said Istel. "They swarmed him."

"Are you sure? Maybe he's just hurt—"

*He's dead, Dek.* Teslin squatted beside Istel, arms on her knees. Fog swirled around her ankles. The handcart's wheel spun through her left shoulder, pushed by the wind and the rain. Her armor rippled like a sheet where the spokes passed through.

A soldier didn't survive if she panicked easily. A soldier took what happened, and adapted to it, and kept going. So there was no point at all insisting that Teslin could not be there, no, when it was obvious that she was. And just as obvious, "You're dead, Teslin."

*Can't argue that.* Teslin's mouth twisted. *The skraeling said you'd need help. Guess you do.*

"Help." Jari had needed help and died anyway. The Sixth still needed it. But there would be runners on their way to the Hill by now, bringing reinforcements. Trained Illhari troops could handle a street mob. They didn't need her.

Snow, however, did. Motherless half-blood heretic Snowdenaelikk, whose skraeling partner called up Dek's dead friends for *help*.

Foremothers forgive, but it was good to see Teslin. And where Teslin was—

"Where'd Barkett go? I saw him. Didn't I?"

*Yeah.* Teslin jerked her chin upslope. *Scouting ahead. The svartjagr's carrying on about something. Toadfucking godmagic up there, I think.*

Godmagic. Ask what flesh and bone could do against godmagic except die. And then ask what dying meant anymore, with Teslin *here* and Barkett up *there* and foremothers knew how many more of her dead friends haunting the streets on Veiko's say-so.

And then ask what would happen if Ehkla won whatever it was Ehkla meant to achieve. Ask how many more dead Veiko would have to call on.

Dekklis looked

*through*

past Teslin, to where the barricade hulked between the Bridge and the Warren. It wasn't large. Maybe chest height, and no deeper than the oxcart that made up its bulk. But anyone trying to climb it would leave her back exposed to the Sixth's crossbows and javelins. And on the other side—bet on a nest of Alviri, armed with contraband weapons.

"We won't get over that."

Teslin shook her head. *We'll get past it. Come on, Dek.*

Another bolt slammed into the planking. It had, Dekklis saw, a bit of flesh still attached. She waited for the subsequent scream. Couldn't hear it. Only tunneling quiet, like a wall between her and the battle not fifteen paces away, as the fog thickened around. The rain had stopped, she realized. There was frost on the metal bands of her armor, while the wet wool and linen stiffened and chilled. The smoke and blood smells rinsed away into pervasive nothing.

"Come *on.*"

Then it was Istel pulling her up again, with a pincer grip on her arm. Dragging her toward the Warren, following Teslin's broad, translucent back. They pulled her *through* the barricade as if it were made of fog and cobwebs, as if the Alviri swarming over it were made of mist. Dekklis saw one of them flinch and startle where Teslin walked through him. Briel scythed overhead, solid black shape cutting uphill, keening.

Toward Snow. Toward Ehkla.

Hell.

* * *

Snow shook her head. "You want me to *what*?"

"Kill me. That is why you came, is it not?"

"I came because Tsabrak dragged me."

Ehkla laughed, one sharp peal before pain hitched her airless. Gasp and wheeze, then sibilant: "*He* may think so. But you mean to kill me. You'd have come eventually. I know my enemies."

"Thought we were allies."

"You never did." An ordinary woman would've shaken her head. Ehkla still had the reflex. Turned her cheek a fingerlength and stopped. Held very still while her eyelids creased closed and her breath hitched and stopped. That was a woman fighting for quiet, for control, for some measure of her dignity.

*And she wants you to kill her. That's convenient.*

Laughing God, wasn't it. There were candles here. Snow could burn through the ropes. And with her hands free, she could pull power out of stone and wood. Shape it, even with that broken finger bone. She might bring down the ceiling. Might send fire up the walls. Blast her way back to Veiko, bring this whole side of the Bridge down in fire and blood.

Felt like the God's hands on her back, pushing, sounded like his whisper.

*Do it. Clear your debt. Save your skraeling.*

Her chest constricted. This whole business stank worse than Ehkla's rotting.

"Doesn't matter what I think. Tsabrak says we're allies. So does the God."

"The God." There, Ehkla's old smile, the one like a nightmare. "The God has already betrayed our alliance. Has already betrayed you, too, I think. Those scars on your wrists. Are they new?"

"These? Yeah. My fault. I like to play with fire. Watch." Chin up, shoulders back, Snow walked to the nearest brace of candles. Stretched her hands wide as she could, lowered them until the flames touched the rope still wrapped around each wrist. Fibers blacked. Curled and smoked and parted.

Then the candles flickered, as if the room had suddenly run out of air. In the absence of tallow and smoke, the rot stench was damn near unbearable.

So Ehkla wasn't defenseless. Good to know. Still had some command of godmagic, which might or might not be a match for Snow's second-tier conjuring.

*So find out, yeah?*

The ropes hadn't burned through yet. Down to blackened threads, still silk-strong, that would not yield to what physical strength Snow could manage. But she had enough slack to move her palms apart, to cup the air and draw on what spark remained in the nearest wicks. She flexed her fingers—even *that one*, which made her vision spark—moved the fire here to *there*. It arced off the wick. Licked out onto the ropes. Crackled and flared and spread and devoured, sparing her skin underneath. Bright flare that chased shadows into the corners, that showed Snow the cracked plaster walls covered in sigils and glyphs that gleamed wet and thick.

Columns of them, lines that made her eyes ache and slide away while fear cramped cold in her belly. More godmagic. Cousin to the prayer on Kenjak's pole, in the same way that wolves were cousin to dogs.

*Fuck and damn.*

Snow clenched her fists on her conjuring. Banished the flame back to the candles, except for the sparks that escaped where her broken finger would not quite close. She brushed the fragile corpse of the rope onto the floor. Put her boot on the sparks and ground down. Let her hands drop loose while her wits scrambled like Logi on ice. She knew godmagic when she saw it. That was some kind of ritual, and only one person here could've scribed it.

"That toadshit on the walls," Snow said. "What's it for?"

"To make an avatar."

Bind a goddess to a living body, draw Tal'Shik's power into this world through blood sacrifice. That kind of power had broken the Alviri armies. Would break the Illhari legion, too, if it got loose here.

Snow knew her voice shook. Decided she didn't care. "I'm no godsworn."

"You don't need to be. You need only to kill me."

"Why me? Whole garrison on the Hill would fight for the privilege to kill you. You wouldn't even have to tell them why."

"You're a chirurgeon. Any fool with an axe can kill. But a sacrifice must be done correctly. Properly. You understand that. I cannot die too quickly."

"Ritual murder. Yeah. I hear you. So what, I do this and you go after Illharek? Bring down the Republic? Is that what *she* wants?"

"That matters to you?"

"Not particularly. But I'm in no hurry to replace what we've got now with pre-Purge toadshit, either."

"Tsabrak said—"

"Tsabrak doesn't speak for me. You want my help, you pay *me* for it. What's your offer?"

"Your life."

"Do better."

Ehkla's eyes threw back the candlelight, flame flicker in the gold. "I am not the only daughter of Tal'Shik among my people. There are other godsworn like me."

"Of course there are. They're the ones burning out the Alviri, yeah? Probably crowding up to replace you the minute you fall out of favor. Which you won't, if you get Tal'Shik to crawl into that rotting body with you."

"My sisters will destroy this city and put every Illhari they find on a pole. Half-bloods, too."

"And what will they do to you, hm? They've got no idea you look like this. They did, you wouldn't need me to kill you. *They'd* do it, only they wouldn't make you an avatar. That's why you're doing this toadshit, so they can't touch you. So again, *what the fuck can you offer me?*"

The smirk faded. "Veiko Nyrikki."

"He's yours to give now? I don't think so."

"I tell you this as a favor, Snowdenaelikk. He intends to face her, and if he does, he will die. If you hurry, she will come to me instead, and he will live."

"Veiko did all right last time, yeah? Put out her eye."

First sign of anger, flare and spit like water in hot oil. "He was lucky."

"Yeah? Luck must've hacked you up, too. He broke whatever godmagic toadshit you did to him, put an axe through you, and now you're worried. So is Tal'Shik. So is the fucking God, come to that. That's what scares you, yeah? That Veiko'll hurt Tal'Shik again. And if your goddess goes down, the God will be on her."

"And so Veiko will die, to help the God."

"He won't care so much, long as he gets Tal'Shik. He's crazy like that."

"You care." That simple, that certain. That smug, her white teeth lined up legion-straight in a grin.

And not wrong, no. Dead shot, like an arrow that goes straight past armor and sticks in the heart. A body might keep moving after that, might keep running, but the end wasn't in doubt.

The glyphs on the wall seemed to writhe, like living things in pain. Proof that godsworn did not bargain, no, that they prayed, they asked, they sacrificed and hoped for some favor. Or they walked the other way, Purged and denied, and pretended the gods could not touch them. Extreme reactions, from a people who did not like half measures.

The God had told her, *Kill Ehkla*. It didn't matter what came after. She hadn't promised to save the Republic. But she hadn't promised to build a road so the God could march into Illharek and take over himself, either.

*One thing at a time, yeah?*

"My life. Veiko's life. I do this, *whatever happens*, you don't follow us. You or your motherless sisters or your motherless goddess. We walk away."

Ehkla's face was as blank as fresh plaster. "Tal'Shik will owe you a great debt. I will also owe you."

Imagine Veiko's face when he heard *that*, yeah. Snow swallowed laughter back like slivered glass. Said, raw-voiced:

"All right. Then tell me how you want to die."

\* \* \*

The black river was restless. It churned and frothed along its banks while the dead thrashed beneath its surface like spawning fish. Veiko stood on its bank beside K'Hess Kenjak and looked at the far side, where the forest hunched under a sky smudged to charcoal. Clouds roiled in what should be smooth, flat grey.

It was not a good omen.

Beside him, K'Hess Kenjak shifted his weight, one foot to the other. His armor creaked and sighed like old branches. He did not, Veiko noticed, leave any marks in the river's mud banks.

"The fighting's begun, skraeling."

"Yes." Veiko's own feet sank a knuckle's depth into the bank. He pushed onto his toes and felt the mud pull and shift. Very easy for a man to slip were he to attempt to jump the river. Very easy, even with two good legs. Which he did not have. The pain had followed him onto the glacier this time and grown worse with each step, until it was all he could do to stand steady on both feet.

He supposed that was not a good omen, either.

"Skrae—Veiko." Intense cold, where Kenjak touched his arm. "Something's happening. I can feel it."

"It is Tal'Shik," Veiko said with more confidence than he felt. It could be the whole realm of spirits turning inside out, for all he knew. Could be a perfectly natural event, that storm over the forest, the madness in the river.

*Tell yourself that.*

Kenjak swayed away from him. Paced two steps away, turned, and came back. "You should do something. Cross the river. Go to meet her."

"You are impatient."

"And you're afraid." Kenjak was not. Was angry, as only the dead could manage, lethal and cold as winter.

Veiko shrugged. Did not deny the cramp and twinge in his belly, or the tightness in his throat, or what they meant. The sky over the forest changed again. Purple now in the center, spreading out like a bruise.

Definitely a poor omen.

"Go," he told Kenjak. "Tal'Shik is my concern."

"I might help you."

"No," he said again, and retreated up the bank to flat, dry ground. Drew his knife from his belt. "You have given me what I asked. You have prepared me for this battle."

"I showed you what she cut into the pole, skraeling. I taught you those marks. How is that help?"

Patiently, slowly, as much for his own courage as Kenjak's persuasion, "It is a ritual. A prayer. She will come to me because the sigils say that she must. That is what Snowdenaelikk told me. That is why you had to teach me." Only, Snow had not known what his errand was when he asked to visit the ghost roads. It had been his guess that a ghost could not summon a spirit as great as Tal'Shik, and so Kenjak was safe enough making the marks. Now it was time to see if he'd learned them correctly. If he'd been right at all.

Kenjak followed him up the bank. "And when she finds you, then what? I'll tell you, skraeling. She'll do to you what she did to me."

"No," said Veiko. "She will not."

"Toadshit."

"K'Hess Kenjak. You have another debt. Go and pay it."

"Fool," Kenjak muttered. He spun away from Veiko's bemused stare and walked away. One, two, and the air split and shimmered. Kenjak stepped into the breach on the third step, and it sealed behind him. A faint swamp stink spread out on the air. Faded as the wind skipped off the glacier and tangled in Veiko's braids.

Imagine Snow's lazy-eyed smirk. *Idiot, keep him with you.*

*Do your job, and I will not need him.*

He wished for her laughter then, her corrosive humor that he understood only part of the time. Wished for *her*, narrow and solid, at his back. He was uncomfortably aware of the open sky, the tundra behind him. If he squinted, he could imagine the dark dots of takin moving along the glacier's far edge.

He had thought to meet Tal'Shik in the forest. There was symmetry in that, facing her where she had first challenged him. There were also trees to put between himself and a wurm's talons. She could drop on him from the sky here, which meant he would

*die, skraeling, isn't that what I said?*

need to be quick on his feet. And he would not be. Ehkla had seen to that.

He had also planned on having trees on which to carve the prayer sigils. There was nothing solid on this side of the river but himself and Helgi and the rock-studded tundra. He thought about kneeling and cutting, and how slowly he might get up again. How much time he would need to pull the axe and fight. How much he did not want to meet Tal'Shik on his knees.

Veiko looked at the knife in his hand.

*The power's in the cutting, not the mark.*

Then, feeling foolish, he raised the point to empty air. Thrust it forward and drew it down. The air caught fire in the blade's wake. Burned a vertical line. Veiko let go the breath he had not known he was holding.

Helgi looked at him and waved a dubious tail. Turned himself once and curled into a knot facing across the river. Eloquent *get on with it, then*, and a dog settled in for a wait.

Veiko carved another glyph, then two. He was aware of the wind coming out of the forest, evergreen sharpness mixed with something dry and old. There was a blackness growing in the clouds, soft edged and spreading.

Imagine it might be a wurm's shape. Imagine Ehkla somewhere up in the Warren, cutting her own prayer and calling Tal'Shik. Imagine Snowdenaelikk facing them both and feel sick.

*She can care for herself, yeah?*

Even Aneki did not believe that anymore. He'd seen that plainly enough when she armed Dekklis and Istel. Seen her despair after, when she watched him mix his own poison.

*She wouldn't want you dead, too.*

*I will not die.* And then he had pushed Aneki gently out the door.

The wind shifted. Brought the old blood smell of the river now, and an undercurrent of hot metal.

This was not an unexpected visit, either. Veiko paused, the knife curled in his palm, as Helgi uncurled and stiff-stepped toward the river.

The God stepped out of the forest. Walked easily across the mud and left no tracks and did not pause at river's edge. The water stiffened where he stepped, melted again in his wake. He stopped just on the near bank, some ten strides away. The flames in his sockets flickered madly, as if in strong wind.

"Stop. Veiko Nyrikki. By any debt you think you owe me, I ask that you stop this."

"I owe you nothing." He must not think about what had happened to Snow. The God was not his target.

*Yet.*

Veiko made himself say, "Your bargain is with Snowdenaelikk," and cut the next sigil in the air. "Seek her out if you wish to change the terms."

"She's beyond my reach."

"That is unfortunate."

The God edged sideways. Helgi pivoted with him and snarled, and the God did not try to pass. "Listen. That godsworn toadfucker Ehkla already marked you for sacrifice, yeah? You finish that prayer, you finish her work. Tal'Shik will come and snap you up like a flatcake."

"Perhaps." Veiko blew out a slow breath. Drew another, just as slowly. "But I need only slow her down."

"Why? For Snowdenaelikk's sake? Idiot. She's already betrayed us both. She made a new deal. Switched sides. She's doing what Tal'Shik wants now. Bought her own life and left you here to die."

Veiko's wrists and arms ached. His leg did—deep, wracking shivers that threatened his balance. He would not do well, facing Tal'Shik like this. She would kill him. He knew that, bone and blood.

*Told you to go, didn't I? Fuck and damn, Veiko.*

She had. Snow would not, he thought, blame him if he walked away. She might even expect it.

Veiko studied the pattern of knuckles and skin where he gripped the knife. White, with all the blood squeezed pink to the edges.

"And what do you offer me?"

"I can remove Ehkla's mark. Break her hold over you." The God shimmered like the air over a forge. Rippled. Reached, over Helgi's snarling disapproval. "I offer alliance, skraeling. Protection."

Veiko clenched his fist tight to keep it steady. Breathed, no matter the tightness and heat in his chest. "I have seen what you do to your allies."

The God looked at him. The flames in his sockets stilled completely, so that they looked like paintings of themselves. "She said you wouldn't care about that."

"That you believed her speaks poorly of your wisdom."

The chieftain's son had worn a similar expression when he'd seen Veiko raise his axe.

The God said only, "Skraeling," which sounded a lot like *idiot.*

Veiko turned back to his carving. "You should go now, unless you wish to meet Tal'Shik yourself."

He did not look to see if the God took his suggestion. But Helgi sat down again, stopped growling.

He was on the last glyph now. Paused at the top of the last stroke. Like balancing on the crest of a mountainside, skis on your feet, knowing that once you begin, you will not stop until the end.

He finished the cut.

The glyphs flared, orange fire to white heat to blinding. Turned liquid and red and ran together, like wax, like blood. He pressed the heel of his hand against his chest. His heart drummed steadily, measured, deliberate.

The sky tore like wet linen, and the wurm came through.

Veiko reached for his axe.

# CHAPTER TWENTY-ONE

Dekklis had faced a bread riot once, back in Illharek. New armor, new sword, new rank. She remembered the desperation on the citizens' faces, Dvergiri and Alviri both, and the mob surging against the granary gates. Remembered the black steel sagging inward, the terrible groan of splintering hinges. Remembered her centurion's shouts to *wait, wait, hold your positions you motherless toadshits* changing to *charge* and *get them.*

That had been slaughter.

Cardik's Warren in riot was both better and worse. There was no mob fleeing the legion this time. Fewer smashed shop fronts, fewer bodies. The streets were still slick, but it was rain, not blood, and the screams, no less terrified, were fewer. But the people roaming the streets this time had metal, and they were intent on murder.

That, too, was both better and worse. Dekklis did not need to hesitate when she came upon looters. But she had to keep in mind that they, too, were armed, maybe armored, and that unschooled cuts could kill her as easily as a professional thrust.

She remembered that the hard way, when a wild-eyed Alvir woman lunged out of a burning storefront. Dekklis was just finishing the last of a handful of rioters, who had seen her and Istel and charged like Taliri berserkers. More enthusiasm than skill, easy kills—

—Istel's shout, a sudden shadow on the fire-bright street—

—and she forgot about *easy* and spun sideways, expecting—

*there, your first mistake*

—a straight thrust for a gap in her armor, where the thin plates met over mail. She'd caught the flat gleam of a slash coming up, wild and wobbling. Had time to recognize a legion sword in the woman's hand and wrenched her own up into a block.

*Too slow, too late.*

Dekklis threw herself sideways. Tensed for the hit and hoped it didn't take off half her face, please let it be only minor—

And then Teslin was there shouldering Dekklis aside while the sword punched through her still-translucent chest and scythed upward before popping out just below her left ear.

The Alvir screamed something Dekklis understood more by tone than by vocabulary. But she wasn't a coward, no, came around and stabbed a second time. Better form, but too slow. Teslin shook her head and put her own sword through the woman's belly. A second scream, wordless, which gurgled to moans as Teslin jerked the ghost-blade loose. A final cut, straight down, and the moaning stopped.

Teslin spat. Tilted a look at Dekklis. *You all right?*

"Yeah. Stupid. Didn't see her." Dekklis waved off Istel's offered hand and picked herself up. "Didn't see you, either."

*Not gonna let some toadbelly stick you, Dek.* Teslin rolled her neck and grimaced. *Weird feeling, that. Doesn't really hurt, but. Fucking weird.*

"Yeah, well. Thanks." She wanted to ask where

*the ghost*

Teslin had been, why she and Barkett weren't staying closer. She drew breath and then choked on it. Teslin wasn't hers to command. She was Veiko's now, if anyone's. Take the

*witchery*

miracle for what it was, that Teslin had come in time and saved her.

Maybe the dead could hear thoughts. Maybe Teslin was just that good at reading Dekklis after years together. She poked her chin up the street.

*Barkett's following the svartjagr. Figured you needed to keep your eyes on the streets. Figured you might need mine, too. Crazy people out tonight.*

"You figured right." Dek's shoulder ached where she'd landed on it. She rolled it. Squinted against the glare and fumes coming out of the ruined storefront. The blackly crisp sign over the door gave no hints to its former purpose. Something round. Tankard. Barrel. The smell coming out of it was pure roasting meat. Those might be shrieks spiking up through the fire's roar or raindrops sizzling into steam as they hit.

*Angry dead.*

Hell. Angry living.

"What I want to know," she said, "is why they're attacking *us*. The Taliri burned them out, not the legion."

*Toadbellies,* said Teslin. *Who knows what they think? Rot 'em.* But from Istel, quietly:

"The Alviri carry a lot of old grudges, Dek."

"It's been two hundred *years* since they lost that war. The Taliri are staking their relatives *now*. And these toadshits live here. They're killing their own."

Istel shook his head. Turned his face upslope, so that the fireglow kissed red off his profile. Istel's *I won't argue* face, his lips pulled into a knot under that long Dvergiri nose. He had, Dek noticed, picked up the dead woman's sword and jammed it into his sheath. Held his own sword wet and naked while the rain washed the blood off it.

"What's the extra metal for?"

He didn't look at her. "Snow won't be armed, when we find her. She'll need a weapon."

"She might be in no condition—"

"We're not going after a corpse," he said. "She's fine. Briel would say otherwise."

Teslin pushed between them, arm and shoulder. The fire pinked through, counterbright to the dark cuts of rain. *Listen, Dek. Hate to break it up, but the svartjagr's stopped up there. Perched and hissing.*

Dekklis scraped water off her face. Drew a breath. "Then we'd better see what she's found. Show me."

Teslin spun on her heel. Slipped ahead of Dekklis and started—not running, no, running came with bootfalls and splashing and creaking armor. This was silent motion, grey, mist taken a familiar shape.

Teslin had never been much of a runner. Ask if she liked it better now when her feet didn't slip on wet paving, when she wasn't puffing uphill in mostly full kit. Ask if she wouldn't rather both of those things than what she was.

Ask nothing, yeah, and save her own breath for running.

Almost to the top of the city by now. Dekklis looked left and there was the Hill, with its streetlamps and warm yellow windows. There was a bonfire up top in the garrison courtyard. The troops were probably swarming like bees. But here, in the Warren, only darkness, except where something or someone was on fire. No candles in the windows, no lamps, all the doors shut and dark on the edges.

Families in there, scared and hiding. Not everyone gone mad in the streets, not everyone looting. But the legion, when they won up this far, wouldn't care. They would smash into houses and drag their residents out into the street. If they were Dvergiri, they might be all right. But Alviri would bleed for this. All of them, any of them.

*Old grudges.*

*Blood and fire.*

* * *

Ehkla described what she wanted, with a chirurgeon's anatomical detail. Reminded Snow of her student days, except their second-year project was always dead first before they cut it. Made her wonder what Ehkla had done among the Taliri before turning godsworn to Tal'Shik.

Snow turned the knife Ehkla had given her over in her hands. Motherless thing made her skin tingle. Wicked-sharp tip, fine serrations all along the inner curve. Same weapon that killed Helgi, same one that cut Veiko. Maybe he'd see the irony in what she was about to do with it, if she lived to tell him.

"Wurm's tooth," she said. And when Ehkla frowned, "Skraeling word for *dragon*. Way I hear it, these hurt more than metal."

Ehkla shrugged partway out of her robe. "The skraeling thought so. He screamed."

"He says you did, too. *His* axe was plain steel."

"He surprised me."

"Yeah? Then I'd hate to have you get surprised this time, too. That big toadshit out there offered to rape me to death already. Be unfortunate if he interrupted this ritual because of your howling."

"He will not. And I will not." Ehkla stood up, naked now. Beautiful woman, except for the ruin of her shoulder. "Close the door."

"You think he'll stop to knock?"

"You're a conjuror. Look at the lintel. What do you see?"

Sigils, in a violet one shade off black, danced and writhed on the wood. "Godmagic."

Snort. "They are wards, conjuror. You know that. *My* wards. Tal'Shik will require more than one life to take physical shape, although she needs only one sacrifice. *You* will be safe in this room. Any men in the hallway, however, will die."

"Good to see Tal'Shik's ethics haven't changed. I mean, casual slaughter of her worshippers—"

"They're men. And Alviri. What matter?"

"Your allies," Snow snapped. "And Tsabrak's no Alvir."

"Then let the Laughing God protect him." Ehkla knelt amid the candles. Tipped forward and caught herself on her good left hand. "I will need your help, Snowdenaelikk. To lie down."

"Right." Snow pushed the tooth into her belt. Scrubbed her palms on her thighs. Put her hands on Ehkla's ribs, on the undamaged part of her right shoulder, and eased her onto the scuffed dirt floor. Helped her straighten her arms out, cruciform, while the mauled shoulder seeped a fresh stream of foul. Ehkla did not scream, although she hissed and gasped and shivered. Lay still, finally, panting, belly and face pressed into the floor.

"Begin," half prayer, half sob.

Snow knelt beside her. Moved Ehkla's braid aside. Poked the wurm's tooth in near her spine where the ribs met the long column. Pushed. Flesh and bone parted easily.

Ehkla groaned.

The glyphs on the walls began to glow.

\* \* \*

Ghost Teslin led them on an uphill charge into growing darkness. Thicker shadows, a charcoal sky that offered no illumination. Teslin and Barkett seemed to have some idea where they were going. Maybe they had some special sense she didn't, to navigate Cardik's slums. Or maybe, Dekklis thought with some guilt, maybe Teslin and Barkett had grown up in these streets. Maybe she just hadn't known it. Hadn't bothered to ask.

Teslin would tell her she was being an idiot, Teslin having little use for guilt. But Istel. Dekklis cut a glance at her partner, who trotted beside her as unconcerned as if ghosts were as common as fleas. A woman got to rely on that kind of steadiness. Take it for granted. Never wonder where it had come from, or what it cost him.

Later, yeah, later she'd buy him a beer and ask what he thought about all this. If seeing Barkett flicker from *there* into *nowhere* made his stomach hurt. If he flinched when Teslin came so close that her edges blurred into his. What he thought about rebel Alviri and blood and butchering civilians. She'd ask, and then she'd listen to what he said.

And then they came round the corner, and it didn't matter what Istel thought or what she did. *There*: a plain building with typical cracked plaster walls, a roof that wanted repair, some chipped, poorly done fresco on the front that Dekklis could almost make out through Barkett's midsection. A building exactly like a dozen others, except for the light leaking out at its seams, a violet so deep it hurt her eyes.

Barkett pointed down the alley. *There's an open door that way. Something's happening inside.*

"You reckon?"

Earnest nod that made Dek's chest hurt. Death hadn't sharpened Barkett's wit at all. He pointed again, this time at the roofline. *The svartjagr stopped here.*

Dekklis followed his hand. Guess that the dead saw better than the living, then, if he could find Briel in that shadow. It was the purple glow, she decided. Didn't really give off any light, reflected off pale things and turned what was already dark to invisible. Take it on faith that Briel was up there. Faith and the nagging headache and the svartjagr's fear in her guts.

*We'll take point,* said Teslin. *Just in case there's trouble.*

"There's doubt about that?"

Teslin's mouth quirked. *I think trouble will have a harder time killing us than you. Don't look like that, Dek. It's all right.*

And then Teslin went down the alley and ducked through the door, Barkett crowding her heels. Ask if one ghost could walk through another.

*Don't, yeah?*

Dekklis followed them, with Istel hard behind her.

They found the first corpse just inside the doorway. Big Talir, too large for the stolen armor strapped to his limbs. Dekklis toed his cheek, so that his wide, dead eyes looked sideways, up the corridor.

"No marks on him, either. No blood."

"Maybe conjuring," Istel murmured. "If Snow's here. Maybe something else she did." He added, as Teslin cocked her head, "Snow's got talent with poisons."

*Huh.* Teslin squatted beside the dead man. Traced fingers over his chest, which sank into steel and leather. *Well. If she did this guy, she saved me the trouble. He's one of the ones from the forest. Toadfucker.*

The corridor beyond seemed too long for the house, a forever stretch of dim twilight. Had to be a trick of the dimness that everything seemed to pulse and ripple. There was too much shadow in the center while the purple light collected in the creases between wall and floor. It flowed toward the far door like liquid.

Dekklis closed her eyes. Squeezed and reopened and told herself she was tired, that was all, while her heart skipped and thumped. Maybe that was Briel's doing, Briel's fear, and without it she'd be brave as Istel.

Who was standing beside her, rigid as bone, whose chest heaved like he'd been running. Maybe not so brave.

The ghosts turned their heads together then, at no sound Dekklis could hear. Teslin brought her blade up. Took a single step up the corridor.

*Someone just died,* she said. *Dek, I think—*

The building shuddered.

*Out,* said Teslin. She caught Istel's shoulder, spun him, made a grab for Dekklis, and claimed a fistful of wet sleeve. Dragged and pushed them back down the corridor and out into the alley, across the street, until they fetched up on the far side.

Then, only then, did Dekklis turn around, and—hell.

* * *

Ehkla kept her word. Didn't scream, not once, although the sounds that got past her teeth might've been worse. Sounded a little like Briel had when Snow had first seen her, pinned and stretched on the worktable. Airless squeaks.

Butchery, chirurgery, vivisection. Snow had seen and done all three. This wasn't any of them. This was godmagic. Ritual sacrifice. The wurm's tooth cut bone and flesh like butter, sharper than any weapon should be. And Ehkla's blood wasn't right. Oh, there was plenty of it—the expected amounts for deep cuts into the torso—but it flowed away from the wound in neat channels, ran across the floor as if the whole building had tilted. Ran *up* the fucking walls, to fill the glyphs until they glistened. Snow didn't want to look at those too closely, didn't want to vomit herself inside out. She had to remember what the fuck she was doing and what came next.

*The end of the Illhari Republic.*

Alviri and Taliri allied under the goddess whose cult had led Illharek to smash their alliance the first time. Alviri and Taliri, under that goddess, destroying the Republic who'd later Purged her worship. You could laugh at that irony. Well. *She* could. Dekklis wouldn't think it was funny. Dekklis would take her head off for this. Call it treason, yeah, and Dek wouldn't be wrong.

And Tsabrak. Fuck and damn. Tsabrak was likely dead already if he had stayed in the building. Stupid to be sorry for that, when he'd delivered her here in the first place. Damn sure he wouldn't mourn were their places reversed. Damn sure he hadn't when he'd sent her up the corridor to die.

Except he hadn't. He'd told her she'd survive if she did whatever Ehkla wanted. And Tsabrak knew enough about conjuring, about what she could do, to know that one broken finger, the littlest on her strong hand, wouldn't stop her. He'd marked her, yeah, but he hadn't crippled her. Maybe he'd known after all what the God had wanted her to do. Maybe he was playing his own role in that plan.

Too late for regrets now, in any case. Too late, with one side of Ehkla's ribs already cut from her spine, with the wurm's tooth making short work of the other. The biggest danger was pressing too hard, hitting an organ and killing her too soon.

There were rules to this. Steps. *Ritual.*

The God had rites, too. He favored fingers cut off joint by joint, eyes lanced with hot needles, lips stitched shut with wire. Nothing fatal. The God liked pain better than death, as a sacrifice. But the God wouldn't thank anyone for binding him into flesh, either. It was one thing for him to wear his godsworn like a pair of boots at his discretion. Quite another to be bound into their skin.

Snow paused, as Ehkla's writhing threw her next cut into jeopardy. Crouched on the balls of her feet beside Ehkla's body, with Ehkla's blood rolling past her feet like rivers. Thought about sticking that knife straight down, pinning lung and heart to the floor. Kill her. Have *done.*

And hope Tal'Shik didn't come visit anyway. Or hope she did, so that she didn't stay in the spirit world and finish Veiko first. If he was even alive now, and how would she know it?

*Don't think that. Just don't.*

Snow jabbed again, into the gap between ribs. Drew down hard and fast. For a moment the blood gushed, uncontrolled, drowning the wound rot in its bright copper tang. Two more scores, long across the ribs, so that the skin would yield. And then Snow reached into the slits, one side and then the other, and peeled the ribs away from spine. Stretched them sideways, so that they looked like obscene wings. Blood pooled in the body cavity, spilled out around her boots. Ehkla shuddered hard and stopped moving. Not dead, no, not yet. See her lungs in there, fluttering.

The room congealed into stillness. The candles stood up, rigid and frozen and weakly white. The glyphs on the wall stopped wriggling. The light had gone almost totally violet now. She could feel that power, that *waiting.*

Snow shifted the tooth to her right hand. Reached, carefully, into Ehkla, drew out her lungs and laid them on her shoulder blades. Had to balance the right one when it wanted to slip off the shattered ends of bone.

A body couldn't live like that. Not long. Ehkla didn't surprise her. One more quiver, and she died. Snow felt it, knew it, with a chirurgeon's certainty.

The wurm's tooth crumbled. Dust and ashes sifted through her fingers.

The glyphs glowed brighter than the candles. The blood did, changing from red to purple, running into all the corners and up the walls.

On the floor, Ehkla's peeled-back ribs flexed. Stretched. *Changed.* The ruined right shoulder smoothed out as the rib-wings stretched wide as Snow's fingers, then wider as the bones grew and stretched.

Snow stood up. Retreated toward the door, as what had been Ehkla writhed on the floor. Shadows sprouted out of Ehkla's back, strung themselves across bone, making wings. A coiled shadow between her legs that might be a tail. The avatar—that's what it was, yeah, on its way to becoming a toadfucking *dragon*—turned its head and looked at her, one-eyed.

"Snowdenaelikk," it said, and the air itself creaked like old boards under too much strain. Ehkla's voice, bent and raw, as if the throat couldn't quite hold the syllables. Her neck stretched and uncoiled, raising a face that was still recognizably *Ehkla*—if Ehkla's remaining eye was orange, sure, with two black-slit pupils—level with Snow's own.

Snow bared her teeth. "Tal'Shik," she said. "Time to keep your bargain, yeah? Let me go."

"Sssssss." The jaw that had been Ehkla's unhinged, dangling loose, held only by flesh. A tongue curled from the mouth, thick and pointed and absurdly pink between teeth that were growing, curving into weapons. Laughing at her, maybe. Or imagining how she'd taste.

Snow retreated another step, two, put her back against the door. The wards were still in place. She touched them and felt burning all over her skin, nausea, her flesh grown too small and too tight. They'd kill her if she forced them.

So she was trapped in here, because Tal'Shik wasn't going to drop them. Let Snow go, *sure*, those were the terms, but Snow hadn't asked *let down the wards*. She'd said, *Whatever happens, you don't come after me.* And *whatever* was the wards still up, and Tal'Shik laughing, growing, spreading, a shapeless, boiling violet that matched the glyphs. Against that light, the candles cringed.

Fuck and damn if she'd wait here to die.

Snow took a bite of breath and reached her wounded hand toward the candles. Fire was the apprentice's first friend, yeah, and she was well past apprentice. She crooked her fingers, then flexed them long. The fire fled the candlewicks. Streamed across the open space gap like it had when she'd burned the ropes; only, this time it skipped past her flesh and coiled under the skin of her hands, binding itself to her bones.

Hold that hand still, go *fast*. She flexed her other wrist. Conjuring wasn't godmagic, bound by blood and bargains. Conjuring relied on talent and skill, on whole hands and whole wits.

And luck. Maybe that.

She drew power from the pattern of wooden beams crossing the ceiling, from hearthstones, from planks under cracked plaster walls. Bright lines that she gathered together and held, just so, in one cupped hand. The patterns skeined between her fingers, visible to a conjuror's eyes.

*What is shaped once can be reshaped.*

Pressure built behind her eyes, an ache worse than any sending of Briel's, like the first threat of backlash. The walls trembled. The ceiling beams moaned. Plaster sifted down, fine as flour. She couldn't *quite* hold the power, one-handed. The fire strained her other hand, throbbing through bone and tendon, raising fine blisters on the finger along the bone's broken seam. To reshape a thing—wood, stone, fire—a conjuror needed perfect control, hands and mind together. But to *unmake.* Well.

"I'll let myself out," she told Tal'Shik. "You stay there."

Then Snow slammed her hands together, twining her fingers, never *mind* the white shock of broken bone. The skeins of timber and stone tangled together. Knotted. Then Snow tore them apart, ripping her fingers away from each other, loosing that power. Let herself yell as the finger bone grated. The walls fluttered like lungs—strained against the wards—and burst outward, taking with them the door and the wards on the lintel.

Snow sprang for the hallway. For a moment the ceiling remained intact behind her, sagging over Tal'Shik. Then it came down, a burst of floorboards and plaster and the stone from the hearth in the room above.

Tal'Shik howled.

Snow paused then, looked back: a pile of debris where the room had been, violet godmagic oozing through the cracks. A bubbling snarl that said *living avatar* and *angry dragon* and *be somewhere else.*

In a toadfucked heartbeat, yeah. But first.

Snow stretched her broken left hand back to the rubble. Turned the palm open and up and released the fire. It spilled out of her bones, rushing through flesh too fast to burn it. Raced along the walls, the floors.

*Burn,* Snow wished it. *Burn.*

Which was all fire ever wanted. It surged across the debris, across the violet shadows, up the ruined walls. Found old wood, burst to kindling, and roared as loud as Tal'Shik.

Then she ran.

* * *

The whole house was glowing. Swollen, its walls bowing out and splitting at the seams. Fingers of light reached up toward the sky, spearpoint violet stabbing into the clouds. A section of thatch sluiced off the roof. Then another. But there was honest fire in that mix, too, flame reaching through the seams, catching on the thatch. Something howling inside, something huge, in rage or pain or both.

Dek tried Teslin's grip. "Snow," she said. "Snow's in there."

*No,* said Teslin. *Dek,* no.

And then, there: a shape staggered out of the alley, a pale smudge of hair. Snow stopped in the street, half a breath, steadied and came right at them.

"Got to go, Szanys. Let's move." Following her own advice, no stopping.

Dek shot her hand out. Caught a fistful of sleeve and wrenched. "Where's Ehkla?"

"Gone," Snow said shortly. "We want to be somewhere else, yeah?"

"Dammit, Snow!" as the other woman pulled loose and swept past her.

*What's got into her?* Barkett wore the scowl that meant *something's happened I don't understand.*

"Don't argue with Snow," said Istel. "If she's scared, you should be." And went after her, steady legion trot, as if Snow wore the rank.

Nothing to do but follow Istel, with the ghosts beside her. Down the street, as if they hadn't left a house on fire behind them, glowing. As if half those flames weren't *purple* and Ehkla wasn't back there.

The sky chose that moment to split. Lightning sheeted across it, followed by waves of thunder that rendered the world temporarily deaf. Then rain that made the earlier storm seem like morning mist.

Dekklis sped up. Easier to run downhill, to catch up with her partner and the motherless half-blood at the next intersection. They had their shoulders together against the rain, some murmured exchange that couldn't get through the storm and the pounding behind Dek's eyes. A witchfire hung over Snow's head like her personal lantern. Water streamed down her face, soaked her topknot to rattails. She leaned close to Istel. Opened her mouth while Istel pulled the spare sword, naked, off his belt and passed it to her.

Briel shrieked, and Dek felt her panic like a kick to the chest.

Then Snow was spinning to face

*nothing there*

the shadows collected at the border of witchfire. And not shadows, no, not just: a Dvergir man stepping out of them. Trick of the light, must be, that his eyes looked like live flames.

But the seax in his hand wasn't a trick or imagining. Illhari black steel, Snow's own weapon. Snow managed to catch his cut on the flat of her borrowed legion blade. They stared at each other as the metal scraped and stuck. Shock, recognition, spread across the half-blood's face like fire in oil. Her lips shaped a word, a name, a prayer.

The man reversed the blade, made a sweeping cut toward Snow's face. Less graceful than before, less focused. Snow caught it again, this time edge on edge. Held him there for a heartbeat while he leaned into the crossed blades and shoved. Snow skidded backward in the mudslick streets. A moment's recovery, to get both feet solid under her. Only a moment.

Forever, in a fight.

He chopped the blade crossways at her neck, his full weight behind the stroke. Should have killed her, would have, if he'd connected. But Istel was there suddenly, surging out of the rain, reaching around to swat the attacker's blade. Not a perfect deflection, just enough to knock the strike aside; and then Istel reversed his grip on the sword and punched it through the man's chest.

The stranger's fire-eyes got very wide. Flames—they *were*, fuck and damn, real fire—flared up. His mouth rounded. Blood gushed between his teeth. A normal man would've clutched at the wound. Would've stared at it, and understood he'd just died, and waited for his body to catch up to that realization. Not this one, no, he dropped his sword and thrust his empty hand out and flat-palmed Snow in the chest as if he meant to tear out her heart.

An instant's white daylight as lightning cracked across the sky. Briel arrowing toward them, caught motionless. Teslin and Barkett washed almost invisible. Then the storm-dark crashed in again, crowding in on the witchfire's borders.

The stranger's body slid off Istel's sword. Snow dropped to her knees.

The witchfire abruptly went out.

# CHAPTER TWENTY-TWO

Veiko stood on the riverbank and looked at the empty skies. At the flat grey where there had been swirling dark. At the empty air where the sigils had burned a moment ago. The wurm—Tal'Shik—was simply *gone.*

He was grateful for that. But he wondered where she'd gone. Worried what her disappearance meant for his partner.

Helgi *oofed.* Poked his nose hard into Veiko's thigh. Did it a second time, harder, and a third, until Veiko looked down at him. Then Helgi nipped his breeches and tugged.

*Follow me,* that meant. All right. Veiko shifted his grip on the axe. Held his breath against the pain he knew was coming—and realized, belatedly, that there was no pain. No heat when he ran his palm across his thigh. It was as if Ehkla had never marked him.

He wondered what had happened to break Ehkla's power. Imagined the answer might have midnight eyes and a talent for violence. But that did not tell him where Tal'Shik was. She had been coming. The sky over the forest had been—

He blinked. The forest was gone. It was hillsides now, across the black river. Striped bands of white-and-grey stone jutting up out of the earth at angles. Barren, blasted, with a scatter of warped trees clinging among the crevasses. It was more desolate even than the glacier. No spirits, except the weary trees. Even the sky seemed dimmer. Greyer. A slow fade to twilight in a dull iron sky.

Helgi yipped. Pranced toward the black river and circled back. A slender tributary joined the black river here, trickling out of that barren land. It twisted through the boulders, originating from a massive gash of warped and jagged stones, like a mouthful of broken teeth. The cave opening stretched as tall as Still Waters, gaped wider than an Illhari road. Solid black maw that swallowed the light and the river.

Then Veiko realized where he must be. What souls swam out of that cavern. He wondered if this was what Kenjak had seen first when he died. If this was where Teslin and Barkett had come from when he called them back. He might ask them next time. He could do that. He'd gotten very good at speaking to the dead.

Veiko's chest hurt very much, of a sudden. He breathed past it. Grief was a luxury, and it was too soon for mourning. He would not be here, on this bank, if it were otherwise. Helgi was hunting a woman's soul, not a ghost.

The river was narrow here. Veiko stepped over it. Helgi's paws kicked up dust on the path, little clouds that hung for a moment before they settled again. Moving with speed, but not urgency, toward the cavern.

Take that for a comfort, and follow him.

\* \* \*

Snowdenaelikk was drowning. She wasn't afraid, although she thought she should be. She remembered the Laughing God in the Warren, wearing Tsabrak like a pair of old boots, and how he'd come at her with her own fucking blade. She remembered a red wedge of steel coming out of Tsabrak's chest, with Istel on the other end of it. She remembered a moment's relief before the God had reached for her. And then she remembered the tearing pain in her chest when he touched her, and thinking that must've been what Ehkla had felt, *that* was dying.

This—this didn't hurt. Cold. Dark. But easy. Let it go and slip away, no effort at all. No fretting whether her conjuring had been enough to kill an avatar, or if she'd loosed Tal'Shik on the world. No matter. Let it be someone else's problem.

Except that someone else would be Veiko. Would be Dekklis, and Istel, and the whole fucking Republic.

Snow struck out with both hands. Bumped something in the dark that slipped her grip when she tried to grab on to it. She kicked herself toward it, reached again.

A hand grabbed a fistful of her hair. Dragged her—some direction, fuck and damn, couldn't tell up from down. She flailed at it. Got hold of a wrist, intercepted a second hand that seized on to hers. Then she was sliding up through water, then into air—then landing, hard, on what felt like wet stone.

It was either dark or she was blind, didn't matter, hack and choke and vomit up water that burned her throat with its cold.

Black water, black rock, *black*.

She closed her eyes. Didn't change anything. Opened them again. Called up a witchfire without thinking at all, wished it there and it was without even a shiver of backlash. Conjuring that clean only happened Below, and she was leagues from a decent cavern, so where *had* the God sent her? And then she cupped the witchfire between her two hands and looked at the man who'd saved her.

Oh fuck and damn. Not Below at all. "K'Hess Kenjak."

Must've been the look on her face that made him smile. Showed her the boy he might've been when he wasn't in a legionnaire's uniform and trying to kill her. His hands, she saw, were wet. "It's all right, half-blood. I pulled you out of the river."

The river. *Which* river? The witchfire showed her black water, a liquid mirror winding slowly between the rocks. She thought she saw movement under the surface. Dvergiri faces, pushing up through the water. Dead faces, grey skinned, with wide mouths and blank eyes. She thought she might see Tsabrak among them and looked away fast.

*That* river. Veiko's river. Admit a little fear now. Keep it out of her voice. "Am I dead?"

"You are." Kenjak shrugged. "And you're not. I don't know how it works. Ask your skraeling."

"Love to. You know where he is?"

Frowning now, and older than she remembered him. "Last I saw, waiting for Tal'Shik. He sent me away. Sent me to you."

"That would be my next question. Why?"

"To pay my debt. I owe you a life."

"How did Veiko know I'd end up *here*?"

Kenjak snorted. "He thought you might do something—what did he say? Foolish. And here you are."

"Right." A dead woman's heart wouldn't beat this hard, would it? A dead woman's throat wouldn't hurt every time she breathed. "Is he all right?"

"I don't know."

"You don't know *much*, yeah?"

"I know you're trapped in here." Kenjak pointed into the dark. "The black river runs that way. That's the way out, but there's something blocking the path. Or someone."

She raised the witchfire, marked the steepness of the path. The narrowness of it. Pulled her feet under her and stood up. Take it slow. A dead woman's knees wouldn't shake like this. Concentrate on the slick, black rocks, on keeping her feet underneath her. Not much different than walking a wall, was it? Slip and die. Simple rules. So don't slip. And don't ask if she *could* die here. Again.

"That isn't smart." Kenjak hadn't moved. Sat where she'd left him, with the river lapping up over the toes of his boots. "You have no guide, half-blood. You have no idea what you're doing, or who you might meet at the top. Veiko will come. Alive or dead, he'll come for you."

"Oh, I have a good idea who's up there." Same one responsible for putting her here, yeah. Motherless Laughing God. And Veiko would walk right into him. "I'll find my way."

Ask what a ghost thought of

*stupidity*

honor in a half-blood heretic. Ask what he thought about loyalty. Ask if he thought she'd lost her wits in the river, probably, from the look he gave her.

"Then I wish you luck, half-blood. Better than I had."

\* \* \*

Helgi stopped, stiff-legged, all the fur on his spine ridged. Shadows spilled out of the cave mouth like blood, leaking and spreading along the path and stones. Oozing toward Veiko, living black.

"The shadows are a child's trick," said Veiko loudly. "Any Dvergir can do it."

The shadows stopped. And grew, suddenly, gathering themselves into a man's shape. Vague outline, then hard edges. Turning into the God, whose smile was hard beneath those twin fire eyes.

"I'm not *any* Dvergir, skraeling. No mere ghost. But you know that."

"So you say. And I am not here to speak to you. But you know that."

The flames in his sockets licked higher, brighter. "Snowdenaelikk is dead."

"Even so, I am here for her. Not you."

"But you can't have her. She's mine, skraeling. Do you understand that? She broke her bargain with me. This is the price."

A man's heart could burst, beating so hard. "I will not leave without her."

"I see." The God spread his hands. "What shall we do?"

Veiko shrugged. Waited and said nothing. It was, Snow told him, a maddening habit.

The God was not a patient creature. He came out a little farther. Liquid shadows puddled around his feet, steamed blackly into the silver-skied twilight. "Surely there is something you can offer, skraeling, some payment for her release."

Veiko frowned. Sucked his teeth and looked up, as if the sky might tell him what to answer. Swung sidelong and touched stares with Helgi. The dog bunched himself into a crouch. Watched Veiko intently.

The God drifted another pace closer. "Well, skraeling?"

Veiko looked at him. "I will offer my axe."

"Your *axe*?" The God stared. Then he threw his head back and laughed. The rocks shivered. Melted. "What would I want with your axe?"

It was a fair question.

Step and swing, axe and body moving together. Cut and chop with all his weight behind the steel. Feel it cleave into godflesh, in the crease between neck and shoulder, and slice it loose on the same stroke, so that the blade did not drive too deep and stick there. Pivot and step again, axe held ready.

And hold. Wait as the God crashed onto one knee, his hand clapped to the wound. Blood like molten fire ran through his fingers and burned the stone to dust where it fell.

"I did not say you would want my axe," said Veiko. "Only that it is my offer. And you have accepted. Now will you let her go, or shall I offer a second time?"

* * *

The darkness split. Narrow bands at first, and then whole sections peeling away like the skin on boiled fruit. A flat yellow-grey light crept in after it, brittle as glass, and shattered on the jagged vault overhead. Snow's witchfire paled in that brightness. Smoked and flickered until she let it go altogether. No more need of it, not when she could see all the way to the cave's gaping mouth.

The light showed the grey dog standing on that path, looking down at her. A grey dog several months dead, who put his ears back and grinned at her.

Snow clenched her fists. Didn't run, fuck and damn, no. *Walked*, as steady as she could, while her nails cut crescents into her palms. Helgi would not be here without Veiko. Believe that.

And still, when she saw his tall silhouette, she let her breath out in a gust, and put her hand on the wall, and waited there while her heart tripped and stuttered relief.

*Are you all right?* jammed up in her throat. Of course he was. Here, wasn't he, with Helgi prancing beside him. Strong strides, easy, as he came down the path, the axe swinging in his right hand. Coming for her, because he was a—

"Damn idiot. You shouldn't be here."

He didn't answer. Stopped in front of her and raked that witchfire stare across her, face to feet and back. Then, Veiko-grim: "Nor should you. How did it happen?"

"The God," simply. She thought of Tsabrak in the river. Wondered if Veiko could summon him out of it, and what she would say if he did.

"The God said you broke the terms of your bargain with him."

"The God lies. I killed Ehkla. Carved her up, worse than what she did to Kenjak. Godmagic, yeah? To summon Tal'Shik and bind her into Ehkla's body. She *did* die." She held her eyes wide against that memory. "It just didn't last."

"So she is not dead."

"She didn't *stay* dead. I tried again. Conjured up fire, tried to pull the whole building down. But I don't think it worked."

Veiko was frowning at her. "That was not wise, calling Tal'Shik into a body."

"What's wise, Veiko? Tell me that. If I killed Ehkla the way the God wanted, Tal'Shik would've killed you over here."

She expected argument. Protest. A flash of skraeling pride, like summer lightning. Got a grim stare instead, and a quiet, "That is likely. Instead, the God killed you."

"But you sent Kenjak to me."

"I did."

"Good thing, yeah?" Her voice dried up. Safer, easier, to look at her hands, than to hold that stare. She rubbed her thumb across the God's mark on her palm. It ached like an old bruise.

"There's blood on your axe, Veiko."

"The God and I reached an agreement concerning you."

"Did you kill him?"

"Those were not the terms."

As soon argue with that logic as reason Briel off a flatcake. "*That* was not wise, Veiko."

An almost-smile that faded as fast as winter daylight. "I did not want a dead partner."

Now the shakes started, damn them, settling in voice and knees and hands. "Isn't that what you've got? Kenjak pulled me out of the river. I think that means dead."

Veiko folded his hands over hers. Warm fingers, strong and steady. "It will not last."

"That's supposed to make me feel better?"

His mouth pulled up on one side. "No."

"Good."

"But among my people, it would make you a noidghe."

"Dvergiri don't have noidghe."

"Perhaps," said Veiko, "they do now."

\* \* \*

Clear dawn, with the battle sounds drifting in on the river mist. Dekklis shared space with Briel on the windowsill and watched the bruised sky over the Warren. It had glowed through the night. Still did, proof against any light out of the east. But the fire had not crept across to the Bridge, and neither had it jumped across to the Hill.

Ask if that meant Tal'Shik was contained. Ask if that meant Snow had managed, after all, to kill Ehkla. Ask if Snow were really dead, for that matter. Her eyes were closed. Her skin was cold. No breath that Dekklis could find. But Teslin and Barkett said she wasn't.

Dekklis couldn't tell the difference anymore. Oh, she was reasonably certain that she herself was alive. That Istel was. And so was Aneki, who had met them at the back gate. Who had not asked why two of the four troopers that brought back Snow's body were as insubstantial as mist. Who had not asked why, in a rainstorm, Dekklis and Istel were frosted with ice. Who had not asked how they'd got through the fighting on the Bridge. Aneki had only opened the gate and led them inside and up here, where Veiko was already stretched like a corpse on his blankets.

Not dead, Teslin had said. Not him, and not Snow.

*I should know, Dek. I'm telling you.*

Dek hadn't argued the point. Had sent Teslin and Barkett back into the streets, twice and three times, to bring back news. They reported fighting still in the Warren. The Bridge fires gone out. Fighting at the east and south gates of the city, where bands of Taliri were massed outside in what had been Cardik's farmland.

A lot of dead out there, yeah. A lot more dying.

She should be out there herself, with the Sixth. Should be sticking metal through someone living, instead of watching the varying definitions of dead. She'd made an attempt, when they'd got Snow back here, to turn around and go out. Aneki had stopped her. Spread arms in the doorway—

*Want to get killed, is that it? Safer here.*

—and argued. Aneki would have moved if Dekklis insisted. A sword could be very persuasive.

But only one sword, because Istel meant to wait, like the dog or the svartjagr or Aneki, until something happened. So she could argue with that stubbornness or go with it. Sit. Wait. Watch.

And so the night crawled past, and the rain changed to ice, and then snow, and then stopped altogether when the sun poked cold fingers into the sky. Pale, heatless yellow, smeared against smoke and the violet glow off the Warren.

Teslin touched stares with Barkett. Cleared her throat. *Got to go, Dek.*

*Will you come back?* clogged in the back of her throat and burned there. Couldn't bear a *yes,* hell and damn, couldn't face a *no.* Bad enough to grieve once and know someone was gone. Worse, far worse, to know that it wasn't true, that they went *on* somewhere, some place she couldn't reach.

"You be careful, yeah?"

Teslin nodded. Clapped a hand on her shoulder. The touch might have bruised her once. Now it only chilled her down to bone. Ask if that was pity in a dead woman's eyes. Ask if it was grief.

Dek had no shortage of either. Clamped her teeth shut on the sound she wanted to make. Turned back to the window and leaned out as far as she could. Told herself it was cold stinging her eyes, that was all. Behind her, Istel swore until he ran out of breath.

Briel *chrripped.* Snaked her head around and looked at Snow, who was sitting up and looking down at a shirt on which the blood and rain had long since dried. She brushed at the stains. Frowned. "My skin feels tight."

"That feeling fades," Veiko said from his pallet. He rolled onto an elbow. Patted Logi's head.

"What are you talking about?" Dek blurted at the same time Aneki said, "Rot you both, scaring me like that."

Snow held out a hand to the svartjagr, who minced and fluttered from the windowsill as if she hadn't been keening and fretting the whole night. "Sorry. Didn't plan that."

"You were dead," Dekklis said.

"Well, she's not now," said Aneki.

Maybe Aneki didn't see the problem with a corpse sitting up and talking. Maybe Aneki hadn't spent the balance of her adult life dividing the world into living and dead, enemy and ally, and never worrying about what happened after. Dead was dead, that was all, and now it wasn't.

Snow swung her feet over the edge of her bed. Winced and closed her eyes and touched the back of her skull. "Did you drag me back here by my feet, Szanys?"

"Should have, yeah? You're welcome. Could've left you up in the Warren." Dekklis had to sit down, suddenly. Landed hard on the hearthstones, palms and ass together. "Teslin carried you. We walked through this fog that came out of nowhere. Five steps, I swear that was all we took, *five*, and we went from the Warren to Still Waters' back gate. There was ice on my armor. You tell me how?"

Snow was watching her. Not smiling now, not even a smirk, eyes narrow and knowing. "I can't."

"It is the ghost road," said Veiko. He was sitting up now, bare to the waist, sifting his braids through his fingers. Maybe his hands shook a little. Maybe that was the uneven firelight. Shadows under his eyes, purple as the sky over the Warren. "It is how the dead walk between worlds."

"The dead shouldn't walk at all."

"What should be and what is are not always related."

"They're gone. Teslin and Barkett. Just gone."

"No," said Veiko gently. "They are only dead."

And what could she say to that? Throw her hands up, spin and stalk the too-short distance between window and hearth. Lean against the cool sill, fold her arms. Feel her heart beating hard in her chest.

"So what now?"

Expecting—hell and damn, what? A plan. An idea. Words, of which Snow never had any shortage. Got only silence and Snow looking deliberately somewhere else. At the floor. At the table. At her partner, finally, for a long moment.

Veiko said nothing, either. But he shrugged into a shirt, and a sweater after it. Found his pack and began to fill it, with the efficiency of a man used to moving.

"You're leaving?"

Snow squinted at the window. "Before the sun gets much higher. Yeah, Szanys, we are. This city's not safe."

"You reckon? You maybe think you had something to do with that?"

Istel grunted. "Not fair, Dek."

"You shut up," she told him. Damn near choked on the words, on the anger.

Aneki slid into that silence. "I'll give you what provisions we can. Don't you argue with me, Snow."

"I was going to say you should come with us."

Aneki shrugged. "Still Waters is my place. Not going to leave it."

"If the legion fails—"

"We'll survive an occupation. Brothels do."

"The Taliri might come looking for me. Ehkla, maybe, if she's still alive."

Dekklis snapped, "How can you not know that?"

Snow wheeled around. "Because she was turning into an avatar when I dropped the roof on her and set the place on fire. I don't know how well avatars burn. I don't know *if* they do. Wasn't going to wait, was I? Any more than *you* did."

"Doesn't matter now." Aneki shrugged. "You won't be here, will you? Whoever comes looking, they won't find you."

"Tell them where we have gone," Veiko said. "If they ask. Do not try to protect us."

"Protect you? I'll tell them I sold you to the legion. Not that far from the truth, is it? Just be seen leaving with *them*, yeah? Out the front door."

It was like listening to people discussing the quality of their wine while their house burned around them. Dekklis chopped her hand at the window. Sent Briel hissing up Snow's shoulder, startled a yip out of Logi. Even Aneki flinched from the motion.

Snow only looked at Dekklis and smiled, very faintly. "Something to say?"

"You didn't ask, but let me tell you, since no one else has. Your revolution is still out there in the streets."

"Not mine. Tsabrak's. And he's dead."

"You armed them. *You* did, as much as him. And there are Taliri at the gates."

Snow grimaced. "Reckoned. Those're Ehkla's so-called sisters."

"More godsworn? Hell and damn, Snow——"

"I didn't know before, yeah? Ehkla told me. But I should've reckoned it. Both of us should have, Szanys. So much for childhood lessons."

"I did reckon it. I said——"

"Dek." Istel put his hand on her arm. Squeezed. "It's done, yeah?"

"Right. Done." She raked the remnants of her queue out of her face. "How will you get past all of them? More ghost roads?"

Snow looked at her as if she were a particularly slow child. "I'll conjure us past. Same way we got in. Once we're out, though, we'll need your skills. Can you get us around the Taliri? Get us to Illharek?"

"Get you around—? This city's under attack, you savvy that? We're not leaving."

Snow looked at Veiko. "And you think I'm stubborn."

"It is a Dvergiri failing." Veiko turned those pale eyes on Dekklis. "Your oath is not served if you die here."

"And what would *you* know about oaths?"

Veiko laughed, dry as old bones, damned if she could tell why.

Indignant now, feeling as if she'd already lost the fight: "You don't need *us*. You got away from us once. You can dodge the Taliri once you're out."

"Perhaps." Veiko shrugged. "But I do not know the way to Illharek."

"Your partner does."

"*His partner* knows the roads, not the woods. And his partner can't get an audience with the Senate. I'm a half-blood. Think the senators will listen to me if I say Tal'Shik's come back?"

"You're a heretic, too. Don't forget that."

"Reformed. Listen, Szanys Dekklis. It has to be you who tells them what happened here. If they're not warned, if they don't act, the Taliri burn their way to Illharek's gates and this happens again."

"Now you love the Republic. Toadshit. I think you're worried for your own skin."

"Maybe I am. Maybe I'm thinking of you and Istel, too. Don't want you to end up on a pole on the Market Bridge."

"You know what the legion does to highborn deserters? The pole might be kinder."

"They won't touch you. Your mother's a senator. You say Tal'Shik's back, they'll listen."

Like walking into a blind alley and finding yourself surrounded. Know how it'd end, yeah, and fight anyway. "Maybe she isn't. You might've killed Ehkla. You said—"

"That I wasn't sure. I'm still not. That there's not a dragon burning Cardik right now says I did something right. But whatever happened to Ehkla, Tal'Shik's not finished. You know that. Lessons, Dek. She's going after Illharek."

Dekklis looked at the rings glinting high in Snow's ear, at the rain-draggled topknot. "And you will be doing what in Illharek? Examining the Academy's archives? Finding new poisons? New heresies?"

Snow glanced sidelong at Veiko. Whole conversation in that look, which ended on Snow's grim "Something like."

Veiko didn't look any happier. Lips tight, eyes narrow. But he wasn't arguing as he traded bloodstained silk trousers for worn leather.

At least someone's partner stayed faithful. She could feel Istel's eyes on her. Knew what he wanted. She could test his loyalty, sure, order them both back into the streets. She'd have to cut him down when he refused or watch him walk out with Snowdenaelikk. Or admit that Snow had a good point, ever and always.

"Illharek," Dekklis said. "We'll go with you. Damn you, Snowdenaelikk."

The half-blood grinned like a midwinter sunrise. "I think you're too late for that."

# ACKNOWLEDGMENTS

So many thanks! In no particular order:

To Lisa, for being a fabulous agent.

To Tan, for reading every draft, even when there was a baby on the way.

To my parents, who always kept me well supplied with books and who taught me how to use my powers of epic stubborn for good.

To Stephanie, who helped with query letters and synopses.

To Colleen, who wouldn't let me quit.

And finally to Loren, for being the most metalhead cheerleader ever, my partner in all things, and for making all the coffee.

Without these folks, this book wouldn't be here. Thank you.

# ABOUT THE AUTHOR

*Photo © 2015 Tan Grimes-Sackett*

K. Eason started telling tales in her early childhood. After earning two degrees in English literature, she decided to stop writing about everyone else's stories and get back to writing her own. Now she teaches first-year college students about the zombie apocalypse, Aristotelian ethics, and *Beowulf* (not all at once). She lives in Southern California with her husband and two black cats, and she powers everything with coffee.